LIN TREADGOLD is a retired trainer c  owned her own training school for tw 2002 and moved to Holland to join 1 space in her life, she became a writer a

Lin is a member of the Romanti The Society of Authors. *Goodbye Henrietta Street* was a contender for the Joan Hessayon Award with the RNA, in 2014.

Goodbye Henrietta Street

LIN TREADGOLD

SilverWood

Published in 2015 by SilverWood Books

SilverWood Books Ltd
30 Queen Charlotte Street, Bristol, BS1 4HJ
www.silverwoodbooks.co.uk

Copyright © Lin Treadgold 2015

The right of Lin Treadgold to be identified as the author of this work
has been asserted by her in accordance with the
Copyright, Designs and Patents Act 1988.

All rights reserved. No part of this publication may be reproduced,
stored in a retrieval system, or transmitted in any form or by any means,
electronic, mechanical, photocopying, recording or otherwise,
without prior permission of the copyright holder.

This is a work of fiction. Names, characters, places and incidents either are
products of the author's imagination or are used fictitiously. Any resemblance
to actual events or locales or persons, living or dead,
is entirely coincidental.

ISBN 978-1-78132-346-5 (paperback)
ISBN 978-1-78132-347-2 (ebook)

British Library Cataloguing in Publication Data
A CIP catalogue record for this book is available from
the British Library

Set in Adobe Garamond Pro and Cheddar Jack by SilverWood Books
Printed on responsibly sourced paper

To all the people of the Isles of Scilly

'Richard'
This time tomorrow you will be going,
Luggage in hand down the narrow stone quay,
Fishermen say the wind will be blowing
West, when you go on the tumbled grey sea.
This time tomorrow, you will be leaving
Waving your hand as you clamber aboard.
Telling us there, and we half believing
That you will be back, our friendship restored.
We shall be standing and watching your boat
Dip in the waves as she takes you away,
Straining our eyes as the grey of your coat
Blurs in the distance to uniform grey.

And I, I shall say, as I turn away,
The tears on my face are only salt spray.

From *Love Poems from Scilly* – in memory of poet
Anne Lewis-Smith, died 11 May 2011

Chapter One

What was she doing going away without him? The day before, she had left Rob at Darlington station and now she wondered why.

'Luggage for St Mary's in this container. Please stand in the queue.' A young man wearing a navy-blue boiler suit directed passengers towards the ship's gangway.

Pippa waited in line as she stared into the green-blue water. Was it possible she could find happiness again? In all her thirty years, she had never been on holiday alone.

The ship's whistle, deep and throaty, resonated across the quay and into town. It was time to leave Penzance. The salty tang of the bacon sandwich from breakfast lingered on her lips. She leaned over and gazed into the water as mirrored swirls reflected the ship's hull. Thank goodness she had remembered to take her travel pill after breakfast.

'Lovely day. Great weather for a trip to Scilly,' someone remarked as passengers stood in line.

Pippa sighed. 'Yeah, I'm just glad to get here. The journey was longer than I remember.'

The familiar odour of fish and lobster pots, stacked on the quay in neat rows, reminded her of home. At last, the islands were within reach, just a few more hours and she would be there.

As she waited at the bottom of the gangway, a member of the crew clipped her ticket.

'You're not on the day trip then?' he grinned.

'No, three weeks.' Pippa hoped to start moving forward in the queue.

'Lucky you,' a woman remarked behind her. 'I hope you'll find enough to do. It's a small place, you know.'

'Yes, I will. I came here five years ago, it's been a while.' She had done her homework, read the leaflets and brochures about life on St Mary's. The photos, taken on the last trip of narrow streets and busy harbour, had remained in her thoughts.

She searched for a seat on the upper deck and a place for her heavy rucksack. Had she really done the right thing coming here?

The sounds of crashing on the ship's hull made her lean across the rail to look. The dockers were removing the gangway from the ship.

'Let go aft' came a voice from a ship's officer holding a walkie-talkie. It wasn't long before the gap between the quay and the ship widened and they left Penzance at a leisurely roll.

Pippa closed her eyes against the sun, and for a brief moment she reminisced of her days before life had flung her into a dark-ened room. This was the same seat where she, Rob, and Daniel had squashed together five years earlier. She looked out to sea in a moment of regret, and sighed.

The breeze from the previous night had lost its strength and the pungent salt air lifted her senses as the ocean rocked in glassy curves along the coast. She searched in her pocket, found her sunglasses, and pushed the loose ends of her auburn hair into a ponytail. There had been no point in unpacking, and the night at the Youth Hostel had afforded little privacy. On arrival at the holiday cottage, she would shower and change into something more suitable.

The ship sailed past Newlyn and Mousehole, with the Minack Theatre nestling in the distant cliffs above Porthcurno. The ship rolled like the gentle rocking of a baby, and an hour later, Land's End appeared as a grey line on the horizon.

Next to Pippa sat a family with two children. The boy, looking white in the face, asked, 'Are we nearly there yet, Dad?'

'Not long now, son. In about an hour we'll see the islands.'

Pippa stared at the child, his sweet young face attempting a smile at his sister. Not wishing to meet his eyes, Pippa turned away. Without warning, the boy ran to the side of the ship and threw up. *Oh God, poor kid, I know how that feels.* In her pocket she found a packet of tissues, which she handed to the child's mother.

'Thanks, he's not usually this bad,' said the woman. 'William, come here, darling, the nice lady has given us a hanky for you.'

It seemed almost every parent had named their son either William or Harry in the last few years. Pippa moved away; there were too many memories.

As she leaned on the rail, gazing out to sea, she recalled the conversation at the doctor's surgery back home in Whitby. She'd told her GP she was going to the islands for a break; only *he* understood.

'You know, Mrs Lambton, you ought to contact the local bird club and meet like-minded people. It'll do you a lot of good. If you go to Scaling Dam, there's a bird hide along the shore. You should try birdwatching, it's a very healthy hobby and not just for men. Women do it as well! Also, you must take a break somewhere and relax.'

She went home to Rob and told him what the doctor had said.

'I'm not interested in all that stuff, it's not for me.'

He'd laughed when she'd bought a new waterproof jacket from the sports shop in town; she needed something to keep her warm. But Rob, thinking his comments amusing, remarked, 'Where's your deerstalker? Bloody hell, Pippa, you'll be buying a rifle next.' She'd felt impatient at his silliness, but held her tongue, often wishing she really had bought a rifle. Well no, but... *Hell, why does every word need to be planned?* Over the months, she realised how Rob's attitudes were more of a challenge. He'd applied to do a counselling course for his job. He told her it might help to sort his mind, but instead it made him worse. He had become more self-aware and she began to think he disliked what he saw.

His words came flooding back. 'For God's sake, Pippa, you can be so bloody stupid at times.'

If I had bought that rifle, I probably wouldn't be here now. Pippa sighed. The idea of disappearing to a remote island was the right thing to do.

She recalled the day she went to the cemetery and met a man, who said, 'Maybe one day you'll find direction around the corner, where it's been waiting to meet you,' Yes, of course, that was it! She needed direction. That was her real reason for coming here. The man was right, perhaps it was all "just around the corner", but five hundred miles away.

Pippa's attention was suddenly caught by the clown-like puffins and guillemots rafting on the sea. A puffin flew across the bow of the ship. She used to think they were much larger. In recent years, everything had become larger than life: the agony, the sorrow, and the guilt. It had all been too much.

Splash! A couple of bottle-nosed dolphins surfaced in the ship's wake, and with enthusiasm everyone stood on deck, dolphin spotting.

'Look, there's one. Dad! Get the camera, quick.'

Pippa smiled. *He'll be lucky.* She looked behind her to the place where they had sat on the previous visit. Daniel had spotted the basking sharks first. 'Mummy, look at the big whale,' he'd said.

With a wonderful sense of freedom, he'd learned so much about the wildlife through the local young birders club. 'Aw, Dad, won't you come as well?' he had pleaded. They always left home feeling sad that Rob wasn't with them. She'd had to make excuses for Rob's lack of enthusiasm. Instead of walking the beach with Daniel, Rob spent too much time down at the pub with Terry and his mates. It was all too convenient having a pub on your doorstep. There had been days since losing Daniel when she could have hidden away in a corner with some pills and a strong sense to take the lot. Daniel's face kept her going. What would he have thought if she had given up on him? She was about to cry, but stopped herself. It was no good crying now; what was the point?

*

10

The ship continued to roll, and the child she had helped earlier looked very white in the face. 'How's he doing?' asked Pippa.

The mother smiled. 'He'll be okay once we get to the other side.'

Pippa turned her head away to look out to sea again; the dolphins were gone.

She turned her gaze towards the horizon and her thoughts changed to best friends, Joan and Terry. They had always been there for her; soul mates all their lives, but where was Rob when she needed him – or did she need him? Of late, he seemed very confused about himself. She craved his love and affection, but somewhere a great hole had opened up and nothing remained to bridge the widening gap. Strange emotions had willed her to come here and she found it hard to explain.

Her eyes scanned the horizon for St Martin's, Tresco, Bryher and St Agnes, firing thoughts about her impending arrival at "Gilstone Cottage". She planned to sit on the beach with the palm trees waving in the summer breeze. Oh yes, this trip would be a soul-searching experience, for sure. She focussed her binoculars as the blue-grey of the islands appeared on the horizon.

Pippa swallowed hard and shuddered with a sense of "I always wanted to be here", as if an old friend on the other side awaited her with a longing to put their arms around her, kiss her, and say, 'I'm so very glad you're back. I missed you. You're going to be fine now.' If only it were real. This vivid imagination, this indulgence, provided a sensation of belonging and hope. Today, she knew what lay ahead: a bag of happiness waiting to be unwrapped.

She leaned over the rail and looked down at the azure sea at the way the ship cut through the swell. A gull flew overhead; its call reminded her of home and Rob. Her doctor had been right, she needed the break; surely Rob must have realised, he was supposed to know about these things. *He's a nurse, for God's sake. Why doesn't he understand?*

The greyness of the horizon turned to green as she recognised the shapes of the rocks. A helicopter drummed across the sky, about to land at the airport, down, down, down, to disappear over the hill beyond.

The ship rolled across Crow Sound towards *The Road*, a blue lagoon where the sea once flooded the palm of an imaginary hand, leaving fingers of land protruding high above the waves. Pippa gazed into the depths of the water as the ship slowed and the crew prepared to dock. Fronds of kelp and bladder wrack swayed in the tides, and the white sand revealed a playground for crab and lobster.

The ferry entered the harbour and the drumming of the ship's engines quietened, then stopped. The harbourmaster's voice echoed from the quay and made her turn. With a look of mock impatience, he gestured to the crew as if using sign language to the deaf. The First Officer came out from the bridge to see who was making the commotion.

'Hey, you lot! You're like a pack of amateur sailors on a week-end cruise. Get that blummin' ship further down the quay!' He used his thumb in a backward gesture and rolled his eyes in mock impatience. 'Honestly, you'd think we'd never done this before.' He grinned at the passengers. 'You might realise, folks, you've arrived on St Mary's. Welcome to the islands, everyone.'

Pippa sensed the holiday laughter coming from the quay. The call of the gulls made her feel as if she'd belonged here all her life. It brought to mind the atmosphere from her last visit, the working relationship between shore and ship. She had seen the well-practised routine before. They were great people: a community where goal setting was all about the challenges of living in a remote location. The setting of the islands had captured her thoughts from the first moments she stepped on them with Rob and Daniel. They'd taken a holiday in Cornwall and wanted to explore the Isles of Scilly. 'Let's buy a ticket, it sounds lovely,' she'd said. Rob, as usual, wasn't keen. He was worried in case he was seasick and made a fool of himself.

'Come on, Daddy, it's a big ship. We have to go on it…please.'

*

12

Pippa waited until the doors were open and she could walk ashore. *Freedom at last!*

Once again, she watched as the crew wheeled the gangway into position.

'Are you sure you want this 'ere? There are too many people wandering around. Harry, mate, get this area roped off before we unload, please.'

With the chatter of tourists on the quay, Pippa pulled herself back to reality as the dockers tied the ropes. Within minutes, the ship's crane had extracted cargo from the hold. Luggage containers were winched off first, and then a car, followed by scuba-diving gear.

The forklift driver shouted instructions to his colleagues on the quay and poked his head around the cab. 'Stick them over there.' He pointed towards a container.

Pippa spotted the lorry taking delivery of luggage to the hotels and holiday cottages. She had seen it all before. Fascinated, she watched what appeared to be organised confusion, and the way they steered every piece of cargo onto the quay.

She loved how the granite harbour glinted in the sun, and the many coloured boats, anchored in the bay, nodded on their moorings. Day-trippers returned from the outer islands, binoculars hung around their necks, and rucksacks slung over their shoulders. The salt air, once again, tasted of summer holidays and the happiness she craved.

Pippa puffed out her cheeks as she lifted her heavy bag to her shoulder. *Hell, how much stuff did I pack in this thing?* It was only a ten-minute walk to the cottage, but she changed her mind about walking as she spotted a taxi and poked her head through the passenger window.

'Gilstone Cottage, please.'

'Have you come far?' he asked.

'I've travelled down from Whitby in Yorkshire.'

'Oh, okay. You got the same things as us, 'aven't you?' He

wrinkled his brow and chuckled as he steered away from the cobbles on the quay and turned the corner by The Mermaid pub.

'Birds… I love watching the birds down here, and the sea is bluer.'

The taxi driver smiled. 'The Birdman is away this month, but I'm sure you'll find someone doing a birdwatching tour from the Wildlife Trust, or whatever they call it these days. They got an office up the hill.'

Pippa prayed there would be no more questions.

As they drove along Hugh Street, her memories were all too clear. She wondered how she would be able to ignore the images. She recalled Daniel walking by the shops with a small backpack on his shoulders as she passed by the place where they had bought ice creams. She saw the toyshop on the corner with the buckets and spades, but the old bus in which she'd toured the island caught her eye. They still had it, parked and empty; she imagined herself coming down the steps.

Visitors and locals cycled along the street, and an elderly woman sat with her eyes closed in a deckchair outside her pristine cottage. Two minibuses stood near the red phone box in the centre of town, and a vision came of Rob, *yes, Rob again*…with Daniel on his knee, licking their ice creams on the square. *What would all this mean, being here alone?*

If only she could live without blame or forever seeking Rob's approval. *What if things had been different?* There had to be a degree of acceptance, a lessening of despair. Leaving Henrietta Street for a while might make things easier, a time for reflection, and a chance to consider what to do next. Her old friends and neighbours, Joan and Terry, had moved away to the edge of town; perhaps it was her time to move on as well.

The driver stopped near the museum. 'Have a nice holiday,' he said.

Pippa paid him and he handed her the rucksack from the boot. A piece of paper pinned on the green wooden door caught her eye.

Dear Mrs Lambton,
Go in, I will come with the keys later. Your food delivery is in
the fridge.
Regards,
Janice Stowes

Pippa stepped inside the old stone-clad house. She felt like Alice peering down the rabbit hole, needing time to adjust from the sunlight as she explored the living room. The cottage was bright and clean, with 1970s-style furniture, basic but pleasant. The description in the advert had been accurate: "in the centre of town and easy access for the boats".

She stepped into the conservatory where a door led to a small back yard. A vase of flowers stood on a table to welcome her.

She heard a knock and the front door opened.

'Helloo, Mrs Lambton… Sorry I wasn't 'ere when you come. As you can see, we don't usually lock our doors on the island; the crime rate is very low. They can't easily escape from St Mary's,' she jested. 'Still, 'ere's the key. We 'arve a lot of people milling around the place when the boat comes in. So maybe it's best to lock up.' She placed the key on the dining table.

'Ah, you must be Janice! Great to meet you. Thanks for fitting me in.'

'That's fine, m'dear, a pleasure to 'arve you. 'Bin 'ere before?'

'This is my second time on Scilly,' explained Pippa.

'Okay. I 'ope you enjoy yourself.'

She felt Janice was dying to ask why she was alone; perhaps good manners restrained her. Pippa had spent her life volunteering information, and felt it was good to stand back and be anonymous for a change. Instead, Janice merely pointed to the instructions on the cork notice board for the smooth running of the cottage.

'I 'ope you will be comfortable. If you need anything, just ask. Electricity is on the meter, but you'll need ten pence pieces. We don't mind if you want to use candles, as long as you're careful. My place is the last 'ouse near the pharmacy on the 'arbour, it's called *First and Last Outpost.*'

Pippa smiled; she liked the name of Janice's house, and, of course, these islands were the last English outpost before the USA, so it made sense. She also liked Janice and her Cornish accent, and wished she could stay longer. 'Did you get my cheque?' Pippa asked.

'Er, I think so, er…yes, I did.' Janice nodded.

Pippa thought Janice's business methods seemed very lax. While on the phone from home, she had insisted on sending a cheque for the deposit and had asked what would happen if she couldn't make it. Janice replied that she wasn't bothered. 'There's always someone to fill the space in the summer.'

Pippa smiled and realised Janice had edged towards the door.

'Have a nice 'oliday, dear, and let me know if there is anything I can get you. Bye.'

Pippa gazed through the lounge window as Janice hurried in the direction of town. She sighed. Now that the owner of the house had gone, perhaps she could relax her thoughts and explore.

She unpacked her bag and placed her shorts, jeans, and T-shirts into the old tallboy dresser in her room. Perhaps if she took a stroll after lunch she could walk around town and go back down the quay. With Rob not being here, the holiday would be more relaxing. No – that sounded mean. *If only Joan, Terry and Rob could see me now.* It was astonishing to think as best friends they had been together all these years, but how much longer could they live like this? Was the tension between them just her imagination? Now she was here, it was as if something marvellous was about to happen. All she wanted was a guilt-free holiday and a second chance in life. Surely, this beautiful place would provide her with the respite she needed.

Chapter Two

Rob yawned and longed for the freedom to spread his legs under the bed sheets. He squeezed his eyelids together. *Bloody night shifts!*

The light flashed on the answer phone; he listened to Pippa's message. 'Hi, Rob, I'm in Penzance. Sorry I missed you. Bye.' The communication was always short and sharp. Living without her for three weeks had to be a test of his feelings. Did he want to be part of her anymore? He couldn't leave Whitby, but the house wasn't his to sell. She ought to have signed over to joint names after her father died, but they never got around to it. He scolded himself for not pushing the issue.

He often told his patients, 'If what you are doing isn't working, you should change it' – a phrase he'd learned in his training. God! How he'd tried to change.

'Daniel is all around us, I can't stand it,' he'd told Pippa.

'Well, that's normal, Rob, what do you expect? He was *our* son.' Aware of the tearful tone in her voice, he hated himself for being so cold. *What was I supposed to say?*

'We have to move on, it's your choice,' he'd said.

'Are you threatening me again?' *More tears!* He knew she had cried too many times and he ought to be sympathetic, but with Pippa, those feelings wouldn't come. He never wanted to appear mean and resentful, but sometimes he couldn't help himself. The course wasn't making things easy, even though he might learn something from the study. His tutor had said he should try being more true to himself.

Recent arguments washed across his thoughts. 'You're provoking me, Pippa. I don't need this. Sometimes my life is better when you're *not* here. We have to stop playing mind games.' Why did he say those things? It just came out that way. 'I didn't mean it, sorry.'

'Yes you did, Rob. I get the message.'

He recalled how she'd stormed off out the back door into the yard for a breath of fresh air and he'd followed her. 'I think we ought to go for divorce. This isn't working, is it?

'Rob, for Christ's sake, leave me alone. I need…need *understanding*! Love! Not *this*!' Then she was gone…

Rob caught a glimpse of the end of Breakfast TV and finished his sandwich as he pressed the remote buttons, channel hopping. He hoped to see the news about the FIFA World Cup, but he'd missed it. *Damn! Now – what should I do?* He closed his mouth after a huge yawn; the cold egg and bacon sandwich tasted like cardboard.

The phone rang; he decided not to answer it. He knew it was Joan calling, but now was not the time. Exhaustion pulled him down, that was all, and he didn't wish for further intrusion. No, he would leave it to ring.

He switched off the TV and made his way upstairs. Alone at last, he now had a chance to get his mind around the days ahead. He shook his head in sheer frustration and weariness.

As he passed the bathroom, he paused for a moment as sunlight peeked through the cracks in Daniel's room. The nameplate was no longer on the door; all he could see was the outline of an empty space where the sticker used to be.

He turned the knob and went in… *Oh my god, what has she done? When? Why didn't she tell me she had taken "the shrine" away?*

He stood back, staring at the changes. The heavy feelings in his chest began to creep in; the memories, the day of the accident, and Pippa's time in hospital.

The bed, now in a different place, was made with a fresh duvet cover and no sign that Daniel ever existed. He glanced at the teddy on the windowsill and confused feelings of anger and resentment dominated his thoughts. *Where the hell's the rest of Dan's toys?* He opened the old oak wardrobe and discovered an overloaded black bin liner. A piece of Lego protruded from the bag.

He looked in the drawers. 'Oh my God, Dan's clothes are all gone.' He sat on the bed in what seemed like a different room and a dreadful ache cramped his chest. For the first time since Daniel died, he cried. *How could she?* His father always told him to stand up and be a man, but now his hands had become salty-wet from the tears. He rolled on his side and lay on the bed where his son had slept. *Why? Why?* Those dreadful feelings of hate for Pippa began to return. *Why had she done this without saying a word? I never thought...* He wanted to be there too, take things slow, with dignity, not sling Daniel's possessions into plastic bags, and stuff them in the wardrobe! Then he remembered he had asked her to do it.

He lay back on the bed, staring at the ceiling and imagining himself as his own patient in one of his counselling sessions, but this time someone else, an imaginary middle-aged woman in a grey suit, asked the questions.

What do you feel right now?

Betrayal.

What does betrayal mean to you?

My parents, my lost life, my son, my wife.

What are your feelings right now?

I'm angry.

Tell me about your anger, Rob.

Pippa has gone away when she should be supporting me.

Do you love her?

I don't know.

How do you feel about her?

I don't KNOW!

He had to stop punishing himself.

How am I supposed to respond? He'd never cried in front of Pippa. Why should he start feeling this way today, and why did counselling never work when you tried it on yourself? Sometimes he had been two people. *Pippa was right.* At work: the caring Rob, his patients praising him, but the Rob at home had no sense of who he was any more, and now had a wife who was somewhere else.

He stood to look in the mirror and stroked his hair. He ought to go and have it cut; his last visit had been two months ago. Maybe this time he would ask the hairdresser to cut it shorter; he might grow a beard and re-invent himself. He knew he'd lost weight where the other guys had put on a few pounds since their marriage; he looked more like a stick. Maybe he should be grateful he wasn't fat. If he stopped smoking… He'd been through all that many times with Pippa. He tried to pull himself together and muster some enthusiasm, but for now, sleep was a priority. He stood with resentment and left the room.

He didn't bother taking off his clothes. Pulling back the covers, he puffed up the feather pillows. Pippa hadn't made the bed; she hardly ever did. When one of them got out, the other got in. He took a deep breath and squinted at the clock through tear-filled eyes. *What time is it?* He ought to snatch a few hours until Pippa called him and then go to the pub. He had the evening off – darts night and free food but at least he didn't have to cook! He raised his hands to his face, pressing his fingers into his brow in frustration. Once he got his head down, he promised himself he would be calmer.

He took off his shoes and socks, undressed down to his boxers, and listened to the ticking clock. He lay on the bed with the curtains closed and the sound of tourists walking outside on the pavement. If only he could shut everything away in an instant.

Half an hour elapsed and sleep still eluded him, his mind rippling with recollections of his childhood and the sadness. Aware of the clock, "tick-a-tock, tock-a-tick"; the sound became as intrusive as tinnitus.

He must have dozed off for a short while, and in his dreams he heard the voice of a child. On waking, he thought he saw Daniel standing at the end of the bed. 'Daddy, I want a drink. Daddy, I'm cold, can I come into bed with you and Mummy?' He shut his eyes in case it was real. *I can't do this!*

Once again, sleep evaded him and more thoughts flooded his mind. As he lay there staring at the ceiling, the faces of Pippa and Joan soared across his imagination.

He recalled how he used to picture himself with two girlfriends, lying in bed with one on either side. *Hell, how self-assured I must have been in those days.*

Perhaps the lure of Pippa's independence had brought them together – or was it something else? *Had I really loved her? It all felt so safe.* He recalled lying on top of her, panting and moaning in pleasure. He'd become worried in case she got pregnant, and he'd thought about Terry giving out packets of "Johnnies" he'd nicked from a broken vending machine. He had heard they were not reliable, and sighed with relief when two weeks later Pippa told him she had "come on". He needn't have worried; the sex was as good as he'd imagined. He thought he was in heaven. Oh yes, he'd been proud of her all right, but love was only a word he used. It's what you did with it… *I was never in love. I know that now.*

'Perhaps one day you might discover more about your real parents,' Pippa reminded.

'To be honest, Pippa, I'm not that interested. Why should I want to know them? My mother abandoned me.'

'But, Rob, there are reasons why people do these things, it might not have been her fault.'

'She had me, didn't she?'

'Anything could have happened, don't judge, Rob. Anyway it's not for me to push the issue.'

Pippa didn't want any more children – or sex. She thought she might get pregnant again, and history had a habit of repeating itself.

His hand rested against his groin. *Right now, a good fuck is the answer.* He must try to break this barrier between them. *I need to be stronger; no more excuses.* All he could muster was a "do-it-yourself" job when she wasn't around to listen. At least, he hoped she wasn't listening.

Maybe she was right, it was time to go looking for his real mother. Of late, it had been impossible. Now that Pippa had gone away for three weeks to gather her thoughts, he also had more freedom to consider the future. Two things his counselling course couldn't tell him: who is the real Rob Lambton and where did he come from?

Through the half-open bedroom window, the intermittent odour of smoked herring drifted from the kipper smokehouse. Whitby kippers were his favourite, and the town had so much to offer. Why would Pippa want to go to Scilly? Rob's own experience of the islands was not so different from being at home. They had a harbour with boats and fishermen. Scilly felt like a busman's holiday. He'd often told Pippa, 'Give me a mountain in the Lake District any day.'

Now that Joan and Terry had moved away, what else was there? *They've got young Jordan to think of, I suppose.*

For a moment, Rob's thoughts turned to Terry. Why hadn't he been back from the oil rigs in ages? Rob never dared to ask Joan in case he upset her.

It was the phone call, the one all parents dread, the one he would never forget. He'd thought about the tragedy too many times and he wished he could stop doing it. He promised himself another dog was out of the question. She had been the cause of his son's death, running out into the road like that! Why did Dan run after her? Pippa should have held tighter on to his hand.

He slipped a cigarette out of the packet from the bedside table and put it to his lips. His thumb flicked over the lighter and he hesitated a moment before inhaling. His mind still on Pippa, he blew relaxed smoke rings and watched himself in the mirror as a series of perfect O's chased each other. He kept promising Pippa that each cigarette would be his last. Would it be this one? Hell, no. Now was not the time to give up, not yet. Perhaps if he put the radio on, he might fall asleep. He stubbed his cigarette into a half-full ashtray and wriggled into the mattress.

He reached over to the radio and pressed the switch. At least he'd smoked this ciggy without Pippa niggling at him about smoking in bed. He knew he ought to practise what he preached, all those campaign posters at work. He would fall asleep listening to Radio 4, and the voice of Brian Redhead on the *Today* programme might help him drift away. It usually did.

Chapter Three

Pippa headed into Hugh Town; the aroma of fresh-baked bread wafted across the street from the bakery. At a steady pace, she made her way towards First and Last Outpost. At the front of Janice's cottage, in a small patch of garden, a flush of exotic flowers lined the path. The sway of the old granite wall provided a refuge for pennywort and mesembryanthemum. Spikes of tall agapanthus with blue trumpet-shaped flowers stood tall through the foliage.

As she continued towards the harbour, she noted the souvenirs on sale outside the old-fashioned shop windows. Brightly coloured tea towels, with pictures of puffins and seals, were hung on string and pegged out, as if on a washing line.

Pippa very quickly became aware of how she once walked this spot with Daniel and Rob. Wearing his red *Start-Right* sandals, Dan had complained about having to walk so far, his legs were tired. She thought she could hear him talking to her. 'Mummy, my legs hurt – carry me.' She recalled how Rob had picked him up and lifted him onto his shoulders.

She told herself not to crumble on the first day of her holiday. *You can do this.* Joan often warned her not to keep punishing her grief.

She made her way down to the quay where notice boards provided information like shopping lists. Today had moved on; tomorrow's boat trips already advertised.

Tourists strolled along the harbour, and the *Scillonian,* still tied to the pier, reminded her of an old dog waiting for its master.

Pippa walked almost shoulder to shoulder to meld with the crowd. If she made enquiries for the birdwatching tours, it would be a start. She picked out snatches of conversation and listened as the atmosphere rang with voices.

'Don, what time you taking *Lily of Laguna* out tomorrow?'

'Mick, is your puffin cruise booked now?'

'And normally he has fish for breakfast.'

She smiled to herself. It was like Whitby; only the accent was different.

The name Don was one she recalled from her last visit. *Oh yes, I remember him.* His infectious laughter and humour had made her smile. She wanted to go over to him and say, 'Hi, remember me?' but he wouldn't have remembered her, for sure.

Tourists wore the usual summer clothes: shorts and sandals. Others donned weatherproof clothing for the deeper water out at sea. Pippa watched as day-trippers mingled together, each on a mission of pure leisure. A breeze blew across the stone pier, and the anglers reeled in their tackle due to the fast falling tide. She followed them along the quay, their rods in one hand and a small catch of fish in the other.

With the bustle of life in the harbour, she reckoned she might be lonely if she didn't push herself forward and join in. From her life in Whitby, she knew too well the ways of local people. You had to introduce yourself and be part of the scene.

The morning trip returning from St Martin's moored alongside another boat. Passengers disembarked by walking across both vessels onto the granite steps.

A well-tanned man with blond hair caught her eye. She saw him packing up his telescope and making conversation with the skipper. He had his back to Pippa before turning to one of the passengers and assisting her to climb the harbour steps.

'Bye, and thanks,' said the woman.

'Hope you enjoyed the trip.' The man continued to help the other passengers. He had a slight foreign accent; perhaps he was

German? Pippa found it hard to tell as his English was excellent and he pronounced some of his words like a Cornishman.

'Many thanks. Mind how you go, Mrs Dewhurst. Don will take you back to St Martin's at four o'clock. Oh, hello Sam, didn't realise you were on the boat today, how's your mum? Take it easy, madam, step on this one first then hang on to the rail, the steps are wet, be careful now. Well done...bye.'

Ten minutes later, Pippa gazed into the empty boat. 'Excuse me,' she called. 'Can you tell me if you are doing any more trips today?' She felt her awkwardness might show and wondered if her question was stupid.

The man removed his sunglasses, looked up at her and smiled. He climbed the steps so he could hear her, and she saw how tall and attractive he appeared, with eyes the colour of the sea. She looked away from him, hoping she wasn't being a nuisance.

'I'm sorry, but *Lily of Laguna* isn't going out again until tomorrow. You could try the other boatmen. We have a couple of repairs to do.' He paused for a moment. 'Erm...if you want to come with us, you can buy a ticket for tomorrow on this boat, if you like.' He smiled at her again.

Pippa brought her hand up to shade her eyes. The sun's reflection on the water dazzled her. 'Thanks very much, I'd love to.'

'Was there anything in particular you wanted to see?'

'I'd like to learn more about the islands, and maybe do a spot of birdwatching.' She touched the binoculars around her neck. 'I've just started and I'm not very good at it yet.'

'Well... I do the birdwatching tours, and most of my visitors are learning like you. My colleague, Martin – everyone calls him The Birdman – is away now on tour in West Africa, but I'm here if you want to book a trip tomorrow, yes?'

She hesitated, then nodded. 'Oh, of course, I heard about The Birdman, and yes, that would be excellent.'

'I'm doing a guided walk and so far we've got seven bookings. I expect more later. We are going to St Martin's. How about the morning trip?' He smiled straight at her, as if willing her to say "yes".

'Okay, I'll get a ticket,' she said, realising her own enthusiasm. *God – what am I doing?* She found herself saying "yes" for the first time in ages.

He began to walk away from her. 'Come on, then' he beckoned 'I'll help you. I'll see if Andy is in the kiosk and try to get you one of my special tickets.'

Unsure of herself, Pippa followed him a short distance along the old granite quay. He stopped and turned around to face her. 'It's a great place this, you know. We have a lot of history in these islands.'

'Mm, I bet. So exactly who is this Birdman?'

'Oh well, we've always had a Birdman around the place since the late 1700s. His job was to collect puffins for food, an important source of meat in times of famine. These days it's a title handed down through the generations. Of course, now nature conservation is the key issue.'

Again, he smiled at Pippa; his blue eyes seemed to read her thoughts.

'Anyway,' he added, 'I'm here doing these tours until my colleague returns in a few weeks' time. He's the expert. My usual role is to manage the nature reserve.'

It was what she needed. Someone she could recognise and with whom she could converse on her daily strolls down the quay.

He turned towards the boatman on duty in the kiosk. 'Just one ticket for tomorrow for the nice lady with *Lily* please, Andy.'

'Two pounds to you, ma luv,' said Andy, giving Pippa the change from a five-pound note. 'You're lucky to catch me 'ere at this time, I only opened up for that big cruiser we 'ad this afternoon. Just finishing up for a cuppa tea.'

Pippa thanked him and turned to her guide. 'So I suppose you're the expert now, then?' She hoped her question wasn't too impertinent. 'I'd like to find out more. I'm here for three weeks, so what do you suggest I do?'

She heard Andy chuckle at the word "expert". He looked at Sven and grinned.

'I suppose I am, really, if you put it like that. I think I had better introduce myself. I'm Sven Jørgensen. I originally came from Norway, but I live here now.'

She took his hand; his grip felt genuine and welcoming. *Norway, eh? Gosh, he's so suntanned. He must spend hours on these boats every day.*

'I'm Pippa. How long have you been here on Scilly?'

'Oh, it must be, erm…almost six years now. I work for the new Scilly Environmental Trust and generally make a nuisance of myself. I'm actually an ornithologist. If you are interested in birds, then I'm your man!'

Pippa giggled to herself. His long blond hair and suntan made her wonder whose man he really was. How silly, she hadn't realised he was the main tour guide for the islands. She was only trying to cheer herself up. He must have thought she was some dizzy woman on holiday trying to make out she was a proper birdwatcher. Still, he seemed helpful, which was something she needed right now.

'Listen, erm…' He scratched the side of his nose. 'The slide show is on tomorrow night in the church hall – perhaps you can come? You will learn a lot about the history of the islands and the bird life. Bring your family and friends.'

Pippa replied without hesitation. 'Okay, sounds like a great idea. Although I don't have anyone I can bring, but I will come, I promise.'

'Oh I see, well…' He hesitated for a moment.

Before he could finish his sentence, Pippa filled in the details. 'I'm just taking a break, you know how it is, a spot of respite, you might say.'

'Respite?' echoed Sven.

Annoyed with herself for hinting she had a problem, she disguised it with her next piece of information. 'I've been to Scilly

before, but I enjoyed the atmosphere so much, I've come back for a longer stay.'

If only she could stop being in eternal grief; would it always be this way? The short answer was—yes.

'Give me a second. Are you walking back into town?' asked Sven.

Pippa nodded. 'Yep.'

'Let's walk back to the boat. Just got to pick up a few things, and then I'll walk up that way with you.'

Pippa followed him.

'I'm pleased you came, it's a great place to start learning.' He looked at Don in the boat. 'Mate, pass me my bins and 'scope, can you?'

Don obeyed, giving Pippa a sideways glance. 'Watch 'im, young lady, he has an eye for all the young girls.'

'Thanks, Don.' Sven grinned, rolled his eyes, and ignored t comment.

Pippa chuckled at his apparent shyness. She liked the he spoke, his Norwegian accent, his politeness, and gentle He had well-cared-for teeth beneath a kind smile. He would, i be a useful person to get to know for the information she about the wildlife tours. After all, she had come here to learn

Having changed from his boots to a pair of open-toe Sven tied the laces together, and slung the boots over his He wore cut-off denim jeans, revealing long suntanned the hairs had bleached in the sun. His white T-shirt accentuate his tan. He struggled to organise himself strap here and another one there, boots dangling an a bag to carry it all.

'See ya, Don. I'll be back down here later, as up his hand in a gesture of farewell to the skipper continued walking with Pippa. They paused for their backs against the granite wall as a lorry loa turned the corner.

'I remember Don from the day trip I had

He was telling me about Tresco and the gardens,' recalled Pippa. 'Yeah, he seems to be a good laugh. Nice guy.'

'Ah yes, you said you'd been here before. Where are you staying now?' asked Sven.

She was glad he didn't ask her about the last trip. 'I've hired a cottage near the Museum: Gilstone. D'ya know it?'

'Ya, sure, the old place is now owned by Janice Stowes. The house used to belong to her mother before she got Alzheimer's and went into care. Janice is a very nice lady, although a bit disorganised at times, but she has to visit her mother every day, so it's understandable, I suppose. Her husband co-owns a boat on Bryher. Are you really by yourself then?'

Pippa had never been to the island of Bryher; it was on the agenda.

'Well...yes.' She gave a half smile, desperate to move the conversation elsewhere. 'I suppose I'd better find something to do this afternoon.'

Sven turned to her. 'Look, er... I could murder a cold drink right now. Would you like to walk up to Porthcressa with me? The restaurant is open and I could tell you more about this place, which birds are here at this time of year. Perhaps I can help you decide how you want to spend your...what did you say? Your "respite".'

'Oh, that would be lovely. Much appreciated.' Pippa smiled. 'You look overloaded. Here, let me carry the boots.' Pippa held out her hand as if she was playing "mother".

'Yeah right, you noticed the clutter. I'm like the Loaded Camel up at Porth Hellick — that's a rock formation, you'll see it soon on your travels around the island. Yesterday, I lost my rucksack overboard in the wind, the sea got a bit rough. The bag sank to the bottom before we could pull it out. I had some lead weights for thing, no wonder it went down so quickly'

'Good job your "bins" weren't inside, eh?'

She saw the word *Zeiss* on his binoculars and realised it was mous name of quality.

'Oh no, I never keep them in my bag, all part of being a good birder. You never know when you might need them.'

Pippa loved his politeness, and the way he said 'yeuw' instead of 'you'. Sven stopped outside the Porthcressa Restaurant and dropped his heavy gear on the lobby floor. 'I'll leave it and pick it up when we've had coffee.'

'Can you trust dumping your bag?' Pippa asked.

'Oh, yes, we never worry too much on St Mary's about theft. This is an island.' Sven led the way through the empty tables and outside on to the veranda. He drew out a chair for her.

Aw…how kind. Rob had never done that all their married life. Small gestures made a difference.

Pippa captured the view, her mind on the glassy sea and the wonderful scenery. 'Wow, this is lovely,' she said, staring out beyond the bay.

Sven sat opposite her. 'I know, this is one of my favourite views, too. I see it every day from my bedroom window. Don and I often come up here when he's not on the boat. It's a great place to relax and have a beer.'

The waitress came towards the table with her pad and pencil. 'What can I get you, Sven?'

He passed the menu to Pippa. 'The usual beer, Christine, please.'

Pippa scanned the list at the choice of iced cakes.

'I'll have a coffee and…oo, yes…a lemon gateau, thanks.' She looked up and smiled at the waitress.

'Good choice. Try the Black Forest one next time you come,' recommended Sven.

'You must have loads of friends?' asked Pippa.

'Yeah, sure. My colleague Martin – you know, The Birdman I told you about? He's the big boss around here, makes all the decisions when he's back in town. Just now, I deputise for him. It's the first time I've been in charge. I may not be here much longer when my contract runs out. I have to wait until he gets back. He lives with his wife just over the hill.' Sven pointed behind him towards The Garrison. 'It's not like on the mainland. Here everyone knows who you are, and sometimes things can be rather intrusive. Do you have lots of friends back home?'

'Yes, two very good friends and a couple of school friends.'

Pippa sat, resting her chin on clasped hands, hanging on to his every word.

'We have some great birds around at the moment,' he said. 'You'll find the common birds have no fear of people and the thrushes will come and feed from your hand.' He carried on listing the birds. '…Peregrine, roseate tern, puffins, guillemots, razorbills, all the usual stuff.'

Pippa's mind began to wander; some of the names she didn't know, but she felt she could listen to his accent all day. His English was good, very good. Thrilled at her invitation for refreshments, she welcomed it during her first few hours on the island. He knew his birds, for sure. She jolted herself back to the conversation.

'…and you can do the Shearwater trip if you like. You should see life here in October when all the Twitchers arrive. The place gets busy again. Oh yes, never a dull moment, I can tell you.' Sven laughed.

Pippa wondered why people would travel hundreds of miles chasing after rare birds only to tick them off on a list. Surely they weren't real birdwatchers.

The coffee and cake arrived, and Christine lifted the glass of beer from her tray and placed it on the table. She smiled at Sven and cleared the other glasses.

'Where did you say you lived?' asked Sven.

'Whitby, it's on the Yorkshire coast. I live close to the harbour. I was born in the town. I suppose this is why I have this affinity with Scilly. It's just so much nicer here, though. I adore the islands and the blue sea – although Whitby is larger, and we have a lot of ancient history in the place. It's also famous for the Dracula stories, did you know?' Pippa chuckled, enjoying the role of tour guide for her hometown.

'Oh, I didn't know that. Spooky, eh?' Sven leaned on the table and mirrored her clasped hands. A moment later, he picked up his beer, supping the head from the top of the glass. He wiped his lips on the back of his index finger. 'So…what birds do you see in that part of the world?'

Pippa felt the usual dread of questions, and hoped he wasn't going to ask her those things. She would have to tell him she didn't know. An involuntary movement of her hand caused her to drop a spoon on the floor, and Sven bent to pick it up. There was no nicotine on his fingers like Rob's. How she hated cigarettes. They had put her father in hospital, the very same place where Rob worked. How could he not realise smoking was bad for you?

'Thanks, sorry,' she said, slightly embarrassed as Sven handed her the spoon. 'Ah yes, birds, the same as here, I think, but not so many. I know we get a few gannets in August.'

He smiled at her, ignoring the incident. 'So what got you into birding then?'

'Well, my father used to work on the Balmoral estate in Scotland before he married my mother, and then in later years he was always interested in the wildlife on the Yorkshire Moors. He was a volunteer grouse beater. So I knew the names of a few birds before…' she almost mentioned Daniel and stopped herself, 'my dad passed away some years ago… I miss him a lot.'

Sven empathised and drew in closer to hear what she was saying above the noise of the mewing gulls. 'I'd like to go up there sometime.'

'I live very close to the Abbey steps in the famous old Henrietta Street. Did you know there are one hundred and ninety-nine of them to the top? My friend always gets it wrong. You can see the jawbone of a whale representing an archway on the cliffs in Whitby. I think it was presented to the town's folk from the people of Norway,' she hinted.

'Sounds like a great place if they are friends of my country,'

Pippa felt the warmth of his smile, and was glad she had told him. She listened as he explained his father was Swedish and had married his Norwegian mother. They lived in Trondheim, his birth-place. 'I'm hoping they will come next year and visit me – they've never been here,' he said. 'The travel takes three air flights, and that makes the holiday very expensive. My mother is a bit interfering sometimes, you know like mothers can be, but she means well.'

Pippa lowered her gaze as Sven continued his conversation.

'I've got no idea how she would cope in my little cottage, as they have a big house. I don't have any brothers or sisters.'

Pippa looked up; she was an only child too. 'Is your father also into nature?'

'No, my dad was an engineer. It was my grandfather who used to go seal hunting, but he changed his thoughts over the years and showed me a lot about wildlife, just as your father did for you, I suppose. Have you done a lot of travel then, Pippa?'

It was the first time he had used her name, and he made her feel she belonged here.

'No, not really, well…normal living stuff, you know how it is. I spent most of my days living in my dad's house in Whitby. My mother died when I was twelve.'

Sven lowered his eyes. 'Sounds an interesting place, and losing your parents at such a young age couldn't have been easy. I'm glad I met with you anyway. It's not every day I am able to take a lunch break like this, so thanks for the company. When you take your trip tomorrow on *Lily*, I'll show you some really good birds.'

'That would be lovely,' replied Pippa. 'I'll look forward to it.'

She caught him glancing at her left hand and was clearly grateful he refrained from asking questions.

'Sorry, but I'll have to go. Our secretary, Margaret, has some work for me. Lovely lady, she retires soon. Then I'm going home for a rest, I only live over the way.' He pointed up the beach. 'It's the white house called Beachside Cottage a little further up the bay. I'm pretty lucky, really – the house belongs to the Trust.'

'Mm…that's a nice name for a house. Sounds like a great place to chill out, eh?'

He stood tall beside the table and smiled down at her. She wondered if this was another invitation for the future: more boat trips, and perhaps another coffee.

'The refreshments are on me,' he said, reaching for his wallet in the pocket of his cut-off denim shorts.

Pippa couldn't help feeling star-struck by his presence. 'Thanks, Sven, that's kind of you. My turn next time, eh?' she offered. 'And thanks for the chat, I really enjoyed it.'

'Bye, Pippa, nice to have met you. See you at the boat tomorrow.'

He left the table and her eyes followed his path as he walked into the distance, overloaded with equipment and shoes. *Oh my, he's lovely.* She shook her head and smiled at her pointless thoughts.

Alone with her lemon gateau, Pippa's eyes searched the shore. Most of the people on the islands appeared brown and weathered. It seemed that summer had brought out the best in everyone.

As she lingered at the wooden table, she gazed out on the bay, listening to the sound of terns screaming along the water's edge. A gull perched on the sea wall. It had its eye on the lemon gateau, and a battle of wills between Pippa and the gull ensued. Finally, Christine came out with the sweeping brush.

'Darned gulls, I wish people wouldn't feed them.'

Children paddled along the shore, and Pippa's thoughts turned to Daniel. She remembered he had sat by the rocks with Rob and played with the new bucket and spade. They had looked so happy making a sand castle, pressing limpet shells into the sand for the windows, driftwood for a roof, and seaweed as a flag on the top. Pippa quickly looked at her watch; it had become a habit when she thought she was about to cry. It always seemed to take her mind off the negativity so often invading her thoughts.

The town fell quiet, and a few late afternoon shoppers crossed the street. Day trippers were about to leave with the *Scillonian*. Pippa took in a deep breath of sea air. She felt a moment of bliss pass over her; perhaps these moments would last longer. She hoped they would.

The pale shingle along the shore tempted her to walk down to the receding tide. Alone with her thoughts, a good feeling kicked in as she looked towards the house Sven had indicated. There were many small cottages in the distance at the end of the beach, all painted white and facing out to sea. She looked through her binoculars and thought how lucky he was having palm trees and wonderful flowers outside his front door.

She sat a while longer, enjoying the sounds of the birds before removing her sandals to walk barefoot to the cold, clear ocean. The large grains of sand hurt her feet. The sea looked tempting and the glinting ripples crept back and forth along the shore. She splashed her feet in the water and made a sharp retreat – it was very cold. She tiptoed across the sinking sand, leaving footprints behind her; the sea lapped over them, and soon they were gone.

With her back against a granite rock, she closed her eyes to listen to the sounds of Scilly. The lapping waves on the shore and the call of the terns, "Kree-ah, Kree-ah", made her smile. She opened her eyes and watched a gannet plunge-dive into the sea beyond the bay. She almost heard the splash. The sounds made her want to stay until sundown, but she had to phone Rob.

She slipped on her sandals and plodded over the sand towards the red phone box at the town park and then cursed, remembering Rob might not be at home for at least another hour.

On arrival at the cottage, Pippa headed for the shower; the warm water down her spine was a welcome relief as she rinsed the shampoo from her hair. She thought how much she had enjoyed her conversation with Sven. He seemed very caring and was obviously having great fun in his life. Did he have a wife and kids? What exactly had brought him to these islands? He must have been here on her last visit, but the time had been too short to notice. Now she was here again, three whole weeks would be perfect.

After stepping from the shower, she towelled her body, dressed, and allowed her hair to dry in the sun. Her mind wandered to thinking how brave she had been to come here alone.

The call to Rob could wait a little longer. Now…what should she do during her holiday? She needed more self-control for a start. Perhaps she should get involved with lots of outdoor activities to keep her mind occupied. If Sven was around, she could go on his trips to the different islands and learn a lot more about the wildlife – perfect! All she wanted was Rob to tell her he loved her – and when had he last done that? Ten years ago? Three little words – that was all. He was right, they had grown up together and marriage had brought nothing but sorrow. Her father had warned her, 'You never know someone until you live with them.'

She didn't know why but the negative feelings had crept back again, and she scolded herself. *Day One – Stay positive! Joan's advice.*

Pippa's hair had dried and she wandered back to the phone box, taking her time. Inside her thoughts, a deep reluctance held her back. It would be the same old conversation for sure.

Walking around the perimeter of the park, she noticed the blue spikes of agapanthus standing tall over the wall and couldn't help thinking how wonderful it would be to live here. Sven was lucky, she thought. He'd made a great choice in his life. She entered the red phone box and took out the coins from her purse, then dialled the number.

'Hello, Rob?' she shouted. A roaring motorbike drowned the conversation; the rider sped away down the narrow street. 'Can you hear me okay? I'm fine, doing a bit of exploring. I met some nice people and had coffee with someone who does birdwatching and wildlife tours. Are you okay? Nice weather at home, is there?'

Rob didn't get a chance to answer when the "pips" sounded, and she put more money into the slot, which seemed to eat up the coins like a gaming machine.

'I'm washing up,' he said.

She heard the faint clinking of pots.

'Hang on while I dry my hands.'

Pippa pictured him with a hunched shoulder, the phone to his left ear and a tea towel in his hand. She also "saw" his unwilling face; washing up was something he hated.

The motorbike returned down the street, and she listened hard with her finger closing her right ear.

'You didn't tell me about the room,' scolded Rob.

'What room – oh, you mean Dan's room? Yes, sorry Rob, I was so busy packing, and with you being at work I didn't manage to tell you. I wanted it to be a surprise. Sorry.'

'Pippa, how could you do that? Fail to tell me you stripped the room?'

'Well, you asked me to change it lots of times, and you never go in there.'

'I thought we might have done it together.' Rob sighed.

'Sorry, Rob. These days communicating with you is so hard in case I do something else wrong. You're never around when I need you.' She recalled the number of times she had to walk on eggshells, doing things behind his back just to keep the peace.

'Well, you surprise me, Pippa. Don't you think *I* might want to be involved in this? It was very thoughtless of you.'

'As I said, that's exactly what I wanted, to surprise you. I'm sorry, Rob I didn't mean to be thoughtless. Honestly I didn't. It's just my mind these days isn't clear. Don't you understand how *I* felt when I tidied up that room? I know I should have shared the task with you, but you weren't there. I was going away and I thought you might have been pleased or even proud of me.'

Rob answered something down the phone, but Pippa's head was now full of Daniel and she wasn't really listening.

She didn't want to tell Rob she had broken Daniel's name-plate on the bedroom door; he might have complained at her again. As she'd pulled at it, she'd heard a heart-breaking *crack* and had sucked in her breath. 'Oh no, I didn't mean to do that,' she'd wailed, holding the two halves in her hand. 'Not this as well.' She wished she hadn't bothered.

'Okay, sorry, Rob.' It seemed she was always saying sorry to him, always apologising, and he blamed her for a lot of the bad things in their lives. She had felt guilty enough when Daniel had let go of her hand – not that she remembered much about it.

'Okay. Enough said, I suppose,' said Rob. 'I want you to think while you're away, you know…what we talked about?'

Her mind seemed all over the place. 'Pity I missed you yesterday, I did try to phone you,' she butted in, trying to smooth things over.

Pip, pip, pip, pip, pip. The pips stopped and she hurried through the last few words in case she got cut off mid-conversation. 'Oh, must go, the money is about to run out, it's all I've got in change for this call. Gosh, you don't get much time, do you?'

'Okay, take care then,' replied Rob, and as suddenly as he was there, he was gone.

'Bye.' The farewell was just in time, followed by a long final tone.

A tear came to her eye. *Is this how it feels to be divorced – disconnected – five hundred miles apart?* A tear dropped onto her T-shirt. *Damn him, why does he have to be like that?*

After dinner, Pippa walked down to the harbour. The local pub, *The Mermaid*, looked tempting, but she became anxious as she stepped inside. She didn't like going alone into pubs, but felt drawn to the friendly sounds coming from within. This was Scilly, you could do anything out of the ordinary here, and mainland rules didn't always apply. Anyway, going into pubs alone wasn't illegal, so what did she have to worry about? Nothing. It was all about having a good time and making the most of the island life.

The pub was frequented by the pilot gig teams – you could tell from the oars hung from the walls. The gigs were handed down through generations; famous names cheered by the tourists: Bonnet, Golden Eagle, Czar, Men-a-Vaur and more.

She squeezed between locals standing at the bar and heard singing from the room below; a song she knew well from the folk club at home. The sounds of local folk singers, serenading their sea shanties, tempted her to go down the steps to the next room. She poked her head through the door.

'For we're going to cross the water / Heave away, me jolly boys, we're all bound away.'

Pippa ordered rum and cola and sat at a table on her own with a view of the harbour, but it wasn't long before conversations sucked her into the friendly atmosphere.

'Don't sit there on yer own, girl, come and join us,' said a voice from the next table. Before she could answer, the man introduced his friends. Beer glasses stacked together on the tables showed the fun had been going on for some time. 'It's Harris's birthday – he's seventy today,' the man called above the noise.

He introduced himself. 'I'm Charlie James. This is Mark, Sue and Lydia' they nodded '…and Jan and Marijke from Holland.' Charlie pointed to a bearded man at the bar who held up his glass; they acknowledged each other. Pippa assumed this was Harris.

'Sorry, I didn't catch your name,' she said, turning to the group.

'Marijke van Diemen.' The woman held out her hand to Pippa as a welcome. 'Dit is my husband, Jan.'

Pippa smiled; she thought Jan seemed frail as he held out a skinny hand.

She wondered if Charlie had gathered all the waifs and strays on the island and put them together on one table. She sat down next to Lydia who appeared to be about the same age as her. The group rallied and encouraged her to sing along with the sea shanties. She remembered the songs from the local folk club at home.

Charlie James looked about fifty years of age, tall and slim. Pippa realised he was rather worse from the beer he was drinking. She was unsure about him; she got the impression he needed to be in the limelight to show he was in control.

'Ignore Charlie,' whispered Lydia when the singing finished. 'He can be a bit of an idiot when he's had a few pints. He works with Sven Jørgensen, "The Viking" – you know, the guy who runs the bird tours? Charlie's a volunteer with the Wildlife Trust.'

Pippa smiled at her nickname for Sven.

'Where do you live?' asked Lydia.

'I'm from Whitby, up north.'

'Oh right. I have an uncle, he lives near Scarborough. He has a farm. We used to go for holidays when we were kids.' Lydia gave a reminiscent smile.

The music rallied again and everyone joined in the chorus. Pippa found herself laughing, something she hadn't done in a very long time.

As the music played on, she sensed an atmosphere of belonging. For sure, it was like Whitby, but a lot more captivating, with its sandy beaches and palm trees blowing in the Atlantic breeze. *If Rob hadn't been so stubborn, he might have enjoyed this.* But no, under the circumstances... They both needed a chance to think about their future.

Looking out the window, she watched the melting sun between the two hills on the island of Samson and caught a glimpse of Sven on the quay with Don. Her eyes followed his every move as he stood, hands gesturing, passing the time with his friend. He waved at one of the boatmen as they headed out into the bay. Pippa stared, mouthing the words of the song.

'Come on, girl, sing up,' said Charlie, encouraging her to join in.

Marijke said, 'I know some of these songs, they are wonderful. We really like de English folk music.' Pippa turned to her, smiled and joined in the singing again. '*Way haul away...we'll haul away, Joe.*' By the time she looked again, Sven was gone.

'I have to dash now,' announced Lydia as she glanced at the time. 'I'm catching a boat back to Tresco. Don Trewin promised me a ride back before it gets too dark.' She stood. 'Nice to meet you, hope to see you around town. Bye.'

The partying continued, but the night had beaten the day. Pippa needed to visit the Ladies' room and met Marijke coming out of the adjacent cubicle.

41

'Are you going up Hugh Street?' asked Marijke. 'We could walk up together. I was meaning to ask, are you on your own here? Do you always spend holidays by yourself?'

'Yes, I'm on my own, but it's a long story, and too long to tell you all the way up Hugh Street. Anyway there's a lot to do here. I'll be fine.' Pippa smiled, trying not to say any more, and Marijke seemed to understand. Smiling your way out of sadness could make it easier to cope; she mustn't get like Rob, always inside himself, never practising what he preached. The three of them walked on through the lighted street as people left the pubs along the way. Marijke told her she lived near Utrecht and that her husband Jan was here for a rest after a serious operation to relieve his cancer.

'It's the perfect place, don't you think?' Pippa asked her. 'I do hope Jan feels he can enjoy his holiday, despite his illness.'

Jan replied, 'I wish I didn't have to go home next week, it's been wonderful.'

Pippa slowed her pace and bid farewell to Jan and Marijke. She switched on the light in the porch and closed the door.

Janice had told her Hugh Town was one of the safest places in the world. Everyone looked out for everyone else; it was that kind of place. Pippa locked the door as she was used to doing at home. She walked across the echoing stone floor to climb the stairs to bed. What would tomorrow bring? She looked forward to seeing Sven again; it was important to get to know people. Anonymity was pleasant for a while, but not every day.

She lay awake for a while with good feelings, and despite her memories of Rob and Daniel walking down Hugh Street, the whole place seemed more captivating than she'd found on her last visit. She looked forward to meeting interesting people and discovering more about the nature of Scilly and island life. Now was the opportunity to be herself, independent and happy. The drink had played its part in allowing her to drift away into the night.

Chapter Four

Joan Marshall's coffee was lukewarm. She had been chatting on the phone to her mother for the last half hour. As she sat on the kitchen stool, elbows on the work surface, she twisted her short mouse-brown hair around her fingers.

'Yes, our Mam, I'll ask him, but it's difficult. He's on the North Sea. He can't get into much trouble out there.'

'It's important, our Joan. Jordan needs his father. You have to be straight with him, love. He can't be away all this time, surely?'

'Well he is, and it doesn't *bother* me.' Joan knew she'd told a white lie. 'I mean, it's a job and he earns good money. Anyway, I never see you and Dad now you're in Devon. No big deal these days.' She thought about what she'd just said. It didn't really make sense, but at least she knew what she meant. 'Anyway, our Carole baby-sits for me, and Rob is repairing Terry's old Matchless bike. Pippa's gone away for three weeks, so now I'm relaxing.'

She peeked around the door into the lounge. Her two-year-old son, Jordan, sat watching a TV programme, singing along to *Postman Pat*. He seemed happy enough. Joan smiled as she watched him mouthing the words in his own way. Her mother was still talking on the other end of the phone and Joan hadn't really listened to a word she'd said.

'Our Mam, listen, I gotta go now, and please don't worry. I'll phone you soon, okay?

'Okay. Take care, love, and don't forget what I said… Dad sends his love. Bye.'

Joan raised her coffee cup and took a sip; it had gone cold. A pile of washing lay on the floor ready to go into the machine. If only Terry were here. The tap in the bathroom needed a new washer and the front door weatherboard kept sticking. They were nothing more than the usual domestic irritations, where a man's strength proved an asset to his wife. Only Rob had been there to help her with the occasional emergency. Pippa had asked him a few days before she left if he could help to fix Joan's showerhead in the bathroom. He was good like that, and she was grateful for their friendship.

When is Terry coming home? Is this how it was always going to be? She hadn't realised when he got the job that having her husband away was going to mean months without him rather than weeks. Most oil rig workers were only away for about two or three weeks at a time. *But, three months?* Something inside her felt wrong. Did he not want her any more? She'd tried so hard to please him. Was this an excuse not to come home? She must stop thinking like that, but the last time he'd phoned was over a week ago. She missed him more than ever, but understood he was earning good money now. Even so, she wanted desperately for him to come back to her, to see Jordan, and be a father again. Now they were living on the edge of Whitby town, their lives had changed in the social sphere. She wasn't sure which was better: having the money or having Terry back. She felt lucky to be able to buy the things she could never afford when she lived in Henrietta Street. Thank goodness Pippa was still there for her. She'd kept asking when Terry would be home. She couldn't tell her friend exactly when. Why Terry evaded the issue with every phone call, she wondered, what was he thinking – or doing? She must find a way to ask him so it wouldn't sound as if she didn't trust him. She sucked in her breath in a moment of forgetfulness. *Oh yes. Rob. I promised to call him. Maybe have a word with him about the bike before Tel gets back. It's pointless having a motorbike that isn't being used.*

Rob and Pippa had always been there for her, and when Daniel had suffered his fatal accident, she'd felt it like the loss of her own child. She'd looked after Daniel as a baby to help Pippa attain her teaching qualifications. At the hospital, she'd kept a constant vigil over her friend, waiting for her to recover consciousness on the day of Daniel's accident. *After all this sadness, no wonder she needed a break.* Joan couldn't see herself without Jordan. The agony and pain suffered by Rob and Pippa, she felt it too.

She pulled herself out of her thoughts, wondering where life was going to take her next. She ought to phone Rob and ask about Pippa's trip to Cornwall.

She dialled Pippa's number. 'Hi, Rob, it's me. I thought I'd give you a ring. Did Pippa get away okay?'

'Yes, no problem. Trouble is I'm not sure if this holiday is going to make a difference.'

'Aw, Rob, don't say that. You'll have to be patient, love.'

'Don't you think I've been patient for long enough, Joan? It's my job to be patient. I'm in nursing, for God's sake. It's something I do, I look after depressed people! Sorry, Joan love, I didn't mean that to sound so harsh. I'm very tired, that's all.'

Joan turned down the corner of her mouth, glad Rob couldn't see her. She didn't relish change either. 'Yeah, I know. These things take a long time. You were both so young to lose someone in that way. I appreciate your agony, Rob. I was there too, remember? You know, you ought to try to understand, considering your job an' all that. You really should talk with Pippa when she gets back.' Joan knew she was scolding, but she also knew Rob wouldn't take it the wrong way. She heard Rob sigh and she changed the subject.

'Have you eaten? Can I do any shopping for you?'

'No, not really. I got food in the freezer and I opened a can of beans for breakfast and made some toast and a bacon sandwich. Will that do?'

Joan smiled. She'd imagined him on the other end of the phone looking annoyed at having to fend for himself for a change, but it seemed he was coping fine.

'What on earth are you both going to do with your future lives, Rob? I mean, it's all so tragic.'

'I don't know.' Rob sighed. 'I ought to give us a chance to start again. I mean, we can't carry on like this, can we – you know, the way things have gone?'

Joan was about to make a suggestion about marriage guidance; she hated to see her best friends falling apart. The four of them had been good mates for as long as she could remember. To lose Pippa and Rob right now would cause her much sorrow, but Rob always seemed such a great person, it might have been fine except for their tragedy. Rob spoke, interrupting her thoughts.

'Well, honestly, the house is a shrine to Daniel, and we do nothing but argue. We either have to move house or move on without each other.'

'Oh come on, Rob, don't be like that.' She hesitated for a moment. 'But you do love her, don't you?' She picked up her pen and began to doodle a heart on a pad as she waited for him to say something.

'I don't know anything anymore. Look, I must go. I've got all kinds of things to sort out, but I need my sleep first. I'm absolutely knackered.'

Joan sensed his agitation. She wanted to talk about Terry, but Rob's mind seemed to be somewhere else.

'Okay, Rob, sorry to bother you when you're tired. Just think about what I said, won't you? Don't do anything rash. See you soon, love. Bye.' Reluctant to close the conversation, she sighed. He'd had a bad time and, like Terry, he could be evasive. Perhaps it was a man thing. For a moment, she felt helpless. Her best friends' marriage falling apart was like watching yet another tragedy unfold, and worse still was not being able to do a darned thing about it. Would Rob ever get back on track with Pippa? A two-year counselling course might have helped him to understand his patients; it certainly wasn't helping him in his personal life. He just seemed the "wrong type" to be studying that kind of thing. She knew he was a good nurse, but a psychologist – no! She smiled to herself. Rob was fine; just a bit muddled, and who could blame him? Over the last few years, his and Pippa's luck had run out.

Now she came to think about it, Pippa had mentioned things weren't right when they'd met in town for coffee. She'd told Joan that Rob depressed her, and he was never at home when she needed him. *Hm… I know how that feels.* She knew that Rob had tried to help Pippa through the stress and grief using his professional knowledge, but it was different with family members – almost impossible. They were all in this together. Joan sighed. *Where are we all going in this life?* All she wanted was for Terry to come home, and for Rob and Pippa to settle down again. She hoped it was a passing phase in their lives.

The calendar on the wall made her look back at the last time Terry was home. Thumbing through the months, she found his birthday and, coincidentally, the anniversary of when Dan had passed away. She and Terry had gone out to the pub to celebrate when a mate of Rob's had given them the dreadful news. Only later did they learn that the situation was far worse than they'd expected.

Only weeks before, they'd all spent Christmas together at Rob and Pippa's house. It had been fun, and the five of them had taken a trip to the steam railway on the *Santa Special* and scoffed their mince pies and coffee on the train. Terry and Rob had played football with Daniel after New Year. Some weeks later, Dan was gone. It had left a void in all their lives until Jordan was born.

Now Joan began to think about their future. *How will we cope when we are all forty-five? Will we still have each other?* Somehow, she didn't think so. It was her birthday soon, and being thirty-one wasn't something she relished.

She felt a tear in her eye. 'Come home, Terry, I miss you,' she whispered. 'I can't do this on my own any more.'

By now, Pippa would be on her way to Scilly. What was it about the islands that was so special to her? Was she running away from all the turmoil?

Joan remembered when Pippa used to plait her auburn hair; it was so long she could almost sit on it. And the nights when they all went to the Youth Club, the girls showing off as they did in those days. Pippa was a fun-loving person. An Irish mate of Rob's at the pub once described her as having "great child-bearing hips". Was it supposed to be a compliment? Joan was never quite sure. Pippa seemed a lot more attractive in the last few months, almost as if her grief made her stronger, even more determined. Of course, there had been the bad days as well; days when she didn't want to leave the house. Before Daniel, they'd all been good mates. Joan knew Terry from school, and everyone said how well suited they were.

Joan rallied. She had to trust Terry; he was working away from home, nothing more. He was her husband and she'd always supported him in every way, but when he was home, something was off – different. For one thing, their sex life had deteriorated since Jordan had been born. Perhaps Terry had a complaint, one of those where you "can't get it up"? She'd thought he'd be extra keen after all that time away. When he first came back, she'd made sure Jordan was with Carole, bought new perfume, set the scene, but Terry had fallen asleep in front of the TV.

She'd wanted to tell Pippa she felt disturbed by his behaviour but, knowing Pippa, she would have said it was normal, probably told her to stop worrying so much.

Joan knew precisely when she must have conceived with Jordan. She pretended it had been fun; in truth, the whole affair had seemed unexpected and quick, although Terry said he'd enjoyed being with her. She would have to speak with him and get him to find some help. She gave a deep depressive sigh. Next time he called home, she would have to be stronger with him.

Jordan was still watching his favourite TV programme. There was enough time to put in the last of the washing before *Postman Pat* finished and she would take the youngster to the bathroom for a scrub.

Chapter Five

Terry Marshall arrived in Aberdeen after a helicopter ride over the North Sea. He yawned; how he hated mornings. The headache he'd woken up with still hung over him. With his boarding pass in his shirt pocket, he waited. Some narked Scots woman had served a foul-tasting cup of coffee and complained when he'd given her a twenty-pound note.

Sitting beneath the loudspeaker, the airport announcement startled him.

'Ladies and Gentlemen, due to a technical fault, flight 226 to Teesside will be delayed by thirty minutes. We apologise for the inconvenience.'

Terry checked his watch. How much longer would he have to sit here? Recently he'd come to accept the way of things in his life: things that, if he couldn't change, must be endured.

One hour after the first announcement, Terry boarded the plane and took his seat next to a woman reading *Anna Karenina*. He closed his eyes and didn't speak to anyone except for a curt 'No thanks' to the air stewardess who served the usual coffee and chocolate-chip cookie.

Upon arrival at Teesside airport, a hire car awaited him. He ran through the rain, but by the time he put the key in the lock, his shirt was soaked.

After driving through the industrial dismay of Middlesbrough, he stopped at a pub for lunch before making a call to tell his mother what time to expect him. He put the money in the pub call box and waited.

His parents only ever answered the phone with a 'Hello'.

'Hi, Dad, it's me.'

'Hallo, I thought it might be you. How are you? It's your Dad here.'

'I can tell.' He smiled, knowing his father's hearing was not very good. 'I'm fine, Dad.'

'Where are you, son?'

'In Saltburn. I'll be back in less than an hour. Is our Mam there?'

'No, she's with Carole. They've gone round to a jumble sale thing. I hear Jordan's been sick for a couple of days.'

'Is he awright?' Terry knew he should have phoned Joan earlier, but he needed time to think. He had put off calling her.

'Well…yes, I suppose he is. I was with them yesterday for a short visit.'

'Dad, you didn't say anything to her, did you?'

'What about?'

'You know what I mean, Dad!'

'Listen, son, don't you think it's time you two had a talk?'

Terry wasn't listening. He knew he had to pluck up the courage to tell Joan what he'd done to her. All the bleak facts in his life began to scream at him like the unrelenting nightmares he'd had as a child. He wanted to tell her, but each time he'd phoned, he couldn't do it. It had been a challenge to admit his shortcomings even to himself. When young Daniel died, it was impossible to explain, especially when they had all been involved. There was always too much going on.

'I'll talk to her later, but I'll see you around three o'clock, Dad. Okay? Bye.'

He left the pub and crossed the road to the car to drive down "The Bank", a local beauty spot overlooking the sea. He would take the usual route along the coast toward Staithes and Runswick Bay.

First stop – his parents' house. After all, they were closer than home.

Each day he had felt himself sinking into a void. He couldn't possibly tell his mother. How he would approach the subject, he had no idea. Should he first come out with his confession to Joan, or should he build up a story? He had no experience of these things. His chest tightened when he thought about it. He'd pretended he was fine. Perhaps he was mentally ill. Was it possible to be out of your mind and not realise it? He couldn't hold back on her any more. It wasn't working – couldn't work.

He was almost in Whitby, and as he drove along the sea front at Sandsend and up the hill towards the golf club, he switched the windscreen wipers to intermittent wipe.

The road was almost dry as he turned the corner into Endeavour Crescent, and he caught sight of his mother stooped in the garden. As he stopped the car, she stood and then came to meet him, her arms held out. He closed the car door behind him.

'Terry, pet, hey, how are you? Did you have a good journey?'

She embraced him, and he loved her for it. Hugging your mother was good, especially after being away for so long. He knew how much she cared, and at this moment, he needed her. 'Yeah, our Mam, I'm fine.'

His father came into the hall. 'Ah, you made it, son! Well done, great to see you.' He patted Terry on the back as he used to do when he'd been a good boy in school.

Terry smiled, but inside him he wanted to curse; nothing much had changed.

'Let me make you a cuppa tea, love,' said his mother, fussing him as usual.

'Thanks, Ma.'

'I'll have one too, Phyllis love.'

Terry poked his head through the lounge door. The furniture stood in the same place as it had been for the last twenty years, and he sensed the aroma of his mother's home cooking as he sat on the sofa.

He waited for his father to speak first. A silence came between them, neither of them wanting to open the conversation.

Terry looked around the room. 'Nice to be back, but…' He leaned forward, lowering his voice to a whisper. 'Before you ask, yes, I *am* going to talk with Joan. You haven't said anything to our Mam, have you?'

'Course not, but for God's sake, son, stop telling me about it. It's Joan you have to tell.'

'I will, Dad, but it isn't something you can just blurt out, is it? I have to work out what to say to her.'

'Terry!' His father looked him straight in the eyes and wagged a finger at him. 'Just tell her! You're being unfair to Jordan as well. There's nothing to stop you from continuing your life as a family, is there?'

'I don't know, Dad. I can't exactly see her being pleased about it – hush, here's our Mam.' He sat up straight, pretending everything was fine.

Phyllis entered the lounge with a tea tray bearing her best Royal Albert cups and plates. It was a call for celebration; her son was back. It also seemed as if she had polished the chocolate on the McVitie's digestives. She seemed to notice that the conversation between Terry and his father had stopped abruptly. 'Talking about me again, eh?' she said with a smile.

Terry realised he would never be able to explain things to her. It didn't bear thinking about. He gazed at his mother as she poured the tea. *She must never know.*

After a while, his father excused himself to finish the model aeroplane he was making for Jordan. Terry had the feeling his father had left the room with some impatience – or was it a good excuse to leave? Perhaps it was an opportunity to talk. He wasn't sure.

Phyllis sat with a cup on her lap. 'How was the journey?'

'Long.' Terry nodded.

'How's the job going?'

'Very good.'

She settled back in her chair, and the inevitable questions Terry had been dreading began to pour out.

'Why has it taken you so long to come home this time? Little Jordan has waited for his daddy. He used to talk about you a lot until the last few weeks or so. Joan keeps a picture of you on the table so he can see you. Children of that age can easily begin to forget who you are, Terry. What's going on? Why didn't you go home first?'

Terry felt pushed into a corner, and the only thing he could do was tell a lie.

'It's work, Ma. Joan understands, honest. Anyway I'm going round there soon, thought I'd call in here first as it's en-route.' He was glad he could steer the conversation elsewhere. *Not now, Ma, leave it.*

'You look a bit tired, pet. Why don't you go and have a nap first? I just remembered, Joan's gone to the nursery-school fête this afternoon, so you got some time before she gets back. I think she's going into town with Carole afterwards.'

Terry hoped his relief didn't show. The gap gave him the time he needed. 'Yeah, good idea, I'm knackered.'

'Do you want me to phone Joan for you later, tell her you've arrived?'

'No! I mean, no, don't do that, erm… I want to surprise her.'

'Oh, okay, I'm sure she'll be thrilled.'

Terry didn't want to hear those words; he knew "thrilled" was the last thing Joan would be. How would he begin to explain his extended absence?

He went upstairs and lay on his old childhood bed; it took him a further hour to get to sleep.

By the time his mother woke him, it was almost five o'clock.

'Are you going to see Joan, our Terry? I didn't want to disturb you, I know what a long journey you had today.'

'Oh er, yes…erm…what time is it?' For a moment, he was back on the rig with the North Sea swell knocking underneath. He checked his watch. 'Bloody hell, I'd better go home.' He tried to make out it was a dreadful mistake.

'Good lad,' said Phyllis as she went back down the stairs. It seemed she'd forgotten how much of an adult he was these days.

He made his way to the bathroom to splash cold water on his eyes, and dried his face before going to the phone in the hall.

Oh, God, this is it. Remember what Frank told me on the rig. 'Approach it step by step, tell her how much you care and how it was at the time, tell her how it is now. No lies.' No, he wouldn't say anything now with his mother lurking around the house. He would go home, but first he wanted to be sure Joan was there.

He picked up the receiver and dialled, then put it down again. He sat for a few minutes longer before he tried for a second time. He listened to the *burr burr* of the ring tone, but Joan didn't answer. *Where could she be at this time?*

Perhaps he should phone Rob, go to the pub until she got back. He was sure Pippa wouldn't mind. Anyway, Rob was a nurse, he would understand these things. Approach the subject in small steps; perhaps get Rob's help to explain it all. After all, he was into counselling. His best friend would be the perfect confidence booster. Right now, what he needed was a chat with his best mate. He would try phoning Joan again in an hour, and began to plan his opening words.

Chapter Six

An ambulance stood on the side of the road in Hugh Town; multitudes of faceless people called out her name.

'It's your fault the dog's in so much pain,' Pippa shouted.

Rob, or someone whose face she couldn't quite see, lay dead on the pavement at her feet. Someone placed a mask over her face, stifling her breathing. They were taking the animal to the beach to be buried at sea and it was still alive. Pippa shouted, 'Give me the dog, it's not dead.' She called out into the room and, with ghastly clarity, a terrible vision flashed inside her eyelids. Fighting for breath, shocked, she gagged at the non-existent oxygen mask, unable to focus. She sat up in bed with a start. So, the nightmares were back! Cursing to herself, she stretched her eyelids with her fingers. *Where am I? What day is it? Ah yes, Saturday. Oh hell, I'm meeting Sven in an hour.* The window was open; she dragged herself out of bed and gazed into the yard below. Perhaps one day there would be lovely dreams, but as long as there was still trauma in her head, the nightmares would never go away. She'd forgotten how to dream; her inner-self screamed as she squeezed her eyelids together. *It must have been the alcohol.* She had a headache and reached into the drawer for the Paracetamol.

With a need to feel good for the trip to St Martin's, Pippa took a shower and washed her nightmare down the plughole. She must hurry otherwise she would be late. While rinsing her hair, she closed her eyes to avoid the stinging effect of the shampoo as the shower streamed over her face. The reassuring warm spray cascaded down her back. She turned off the tap. Within minutes, she was drying her hair, putting cream on her face, and rushing around the room to find suitable clothes. The new shorts and strappy top she had bought in Whitby suited her. The folding backpack Janice had left for the visitors hung on a peg; she grabbed it to carry a bottle of orange juice and her raincoat. Remembering what Sven had told her yesterday about the binoculars, she placed them around her neck rather than in the bag.

On the way down to the harbour, everyone seemed to be walking in the same direction. She picked up her pace; the boat was due to leave in ten minutes. Her hair still damp and her binoculars swinging, she hoped she didn't look as bad as she felt, and that the small pimple on her face had faded.

Sven was already at the boat helping passengers to board. Pippa watched him standing there. He was always smiling. She saw how relaxed he was, joking with everyone as they straddled across the boats, reminding them to take it easy.

Pippa stepped down to the boat and Sven greeted her as he helped her on board.

'Hi there,' he said warmly, taking her hand. 'Steady now, don't fall in, will you?'

Pippa grinned and found a seat at the front as Sven picked up the microphone in the wheelhouse, tapping it to ensure it worked.

'Gud morning, everyone. Welcome on board *Lily of Laguna*. My name is Sven, and I hope you all brought your sea-sick pills. I don't want a mess in Don's boat *again* this week.' He chuckled. 'If anyone is sick I get the sack!'

Pippa smiled; he was quite a character for sure.

'How many people have we got this morning?' Sven counted the heads, moving from the back of the boat towards the front, and catching Pippa's eye. 'Fifty-four, fifty-five, fifty-six…glad you could make it,' he said to her above the noise of the diesel engine. Turning to the passengers, he continued, 'fifty-seven, fifty-eight, fifty-nine…' He looked at Don and put up his thumb; the boat was full. They were ready to leave.

He picked up the microphone again. 'Now today, folks, we are going to St Martin's. It's a very beautiful island, and those of you who have the wildlife tour tickets, please wait for me when we get there. We will land at Lower Town because of the tide. Later, we will gather at the other side of the island at Higher Town Quay for the return journey. I will guide you through the birdlife and the footpaths, and tell you a little of the history of St Martin's, so enjoy yourselves. It's a lovely day and the weather forecast is excellent. Thanks, everyone.' He put the microphone back on the hook and Don reversed from the pier.

Pippa looked up and smiled as Sven stood beside her. Her sense of belonging to the islands: she felt it again, just as she'd done on the ship. Why did she feel that way?

'Did you sleep well at Janice's?' Sven asked.

'Not too bad – I had a bit of a nightmare. I think it may have been the rum and cola. I was persuaded to join a party at the pub last night – which isn't like me. I don't usually drink much, let alone go into pubs on my own.'

'You weren't at Harris's birthday party, were you?' Sven raised his eyebrows and smiled.

'Well, I think I was. Some guy called Charlie James invited me.'

Sven laughed. 'I couldn't make it unfortunately. Trust Charlie, he's a bit of a character. He's also one of our volunteers and takes charge of the nature-reserve team when I'm not around. So, are you all right? I'm not going to get the sack, am I?'

'God, no!' Pippa made a face of revulsion and Sven laughed again.

A moment of shyness made her turn outboard of the boat and put her hand into the clear water. She gazed at the fronds of loose bronze kelp swaying on the surface. As the boat left the harbour, she closed her eyes for a moment in the bright sunlight and listened to the sound of the water lapping against the side and the gentle chugging of the engine.

The boat sailed into Crow Sound and Sven glanced at Pippa sitting below him, catching her eye.

'I'm sure I can help you learn a lot today. You know, you remind me of when I started to learn about birds. I used to watch the geese outside of my grandmother's home near Trondheim. She realised I was interested and bought me my first field guide.'

Pippa smiled. His personality and good looks seemed to shine with the morning sun, and she loved the way he spoke.

'I learned most of the Latin names by the time I was sixteen, and then went on to study at university. You see, you have to start at the very beginning and not feel awkward about it. Just go for it and become your own expert.'

'Yes, you're right I suppose, but I don't think I'll ever be an expert.'

Sven paused for a moment, looking back at Don in the wheel-house.

'Well, this could be your lucky day,' he said with a grin. 'Any-way, I'm expecting my colleague back soon, and then I can get on with my real job: managing the nature reserve and the bird records for Scilly. I enjoy doing the tours, but I also love going into the schools and doing hands-on work on the reserve. It's more my kind of thing, I suppose.'

Pippa nodded; she knew what he meant. Her time teaching in the infants' school had provided her with the job satisfaction she needed when Daniel was growing up. She'd taken a two-year course, including training with special-needs children for her NNEB qualification. She had loved it and hoped one day she might have the confidence to go back to work. But not yet. Perhaps when she got home she might have the confidence to return.

As the boat crossed to St Martin's, Sven stood riding a gentle swell. Pippa looked up at him from her seat, and the two of them exchanged the occasional glance and smile. There was something very worldly wise and experienced about him; with his binoculars around his neck and his keen eye scanning the ocean for birds, he seemed to lead in everything he did.

'Puffins on your left, everyone. Razorbill.' He pointed ahead.

'Look, and there's a shag too.' But the bird had disappeared under the water before he could finish speaking.

The passengers held up their binoculars, as if they were at a tennis match where everyone watched the ball, their heads turning in the direction Sven had pointed. Pippa thought most of the people on the boat must be experienced birdwatchers as they carried expensive optical gear. Her "bins" were old and needed careful adjustment. She didn't feel comfortable, but Sven encouraged her. He seemed kind and helpful – something she needed right now. She listened to him all the way, and most of all, he fascinated her.

Pippa wondered how it might have been if she hadn't met Joan, Terry and Rob. What if her life had turned right instead of left? What if she'd met someone like Sven? *Bloody hell!* Such fantasy would get her into trouble one day, she was sure. Too late, she had chosen this path and it had been a disaster. *Stop it.* She pushed her mind back to reality; they weren't too far away from landing on St Martin's.

A seal popped its head out of the water, its whiskers and dog-like head looked appealing. 'Grey seal on the right!' Sven announced.

Heads turned and Pippa joined in. The seal was closer now and she saw the black speckles on its skin and its dark loving eyes, nostrils pulsating with each breath as it kept disappearing under the water and reappearing in a different place.

'Great, eh?' Sven remarked. 'How anyone can hurt them I'll never understand. They're so friendly when we go diving. Sometimes I have to give them a gentle tap on the nose to stop them from being too close – they do tend to nip if I don't watch out. There's one seal, she adores me.' He chuckled. 'I call her Sasha. She seems to know me underwater, but when I approach her on land she won't come near me.'

Pippa smiled to herself. *Gosh, he's a diver as well, is there anything this guy can't do?* She realised she had so much to learn and hoped she had enough time to fit it all into her schedule. She sucked in her breath sharply. *Oh heck, I forgot my suntan lotion, how stupid of me.*

At least her headache had subsided, thank goodness. Since Daniel, she had developed a habit of forgetting things.

Sven interrupted her thoughts.

'I'm glad you decided to come, I have loads to show you. The boat is fine now, a little engine overhaul. It was nothing serious, but we have to make sure.' He squinted as the boat changed direction into the sun. His blond hair had turned wavy in the salt air. 'It isn't easy to get spare parts, we have to order them and sometimes it can be days, even weeks, so we have to compromise now and again, find alternatives.' He turned to Don in the wheelhouse. 'Okay, mate?'

Don nodded, the noise of the engine drowning his words.

Pippa reached in her pocket and found her green hair band. Sven watched her as the sun's rays highlighted her auburn strands. 'Ya,' he said, 'it can be windy once we get out of the lea of St Mary's.' He lifted up his binoculars to watch a shag on a rock in the distance as Pippa tied back her hair. Don steered with one hand on the wheel, spray flew across the bow and passengers hung on to their hats. The smell of diesel fuel reached Pippa's nostrils, and she turned to face the fresher air.

The boat, now in the lea of the island, rocked gently towards St Martin's and the Eastern Isles. With the blue sky, lapping waves, and a very helpful guide, what more could she want?

On arrival at the quay, Sven threw a rope to someone waiting on the edge of the pier. He tied up the boat and the passengers disembarked.

He counted fifteen in his group of birders. They walked up the path and stopped on the higher ground. He explained the archaeology and the rise in sea levels.

'If you all come along to the slide show tomorrow night I'll be able to show you more.'

As Pippa stepped from the boat, there was less wind. She loosened her hair again as they walked up the main path towards Higher Town.

'The sea air can make you burn very quickly,' Sven told her, 'so be careful, especially with your fair colouring. Have you got sun cream with you in your bag?'

'Actually, I forgot it, I came out in a hurry this morning,' Pippa replied, annoyed with herself for leaving it behind on the kitchen table.

Sven opened his rucksack and pulled out a bottle of Factor 30 sun cream.

'Oh, thanks very much, I should have thought about it.'

She watched as he opened the lid and tipped up the bottle. The cream spilled on to her fingers and she smoothed it over her face and arms. She was already turning red from sitting in the boat.

'Here, let me put some cream on the back of your neck – and you'll need it on your shoulders as well. You missed that bit there, do you mind?' He pointed to the spot.

Pippa turned to face him and their eyes met. 'I bet you offer this service to all the ladies.' She laughed away her words.

'Oh! I wish. I always carry lots of sun cream with me. There is usually someone who needs it – better to be safe than sorry, and I have to take care as well.' He put the lid on the bottle, holding it between his teeth and screwing the bottle to the top. His fingers were already moving towards her skin as he dropped the bottle on his rucksack.

He gestured a circular movement with his index finger.

'Turn around,' he said. 'I'll do it for you, if you wish?'

Oh gosh, this will be interesting. Pippa gave a dry smile. 'Er, thanks, that would be helpful.' It had been a while since she had felt a man's tender touch.

With the tips of his fingers, he slowly massaged the cream into the nape of her neck. If the circumstances had been right, she would have let out a satisfying "ahh", but opted to remain quiet and tried to keep her lips together to avoid a giggle. *Heavens, what would Rob say? Hm, probably nothing.* She must stop feeling guilty.

'Okay…done! That should help a lot.' Sven gently patted her shoulder.

'Thanks, Sven, that's really kind of you,' she said politely, not daring to say any more. *But, oh, that was so soothing.*

She knew they would have to catch up with the rest of the group quite soon. She picked up her rucksack and walked on.

'Hang on, wait for me,' Sven called as he wiped the cream from his fingers. He quickened his step along the narrow concrete path. 'You know…where I come from, you have to wear lots of cream, otherwise your whole face and lips crack in the sun. I have a friend back home who was eating his breakfast and his own blood at the same time – delightful, eh?'

Pippa grimaced. 'Ergh! I don't intend to get *that* sunburned. I'll be careful, I promise.'

They walked on up the track, side-by-side, taking in the sea views with the warm breeze blowing gently from the southwest. Pippa felt Sven's eagerness to continue with the guided tour and they joined the group who were sat on a large rock at the top of the hill, gazing through their binoculars.

'Sorry about that, folks. I loaned the sun cream to Pippa here. Does anyone else want some?'

'Yes please, Sven, thanks. I forgot mine too, do you mind?' A woman wearing a blue top and denim shorts came forward. Sven handed her the bottle. Pippa thought, *thank goodness I wasn't the only one who had forgotten the sun cream!* This time Sven didn't offer to help and Pippa felt privileged. No one had paid her that kind of attention in a very long time; it was an odd feeling. She remembered the people on Scilly were very open and friendly, which reminded Pippa that Sven was only being kind.

Now alone with her thoughts, Pippa felt where his fingers had massaged her neck. She didn't listen too hard and her mind wandered to looking at Sven in a "what if?" kind of way. It was his accent, his caring that made her heart quicken. She wanted to be loved again, that was all. Surely that wasn't asking for much? She must stop thinking like that.

*

Sven ambled silently for a while, some distance behind Pippa. Who was this pretty girl, alone on holiday? What had brought her here? Curious to know more about her, she had ignited his imagination. He admitted to himself he liked her, but she was just another tourist on holiday, here today – gone tomorrow. What chance did he have? Soon, she would leave. What was the point in pursuing a relationship under those circumstances? Anyway, she was married – but still, there was something odd about her situation. Perhaps it would not be too imposing to try to find out. He realised he had become just as nosey as some of the residents of Scilly. Living on an island was great, but not for long-term romance. Two-week partnerships were not on his agenda. He wanted something stronger and more meaningful. He would be thirty-something soon; without a girlfriend, people might think he was shy, or even a bit weird…*that's stupid, but…* He hadn't fancied anyone since Astrid, back home in Norway. Oh yes, there had been plenty of opportunities, but it seemed they were all after his good looks. He hated that. He wanted a girlfriend who could get to know the real Sven, instead of him being the so-called "icon of the islands". He had talked constantly about birds during his coffee break; maybe he should have asked more questions. There seemed to be sadness in her expression and she had seemed so eager to learn. He would ask her, but not at this moment. He was working. Spending too much time with one person wasn't professional.

He stopped along the path and turned to his birders.

'The main industry of this island is fishing for lobster and crabs, but it's the fine beaches which attract the visitors and the birdlife.'

'Is this tormentil?' a woman asked, pointing to a small yellow flower.

'Yes, well done, and the little pink flower over there is sea mallow. Most of you will have seen it all over the islands. It's well known that you could put all the inhabitants of Scilly on those beaches and still have room to spare. If you wanted to take off all your clothes on some of the islands, no one would see you.' The group laughed, and he continued. 'Except…the residents of St Mary's… they all get out their binoculars every afternoon.' He had wanted to say those words for quite some time, especially considering his next-door neighbour, Nanette Bell. She always had her nose pressed to the window every time he left the house.

'As we look out on to Chapel Down we can see the Daymark, a navigation aid to shipping, erected in 1683 by Thomas Ekins, first steward of the Godolphin family to live on the islands…' He turned around and pointed towards the higher ground. 'If you would like to look through your binoculars, everyone, I can see a male stonechat sitting over there on the fence.' He erected the telescope and encouraged the group to look through it one by one. Pippa was amazed; she had never seen a stonechat before. Its black head and orange-pink breast were striking and so clear in the 'scope.

'You know, folks,' said Sven, 'these islands are so fragile, everything we do here has to be carefully monitored, far more so than on the mainland. In the summer, we have to conserve water, and if we get bad weather in the winter, we lose some of the less hardy plants to the wind and rain. We often have to lay down a few more rules and regulations to ensure the islands remain protected. Should there be a disaster like the Torrey Canyon, which almost ruined everything, it would take tens of years to repair the damage. Life on these islands is not the same as living on the mainland.'

Sven suggested that Pippa make a bird list during her stay on the islands. 'You never know, one day you can look back on your list and see if these birds are still nesting and visiting us here. If they aren't, we might be in trouble. These islands are unique, there's probably nothing quite like them. There is such a rich treasure of archaeology and wildlife here, we have to spend every moment conserving the nature. We depend on our visitors to help us, and this is one of the reasons I do the tours.'

'I'll buy a notebook in town when we get back,' Pippa said with enthusiasm.

'Now everyone,' said Sven, 'look through here.'

He focussed the telescope and each person took a turn.

'Ah, yes, it's a linnet. Great, eh?' said a man in the group.

'They're so pink on the breast, aren't they?' Sven agreed. 'You can usually tell linnets by their undulating flight, and they have a variety of calls – listen…'

He paused to let everyone hear the 'djit djit' of the linnet.

'The song is almost like "linnet linnet". Okay, now let's move on down the shoreline. Oh look, folks, a rock pipit as well.'

Looking towards the shore, Pippa spied shags floating by, heads turned to the sky making them look like haughty passengers on a raft. Behind her, she felt Sven watching her every move, but was it her imagination, her loneliness, the need to have someone to be there for her? Each corner they turned, she found something new.

Sven had led her in her quest to become a birdwatcher; there was something satisfying about helping her. He remembered when he was learning about birds and how inadequate he'd felt compared to the local experts in the bird club back in Norway. He knew how Pippa must feel.

Having spent the whole morning with his group, Sven stopped for lunch at the café in Higher Town.

'May I join you?' he asked Pippa, thinking she looked distant sitting on her own. Perhaps now was his chance to talk with her.

'Yes, fine.' She nodded with a smile.

He set his plate on the table then took a bite of a cheese and pickle sandwich. Pippa waited for him to finish munching, anticipating his next sentence.

'So, you said you're from Whitby, eh? I've never been there, but from what you told me yesterday, it sounds beautiful.'

He had wanted to ask her what was her connection with the islands? What was she doing here alone on holiday?

'When we get back I have to set up the slide show. Would you like to come early and help? I mean, if you're on holiday I don't want you to be working, of course, but I thought, seeing you're by yourself, you might like to come and be part of the scene.'

Perhaps this was an imposition, but he sensed her sadness and he was anxious not to lose sight of her. There was nothing wrong with being curious.

'I would love to help! Thanks. It's not often I get the chance these days to be involved in something like this.' Pippa's heart gave a skip. It was as if Sven knew her well. She wanted to get in with the right-kind-of people: the real birdwatchers, the ornithologists. She would show Rob that birdwatching wasn't just for old men in wax jackets and woolly hats. Here she could learn more, and show him what Sven had taught her. It might also make Rob see she was trying harder to gain her confidence.

By the time Pippa got back to St Mary's she had a bird list of twenty species. It had been thrilling and a great morning for birdwatching. Sven showed his knowledge of wild flowers and insects like a true expert. Above all, she liked the scarlet pimpernel and sea holly, and the different kinds of bees. For sure, she would never see bees as one species any more.

When they arrived at St Mary's she was the last to leave the boat.

Sven held out his hand to Pippa. She drew back for a moment, but encouraged by his willingness to help her, allowed him to assist her to dry land. As the boat rocked, and with his hands full, Sven muttered through clenched teeth with a pen in his mouth.

Pippa gave a laugh. He was obviously used to multi-tasking. 'Thanks, Sven, it's been great,' she said as she stood on the damp granite steps.

Taking the pen from his lips, he turned her hand and wrote the time of the slideshow on the back. 'In case you forget the time,' he said.

'Oh, I won't forget,' said Pippa as she walked up the steps. 'See you later, then. Bye.'

It was as if her heavy heart had become normal again. Sven was right; you could sit on a beach having cast off all your cares and let the breeze and the sun do the rest. When was the last time she had felt this way?

Walking into Hugh Town, she thought about the morning on St Martin's. It felt great that Sven had wanted to know her and offer his support. She smiled to herself; she had almost flirted with him, and hoped he hadn't taken it the wrong way. *But it was just a bit of harmless fun. He's cute and he cares.* If only Rob could be like that, it might help their relationship. He was all or nothing, and what had happened to caring? He was just as inside himself as she had been. Sven seemed so…different. Perhaps when she got home Rob might have missed her and things would change. That was her reason for coming away, wasn't it? She only wanted to be strong, that was all.

It was mid-afternoon, and after a cup of tea at the bakery she decided to walk to Star Castle and take a stroll around The Garrison. The last time she was there, she discovered a wonderful viewpoint and wanted to go back and see it again. Halfway up the hill, she found Jan and Marijke seated on a bench. With each step closer to the couple, Pippa noticed how Jan's bones seemed to float under his skin. It was sad to see him in this way; in the sun she could see he was obviously very ill. Whatever Marijke must be feeling, she felt with her. *How brave to come all this way.*

'Good afternoon, you two. Enjoying the sun?'

Marijke smiled. 'Hello, Pippa, nice to see you again.'

She stopped for a few minutes to tell them about her trip.

Jan raised a smile. 'Ja, you should make the most of the day while you can.' His thin faced peeked out from under his cotton sun hat.

'I know, it's beautiful, isn't it?' Pippa glanced at Marijke. Perhaps they should all make the most of what they had, she thought.

'You're right, we should enjoy every moment.' She was about to say, 'As if it were our last,' but realised the last part of her comment wasn't appropriate and felt silly for a moment. Instead, she said, 'Have a great time, I'll see you both later.'

As she bid them farewell, she appreciated her luck at not having experienced such physical suffering as Jan. Her mental torture had often caused her to think she should end her life. Thinking about Sven, his job as a wildlife tour guide and the people of the islands made her realise how worthwhile it was to carry on living. No wonder Jan had come here to recuperate; he might not be around for many more months. At least she wasn't ill; it was the "forever grief". Just a few days without it would help.

She found the seat where she had once sat with Daniel. A warm breeze blew across The Garrison, and she rested her back against a plaque of remembrance to someone "who loved these islands". It was comforting to think that years earlier they had also sat here. Over her shoulder, she looked up at the stark greyness of Star Castle Hotel and the flag flying on the top. *There must be many ghosts on The Garrison, all that history.*

The breathtaking view provided solace, with most of the islands spread out like fingers into the Atlantic Ocean. The blueness of the lagoon shimmered in the sun, and the shapes of the rocks and the small coloured boats made this the perfect spot to sit. The smell of chamomile drifted across the path bringing more memories. The last time she sat here was when Daniel had gone to play football with Rob; she'd brought her pencils and sketched the view. She'd almost forgotten how to do all that. It would be good to try again.

Two yachts sailed in opposite directions, one to St Agnes and the other into St Mary's. Pippa sighed. *Are Rob and I like that, always pulling away from each other?* Behind her, two young men pounded the path as they jogged along; she felt their footfalls through the seat, and as their voices became louder, she heard every word.

'Well, yes, because I thought I'd studied big-time and didn't think I'd done too badly.'

'Mm, you know what? I think...'

Their voices faded, the breeze blowing away the conversation.

Pippa sat alone. The overwhelming view, the vivid colours of the ocean and her grief caused her to cry. The grass grew tall over the seat and she felt hidden by the wildflowers. She sucked in her breath with a sob, hoping not to make a fool of herself, but hey – it wasn't silly to feel this way. The scent of the chamomile and fennel produced a conflict between euphoria and sadness. The stunning view all but stopped her breath.

Something made her turn around: she saw a figure coming up the path, a child with blond hair and a small football under his arm. The image of the child came closer. 'Oh my God, no… Dan!' she whispered. He was smiling back at her. She put her hands against her chest. *He looks like Dan!*

The child kept moving towards her; he was waving, and a tear dropped down her face as she thought she saw her son smiling back at her. It couldn't be.

Her eyes turned towards the ocean, the colours and the light. Was it really an image? Was Dan trying to tell her something? She dared not look again.

Further down the path, the child's mother appeared, breathless from running after him. Pippa turned again and watched as the woman caught up with the boy and took his hand. 'Keep hold of his hand,' she whispered to herself. 'Keep hold.' Mother and son walked back the way they'd come and were soon out of sight. Pippa allowed her tears to flow without guilt; she had now given herself permission to cry. Her grief spilled beyond the distant islands, into the Atlantic Ocean. She sobbed her heart into the sea and never wanted to leave this place. Now that Dan was gone, it seemed futile to go home, knowing she had lost her way with Rob. What should she do? She wished she could stay here forever, but she wasn't being realistic; she would have to go home at the end of the holiday. Henrietta Street had been her life; she couldn't just leave it all behind. She should never have tried to hold onto the dog and Daniel at the same time; she should have known better, although Joan kept telling her to stop blaming herself.

She would never find her true self through guilty eyes; moving on was the only option. She paused in her thoughts, took out a handkerchief, and blew her nose; someone was coming up the path again.

It had been her mission to find a way to survive. Her sobbing stopped, and very quickly something transformed her fragile state of mind. It was like a balloon bursting, struck by a pin. Bang! The moment was over as quickly as it had arrived. The balloon deflated. She took a deep breath and began to feel a change. The tears stopped, and, like the blown seeds of a distant dandelion, it felt as if all her cares had floated away. Here was her special place too, as it had also been for the family who had donated the seat. She understood their passion.

With tears on her face, she stood to walk down the hill. Like the day when she had changed the room at home, today she felt proud of herself for getting this far. Rob shouldn't have scolded her; all she wanted was a nice conversation with him on the phone, a kind word here and there. Today Sven had been there to listen to her. He was good and honest, and she gave herself a mental pat on the back for her progress, thankful for his support. At home, no one seemed to understand about conserving nature. These days, people took too much for granted. Perhaps the next time she went to the bank, she would put some money in the Wildlife Trust collection box, her contribution to nature. Here you had to protect your lifestyle; nature stood hand in hand with lifestyle. Back home no one wanted to listen to a woman who wanted to go birdwatching. When all her friends were out celebrating, she had felt stupid and selfish when she'd mentioned to Rob that she wanted to go to the hide at Scaling Dam. Only her doctor had taken her seriously. When she got home she would go and see him again, and ask if he knew of a local club she could join. It was his hobby too. They were all good and positive ideas, and she made up her mind she would take things one day at a time. It was a time to make good plans for the future.

On reaching the town, Pippa put on her sunglasses and hoped no one would notice her swollen eyes. It had been a beautiful yet overwhelming day, and there was still more to come.

Chapter Seven

The phone rang. Rob picked it up.

'Hi, Rob, it's me – Terry.'

'Oh, hi, Tel. Where the heck are you?' Rob wanted to ask another obvious question, but refrained. Perhaps he should wait and give Terry a chance to explain.

'At our mam and dad's.'

'Oh, I see, you're in Whitby, eh?'

'Fancy a drink?' Terry asked. 'I phoned Joan but she's not at home.'

'Yes, I know,' Rob said. 'She's round at Carole's, I think. She phoned up earlier asking my advice about Jordan's cough.' *Shouldn't he know where she is and not me?*

'Oh, okay. I only got home this afternoon. Can we talk?'

'As long as it's nothing too heavy, then. I've been dealing with patients and their problems all day, and I'm on my own here.'

'Why? Where's Pippa?'

Rob explained how she had gone to Cornwall.

'Cornwall? Bloody hell! What's she doing down there?'

'To use her words, she's gone for some holiday respite. Terry, mate, if you like I'll meet you at the Harbour Inn within the hour.'

'Okay, see you then.'

Rob replaced the receiver.

Rob looked up from his beer as Terry walked into the pub. He noticed Terry's weather beaten face, and with a new moustache he didn't seem to be the same guy who had left Whitby a few months before.

The way he dressed in cord jeans and short-sleeved shirt instead of his usual denim jeans and T-shirt. Of course, he was earning good money now.

'Hi, Tel mate. Great to see you. What can I get you?' He patted Terry on the back.

'Pint of Theakston's, thanks.'

They stood together at the bar for a moment before finding their usual seat near the window overlooking the harbour. It was like old times as Rob told him more about Pippa's sudden decision to go to the Isles of Scilly and her departure a few days before.

'Really?' Terry said. 'I know how much she loved it down there, but I didn't think she would go without *you*.'

'It's a long story… Anyway, I fixed the brakes on that old Matchless of yours and I managed to find a guy who deals in headlights. Don't leave it in the damp, Tel, I put a cover on it for you last week.'

'Yeah, thanks.'

Rob was still recovering from his discovery that the "shrine" was gone, and he didn't want to talk about Terry's problems. 'Didn't Joan want to come down here for a drink?' he asked.

'No, er… I'll pop round home after this,' Terry said. 'I only got back this afternoon and I was so tired I slept at our mam and dad's for a couple of hours.'

Rob found it hard to believe Terry hadn't seen Joan yet. What should he say to Terry? It had been too long. Turning up like that, there was no time to prepare his man-chat. He thought Terry felt his awkwardness too.

'I wanted to ask you something, Rob.' Terry fiddled with his glass, turning it in his hands. 'How has she been doing without me?'

'What d'ye mean "without you"? It sounds a bit final, Tel.'

'I know what you're thinking,' Terry said. 'It hasn't been easy for me either, you know.'

'So what's wrong? I didn't think working on a rig took you away that long.'

Terry sat holding his beer. Slow supping appeared to give him time to think about his answer. 'There's something wrong with me,' he said, looking awkward, 'and I thought, you being a nurse, you might understand. I've been getting some advice from someone at work.'

'You ill, Tel?' Rob said.

'I don't know. I get these strange thoughts.'

'What kind of strange thoughts?' Rob began his counselling, thinking Terry meant schizophrenia.

'Look, here isn't the place to discuss it. Can we go round to your house after this, Rob, seeing Pippa isn't there? Would you mind?'

'Sure, if that's what you want, but remember I'm a nurse and not a doctor.'

Rob supped the last of his beer and put the glass on the bar. They walked along the narrow street away from the bustle of tourists, and as they reached the house Rob opened the front door.

'Sit down, Tel.' Rob pulled up a chair and faced Terry. 'I'll make us a drink in a minute. So, mate, what's up? You look tired.'

'Well, it's like this, see. I can't...you know, do it... Well, I can, but not with Joan.'

'You mean you're impotent?' Rob tried not to counsel his friend.

'Nooo, not that.' Terry seemed to find it hard to say the words, as if he needed Rob to say them for him.

'Then what?' Rob looked baffled. His training had taught him to remain calm and allow his patient to do the talking.

Terry looked down at his feet, and then his hands, and then the button on his jacket, and then he couldn't speak. There was more silence. He breathed heavily and sighed while staring out of the window.

Rob waited a few more seconds, and was about to say something when Terry spoke first.

'I'm not the man you think I am,' Terry blurted out.

'What do you mean, Tel? Are you trying to tell me you think

you're, you're…homosexual?' asked Rob, thinking he couldn't possibly have it right.

Terry looked shocked that Rob had come straight to the point. 'Well, yes…erm, oh God, this is so hard.'

Rob's stomach felt as if it was sinking. He'd dealt with this before with his patients, but Terry…He tried not to show his feelings. How was he going to deal with this smack in the mouth? *Mustn't judge, stay professional – shit, what do I say? Best friend.*

'What? Are you sure?'

'I've got this mate on the rigs, Frank. Well, we kind of…did stuff, if you know what I mean?'

'Bloody hell, Tel, how long has this been going on?' Rob found it hard to stay calm. Joan didn't deserve this, but he knew he had to remain unbiased.

Terry's story came flooding out. He kept taking a deep breath with every sentence, almost sobbing.

'I hadn't realised, you see…even when Joan and I got married. I thought I had just gone off her, you know? Stopped fancying her.'

There was more silence. Rob waited, but all he could hear was Terry's laboured breathing. 'You could be bisexual, you know?'

'No, I don't think so. I've been through all this with Frank. I had to go away on the rigs to sort myself out. It was an opportunity to think about what I'd done. I married Joan because it was the right thing to do, a kind of pressure from you guys, and we had Jordan to think of too.'

'I see,' said Rob. 'I hope you're not blaming Pippa and me?'

'No, no, of course not. You and Pippa got married, had Daniel, it seemed right – and then, later, Jordan came along. Sad to say, it was the one time I enjoyed sex with Joan, and the outcome was our son. Since then it's been very half-hearted. I haven't exactly been a good husband, I know that. I don't regret having Jordan, he's a great kid, but he's always been Joan's son, and somehow he always goes to her and not me. I've never felt like a father to him.'

'Well, I hope that it goes without saying you don't regret it, but kids do that. Sometimes you are the best dad in the world, and other times you can't get through to them, Anyway, go on…'

Terry sighed. 'Little Dan was involved in that dreadful accident, and it was all too much. There was no opportunity to talk about it to anyone. About three months ago, Frank was there for me, and it was a huge relief in my life. My dad knows, but you know how it is with our dad, his brother, you know the story…but our mam would never understand. She's already in denial about Uncle Ronnie. She probably thinks it's a hereditary disease or something. Confessing to her about me would kill her. I can't do it. She's so old-fashioned, I know she would never understand. Even now in the eighties you'd think we could talk more about these things, but it's not like that. She still lives in the past, and she's a homophobe for sure. It comes from her upbringing. Frank told me *his* mother was exactly the same.'

'God, Terry, how will you tell her? And for goodness sake, you have Jordan. You have to be bloody sure about this.'

'I am sure, honest I am. I've never been surer in my whole life than now.'

Rob was shocked but still trying not to show it, being ultra careful with his emotions. He found it hard to be in counselling mode with a friend, always nodding in empathy and using a gentle smile to show congruence. There was no point in trying to use his skills on his best friend; he could only support him, but couldn't help using "those kinds of questions". It confused him. But…his best friend and poor Joan were all he could think about.

'Yeah, well, that's the problem,' said Terry. 'I've spent all these months wondering *how* to tell her. I thought you might help me through it. I tried to do the right thing, but when you guys got married I ignored my feelings and went with the flow of things.'

'Look, mate, try phoning Joan from here. She'll be back now – see if she'll talk to you, at least,' Rob said. 'She's so innocent sometimes, she has no idea, and I'm sure she's in denial about you being away for so long. Anyway, I suppose it will be a huge relief not having to live a life of secrets anymore. Believe me, I *know* how that must feel.' He tightened his lips with more sadness in his heart; his adopted parents had left it too long.

He glanced at Terry; there was perspiration dripping down the side of his face. Rob handed him a box of tissues and Terry wiped his brow.

'Go on, Tel, do it,' Rob urged. 'Call her.' He saw the red light flashing on the answer phone and reminded himself to check his messages as soon as Terry had made the call. He had wanted to explain his situation about Pippa, but now it wasn't going to happen.

Terry hardly mentioned Jordan. He was a cute kid. Rob wondered how this might affect him in school; would he be teased? He would need a father figure. Surely Terry couldn't just disappear with the love of his life, this Frank person. He had to think of his son. Rob pushed the phone into Terry's hand and went into the kitchen while Terry dialled the number. He cupped his chin in his hands over the work surface then ran his fingers through his hair. *Today's been a bloody awful day and it's not over yet. Hell! Terry – gay! It must have taken some courage to tell me. God, poor Joan.* He switched on the kettle and prepared two cups for the coffee. He sat on the kitchen chair, listening and waiting to see if Joan would answer the phone.

'Hi, Joan, it's me.' Terry waited, holding his breath for a few seconds while she replied. There was a brief silence.

Chapter Eight

On arrival at the church hall, Pippa found the door locked. Not sure if she'd made a mistake, she waited for a few minutes. She looked down at her hand and saw a faint inky number seven, which she had attempted to wash off in the shower.

Moments later a green van arrived with Sven at the wheel.

'Sorry I'm a bit late. I had to take a boat to Bryher, only got back forty-five minutes ago. I had to dash home, get changed and come down here with the projector.'

Pippa smiled at him. He was very attractive with his tanned skin but also his blond hair and – oh yes, those shorts! The perfect tonic for a sad mind, she thought. 'Here, let me help you with all those things. You always seem to have so much stuff with you,' she offered.

Sven paused to get the key from his pocket. 'Can you open that door for me, Pippa? Do you mind?' He handed her the key.

She took it from him and the metal fob felt warm. She held the door open as he brought in the boxes of slides and the projector stand.

'Are you okay? Too much sun, I think,' he said, gazing on her burning cheeks.

'Well, maybe a bit, although I'm looking forward to the slide show! I'll be fine.'

She held out her hand, offering to carry boxes of slides and leaflets. The feelings of grief she had experienced on The Garrison would not spill into the evening. She would like to have told him about herself, but it was wrong, very wrong, and she feared she might chase him away. He might think she was whining – and why would he care? She scolded herself with a look of despair.

Sven's eyes scanned the room as he turned the wing nuts on the projector stand. He caught a glimpse of Pippa talking to someone who had arrived early. She was placing the leaflets on the table. His gut feeling was to feel sorry for her. What was it about Pippa? Sadness, yes, that was it! Her holiday just didn't add up; why *was* she here alone?

Their eyes met as she came towards him, and he opted to say something to avoid embarrassment. 'Sometime soon, I could show you how to improve your bird identification skills. I'm sure you would find it helpful.'

Pippa smiled at him. 'Great, thanks a lot.' *Wow! Now there's an offer.*

She could still feel the tightness in her chest and needed something to distract her. The slide show would be interesting and might take her mind off her time on The Garrison.

Sven plugged in the projector and tested the slides before the rest of the audience arrived.

'I bought a notebook this afternoon,' said Pippa. 'Thanks for the idea.'

Sven put up a thumb in approval. 'Great!'

Within half an hour, the hall had filled with people, and Sven tapped the microphone.

'Good evening, ladies and gentleman, welcome to the slide show. I look forward to taking you on a grand tour of the Isles of Scilly. There is a lot more to these islands than flowers, puffins and seals, so sit back and enjoy the scenery.'

He projected a map of the islands on to the screen. 'First, I would like to show you the reason why Scilly is a group of islands. It wasn't always like this.'

Pippa listened, glad she had decided to come.

'The area known as Crow Sound and The Road, where some

of you were on the boat with me today, was once a place where you could walk on dry land. With the rising sea levels it formed a lagoon.' Sven pointed to the screen. 'You will literally be up to your waist in the sea.' He showed a picture of a group of walkers wading across Crow Sound. 'At a very low tide you can walk from St Mary's to Tresco, but you have to play safe and get some proper advice, otherwise it can be very dangerous.'

There were magical names like Wingletang Ledges, Porth Hellick Down, and a tiny island rock named Daisy, which sounded like something out of a children's book.

'On the granite rocks, the ships *HMS Firebrand* and *Association* were wrecked in 1707.'

The slide show continued for an hour, and as Sven came to the end of his talk he smiled at his audience.

'Thank you very much, ladies and gentlemen. I hope you enjoyed the show. Drive safely along the "motorway" when you go home tonight.'

Everyone laughed then clapped. They stood and began to leave the hall. Some of them waited in line to talk to Sven. He shook hands with some of them, and Pippa wondered what she should do next.

She saw Jan and Marijke leaving and waved to them. By the look on their faces, they had also enjoyed themselves.

'We hope to see you down at Porthcressa soon, Pippa, don't forget,' Marijke called as she held onto Jan's arm.

'Yes – will do. I'll make a point of it.' She watched as they walked through the exit. *Poor chap.*

Instead of hanging around looking lost, she packed up some of the gear, thinking she was helping Sven.

As the hall emptied, he came across the floor and spoke to her. 'I saw you laughing. Did you enjoy the evening?'

'I loved it all,' Pippa enthused. 'You're so knowledgeable, I find it amazing. Your presentation was great. I wish I could do that.'

She recalled her days teaching at the school in front of an audience, and could hardly believe she used to have the confidence to give a presentation to parents.

Sven smiled warmly at her. 'Practice, I suppose. No, I do it because it's my life, but we all have to start somewhere. Maybe this is your chance as well. Thanks for helping out, by the way. I felt it was a bit of an imposition asking you like that, but I thought as you're on your own, it might just bring you into the way of things here.'

It was 9.30 in the evening. Sven gave Pippa the box of slides.

'Maybe you can put these in the van for me, is that okay? After this I'd like to invite you back to Beachside Cottage for a coffee for being such a good help.'

Pippa felt her arms go stiff and hesitated.

'Maybe another time, Sven, thanks.' *What would Rob say?*

Sven wasn't used to refusal.

'Are you sure? Erm… I would like to, it's not often I get the chance to help a novice birdwatcher. It means a lot to me, and I don't bite.' He chuckled.

'Okay, I'll come round, maybe learn more about island life with the locals,' she said with some secret delight.

'I'll walk you back afterwards. You'll be okay here, it's very safe,' he assured her. He liked Pippa's enthusiasm to learn and her shy personality. He didn't want to frighten her away, but if she was only here for three weeks, he wanted to know her better. He was going through one of his "doing-this-all-by-myself" weeks. He wished Martin would return soon, and Andrea, his wife, hadn't been to see him in a fortnight. She had left the islands to be with Martin in Bristol. He enjoyed going to their house at the weekends for her special fondue evenings and her delicious chocolate cheesecakes, and the visits she paid him. How he wished he had an "Andrea" of his own.

Pippa's curiosity about Sven made her want to be part of his easy happiness; it gave her a sense of security, but most certainly she didn't wish to give the wrong impression.

'Well, if you're sure. I don't want to put you to any trouble at this time of the evening, especially as you've had such a busy day.' She didn't know if she was doing the right thing; she was married, Rob wouldn't like it – or would he even care? *It's all innocent, anyway – no need to feel guilty, it'll be okay. Why not live a little?*

'It's a pleasure,' Sven said. 'I'd be delighted to make you a coffee, unless you would prefer something a bit stronger – but I've only got cider and beer.' He smiled.

'Okay, Sven, thanks, lovely, coffee will do.' His little cottage by the beach sounded homely. She was curious to see how the locals lived; perhaps it was like her own seaside house on Henrietta Street.

On the way to Beachside Cottage, Sven opened the conversation. 'Do you get much time to do the things you enjoy? My social life hasn't been too good of late, I'm always so busy. All that will change when my colleague returns.'

'I used to teach five-year-olds, but I gave up for personal reasons.' She had to keep her bereavement out of the conversation. *Talk about something else.* 'You obviously love the life here.'

'Ya, sure, but it can be a bit insular at times. Everyone knows who you are, and coming from a big city in Norway, I wasn't used to such a small community at first. But now, I suppose I am part of the scenery. I don't mind, but it did take me some time to integrate, and then it all began to fit into place.'

He took out the ignition key, and Pippa got out of the van and closed the door. She heard the sea lapping on the shore and breathed in the air of seaweed on the receding tide.

A row of white cottages stood at the bottom of the hill. The spread of pink Livingstone daisies on the wall of Sven's house had closed their blooms in the evening air. Sven opened the gate and gestured politely for Pippa to walk in front of him up the path. There was a conservatory, like the one at Gilstone, and the overall picturesque design reminded Pippa of how she used to draw a house for Daniel. Sven opened the door and led the way inside. 'Take a seat. I'll make us a drink.'

The interior of the cottage seemed a mixture of the old and the new. Antique-style furniture filled the walls – a glass cabinet and a chest of drawers, an old dining table – but there was a modern sofa, and a few pictures of birds and paintings of Scilly.

The washing up from the morning lay in the sink, and Sven apologised for the mess. Pippa thought that, for a bachelor pad, it wasn't too bad. The views of the bay from the window were unrivalled. Her first impressions made her want to stay longer.

Sven filled the kettle. 'So, Pippa, have you found your respite today?' he said as he flicked the switch. 'Sorry it's only instant,' he remarked, pointing to the Nescafé. 'I couldn't help think you looked a bit tired earlier on, all that walking, eh? I hope you don't mind me asking, but do you normally travel alone? It's not often I meet someone of our age group who takes a holiday by herself. Sorry if I'm being nosey.'

Pippa didn't know what to say; was he being nosey or just kind? Instead, she nodded. 'Nescafé's fine.' It was all fine; she felt so very comfortable with him, to the point where it had become surreal. 'It's okay. I've had a rough few years,' she warned him. 'But you don't want to be bothered with my problems.'

'Try me if you like. Anything I can do to help?' He paused for a moment. 'Milk? Sugar?'

As he passed her the spoon to stir her coffee, she felt his brown hand brush against hers. There was something interesting about him; it was like wanting to feel dress material for its quality; those hands that had earlier soothed her sunburnt neck.

Sven sat to face her. 'I'm a good listener,' he said.

'Right…well… I have to warn you it's not a pretty story.' What was she doing revealing her sadness to an almost complete stranger? But after all, he had offered to listen, and she needed to offload. Would she be making a fool of herself? Nevertheless, it felt right; something told her she was safe here; she didn't know why. What if she told him about Daniel and then there were no more cups of coffee, no one to talk to during her holiday? Sven might even ignore her on the boat trips – but if he knew the guilt she had suffered, perhaps he would understand her better.

'I don't mind, honestly,' he repeated, 'if it helps you to talk things through. You know, they say in my country "a problem shared is a problem halved". Isn't that the same in English?'

Pippa nodded again. His kindness had overwhelmed her and she felt her breath sucked from her lungs. She performed her calming and distancing routine in her head and thought about how to explain it all. *Slowly breathe in and out and focus on something interesting.* The older couple smiling out of the photo on the dresser were obviously his parents; Sven looked more like his mother. Pippa bit her lip and the whole story unfolded as Sven's sympathetic expression waited for her to speak.

'Someone died…someone very close to me.' She cradled the mug in both hands, pursed her lips and blew the steam across the cup. 'Think of the worst thing that could happen in your life and that's what happened to me.' She took in another breath and slowly let it out again, blowing the heat away.

Sven sat still, his eyes fixed on her face, waiting for her to say more. There was a brief silence.

'You don't have to do this, Pippa. It's my fault for pushing the issue, sorry.'

'No, it's okay. Do you really want to hear the rest?' She sighed.

'Only if you want to. As I said, it might help,' he assured her. 'It just kind of shocked me, that's all. Please do go on.'

'Well… I'm here for some peace and quiet as I mentioned yesterday. It's been a terrible thing. You see, my son died three years ago.' All she could see was herself in hospital and Rob telling her Daniel had passed away. Then there was the funeral and all the dreadful things she'd had to endure.

Sven pushed himself against the chair-back for a moment. 'Oh God, I'm so sorry, I didn't realise… I thought…well, I'm not sure what I thought. Something told me there might be a story behind your coming here – only a guess.'

'Was it that obvious? I decided to have a holiday for three weeks to see if I could get some respite from all the grief and bickering which has been flying around my house for the last three years. It's been awful. I suppose I am a target for curiosity by coming here alone.'

She wasn't sure if her mind was operating as it should. For a brief moment she didn't want to be with Rob any more. She wished she could stay here with Sven, just talking, nothing more. His cottage, with a wood-burning stove; how warm and welcoming it would be in winter. The situation called her to an outpouring of her grief. She sensed a welling-up of tears; she mustn't cry, *must not* cry… She glanced at her watch; she ought not to have taken up so much of Sven's caring nature.

'It's okay, no rush. Go on, Pippa, I'm a good listener.'

She gave him a thankful smile; he could read her thoughts too.

'I blamed myself for a long time, and in a way I still do, but it was my husband's reaction which made things worse. We tried to do this together – you know, heal the wounds as husband and wife, but his work got in the way of his family life. He's a trainee counsellor and a nurse at the local hospital, and I feel it's changed him. He's more detached from our son's death these days. I can see what he's trying to do, but it isn't working.'

'Please accept my sympathy.'

Pippa gave a grateful nod. 'Thanks. You see, Rob and I, and our friends Terry and Joan, we're like family. We all got married quite young and our lives have gone through dramatic changes. Anyway, I don't wish to bore you, but Rob and Daniel and myself had a day-trip here once, so I decided to come back and see if I could heal the wounds and move on.'

'I'm glad you came. You would have missed out on visiting Scilly, and we wouldn't be sat here talking. I feel very sad for you. I'm sorry, I didn't mean to pry, I was just being…'

Pippa interrupted. 'It's fine, it helps me to talk. I appreciate it very much.' She gave a tight reassuring smile and nodded a 'thanks'.

'So where is your husband? – Whoops, sorreee! I'm being nosey again.' Sven stirred his coffee. Pippa thought that perhaps he wished he hadn't asked about her problems and she tried to smooth things over to help him.

'Oh, it's okay. Let's say since the accident things haven't been the same between us. I'm not sure what'll happen after this. Rob's studying to be a psychiatric nurse at the local hospital. He couldn't come for the summer, his holiday rota doesn't start until August, and he's more of a mountain man. You see, I needed to get away *now* before I went crazy, because I feel our relationship is somewhat...' She sighed and wrinkled her nose. 'Cracked? Hence the reason I came away on my own.' She had bent the story; her marriage was more than cracked and, in truth, she might not have one when she got home. 'Rob and I, we seem to be going in different directions now – he's drowning his sorrows in his work and doesn't have a lot of time for me, and I'm doing my best to get over the accident and trying not to blame myself. Rob didn't want to come to Scilly and so here I am – I thought it might do me some good.'

'But you're still too young just to let things ride for the rest of your life. You should be out there having a good time. I mean... maybe I can help you to learn about the birds, and make a holiday plan. It would also take your mind off things.'

'Aw, Sven, thanks, that's kind of you. All I want is to be normal again and get my happiness back. I mean, I'll never forget Daniel, of course, but you're right, I cannot allow my life to continue in eternal grief. My doctor told me to get out and go birdwatching. He said working with nature would be a good way of healing myself.'

'True, very true. So doesn't Rob mind you coming here on your own?'

'Our relationship is very, well...we argue a lot. I really don't know how he feels right now. He seems mixed up. You see, he was adopted, and with losing Daniel, it seems like his life fell apart twice. He went into counselling to try to help himself and ended up doing it as a job. I think it's made him worse.'

'Oh, that's a shame. Have you tried to work things out?' He placed his hands around his cup and sat forward to listen more intently.

Pippa sighed. 'I can't get through to him since we lost Daniel. Being away from him for three weeks, I can get some space and know how I really feel and see how it goes. It provides him with a chance to do the same. Perhaps it's a trial separation, although we haven't spoken about it in that way. I know he blames me for losing Dan. I was in hospital for almost a week with concussion. I kept on having convulsions for about a month afterwards. It was my friend, Joan, who helped me back to normality. It's been so hard in the last three years and it was a terrible shock. I could accept the loss of my dad to a small degree, but a child you never forget.'

Sven nodded in absolute agreement. 'You're going to need support while you're here. I'm glad you told me. I hope we'll see each other again throughout your holiday.' He smiled, willing her to say 'yes'.

'Oh, that's the nicest thing anyone has said to me in ages.' Tears almost fell into her coffee cup. 'I feel such an idiot sometimes.' She wiped her face on one of the tissues she always kept in her pocket.

Without a word, he put his arm on her shoulder as if to shield her from all the harm out there on the mainland.

A warm sensation came over her. She knew he meant well and was glad he was there for her. She hardly knew him, but at this moment, sitting with a cup of coffee in his kitchen and with his blue eyes looking kindly upon her, he seemed like a gift from heaven. After her sun-cream experience, she knew he was a caring man, and his arm around her shoulder was a lovely gesture of his warm personality and assurance.

'Pippa, I agree you have to move on. I can see you've had a bad time. I think it would be good to help you learn more about the birds. Nature is a good healer, your doctor was right.'

Sven took a deep breath. He thought he had never known anyone so sad, and yet so enthusiastic to learn. She was in conflict with herself and he sensed her pain. For the first time in his life, he wanted to be involved in something he knew nothing about, and couldn't say why. She liked birds and nature, and he wanted to help her through her crisis with this mutual interest.

Pippa dried her tears as he slowly released her and she took out another paper tissue to blow her nose. It was time to feel better; she couldn't let Sven take all her grief.

'Okay, tell me about you,' she sniffed. 'I mean, we only met yesterday on the quay, for goodness sake. I feel rather stupid.' Aware of Sven's concerns, she realised her friendship might be more than she expected. She concentrated on a spot on the wall, taking calculated breaths. In terms of anxiety, she managed to bring herself back down to a five instead of a full-blown ten: a method Rob had shown her.

'No, it's fine, Pippa. I am very interested in what you've told me. It's a pleasure to meet with you – and to think you've had all this, and there's me here enjoying myself and you out there. God! It doesn't bear thinking about, does it? I'm so sorry to hear about your son. You are right about it being one of the worst things to happen to anyone. I'm glad you shared your sorrow with me, I feel very...' He sighed, trying to find the right English word. Instead, he smiled and shook his head in sympathy. He sat closer to Pippa and patted her hand. It was nice sitting next to her without talking. He wondered what he should do next. He began to sense her vulnerability and felt he should say something.

'I'm pleased you have some good friends back home who support you.'

'Yes, but I'm sorry it had to be you who got the blunt end of my grief. Perhaps now, when we go out on the boats, you will understand why I am here and why sometimes I may not look too happy.' She changed the subject. 'So tell me about Norway, and how you got to be here in Scilly.' She sipped her coffee.

Sven smiled back at her, pleased he had helped her recover from her tears.

'Okay, I'll tell you... I'm not married, no kids, working my socks off for the tourists and generally a Norwegian bum having a great time.' He chuckled, attempting to lighten the mood. 'I studied in Trondheim before I applied for a job in Scotland working on the dolphin project, and then I travelled to England and got this job, so here I am. What you see is what you get!' He smiled the kind smile with which Pippa had become familiar.

'I think I'm beginning to like what I see.' She was sure Sven blushed when she said this. He rolled his eyes and drank up the last dregs of coffee. Pippa almost kicked herself; she hadn't meant to say it in that way. She only meant... Oh, what *did* she mean? Never mind.

'I usually hang around with Martin, "The Birdman", and his wife Andrea. She is a true friend and spends a lot of time on her own. I look in on her, when the boss is away. Don't get the wrong idea, I mean, she's good fun and a bit older than me. We tend to keep each other company in the winter months. Andrea is sort of "family" for me – a good friend too. I also admire her ability to organise events, she is very helpful and makes the most of her time on the islands, and...she makes good cakes.' Sven grinned at Pippa. 'She's an excellent cook. Martin is a great person too, I wish you could meet him. He might not be back in time for your leaving here – not sure yet.'

'It sounds like you have a great life. I'm very impressed at your knowledge of birds, but that's your job. What a great job, eh?'

'Oh yes, it's good – and for me it's the best. But – and it's a big but – you could find yourself going off the rails if you aren't careful, because the islands are so small and we all lead this insular lifestyle. Gossip spreads around the population faster than I can make a phone call.' Sven chuckled. 'It's *that* kind of place – you accept it, but everyone has been so good to me. I love it, I'm totally at home here.'

Pippa gestured towards the mantelpiece. 'The photo – is that your parents?'

'Ya, sure.'

Pippa looked at her watch, not wishing to outstay her welcome. Sven had been too kind. 'I'll have to go soon. I have to admit to being tired after such a long and wonderful day. Thanks, Sven. It's been a while.'

As promised, much to her relief, Sven offered to walk her back to Gilstone. He tossed the van keys on the dining table and closed the door behind him. The moon had risen, providing enough light to shine on the sea. Further on and closer to town, Pippa heard faint music coming from The Bishop pub. 'It's so deserted,' she said. 'Almost spooky. It's like a ghost town with music.'

'Will you be okay at Gilstone on your own?' He scolded himself for asking.

'Oh yes. Thanks, Sven, that's kind of you. I didn't expect to be pampered so much on my first couple of days here.' Pippa chuckled. 'I'll be fine, honest.' She wondered for a moment why he was paying so much attention to her, but it damned well felt good, and so what if he was?

They walked through the narrow street together and crossed the road towards the house.

'Here we are, Gilstone,' Sven announced on their arrival. 'Don't worry, you'll be fine. I hope to show you a lot more about the islands, maybe do some drawings for you and provide you with a kick-start into birdwatching.'

Pippa's insides wanted to sing and dance at the opportunity. 'Are you busy tomorrow evening, or is that a daft question?'

Sven paused for thought. 'No…er…I don't have anything planned, why?'

'Well…it's probably my turn for coffee. There's a conservatory at the back of this house, we could sit in there around the dining table – great for drawing. By the way, I also like to draw – well, I did before…you know…but I gave all that up. I'll make us something to eat, too. Glass of red wine suit you?'

'Sure, sounds good to me. There you are, I got you smiling already. Okay, see you tomorrow, eh?' Sven kindly patted her arm. 'Sleep well and try not to worry, you'll have a great time here, I know you will. Good night, Pippa, and thanks. I'm glad you came back to Scilly. I hope our chat helps you to sleep tonight, eh?'

Astonished by his kindness, she took a deep breath. 'I'm grateful for the company. Yes, you helped a lot more than you realise.' She gave him an assuring glance. 'Thanks again.'

'Take care now – goodnight,' he said. 'Sweet dreams.'

She watched as he walked across the road, almost bumping into a cyclist without lights. She smiled. It had been a lovely evening, and most unexpected.

As she closed the door, she couldn't help wondering what Sven had in mind for her. She wished she could stay here longer than three weeks, but reminded herself that it was a holiday, nothing more. Sven's friendship might make it harder to leave. She could still see his face in her head as she got undressed for bed.

Chapter Nine

Terry picked up the phone as Rob made coffee.

'Hello, Joan, it's me. I tried to call you earlier.'

'Oh, Tel, love. Where are you?' Joan sighed.

Terry thought his wife sounded weary.

'I'm back in Whitby. I wondered what time you got in?'

'You have a key, don't you?'

'Yeah, but…we need to talk.'

'Oh, at last, you've come to your senses, have you?' she said, half-joking.

'Can I come round now?'

'Terry, no need to ask, for God's sake – you live here. What's the matter with you?'

Rob eavesdropped from the kitchen. *Poor Joan.* He knew her well; she could be fiery at times, and having heard Terry's confession he was upset for her. He wondered if he should be in there, supporting the two of them – but no, this was something they had to do on their own.

'Where's Jordan?' Terry asked.

'In bed, of course, out like a light.'

'Good, I'll see you in half an hour. Bye.' He replaced the receiver. 'Well, that's it, then,' he concluded.

Rob looked shocked at the short, sharp conversation. Where once he thought there had been warmth and love, they had gone. *Is it like that with Pippa and me?*

'How are you going to break this to her?' he asked. 'I mean, you will tell her, won't you?' He watched Terry's face, knowing he could easily back out. Terry didn't reply.

Rob shook his head, not believing the events of the day. His best friend, whom he had known most of his life, had confessed he was gay. How difficult this must have been. He sensed his own shock; none of them had ever thought of Terry in that way. Why should they? He was Terry, the quiet one, not much older than Rob, only by a few months. They were at school together. Rob realised he would have to get used to it, but it was a stigma his best mate would have to suffer for the rest of his life. The world wasn't ready for this kind of thing, especially in Whitby. Terry had made his choice to "come out". *Can't believe it.*

'Anything I can do to help, Tel?' Rob asked. 'I mean, this is a shock for me as well, mate. I never realised…'

'No, Rob, thanks, I'll have to face her, and you know what she's like. She won't believe me. I've sat for weeks practising what to say. Frank's been very understanding. He's given me lots of support in the last few weeks.' Terry's throat faded to a cracked whisper. 'I suppose I'd better get over there.'

'Don't linger. Just do it, Tel. I can support her if you like, but let's see how things go, eh? Good luck, mate! Call me if you need a further chat.' Rob patted Terry on the shoulder as he went through the front door. 'See ya. Good luck.'

As Terry left the house, Rob began to wish today hadn't happened.

Terry took almost twenty minutes to walk home as he had left the car with his parents. He and Joan had bought an ex-council house at a reasonable price. He recalled when they used to live a few doors down the street from Rob and Pippa, but the house was too small and rented, and they needed an extra bedroom for Jordan. Things seemed different then, easier.

He put the key into the lock. He knew the door always stuck on the weatherboard and he gave an extra push. He ought to repair it; it had been this way for about two years. He'd kept promising to make a new one. It would dry out by July.

Joan stood in the hall; she noticed something wasn't quite right as he walked through the door. He had changed; his hair was different, longer, and his eyes seemed to be searching around the room rather than giving her a welcoming look. He held her in his arms, but didn't kiss her. 'Come on, love, let's go into the lounge and talk.'

'Tel, what's the matter, love?'

'I'm not going to beat about the bush, but first let me tell you I care a lot about you, Joanie, honest I do.' He only called her that when he wanted her to be calm.

Joan's face fell. 'Are you ill?'

'No...no, nothing like that. It's a long story, really, and I've been trying to explain for the last four years. I have a confession to make.' He hesitated for a moment. 'I've not been totally honest with you.'

'You've been leading a double life then?' Joan teased.

Many a true word, Terry thought as the vision of Frank's face came to mind. 'Come on, Joanie, listen to me, love, this is serious. It's taken me a long time to reach this point and I'm not going to allow this moment to pass any longer. I need your understanding. God! This is hard for me. It's to do with my sexuality. You might find this hard to believe, but I'm...'

'Okay, Tel, I *know* what you're going to say – you can't, you know...do it. I knew that, you just need to get some help, don't be scared, love.'

Terry almost sobbed, letting out a loud sigh.

'No, Joan. I don't know how to say this more gently.' He gave another deep sigh; the words he had thought about so many times sounded dirty and betraying.

'Joanie, listen to me, love, I want you to take this seriously. I'm... I'm homosexual. You know, *gay*.'

'Terry, don't be stupid. We've got Jordan, you can't be.' Joan stared at him with horror in her eyes. 'You're crazy. You just need some advice, that's all. You've got it all wrong, pet, it's something you need to talk to the doctor about. You're not one of those, you just made a mistake. You've been going through stress recently, I know.'

Terry took her by the hand and drew closer to her.

'Joanie, listen to me, love, this is serious. I've tried so many times to explain, and I promise you I never went with anyone while we were together. All those times I tried to make love to you and I found it very difficult, all those excuses I made. So much has gone on in our lives, how could I tell you? You're a lovely person, Joanie, but I found it impossible to do those things. It's me who has a problem, not you. It's *my* fault. When Daniel died, we were so involved in helping Pippa and Rob come to terms with it all.' He saw the look on Joan's face and began to hate himself. 'Then I got the job on the rigs – a deliberate move to give me time to think. I didn't "come out" until a few weeks ago. I didn't understand why I had these feelings. I've suffered with depression for too long and tried not to show how I felt. Everyone around us was getting married, it was the right thing to do. I thought I loved you in that way. Being gay was never talked about. I now realise this was something I was born with. It's only in the last few months I've felt confident enough to get some help. You gotta believe me, Joan. I'm so sorry, pet, honest I am.'

Joan's chin dropped. 'Bloody hell – you mean… Is that why you never came home? You mean…' She was now close to tears.

'Yes, I do mean it. Joan, you are so old-fashioned sometimes. Gay men are coming out more these days, and yes, they can have children. I proved that – why not? Don't be so bloody daft.'

Joan stared at him with wide eyes. 'Shit, how do you know you are queer, gay or whatever? What do we do? Born with it, you say? So do you need to see a doctor or anything?'

'No, Joan, I don't need a doctor, for God's sake. Let me explain…'

'But, Terry, I am confused. What do I do? What does this

mean?' Joan panicked, knowing it could be the end of her marriage if she didn't try to make him see it differently.

'Listen, Joan, *please*. I got very down this year. I tried not to let you see how I felt. This guy on the rigs, Frank, he's my...my...well, anyway, he helped me through it. We are partners now. I'm sorry. Anyway, Joan, it's not like you and I have been "at it" like rabbits since Jordan was born.'

'What d'ye mean, partners?' Joan glared, behind time with the words Terry was saying.

Terry looked at her straight. 'What do you think I mean?' He gave a deep sigh and turned his gaze away from her.

'You mean...you and him did stuff together?'

'God, Joan, you are so naïve. You just don't get it, do you?'

Joan stared into the room. She never spoke, nor did she blink. She felt dirty and wanted to get an urgent shower. Her mother had drummed it into her not to go off with strange men; she often talked about "those kind of men", and Joan didn't know how she was supposed to react. She wanted to say, "You should have told me before this". Instead, her anger rose and she burst out with her true feelings.

'Does this mean you are leaving Jordan and me?'

'No, it doesn't have to be this way, Joan.'

'I hate you for it. I don't want Jordan to see you again, especially not now. I don't want him influenced with your lies.' Her breathing became a sob.

'Joan, please listen, love, I can understand your anger.' Terry felt injured and wished he hadn't told her. 'Please, Joan, please understand, I am trying to be honest with you.'

'Honest? Honest? You cheated on me. Don't call me "love".'

'Joan, listen to me, *please*. Being gay is a condition of my thoughts and the way my body works, it's something I can't help. It's certainly not an illness. I told you I was *born* like this, it's not my fault! Joan, you're not listening to me! I didn't mean to cheat on you, it just happened. Being away from home helped me to "come out". I need to know what we're going to do considering Jordan as well. I came here tonight hoping we could work things out.'

Terry's face turned a deeper pink and beads of sweat ran down his cheeks. *Frank was right. 'Say it as it is, keep telling her the truth and show her you really do care.'*

Jordan heard voices and began to cry. 'Mummy, Mu-mmy.'

'I'll go and see him,' said Terry.

'No, you bloody well won't. I'll get him. He needs me, not you. You haven't been here all this time, you'll scare him, and anyway, he doesn't know who you are any more.'

Terry sat back, astounded. *Oh heck, this is unbelievably hard.* Joan's words had stabbed him to the core

She left the lounge in a hurry, her mind numb, crashed into the small chest of drawers on the landing and stubbed her toe. 'Ow, ouch, ow, ooya bugger.' She sat on the floor while Jordan howled, 'Mummy.'

Terry ran to see what had caused the commotion. 'What the hell have you done?' he yelled, halfway up the stairs.

'My toe, my toe,' she cried. 'Bloody 'ell. Ow, ow, oucha!' Her face distorted with terrible pain.

Terry saw his son standing beside his mother. Jordan went quiet for a moment and then screamed.

'It's okay, Jordan pet,' said Terry. 'Here's Daddy. My, haven't you grown?'

Joan groaned in pain.

'What do you bloody well expect? He's two now, and you didn't even send him a card last month. Ow, ouch!'

'Joan, I don't live in a town. I can't go shopping like we used to. I phoned you, didn't I? Are you awright?'

Jordan began to scream again and huddled into his mother, refusing to look at Terry, then ran into the bedroom and hid under the covers.

'The kid's terrified of you. Ouch, bloody oucha, no I'm not awright,' she echoed, rubbing her fingers over her big toe, which began to swell.

Terry ran downstairs, brought a packet of frozen peas, and placed them with care on her foot.

'I'll do it!' Joan yelled. 'Jordan pet, stay in bed. Go to sleep. I'll be alright, sweetheart.'

'Should I kiss it better, Mummy?' Jordan stood supporting a wet thumb.

'No, sweetie, it's okay, just go to bed – there's a good lad.' She looked at Terry. 'He's a really good kid,' she said, sniffing back her tears.

'Here, let me help you downstairs,' Terry offered.

'No, I'll manage, don't touch me!' She hobbled into Jordan's room and sat by his bed.

Terry watched and wanted to hold Jordan in his arms. 'Hello, Jordan, come to Daddy. I'm sure he'll be okay.'

'Leave him, Tel,' she screamed. 'I don't want you near him, influencing him in your ways, it feels dirty.'

'Joan! Don't, please, for God's sake – not in front of the kid. I'm suffering enough, can't you see that?' Terry's tears welled under his eyelids.

He went to pick up Jordan in his arms.

'Mummy, Mummy,' Jordan screamed, twisting and flailing to escape from his dad.

'He's been ill,' Joan said. 'Best leave him, but he's a lot better today, just tired.' She tried to be calm for the sake of Jordan.

She hobbled to sit on the top stair, going down each one hanging on to the banister. 'Leave me alone, don't touch me.'

Terry realised Jordan had become Joan's child and not his own. He felt his role as a father snatched away. She had everything in order; the house looked clean and tidy, with all Jordan's toys neat and in their place. He caught a glimpse of himself in the mirror on the landing and stared deep into the image. He concentrated on his eyes, then his lips, and thought how warm Joan had been when they first met. What had he done to her? He hated himself. They'd enjoyed good times together. He couldn't – no, mustn't – hang onto her any longer; it wasn't fair on any of them. She was still young enough to start again, he must give her a chance; that was the least he could do. She would surely see it differently one day.

He crept into the room. 'It's okay, our Jordan, Daddy's here. I'll tuck you in.' It was as if he had some contagious disease and couldn't give his son a goodnight kiss in case Joan shouted at him again.

Jordan hid under the covers with his thumb in his mouth.

'Goodnight, son, remember Daddy always loves you.'

Terry was leaving in a couple of days and he realised he might not see his son again for some time. The feeling in his chest became a heavy stone weighing him down. *Shit, what the hell have I done?*

He thought about Frank. For the first time he knew what love meant. Frank was good-looking, rugged, and there was a sense of mutual trust and understanding between them. If it wasn't for Frank, Terry thought, I might have been living a lie for the rest of my life. 'You can't go on like this,' he'd said. 'Tel, you mean a lot to me, and we're more than good mates now. You have got to tell Joan.'

Terry went back down the stairs as Joan nursed her toe.

'Is it okay?' he asked her. 'Do you think you broke it?'

'No, it's not okay, thanks to you. God, Tel, what have you done? Where do we go from here?' She was quieter now, her mind on her two kinds of pain. 'Who else knows about this?'

'My dad does, and today I went to see Rob while I waited for you.'

'You mean you told every bugger in Whitby about this before you told me?' she said in horror.

'No, no, it wasn't like that, honest. I needed Rob's support. I had no idea what to say, and him being a nurse an' all that, I thought he might understand. Also with Uncle Ronnie being that way inclined I thought *you* might understand. You've met him and he's a nice guy, you wouldn't know about his sexuality unless some-one told you. Even our Mam doesn't realise, and please don't tell her. It would kill her. Anyway, I'm still Jordan's dad, for goodness sake. I still need to see him when I come home. Even Rob spends more time with him these days than I do. I just can't… Oh, shit, I can't do this.'

'I think you're missing the point, Tel. Whether you like it or not, you've cheated on me. It's not a disease, is it? Is it inherited? I mean… Jordan won't get it, will he? All that AIDS stuff you see on the telly, it sounds horrendous. You might die or something. Have you thought about that?'

'Yes' was all he said with a sigh, thinking it might be too late. 'And no, it's not inherited, don't be silly.'

'And I expect Pippa knows about it?' Joan butted in sharply.

'No, she doesn't. I think she'll find out anyway, but she's left Rob, hasn't she?'

'No, she bloody well hasn't. Did Rob tell you that?'

'I kind of presumed… Oh heck, this is far too much for me to take in.'

'Well, don't presume. You seem to do a lot of that recently. Pippa is away on a break, which brings me back to our situation – what do we do about it? I thought I still loved you until today.' Her bottom lip trembled as she spoke and she sobbed.

'I'm sorry, pet, I thought I loved you in that way too. It became a nightmare for me, I honestly didn't know what it meant. It was as though it was happening to someone else. I suppose I've been in denial about it since I was about fourteen. Joan, you have to listen to me. I'm so sorry it had to be this way.'

He leaned forward to kiss her on the forehead.

'Get off me, Terry, please, you don't understand.'

Terry hesitated for a moment. He took a deeper breath. 'We should talk about divorce. I don't think you'll want me to be your husband anymore. I'll still keep sending money for you and Jordan, but I think you'll be better off without me, both of you. I'll stay in touch, I promise. I'll be at our mam and dad's tonight, I'll tell them some excuse or another. Our mam will freak out if she knows about me. She must never know, it would kill her, she doesn't understand these things, so, please don't tell her.'

Joan looked at him and scoffed. 'It's about time she knew who her son really is.' She stepped back and sat on the stairs, still nursing her foot wrapped in frozen peas. She thought about the bigger picture and looked back at how it had been over the last few years. The news Terry had brought became clearer as she pondered on the passing years.

'When I look at Pippa and Rob, then you and me, I suppose we were all pushed together by our own personal circumstances. It's all been a bloody nightmare.'

'I'll come and see Jordan and send you money as I always did, but we need to discuss this further very soon.'

Joan began to sob again, her bottom lip tucked tight under her front teeth. She sobbed into Terry's arms as she had always done when needing comfort. It wasn't as if she hadn't expected Terry to come home one day, asking for a divorce. It had crossed her mind once or twice since his absence, and she had run through her head what she would do if he left her. In a moment of regret she paused. 'Please don't go, Tel, we can work this out.'

Terry stroked her hand but didn't kiss her; it had to be this way.

'I'm sorry, pet, I find this hard as well. As I said I only wanted to be honest with you. We can't go on like this – just think how it might be in ten years' time. I might have fallen ill with the stress and…well, living together would be awful.'

Joan said nothing and sniffed into the sleeve of her jumper.

'I'll be round at our mam's for a couple of days if you want to talk about it. I think it's best I leave now without prolonging the agony. Talk to Rob about it, he's good on these things. I'll tell our mam we had a disagreement. Dad understands, he'll smooth things over for her, and for you and Jordan. I'm going to have a chat with Uncle Ronnie too.'

'So bloody soon? You mean you came to tell me all this and

now you're buggering off to your mam and dad's? And stop calling me pet! I am not *your* pet anymore.'

'Oh, Joan, don't, please. Look, I'll come and see you before I go back to Aberdeen, okay?'

'Is that it? Is that all you can say to me?' she bawled.

''Fraid so. I don't see any point in me hanging around, do you? You'll see very soon, I've done the right thing for you and Jordan. You won't have to live with the stigma of me living in the area – no one will know.'

He opened the front door. 'I'm sorry, Joan, I'm really, really sorry.' Terry sighed and closed his eyes for a moment; he had become his own worst nightmare.

Joan stood with anger in her heart as she tried to slam the door behind him. The door stuck and she had to push it. She now had a new status in life – single mother. She blew out her cheeks and stood in the hall with her back to the front door, then slid down to the floor. She broke down in a moment of anger and shame. But this…jilted…the end of her marriage.

Chapter Ten

The following day Pippa took a boat to Tresco. She packed her bird book, a pencil and her new pad for the bird records. With binoculars swinging, her mind and stature in birdwatching mode, she stepped on board *Black Swan* with another fifty or more passengers. The morning had been foggy and the sea, now calm, reflected the blue sky. Pippa closed her eyes and soaked her thoughts in the atmosphere of the sea.

The boat slid through the water and the sun glistened in the wake. Pippa arrived on Tresco for a walk around the Abbey Gardens. Sven had mentioned the flowers were at their best this week.

On leaving the boat at Carn Near quay, she walked the narrow path towards the entrance to the tropical gardens. With the heat of the morning sun on her shoulders, she drew in a breath of air, listening to the sound of pheasants clucking.

The echoes of the island rang in her ears everywhere she turned. The black-back gull called a rapid *ha-ha ha-ha* as it flew overhead, and she wanted to laugh back at it.

She paused a while to listen to the "shushing" sound of the lapping sea as though she were listening through a shell. The perfume and the buzzing of bees – it was all here. She had arrived in a special place at a time of her life when she needed inner peace. Her sad-self uplifted as she walked towards the garden gate to pay her entrance fee. No more sadness, only simple peace and happiness wafted through the air on this perfect summer day.

Rhododendrons bloomed, and through the greenery poked

the turrets of Tresco Abbey. Screwed to the wall, a plaque provided a poetic message warning visitors not to take plant cuttings. Pippa stood and read it to herself.

Awake my Muse, bring bell and book
To curse the hand that cuttings took.
May every sort of garden pest
His little plot of ground infest
(Who stole the plants from Inverewe,
From Falkland Palace, Tresco too).
Let Caterpillars, capsid bugs
Leafhoppers, thrips, all sorts of slugs
Play havoc with his garden plot,
And a late frost destroy the lot.

Pippa stood back with a smile. *Quite right!*

She walked the many paths, up and down steps and into small niches where she captured the perfume and the colours. She felt quite splendid sitting on a seat gazing at the flush of tropical plants. If only Rob had been interested in all this, they might have had some mutual understanding. She thought hard about what she really wanted in her life. Perhaps she could make her marriage work; there had been days when Rob was kind and generous, but the chemistry between them seemed to have vanished. He could be so deep; he never wanted to share his inner thoughts. She had needed him to ensure her survival, to understand their shared grief.

Enjoy the moment, she thought with a sigh. What was the sense in spoiling this wonderful cloudless day?

Inside the Valhalla Museum, she gazed at the ships' figureheads on display. With every corner, her eyes fixed upon amazing plants. If only she could name them in Latin as some of the women who had passed her on the path had done. The butterflies drew nectar from the flower heads, and the hum of the bees calmed her. The giant heads of pink velvet proteas reached out towards the sky, and the flame trees' colour made them live up to their name. The tang of pine, combined with the salt of the sea, provided a wonderful ambience to the day. Pippa could hardly believe this was England. Her thoughts and feelings now directed towards calm and less anxiety. It had been a long time. She enjoyed the sensation of the perfumed air and felt the muscles in her thighs working as she ascended the steps of The Long Walk. The palm trees lined the path to the statue of Hercules, which gave her the strength to keep clambering up and up. Although breathless, she made it to the top and surveyed the scene: flowers everywhere – *oh, the gloriousness of it all!* How blind she had been; there really was life after Daniel, and she had found it here in the gardens.

It was now time to move on and see more after lunch.

At the café, she ordered a cheese salad with a bread roll, and dropped the occasional crumb for the thrushes, blackbirds, and starlings. She made notes about her walk and drew pictures of flowers.

She checked her watch. The boat would be going back later, but in the distance could be heard the sound of rotor blades from a helicopter returning to Penzance. Just one more stroll up the wooded paths and then it would be time to leave. As she thought about Sven's visit, she began to make her way back to the quay. Before leaving, she visited the garden shop and bought a straw sunhat to protect her face. She tied her hair in a knot inside the brim of the hat, and strolled towards the boat for the return trip. The flimsy red scarf wrapped around the brim of the hat flowed down her back and she felt like a film star on holiday.

That morning, Sven guided a group of birdwatchers from his native country around the Higher Moors Nature Reserve. He had advertised the tour in a magazine in Norway. He knew he was on his best form speaking his own language; it had been a while. His mind turned to Pippa; maybe he could encourage her to enjoy herself. He thought she needed a friend as much as he did. He knew he probably fancied her, but wasn't sure what he should do about it. The last thing he wanted was to be involved in the break-up of someone else's relationship.

He rode home on his bike and made a mental note of what he needed to take with him to Pippa's place that evening. At least she would go back to Yorkshire having learned a new hobby. Yes, she would go home and forget him, just like the others had done. There was Marcia from Bristol who wanted to "eat him to bits", and Alice who was far too immature for her age. None of them were interested in wildlife. They were visiting for a couple of weeks with parents and friends, then gone forever. *Doesn't anyone want a nice guy with an adventurous job?* He chuckled to himself. Pippa seemed different; she wanted to learn, and he was keen to show her his life and the nature on his own doorstep. Even if he did approach the subject, he would have those feelings of failure again if she turned him down. He had three weeks to learn more about her, but she lived hundreds of miles away. Besides, she might be offended, and then he would feel stupid. Why did he keep doing this to himself? There was nothing wrong in having dinner with her; it might help to cheer her up a little. Her tragedy had been dreadful; he couldn't imagine what it must have been like. What she didn't need right now was him messing up her life even more. All he wanted was to show her the birds and the islands, and take it easy, give it time. He knew himself too well; he must control his impulsive mind.

On arrival at Gilstone, Pippa showered, changed, and made a chilli dish with salad.

At seven o'clock, Sven was knocking on the door, looking more sun-tanned than the day before.

'Come in,' she said, 'and make yourself at home. Though I would think you know this place better than me!'

'Thanks. Actually, I've only been here once before to visit Peter Stowes, Janice's husband,' Sven informed her.

Pippa moved her straw hat from the settee to the coffee table.

'Nice hat,' he remarked.

'Yes, I bought it on Tresco today. Did you have a good day at work?' It was a question she'd often asked of Rob. She felt her question must be rather weird coming from someone Sven hardly knew. Also his work seemed like play. She scolded herself for asking.

'Ya, sure. I was speaking Norwegian. Some mates of mine from home arrived on the islands and so I did a tour on dry land for a change. I prefer it – that is my real job.' He sighed.

She busied herself laying the table, putting out the coasters and two wine glasses.

'Can I help?' Sven asked. 'This is great, thanks for the invitation. It makes a change not to have to cook for myself.'

'No, it's fine, I'll be back in a moment. Got it all ready, take a seat, won't be long.' She made her way to the kitchen. 'Can't say it'll be any better than you would cook, mind you,' she called. 'You've probably got your own favourite Norwegian dish, just as I have with Yorkshire Puddings.'

'Do you know something? I've never had Yorkshire Pudding – you have it with beef, right? I rarely go out for dinner, too busy these days. Martin's wife, Andrea, is into stuff that's more exotic. She's a good cook.'

Pippa wondered about Sven as he sat in the lounge as her guest. His time in the sun and his tousled hair had already begun to do strange things to her feelings. She listened, and sometimes his English wasn't quite right, but it was lovely to hear him speak. It was all fantasy, pure fantasy, and why not? Fantasy was good for you.

'How did you get on today, Pippa? I mean, on Tresco,' Sven called to her.

'It's an amazing place. The gardens are so full of colour, is it always like that?'

He poked his head around the kitchen door and smiled. 'Yes, most of the year round. They plant for all seasons.' The aroma of food wafted his way. 'Mm, that smells really good.'

'It's so full of friendly faces here, isn't it? White beaches and the colours of the Livingstone daisies on the garden walls are a dream.' Pippa stirred the chilli as she spoke.

Sven laughed. 'Well, maybe now you know why I live here, although the winter can be harsh, but it never lasts very long. I'm used to the cold weather, of course. I hope they let me stay here a little longer. I don't know yet what'll happen. My contract may be up soon, although they extended it for Martin's time in Africa.'

'Tell me about Martin – that's The Birdman, right?'

'Yes, he's quite a character, part of the island structure, so to speak. He's a good bloke. I often go around to his place. He and Andrea are lovely people.'

'I get the impression you are part of the structure here too,' Pippa said with a smile.

'Oh, yes, me too, I suppose. I will be sad if I have to leave. That reminds me... I have something to show you after dinner.' He opened his rucksack and took out his mini cassette recorder. 'We can listen to this later. I just wanted to bring some bird calls, you'll need these if we are birding.'

'That looks interesting. Should I put some music on for now? What do you like – Dire Straits, 10cc, Elton John? I expect it's stuff the visitors left behind or Janice has left for the guests. I hope you're hungry.'

'Ya, for sure,' he said in answer to both questions, and he chose a Dire Straits tape he found among the pile of cassettes. 'I love the track "Telegraph Road". It reminds me of our road here of the same name. I sometimes go whizzing down there on my bike.' He chuckled.

Pippa brought in the bowls of food, placed the salad tongs in the dish and put a serving spoon in the chilli-con-carne. She offered him the salad.

'I tried not to make the chilli too hot,' she said. 'Would you mind dealing with the wine?' She handed him the corkscrew, aware that he was gazing at her.

'Tell me more about where you live,' he asked as the bottle went "pop".

She told him about the North Yorkshire moors and the steam railway through the Esk valley. 'I often pack a bag and some sandwiches and go walking on the moors. Rob used to go with me, but these days he's stopped all that.'

'By the way, you'll notice I got a new rucksack,' he said with a grin. 'There's this place down the quay, they've got some really strong canvas bags.'

'Nice one, I like the colour, we almost match.' Pippa pointed to her own blue bag laid on the floor in the corner of the room.

They sat opposite each other, making small talk and eating their chilli. Pippa felt odd entertaining him. It was as if she had taken a jump too soon. Maybe a coffee and biscuits would have been enough. *What would Rob say? Sod Rob, this is my life.* She hadn't meant to feel such malice, but it was all about letting go and getting away from her misery. Surely she didn't need to feel guilty about that?

She brought the fruit salad and Sven offered to fill her dish. She couldn't help that odd feeling in her stomach when Sven looked at her. She wanted to say 'What?' or 'Is there something wrong?' Instead, she averted her eyes from his gaze.

'More?' he said, smiling.

'No, that's fine. Thanks for coming. This is incredible, you, here, having dinner with me, I never thought…' Pippa tried to tell him how much she appreciated his visit, but found it hard to find the words to finish her sentence. His eyes kept following her – and that comforting smile of his! How she wished Rob would do more of that.

'It's a real pleasure, Pippa. Great food, thanks.' He patted her arm. 'Let me help you clear the table, then we can listen to the tape I brought with me.' He helped her move the dishes to the kitchen.

'Okay, shall we take a look at this then?' He moved his chair around the table and sat closer to her. Once again her odd feelings returned: gut feelings. Did he fancy her? *How stupid is that?* Sure as hell, she wished it could be true. Yes, fantasy was good for you, for sure. She giggled to herself. *How embarrassing.*

She watched as he drew a picture of a sparrow and headed the title – 'Basic Bird ID'. *He's good, very good. His drawing is delightful.*

'I used to do a lot of drawing at Dan's school before the accident,' she said.

'Yes, I remember you saying about teaching. I can imagine you won't feel like going back to that, though.'

'Yeah, you're right, I gave up. It's a pity because I'd just started, but maybe, who knows, I might have the confidence to do it again. I ought not to give up on all the hard work I put into it.'

Pippa wasn't used to drinking more than two glasses of wine, and, like the perfect gentleman, Sven kept topping up her wine glass. She leaned forward, nodding here and there as he spoke. She thought he was charming. Her eyes kept meeting his and it was hard to stop. Did he realise?

'Probably it's best to start with the colour of the bird, its approximate size and shape. Try to check on the profile of its beak, especially if you have a good pair of binoculars.'

'Well my binoculars are really old, but maybe I can get some new ones soon,' Pippa explained.

'You might only have a few seconds to make a decision about what species you are looking at, but the tail of the bird shows you a lot during flight, so do a quick check if you can – long tail, short tail, forked tail – you know, that sort of thing. You can look it up in your field guide afterwards. When you are practiced at doing this, you can tell which bird you are looking at from a silhouette in the sky and the call of the bird.' He pointed to the diagrams he had made about plumage, wings, under-parts and head, and the song of that species. He played the tapes, and Pippa listened to the calls of the birds and the difference between the song of the blackbird and the repetitive notes of the song thrush. He showed her how a blackcap sounded similar to a blackbird. She couldn't help but listen to the way he spoke, and some of the time she lost her concentration and wasn't listening to what he said, only how he said it.

He showed her how to tell the sexes of each bird according to its plumage, which was often easy, but in the case of the robin wasn't so. She raised her eyebrows, then remarked, 'I'm glad we can tell male from female, most of the time.' *Shit – did I really say that?* She hadn't meant to sound so silly; it had just come out that way. Anxious she might scare him away, she thought she might have to spend the rest of the holiday avoiding him.

Sven laughed, and said with his usual politeness, 'Yes, me too,' giving her a coy smile. 'Now I want to show you the difference between a willow warbler and a chiff-chaff.' He pointed at what Pippa thought were two identical species in the field guide. 'Can you tell the difference between these two?'

'They're the same, aren't they?' Pippa questioned as she traced the shape with her finger.

'Well, you have to listen to the call. One is a cascade of notes, that's the willow warbler, and the chiff-chaff has the same name as its call, like this…' He played the sounds so she could hear them.

'Oh yes, I can hear why they named it a chiff-chaff.' Pippa laughed through a half yawn. 'Oh, sorry, I think it's the wine. It's been so interesting to learn all these new things.' She hoped she wasn't sounding more interested in Sven than his birds; that would be doubly embarrassing. 'I've enjoyed the evening so much, I mean that.'

'Oh, it's nothing, that's okay. I'll stick around in the next few days and maybe we can do a few trips together on the boats this week – but I am quite busy. It's the time of year, of course.'

'Thanks for all your understanding.' Pippa smiled.

'I can see you're tired, so I'll say, "God natt" as we say at home, and I've enjoyed myself too. That meal was delicious, thank *you*.'

'Come again,' Pippa said, and she meant it.

She stood up at the same time as Sven. He seemed glued into his sandals, shorts, and T-shirt. She had never seen him in anything else. It seemed wrong to imagine him in posh trousers and a shirt. Rob always wore jeans and smart trousers for work. He was quite the opposite from Sven. A thought struck her – she must stop comparing Sven with Rob.

Sven closed the bird book and tidied up the table. 'Can I help with the washing up?'

'No, don't worry. I'm happy to have something to do when you've gone.'

He turned to her and spoke as an afterthought. 'I'm going to St Agnes in the morning so I have to leave earlier. Would you like to come?' He picked up his rucksack and put all the teaching aids inside.

'Oh…well, that's kind of you, thanks, but I er…no, I need to do some shopping.' It was best to show restraint. He was obviously keen to help her, but a line had to be drawn. The respect he had for her predicament was what she needed. Perhaps she should accept the situation, relax, and enjoy the moment. Isn't that what the holiday was all about? No, she would exercise restraint. Sven seemed harmless and his intentions were honourable.

He made his way towards the door. 'Good night, Pippa, see you soon. I'll probably call round in the next couple of days to see how you are getting on. Take care and thanks again.'

'Oh Sven – thanks so much, I've really enjoyed the company.'

He left the house and crossed the road into the darkness. He had wanted to kiss her goodnight, once on either cheek as he would have done back home – but no, another time, when he'd got to know her a bit more. He broke into a smile; recently he had become more English than Norwegian.

The next day, Pippa had promised to have coffee with Jan and Marijke. *Poor Jan.* It made Pippa realise how lucky she was to be alive at this moment. 'Everything sad comes in threes,' her aunt had told her. 'Just live your life and enjoy it, you're too young to hide away like this.'

Marijke interrupted her thoughts. 'Have you had a good time so far?'

'Oh, for sure. I did some entertaining last night,' Pippa said proudly. 'Remember Sven from the boats, the nature warden, the one at the slide show? He was up at my cottage for dinner.'

'You didn't waste time then?' Marijke grinned. 'I mean, it's really good you have found a friend.'

'Well, he's not a close friend really, just a guy who is helping me to learn more about birdwatching. Although I agree with you, he is very nice, but I have to tell you I have a husband at home.'

'Oh, I thought you were single, Pippa. I hadn't realised.'

'Well, things are a little awkward at the moment. We had a sad loss in the family.'

Marijke seemed to understand as Pippa changed the subject.

'Anyway, how are you feeling today, Jan?' Pippa asked.

'Oh, it goes well, thank you. I live by the hour, and if I am lucky I will live by the days.' He gave a weak smile.

Pippa looked at Marijke; she knew that look of despair. She understood.

They sat sipping their tea. If she didn't say goodbye to them soon, she feared she might fall back into grief mode. Perhaps it was a little selfish, but it made her think how lucky she was to be fit and healthy. Maybe there was a lesson here too.

Chapter Eleven

Rob decided he needed a haircut. There was enough time to go down to the unisex salon in town; they would close in an hour. The phone rang. It was as if the person phoning him knew he was about to leave.

'Hi, Rob, have you got a minute?'

Oh no. 'Oh, hi, Joan, I'm just on my way out, love. Can I phone you back later?'

'This won't take long,' Joan said. 'You spoke with Terry?'

'Er…well, yes, but if I can ring you back later, we can talk longer.'

Joan ignored him. 'I think I sorted it out. I'm putting in for divorce tomorrow.'

'Hang on, Joan, don't you think that's a bit on the hasty side? I mean, you only just found out about Terry's predicament.' He thought she was trying to be brave by sweeping her situation under the carpet. *Typical of Joan – always impulsive.*

'Well, I have to be practical about it. Being married to someone who is gay is hardly a marriage, and he's got someone else, this Frank character – did he tell you? What's the point in hanging on, it's all cut and dried, don't you think?'

Rob ignored her question. 'Flippin' heck, Joan, don't you think you should wait a bit? I can understand your anger, but you're very vulnerable right now, I know, and he's Jordan's dad too. You can't treat Terry as if he never existed. Yes, we have to talk, I agree.'

'I don't wish to hang around. I thought I loved Terry as

a husband, not as a gay lover – sorry, that's not my style. He is the father of our child, and that's it! I want to get on with my life.' She hesitated a moment. 'You sound angry with me, Rob.'

'Well, no, no, just shocked at your attitude, that's all. Look, love, I have to go out. I'm on days this week, perhaps we can meet up at the pub. Call me tomorrow and we'll make an arrangement. Sorry I have work. I do want to talk to you, honest I do.'

'Okay, I'll do that then. Thanks, Rob, you're an angel. I need to talk to you too. Bye then.'

He was about to leave when, once again, the phone rang and as he made toward the receiver. it stopped ringing.

Bloody hell, leave me alone, will yer?

After a minute, the phone rang again and, reluctantly, he managed to pick up the receiver.

'Hello, Rob Lambton.'

'Ah, Mr Lambton, this is John Grover from Grover and Pearson, solicitors in Kingston upon Hull, sorry to bother you. We would like to call and see you. It's a delicate matter concerning your family.'

'Why, has someone *died?*'

The voice on the other end of the phone didn't fully answer his question.

'Our Mr Carmichael is in your area this evening, and we wondered if it were possible for him to call and see you. The matter is a little urgent and we need to clarify we've got the right person.'

'Who did you say you are?'

'John Grover, solicitors in Kingston upon Hull.'

'Oh, I see,' Rob said, puzzled.

'We hope our colleague can sort this out for you. I feel sure it will be to your benefit. As I said, it's a delicate family matter. Stephen Carmichael will bring his card, and to assure you, we are in the Yellow Pages and this is a legal matter.'

Rob thought he sounded genuine enough, but these days you couldn't be sure.

'Are you certain you've got the right person?' Rob asked, anxiously hoping to get out of the door. 'I don't have any relatives that I know of.'

'I do apologise for sounding a little evasive, but in this case we don't like to talk to clients on the phone – we need to see you in person. Will seven o'clock be okay for you? Sorry this is such short notice.'

'Er…yeah, fine,' Rob replied. It was bound to be a sales representative for insurance. He replaced the receiver and thought how stupid he was for being taken in so easily. He didn't know if he should ignore the call or wait home and hope this Stephen Carmichael wouldn't be the bringer of more bad news in his life. *Solicitor, eh?* He would try to get back in time – tough if he couldn't.

He was sitting on the settee when the phone rang again. He wasn't going to answer it, but what if it was Pippa calling? Did he care? Well, maybe…and she would shout at him for not being there, so he'd better answer it.

'Hay-lo, Rob Lambton,' he said, sighing. 'Oh, is that you, Pippa?'

'You've been on the phone for ages, Rob.'

'So what if I have?' he said.

'I tried to get through. You sound annoyed, love.'

Rob sighed again and shook his head in frustration. 'I'm busy, that's all.'

'Too busy for your wife, then?'

'No, too bloody busy with other people. I need to have some time to myself.'

'What's up?' Pippa tried to calm the situation.

'Oh, nothing really.' He wasn't going to tell her about the call or Terry. *She can find out when she gets back – if she gets back.*

'How's Scilly?'

'It's great. I've met some really nice people.'

'Lucky for you, eh?'

Pippa's anger got the better of her. 'Rob, what is it with you?

115

Always sarcastic, it's more than I can stand. I phoned to see how you are, not to have a bloody row.'

'Look, Pippa, I'm sorry, but today hasn't been a good day. Joan phoned me, I am about to do my exams, I got time off in the week to do it, and there's you and me, and you know...'

'Rob, do you love me?' Pippa interrupted.

'Why would you ask me something like that right now? I could ask you the same question.'

Pippa thought it was the same old argument over again. Nothing had changed. She couldn't believe he could be so stroppy.

'Phone me tomorrow or something,' said Rob, 'and I might feel different. I mean, where do you see us going with our lives?'

'Rob, I don't know. Can we talk about this when I get back? It's all gone wrong, hasn't it?'

'And where do *you* feel it's gone wrong?'

'Rob, you're counselling me, don't *do* that. You know perfectly well where our marriage has failed, that's a stupid question. I only want to know if you still love me, that's all.'

'I'll tell you what I feel at this moment. I think you're right, it's better we wait until you get home. We used to get on really well, and I think we need to make some positive decisions without dragging the whole damned business into the gutter. We could have a trial separation, I suppose, as we're doing now, but longer.'

'What good would that do, and what the hell is up with you today?' Pippa shouted down the phone in tears.

Rob sighed then relented. He could hear she was genuinely upset. He replied to her question. 'You're probably right. Look, I'm sorry, our lives have been turned upside down, and I don't think it's fair to keep pretending like this. Where we should be finding mutual empathy, it has turned us both into, well...monsters. Personally I don't want to do anything we might regret, but I can't live like this anymore. It's interfering with my job and I can't have that, Pippa. I need to work to live.'

'I do still care about you, Rob,' Pippa said. 'Maybe we should get some help from your lot at the hospital, some counselling.'

'Don't be so bloody stupid. I couldn't let the guys at work get that close to my private life. It would ruin my job. Anyway, I'm already doing counselling, or have you forgotten?'

'Yes, but we could find a private counsellor, marriage guidance.'

'I know too much in that respect. I've learned too much, it wouldn't work for me. I'd be looking at myself coming backwards,' Rob said. 'As each day passes we live with the guilt of Daniel. If we're to be sensible I think we need to start afresh. Let me know how you feel when you come home. I can't see us continuing, can you?'

Pippa realised he was pushing her away. It all felt like abandonment and she didn't want to go there. She and Rob had shared beautiful moments together with the birth of their son. Did he not treasure those moments?

'Rob, how can you do this to me? I was hoping we could patch things up when I got back, and not do this on the bloody phone, for God's sake.'

'Okay, I know. Call me back in the week, I might feel better. Sorry, I didn't want to spoil your break, but I haven't had a very good day and I've tried three times to get out of the house this afternoon – so I'm going. Sorry, Pippa. Just have a good think about it and we can talk soon when I feel less stressed. Please understand, it's been a helluva day. Okay?'

Yeah, right! 'Bye, then, I'll phone you again soon.'

Back in Whitby, Rob's determination prevailed. He had to get out of the house before the phone rang again, and if it did, he made a vow not to answer it.

As he sat in the salon, Rob thought about his conversation with Pippa. He felt some regret about his row with her on the phone. The small talk with the girl who had just washed his hair seemed trivial. The man who was coming round to see him, this Carmichael bloke, he had no idea if it was real or just someone coming under false pretences to sell him insurance.

'You want all of this off?' the hairdresser said.

'Yeah, very short, please, but not skinhead.'

'You sure? I mean, you've got nice hair.'

'Yeah, do it please. I'm trying to create a new image.' Rob smiled at her.

'How's your wife, Rob?'

'She's away at the moment.'

'Haven't seen your mate, Terry Marshall, lately. He used to come in for a haircut often, what happened to him? John used to cut his hair. They know each other from college. It was only the other day we were saying we hadn't seen him.'

'Works on the rigs now,' Rob told her.

The hairdresser snipped away the strands of black locks as the hair fell to the floor. Rob stared through the mirror and his eyes followed the young apprentice pushing a sweeping brush. He would no longer be able to tie his hair back in a pony tail for work. Even the hairdresser had been in a year lower than Pippa at school. There seemed to be no escape from the past in Whitby. Pippa was right. He knew he was good at counselling his patients, but was he any good with sorting himself out? He reckoned the answer was no.

'There you go, Rob, is that short enough?' The hairdresser interrupted his thoughts. He looked more closely in the mirror, glad she hadn't skinned him.

'Yes, that's better, nice and tidy,' he said. 'The new me, eh? Thanks.'

He paid, and once again admired his new hairstyle. He would go to the pub and then return home for the man who was coming to see him.

By the time he got back to the house, Stephen Carmichael was already knocking on the door. Rob apologised for being late.

Chapter Twelve

In three days, Pippa had only seen Sven once. It was on her return from an afternoon trip to the Eastern Isles where she saw him chatting with tourists on the quay. She had missed seeing him and hoped she hadn't chased him away.

'I'll try and catch up with you very soon,' he said, sounding as if he should have done it earlier. 'I've been so busy working. Perhaps we can meet up later when I have more time off.'

'Okay, Sven, don't worry, you know where I am.' Pippa smiled and gave a little wave.

'Sure do,' he replied as she walked past him.

She felt disappointed he hadn't been in touch: almost as if he should have told her he wasn't coming. She became aware of her feelings and scolded herself; she didn't own him, after all. He had warned her he was busy. In the light of her conversation with Rob, she needed company; Rob had provided her with a good reason for feeling resentful. Now Sven was too busy, it was hard not to feel that way.

Walking through town, she had visions of Daniel walking beside her. It had been quite a day and she wished she hadn't bothered to phone home; Rob had depressed her.

Later that afternoon, Pippa lay on Porthcressa Beach reading her *Secrets* book. She loved the Danielle Steele novels. How often she had lost herself within the stories. She had two weeks left, but in another two days she might have to find another book to read.

The sea looked tempting. Despite the Gulf Stream lying in the path of the islands, the temperature of the water was not for the faint-hearted. Fronds of seaweed slipped in and out of her toes and she listened to the sounds of the herring gull as it mewed a call over the shore.

She thought perhaps it was time to leave the beach, but something caught her eye. The spectacle of terns diving – she watched them, the way they dropped like stones out of the sky. Something else made her look harder up the shore.

Recognising the vehicle parked some distance away, she wondered if Sven was home, but no-one was there. Sitting on the sand, wrapped in her towel, she squinted in the sun and turned her back to the town, looking out to sea.

As she traced her finger in the damp sand, she wrote *Pippa & Rob*; it wouldn't be long before the sea would nudge it away. She scribbled out *Rob* and almost wrote Sven's name to see what it looked like. She stopped herself. *What a daft idea.*

With the trials of life left behind, a delightful solitude seemed to take over. Leaving the islands would make her feel sad. Perhaps she and Rob would have another row and all her problems would start again. Why would she want to go home at all? What did Rob want from her? She couldn't bear to think about it a moment longer and she returned to reading her book.

Sven finished his work and arrived home earlier than usual. He scanned the bay with his binoculars looking for birds and spotted Pippa instead. Smiling to himself when he saw her, he had an idea. He walked some distance along the path before using the back road to the beach. Perhaps she wouldn't turn around before he got to her. He removed his sandals and hid out of sight, creeping up behind her.

Pippa felt a pair of warm hands around her eyes. She jumped.

'Guess who?'

'Oh, hello!' she said, placing her hand on her chest. 'I wondered who the heck that was.'

'Fancy a swim then?' Sven said, looking down at his feet as he stood on the sand beside her, hopping on one leg. He stepped out of his cut-off jeans, revealing a pair of tight blue swim shorts. 'If you weren't here, I'd be swimming without these,' he joked as he gazed at her head to toe.

'What's stopping you?' Pippa said, laughing.

She had the urge to put out a finger and touch him. His brown body and good looks overwhelmed her. She wasn't sure what to do about him, or how she was supposed to respond. As he bent down to sit on the sand, she saw how he was brown below the waistband of his shorts. *Maybe he really does go skinny-dipping.*

By now, she knew he was getting too close to her. Something had changed. He was more relaxed and open. She didn't need the stress of a failed marriage, but her marriage was already on a rock somewhere out there in the bay. After her conversation with Rob, it was hard to make decisions about anything.

Without warning, Sven grabbed her hand, pulling her into the sea, and teased her about being a wimp in the cold water. He was behaving as if he were a school kid let out of class to play football. It was a side of him she hadn't seen before. He seemed to have changed from being serious about birds to this other personality, and he certainly wasn't acting his age. She smiled to herself, thinking she preferred him that way.

'Come on, girl, get in the water. It's wonderful. We sometimes swim even with the snow on the ground in Norway,' he said. 'You look nice in that outfit.' He pointed to her bikini. 'Green suits you. It goes well with your hair.'

'What?' Pippa laughed.

'Come on, let's go swimming together. The sea isn't that cold today. I have two days off. I've asked Charlie James to help – I deserve one day off at least.'

'Ahh! Don't! It's freezing.' She let out a squeal of delight as the cold sea shocked her. He pulled her gently by the arm into the salt water.

'My God, the girl is drowning. I have to save her,' he shouted.

Pippa was laughing so much she found tears dripping down her face. He picked her up in his strong arms and splashed her back into the water. Her heart was about to burst being with this man who was so pleasantly unpredictable.

He gazed into her eyes. She had to be faithful to Rob. She knew Sven was only being kind to her in view of her problems, but she didn't want him to feel sorry for her.

He sat on the sand and dried his midriff with the blue towel he had brought to the beach.

Pippa watched as he stretched out to sunbathe.

'Have you got any plans for this weekend?' he asked.

'Not really, maybe go to one of the islands and then I don't know. I don't like to make plans, I just let it happen, and my life isn't into planning things anymore.'

'Pippa, my friend, would you like to spend it with me? I mean, we can take a picnic perhaps. Go on, it'll do you good. You know, I need the company too on my days off, we could be good friends whilst you are here.'

The warm breeze blew gently across Porthcressa Beach and Pippa laid her towel on one of the rocks to dry in the sun. She couldn't help smiling to herself. Was this supposed to be a date? What was she doing? It was a bit sudden. He seemed harmless enough, but rushing into a friendship in this way – she hardly knew him. The look on his face gave her a change of heart.

'Okay, I'll come with you. Nice of you to ask. Being alone here is fine, but not all the time.'

Sven beamed at her. 'Great.'

'Anyway, where have you been in the last couple of days?' Pippa asked. Was that question sounding too possessive?

'Oh, I've spent a lot of time working on the boats and it's been a difficult week. I wish I knew the date Martin was due back, I could do with a longer break. When I work normal hours, I get more time off at the weekends, especially in the winter. Maybe when we go down to the nature reserve, I'll introduce you to the other volunteers before the end of your holiday.'

'Yeah, that would be nice.' As Pippa listened, she built a collection of limpet shells and placed them in a circle on the sand. She wondered if Sven already had a pretty girl among the volunteers. Surely, a chap as good-looking as Sven must have a woman in his life, but then why was he always alone too?

'I'll tell you what,' he said. 'We'll go to Old Town, do the picnic thing and then we could drive up to the bird hide at the nature reserve in the afternoon to listen to the coot and other wildfowl. It'll give you a different perspective on water birds.'

This was the serious side of Sven: he loved the outdoor life. 'You don't mind, do you? I only want to help you enjoy yourself.'

'Of course not. You're right, it's a good idea. Thanks.'

She couldn't believe he'd come out of nowhere and now he was asking her out on a friendly date.

'Now you are really enjoying yourself,' he said, laughing. 'You need some therapy, okay?' It had felt good the other night, comforting her. He saw a different side to her; she was a fun-loving girl who had lost her way, and he wanted to bond with her. He knew very well what it felt like to be abandoned, left out to dry. He couldn't help himself, he was naturally pushy, but he felt she wouldn't mind. He kept telling himself she was married, he couldn't have her, but the other side of his mind told him he could at least find out more about her.

The beach. The lapping of the waves. The moment. He felt himself being part of her. He wanted to hold her hand, to touch her again and take her back to Beachside Cottage and make love to her. He scolded himself for thinking that way, but he couldn't explain his reasons; it felt right, a ridiculous fantasy, that was all.

'I've been thinking about you,' he said, 'and the things you told me the other night. I mean, you cannot live your life as a…erm… what's the English word? …Erm…oh yes, *hermit*. You are a good person and I only want to help you improve your quality of life before you go home. Give you something positive to hold onto. To remember Scilly and the reasons you came here.' He hoped his fantasy would be more than that, but he would have to wait, and patience in these matters had never been one of his stronger virtues.

'Well,' said Pippa, 'you mustn't feel sorry for me, okay?'

'No,' he replied. 'I like you.' He looked at her with a raised brow, lips in a tight smile, worried in case he had stepped beyond her comfort zone.

'Well, I like you too, Sven,' Pippa said politely. 'You've been a kind of rock for me in the last few days, and I want to say thanks for that. You're right, it is difficult for me. I am having a bad time with Rob, our marriage and so on. I appreciate your support.'

Sven liked to be direct. He would dive right in there and tell her. There wasn't much time left.

'No, I don't think you get it, do you?' His happy-go-lucky demeanour changed to a more serious note. 'I *really* like you. I don't want to mess about. You only have a bit more than two weeks here. Is there any chance we could get to know each other better?' There was a short silence.

Pippa gave a nervous smile. 'Oh, that sort of *really like?* Oh, I wish it were that easy. I'm still grieving – you realise that?'

Sven put the towel around her shoulders, his muscular arm lingering between her neck and ear lobe. She felt protected. She fancied him for sure, but couldn't possibly step over the boundaries; yet she needed love. *Oh hell, he's gorgeous, but I can't do this, it's not real. A holiday romance, they never work. I'll end up with more heartache. Shit…what do I say?*

Most of the day-trippers had deserted the beach. They were almost alone, hidden by the rocks. Sven laid the towel on the sand for Pippa to sit beside him. 'Hang on, you've got thirty seconds to think about it while I get the sand off my feet. I want to put my sandals back on.' He was nervous and didn't want to sit in an embarrassing silence while she contemplated his question – and what if he had made a mistake? He'd made one big mistake five years ago, had his fingers burned by someone else's infidelity; what if he was doing it again? What right did he have to pluck Pippa away from her marriage?

Pippa didn't need to think too much. It must have showed. How could she have a relationship or even have a quick fling with him before going home? She had thought the unthinkable. It was an absolute "no-no", but going back to Rob? Sven was making it difficult. She gazed at the title of the book she had been reading; she could have secrets of her own, and not a soul would know.

Alone, like this, she might be able to accomplish her search for happiness. If she allowed herself into this illusion, did it matter? Rob would never know, and probably didn't care, or did he? She wasn't sure anymore. Here, she could put her worries behind her and fling her sad life away.

She slid her fingers across her lips, back and forth as she watched him washing his feet in the sea. She couldn't take her eyes off him. With his blond hair falling over his ears, he was difficult to resist.

On his return, he sat with his legs stretched out, his hands patting the wet sand, and his back against the sun-warmed rock: a place he had sat before where his thoughts often turned into reality. He saw how she had written her name in the sand and scrubbed out another name – he retraced her writing, and with his index finger he wrote *Sven* after *Pippa &*.

Pippa realised what he had done and what might be coming next; she had to be prepared, but now was not the right time – and would it ever be?

'Look,' he said. 'No matter what happens, you need to become *you* again.' He looked at her questioningly. 'Yes? Am I right? It could be you and me together having a great time. All this sadness has pulled you down like a drowning animal. It must have been dreadful to have gone through all that stuff.' He took hold of her hand. 'You're a great person, Pippa. I know we have just met, but it feels right. It's you I care about, and I mean it! I wouldn't want to do anything you didn't want as well.' He thought about what he'd said and wondered if perhaps a "here today – gone tomorrow" relationship would be enough to satisfy both their needs – the holiday romance she had denied herself. No, he had told her the truth: he didn't want that, he wanted more. She was lovely, but would she take the risk?

She pulled away from him tactfully and played with the loose threads of the towel.

'You can go home and forget about me if you wish, but that's not what I want.' He dried her back with the towel. 'I've thought about you a lot,' he said as he touched her smooth skin. Her legs seemed to beckon him to reach all the way to the top. His libido was increasing and he couldn't help himself. It was the green bikini, and the bare flesh in between, which turned him on. He kept telling himself to walk away for a moment, do something else. He wrapped the towel around his waist to hide his desires. Needing to hear the right words before he would kiss her, he could sense her feelings and desperately wanted to be part of her. Yes, he knew her life was still on hold, but he wanted to help her make the changes. It had to be her decision, and he felt his heart beating faster, wondering how she would respond. Should he be doing this at all?

Pippa's yearning to be with him deepened, but she held back, refusing to allow herself to make a stupid mistake. She had to think about it, knowing how he felt about her.

There was silence. Sven was everything Rob had been unable to give her. She raised her head and looked into his eyes. She had only known him a few days and the whole idea seemed ludicrous. His face willed her to say 'Yes', but now, suddenly, she could tell something bothered him.

'Look, first I need to explain to you,' he said. 'Perhaps I understand what you are going through. You see, I also have a story to tell. It's part of the reason I live here. I have also escaped from a trauma. About six years ago, my relationship broke up. I didn't want to tell you the other night because it wasn't appropriate. I had this wonderful girlfriend, Astrid. We were due to get married in Norway. She was the best thing that had ever happened to me. I couldn't stop thinking about her. I suppose I was...what's the word? Erm...head over heels in love with her. She was beautiful and kind and everything I ever wanted.'

Pippa raised her eyebrows. This wasn't what she had expected him to say. 'So what happened?'

'She slept with my best friend, that's what happened. We had the wedding planned, everything, the guests, where we would go for our honeymoon, all the usual things you do, and she was about to choose her wedding dress. I was the happiest man in all of Norway. About three months before the wedding, I had gone out to do some birding with a group from the local club. It was snowing and very cold, and we all decided to stop for the day. I came back earlier than expected to my apartment in Trondheim to discover she was in bed with my best mate. Can you believe it?'

'Oh dear, Sven, I am so sorry,' Pippa empathised. 'It must have been awful for you.' She saw how his eyes gazed upon the sand and his thoughts seemed far away in Norway.

'My God, I bet she had a problem talking her way out of that one.' Pippa asked, 'So what happened after that?'

'She married him! I have no idea why she changed her mind, I gave her everything she could ever want. Her excuse? She didn't know why she had done it. I was devastated. The trouble is I never understood her reasoning either. Something just didn't seem to add up. I searched my soul for months, asking what I had done to deserve it. I left Norway in a hurry, I didn't want to be there anymore. You can imagine what that did to me. My mother said I had run away, but would you want to be reminded of everything? And everywhere you...oh sorry, I didn't mean... You see, I kind of know how you feel, Pippa. I know your circumstances are more traumatic than mine, but I only wanted to show you that two people can find solace in each other, and maybe our friendship will help us move on.'

'I see,' Pippa said. 'So that was why you came here, eh?

Sven looked down, the white sand sifted through his fingers. 'Well, like you, I also came to Scilly hoping to find happiness again, but I made a mistake. Scilly is not the place to find love. Oh sure, I love my job with all my heart, and I've been out with a couple of local girls to date, but they leave for the mainland and that's it – gone! The truth is, I'm a bit lonely here despite all the hundreds of people who visit each day. Many of them are over fifty, unless they want a toy-boy!' he said with a chuckle.

Pippa smiled. 'Oh Sven, I'm sorry. What a pair we are, eh?'

'Do you still love your husband, Pippa?' Sven needed to know.

'That's a hard question. I suppose I do in an odd way, but now it's like he's just a grumpy best friend and not someone I feel like going to bed with – sorry, I didn't mean to talk in that way.'

'It's okay.' Sven hesitated. 'Could you see yourself in another relationship? You see, the thing is, I feel I might be…you know… more than just liking you as my friend.' He smiled and looked into her eyes. 'I haven't stopped thinking about you since we first met.'

Pippa turned to meet his gaze. He was lonely, he was lovely, he was kind and gentle, he was handsome, interesting, and a dream of a guy. How could she refuse? She didn't want to tell him how she felt. It was all too soon.

'How can you say those things, Sven? You hardly know me.'

'Sometimes you don't have to know someone a long time, it just feels right. I didn't invite you for coffee the other evening without being curious about you. There was something that turned on a bright light for me.'

'Aw, Sven, I…I don't know what to say.' Pippa felt tears returning, but this time they were tears of joy.

'Say "Yes"? Please say "Yes".' He scolded himself for sounding so pushy and pleading.

Pippa knew she had to be sensible and it wasn't too late to refuse.

Sven leaned towards her to give her a hug. He pushed back the stray strands of auburn hair blowing in her face and gazed into her green-blue eyes. He'd got nearer to her than he'd expected when he felt her breathing, and her lips became a temptation. He held her close as they lay on the beach, oblivious to the sound of the waves and the terns screaming along the shore. His lips pressed gently against hers, caressing her face, and the feel of her lips on his made him want to hold her closer and be part of her forever.

After a few moments, Pippa pulled back. 'Oh God, sorry… I'm in such a muddle. I don't want you to be messed about.'

Sven was firm. 'Pippa, stop. We are in the here and now, and I'm sorry…no, no, sorry isn't the right word. I feel very good about you. Please, don't stop now,' he begged her. 'Maybe I am going too fast for you. Hell, what have I done? The trouble is, we don't have much time, and it's tearing me up.'

'There we go, both apologising to each other,' she said. Again, she felt close to tears, but refused to cry. 'Let's see how it goes, shall we?' She knew it was a crazy madness, and a huge mistake if she got it wrong. Yes, it was wrong, but oh…so tempting to be part of his wonderful island life.

Sven put his arm around her. His insides were overwhelmed with joy, but what if he lost her through his impulsiveness and stupidity? She was far away from home; her husband hadn't cared about her coming to Scilly – at least, that's how it seemed. Would he be breaking Rob's heart too? Somehow, he didn't think so, but how much did he know about Pippa, and was she telling the full truth about her marriage?

'You're gorgeous, you know that?' he said. 'Come on, let's go home and have something to drink. We can talk there, and if you want a shower you can have one. It's my fault you got soaking wet.' He chuckled. 'I didn't mean to upset you, Pippa, I only want to make you happier.' He stopped himself, thinking he had said too much already.

Taking her by the hand, he led the way to Beachside Cottage.

They plodded up the loose sand and he kissed her on the cheek, touching her nose with his index finger. 'I've thought about you a lot on the boat trips in the week. I couldn't wait to find you again. I saw you today and took the chance to ask you if you could see yourself being a part of me.'

Pippa thought she could listen to him for hours. Sometimes it was like she was listening to a child – his English was good, but the way he expressed himself was childlike.

'Whoa there! I haven't said yes! One kiss…' She could hardly get the words out. 'One kiss, that's all, and… I have… I have dreadful complications!' She found herself hugging him. 'You're a hard man to refuse, Sven.'

Sven stiffened for a moment. 'I don't want this to become a holiday romance, Pippa. I've had enough of all that stuff. At this moment, I feel you might break my heart! Look, erm… I know I'm racing on here, and I did consider your situation, being a married woman, but to be honest it's been difficult for me as well. I don't want to lose you. I felt my luck was in when we met, and on our second meeting, it was great having dinner together. Each time I saw you I wanted to be with you. And…you're a great kisser.' He laughed.

'Aw, Sven, that's so sweet of you.' Pippa melted. 'No one's ever spoken to me in that way.' *Even Rob.* She couldn't blame Rob. She mustn't forget, he had lost his son too, and Daniel had been his pride and joy. Saying what they meant to each other had become harder with each passing year. She admitted to herself Sven had swept her off her feet, but Rob had never spoken to her in that way. Sven was fun to be with, and she needed fun. She had forgotten what fun felt like – but she mustn't forget Daniel.

'Maybe I shouldn't have pushed you. I hope it's going to be all right,' Sven said as they got nearer to the house.

'Too late. I've crossed a line, and I promised myself I wouldn't,' Pippa said as she stroked Sven's cheek. 'But thanks for giving me some hope.' She hugged him again.

For the first time Sven saw the real Pippa. He removed his arm from around her waist and escorted her into his home. He didn't want anyone to see them "together"; he wasn't ready for the population of Scilly to broadcast his personal life.

They arrived at the door of the whitewashed cottage. The colours of the flowers on the garden wall were amazing; Pippa appreciated them even more in the daylight. Wall-to-wall daisy jewels in varying shades of pink and yellow cascaded down the small granite boulders. Tamarisk grew along the edge of the path. A large brown spider had built a web among the feathery vegetation and across the path, and Sven carefully removed the connection to the web and cleared a path without disturbing the spider's trap.

Pippa looked up towards the bedroom window with visions of herself waking up every morning to the pounding of the Atlantic and the call of the wild birds. If she had a relationship with Sven, what could go wrong? Would she have the strength to survive all the stress with Rob? The whole of the afternoon with this wonderful man had changed her life. It didn't matter if it was only for today, it was a memory to be treasured.

Inside the cottage, Sven ran upstairs to fetch a clean towel.

'The shower is at the top of the stairs. Here's the towel.'

He imagined how it would have been to step in there with her, but he mustn't chase her away. He knew he was going too fast.

'Oh, thanks, I shan't be long. I gather you've got shampoo in there.'

'Ya, try de lemon one, it's got a conditioner in it.'

Pippa smiled at his reply and closed the bathroom door behind her. As the water sprinkled to her shoulders, she thought about the afternoon and the kissing: his gentle first-time kiss, and how he'd run his fingers down her bare spine. This one kiss would surely change everything. He had caressed her face and looked into her eyes, and oh…he was so sweet, kind, and everything she had longed for. Maybe she should have a good time and forget about it. It would be something good to remember through her life, but his reply about not making this a holiday romance gave her assurance he was serious about her. She couldn't stop thinking about his rugged but boyish good looks; the ripped muscles in his arms that could be holding her so special. Never had a man allowed her to feel so much like a woman; so free and spontaneous. She smiled to herself and sighed. *Would this really work?*

Since losing Daniel, Rob's aggression had become worse. The relationship with Joan's sister, Carole; for sure, it was only a kiss under the mistletoe, but it was a passionate kiss. Pippa remembered feeling strange about it. Also, that girl from Australia he'd met at the pub; they'd walked down the road together after closing time, and he was two hours late in coming home. Pippa could smell a perfume on him; it certainly wasn't one of hers. She had put it all down to his aching mind, preferring to forget the incident. She'd had to trust him. She was sure he hadn't had sex with either of them, or had he? *How many more females did he like to snog under the mistletoe? He doesn't love me, I know he doesn't.* If *he* could kiss someone else, it sure made it easier to think that in kissing Sven she didn't need to feel guilty about it. Perhaps she was justifying her kiss. It was all so confusing.

Sven watched as Pippa came down the stairs smoothing her T-shirt. He made tea, placing two mugs on the small coffee table. He wanted to hold her in his arms and love her with all of his heart. Her freckled face, the green-blue eyes, and the hair that reminded him of sunset fascinated him.

Sven met Pippa's gaze. 'Well, what do you think about us?'

There was a short silence before she answered. 'Well… I like you a lot, Sven. Our afternoon together, I have to say, it's all rather surreal. I hope you understand. I mean, you're such a great guy, who could resist you?' She cupped her hands around the mug of tea he'd given her and smiled into his face.

He came closer. 'I tell you, Pippa, you'll break my heart when you leave on the ferry.' He kissed her cheek. 'Mm, that shower gel smells really nice.'

'But, Sven, listen to me. I've been thinking. I live 500 miles from you. it's a journey over the sea and a full day's ride on the train to Whitby. How can we have a relationship like that? And how can I go back to Rob and never think of you again? It can't possibly work no matter how we try. I may have lost myself in the last few years, but I still have my sense of right and wrong.'

'Let's talk it through – what have we got to lose? How do you feel about me right now?'

'Well, I think you're adorable and kind and lots of good things.'

Sven smiled back at her with an air of "thanks". 'You told me your marriage is a mess. We've both lost our way in life, so what better thing to do than be together? Make it right again, support each other. If you want to be with someone, you will go to the end of the earth to stay with them. Is Rob doing that for you?'

'Wow, Sven, that's a bit unfair. I mean, Rob has been my rock since my father died, and then Daniel, his son as well, I cannot… just leave him.' Pippa's eyes filled with tears. She thought about what she'd just said. It was true, Rob had been good to her. Was she being dreadfully selfish and unfaithful?

'Sorry, Pippa. I didn't mean to be harsh, it just came out that way. I suppose I've had enough of hanging around waiting for something better to turn up, and I sensed it with you as well.'

Pippa thought for a moment. He was right. Rob hadn't exactly run marathons in recent years to keep them closer together, but he was the father of Daniel. Decisions like this would make it more difficult. It was like another one of her nightmares waiting to be unleashed.

'So what should we do?' she asked tearfully.

Sensing her fears, he reached over to the box of tissues and wiped her tears away.

'Cem here,' he said and held her close, his hand stroking her face, looking into her eyes. His lips kissed her brow, and he worked his way down her face until he reached her lips. She responded as he cuddled her closer to him for reassurance.

'Look, what I suggest is that we discover all about each other during your stay here. See how it goes, enjoy every moment we have left, and if we end up hating each other, then we can say we tried and we both made a big mistake.' He held her hand. 'I know, Pippa, I know I have made this difficult. I'm so, so sorry, but I can't help the way I feel about you. I just seemed to gel with you, that's all.'

'And what about Astrid? Is she still in your life?'

'Well, I do think about her because my mother told me she got divorced this year, but I doubt I will ever see her again – she lives in Norway. I have to start afresh, time is passing me by. So…?' He wondered what else there was to say.

Pippa looked him in the face and smiled. 'You can be so persuasive, but something tells me you're right. All these bad times, perhaps being with you for another two weeks will open new horizons for both of us.' She smoothed her hand across his arm.

Sven hugged her. 'You are very beautiful, Pippa. Mmm…and loving,' he added. 'Welcome to our new life, and let's enjoy every moment together. Let me show you about nature here. I want to give you a good holiday, but I hope we can see each other afterwards. I want to make it clear I don't want a holiday romance. I am looking for a girlfriend with a future. May I?'

She liked the plan, and maybe she shouldn't worry about a relationship with Sven. But, a girlfriend with a future? Had Sven made the biggest mistake of his life? She looked proudly at Sven. How lucky she was to have found him, but the guilt began seeping into her mind as she folded her towel in her rucksack.

'What time are you going to go out tomorrow?' Pippa asked, trying to sound normal.

'I'll pick you up around 10.30, if that's okay?'

'I'll make the sandwiches, and I have another bottle of wine we can drink.'

'You're too good to me, Pippa.' Sven chuckled.

She was about to leave him when his eyes met hers and he drew closer to her. He took her in his arms and kissed her until goose bumps tickled her spine, and she didn't want to let him go. His kisses were soft and gentle. She didn't ever want them to stop, but she thought she'd better leave before they both went too far.

'Sven, this is lovely, but...' She felt her heart racing. 'I'll have to go, sorry.'

'Why go? So soon?'

'Sorry, it's nothing you have done, it's *me*. I need to go home and think about all this. I have a lot more at stake than you do, Sven.' She wanted time to consider her feelings, a place by herself to think.

'Yes, I know. I understand, but tomorrow is another day and we can spend it together. You still want to, yes?' Sven asked, hoping he hadn't chased her home.

'Of course I do, although I'm feeling a little overwhelmed and need some time.'

'Sorry, Pippa, that's me, how I am. I'll try and slow down – promise.' He chuckled.

'There's no need to keep apologising. I don't mind, honest. And don't worry, I need to go home and relax and dream about you,' she said, kissing him back. She squeezed his hand and made her way towards the door. 'I do like you, honest I do. In fact, I think I could fall for you too, in a big way, but I have to think about all this. Do you really want to take me on with all this grief hanging around? I'm not sure you know what you're doing. Give me until tomorrow and we'll talk then.'

Sven hugged her again.

'See you at ten o'clock then. I'll be ready,' she said with a smile. 'Thanks again for a lovely afternoon.'

Sven held her hand as she walked out of the door, then let go and gave her a final kiss goodbye. He watched as she made her way to Gilstone, and as she left his sight his insides still pounded from her touch.

Pippa shook with elation when she arrived at Gilstone. 'Yes, yes and *yes*,' she said aloud with both fists banging the air. 'What the hell am I doing?' She sucked in her breath and let it out slowly, allowing the adrenaline to subside. She had vision of Sven making love to her on a deserted beach with palm trees, and a beautiful affair where he whisked her off into the night under the moon on one of the deserted islands. 'What the hell!' Pippa sank to her knees in tears and sheer relief, remembering what he had written in the sand. 'Pippa and Sven,' she whispered to herself. '*Pippa and Sven, Pippa and Sven. Yes, yes, yes.*'

That evening, Pippa climbed into bed. What else could go wrong? Would Rob ever find out? How mean she was doing this to him. It wasn't Rob's fault Dan had died; it had happened and there was no point in dwelling on it forever. Their relationship was one of those things, impossible to repair. They knew each other too well. All these past years from schooldays, and their lives centring on Joan and Terry, but how could she leave Rob without taking away his home? It was her own house, a gift from her father after his death. How was it possible to kick him out of it and leave her son in the graveyard without flowers? Should she tell Joan about Sven?

Two weeks of holiday romance, and then she would go home renewed and perhaps never see Sven again; nothing left but a fond memory. Then again, she remembered his words about a lasting relationship. She must discuss it further with him to find out what he really wanted of her. Too fast, too fast, why did she always do this to herself?

Chapter Thirteen

Pippa looked in the wardrobe to find her new jacket; outside the rain drizzled down her bedroom window. On hearing the engine of the van and the door closing, she hurried down the stairs and opened the front door. Her heart pounded as he stood there with a smile, waiting.

'I should have looked at the forecast for today. Not to worry,' he said. 'Let's go on up to the bird hide, have our sandwiches, and see if any new birds have flown in. So…good morning, my lovely.' He kissed her on the cheek. 'How are you?'

'Fine thanks,' Pippa said, amused at the words "my lovely". 'I'm all packed – wine, sandwiches, coffee in the flask – okay, let's go.' She stepped outside as he opened the door of the van for her to get in.

Higher Moors Nature Reserve could be a dank place in the rain, and Sven drove there with the windscreen wipers going back and forth. He liked her obvious new jacket and noted the binoculars strung around her neck. Inside him, his heart gave a merry skip.

He parked on the side of the road and didn't bother to lock the van. He strode beside her and helped pull the hood over her head as the heavier rain began to fall. On reaching the bird hide, he took her hand and held her close, shielding her from the weather as they passed through the dripping doorframe. Inside it was very dark and he quietly opened the hatch with a view to the large pond and the reed beds on the other side. They sat on the high seat in the bird hide and made themselves comfortable.

Once inside, Pippa sensed the odour of the damp earth under the floorboards. They had startled a mallard, and the rain splattered on the water, making splashing noises which echoed over the pond. Coots gave a repetitive 'kowk' and a couple of great crested grebes slid along with the mallards. Pippa watched, thrilled by the tranquillity, and listened as Sven pointed out the birds.

'*Podiceps cristatus,*' he whispered. 'A smart looking bird, eh? Another one for your list…' He pointed to the great-crested grebe gliding in the water. 'The female grebe carries her young on her back. Oh yes, see, there they are – small striped babies.'

'Oh, aren't they sweet?' Pippa said with delight, softening her voice.

'And there's a gadwall, Latin name, *Anas Strepera*. Look, there it is…over there.' Again he pointed, this time to the left.

'Oh yes – I see it. To me it's a duck.' She chuckled. 'And you said it's a what…? Gad-wall? The grebe babies are lovely, aren't they? Look…aw look, they're getting closer to us,' she whispered with excitement.

Sven nodded and caught her eye. 'Hm, ja.' He adored her enthusiasm. 'Great, eh?'

Pippa sensed an inner peace, the one she had felt only a few times in her life. She was aware of Sven's breathing as he looked through his binoculars. Beside her was a caring, beautiful man who could lead her into happiness, but she knew it would only be living out her fantasy. She needed more convincing than just a kiss.

'Did you sleep okay last night, Pippa?'

'What do *you* think?' Pippa smiled coyly. 'It wasn't easy after yesterday – my brain was going around in circles. I had so many questions. And you?'

'I suppose I did sleep after a while, but I was also thinking about yesterday. I really shouldn't have pushed you that far, I'm sorry.'

'No, no, it's okay. I really enjoyed being with you, Sven, honest I did – and, well, what more can I say? I came with you today, so it must have been good.' She looked at him, hoping he wasn't about to back down on her.

'It's strange, you know, I feel I've known you all my life,' Sven explained, his words interrupted by mallards fighting on the water.

'We might end up like those ducks!' Pippa turned to him.

Sven laughed, but she was right. They didn't know each other at all.

'So what do we do now, start building a nest?' She chuckled.

Sven lifted the strap of his binoculars over his head and laid them on the bench. He stood up. 'Come here,' he said. 'I want to give you a hug.'

He opened his jacket to wrap her inside. She was close to him, warm and comforted, and he kissed her. It was more of a passionate kiss than yesterday. Lips to lips, he caressed her face, and in his passion he spoke in Norwegian to her. His aftershave and the aroma of the dank earth floor seemed to enhance the atmosphere. She had never been kissed in that way. He pulled her closer, and she turned her back to him to lie in his arms as he kissed her neck and ears. Yes, she could feel his emotions all right. She talked to him, ensuring he stayed focused.

The rain began to pour heavily on the roof of the hide, and for a while they couldn't hear each other speak.

'Perhaps we can go somewhere else after this,' Sven explained above the noise of the rain. He placed his nose into her hair and took in the perfume of her shampoo. 'I think you are a very brave woman, Pippa. Maybe during our time together you can tell me more about yourself. I'm a good listener.'

'Yeah, I appreciate it. You are so nice to me, Sven. I can't...' Pippa stood up and sighed before she cried again. She turned around and gazed into his face, wiping away a stray drop of rain on his cheek that looked like a teardrop. Then he kissed her again, deep and loving, his hands around her face, stroking her hair. 'Pippa, you're so lovely. I really want you to share the good things in life with me, and we can go on the boat together. It will be great fun.'

Pippa put her finger to his lips. 'You don't know what you are saying, Sven, honest you don't. You have to get to know me better. I know I keep saying this, but…do you really want to take on someone with all these dreadful problems?'

Again he kissed her, his hands now stroking her back. She wanted him to lay down with her on the earthen floor of the hide and share her emotions. She mustn't, she had to take her time with this. Life would never be the same again, and what if she got pregnant? Being on the pill was never guaranteed. After Daniel, she didn't want any more kids unless things changed for the better. Anyway, you had to be careful these days with all those warnings on the TV. She felt sure Sven was not jumping into bed with every woman he met, but how could she be so confident about him? They had only just met; it was all so bizarre.

'Mm, I hope you are enjoying this as much as I am,' he said. 'I think we both have to make the best of it. You are right. I think for now we should just go along as we please.'

'I agree, but it's going to be hard,' Pippa replied.

Sven gave her a derisive look and a kiss. 'I think it's already hard.' He chuckled, and then wished he hadn't said it.

'Come on, let's not go down that path.' Pippa giggled. 'There's a picnic to be eaten, and it's lunch-time already.'

'Aw, spoilsport,' he said, laughing at her comment. 'No, I'm only joking, please forgive me.'

Pippa opened the sandwich box and offered Sven a choice. She munched on her salmon and cucumber sandwich as Sven looked through the telescope at the paddling gadwall. Today, for the first time in years, she felt the happiness she had experienced as a child. Sven could be the man of her dreams forever, the end of all her troubles, but nothing was that simple. Where would she live? Here on Scilly? Hell, no, that was way beyond her wildest dreams. Leaving Daniel behind would be impossible.

'Sven, are we really doing the right thing?' Pippa asked. 'I mean, what exactly do you expect of me?'

'I told you, I need someone to share my life and I would hope it's you. We can have a lot of fun together, and I think we both need this. I'm just glad I found you, Pippa. Sorry, but I cannot explain it any better. It just feels right. I hope you feel the same way as I do.' Sven stood, looking into her eyes.

Pippa stood with her back to the hide door and sighed. 'I think I do, it's just I have a lot at stake and I hope you can understand.'

'Yes, of course. Cem here, my lovely red-haired lady. Let's hug, and then we'll go back to Gilstone for the rest of the afternoon – is that okay with you?'

Pippa packed up the sandwiches as Sven downed the last of the wine in his beaker. They would finish the bottle back at Gilstone.

Chapter Fourteen

It was the weekend. Joan phoned as she always did on a Saturday morning.

'Just checking – are you okay, Rob?' she said.

'I think it should be me asking if *you* are okay.'

'Yes, I think I am. What am I supposed to feel? Any news to tell me then?'

'Pippa called and she seems fine. Trouble is, though, I'm in a bit of a quandary about what happens when she gets home. We'll sort it all out, I'm sure.' Rob sighed. 'There's no reason to think we can't have a trial separation, or even a "friendly" divorce under the circumstances.'

'What's all this talk about separation and divorce, Rob? What's it all about? This is news to me. You're not suggesting…surely? You've never mentioned it before. I don't want you and Pippa to split up as well! This is all going wrong, isn't it?' Joan sighed.

'Well, our problems have been ongoing since Daniel. In our case I hope it'll be straightforward. Look, Joan, I'll tell you more about it when I see you. Have you seen Terry?' Rob asked.

'Nope, he's gone back to Aberdeen without even calling here to see me. He promised he would. His mam phoned me. She said, "Now, Joan, you haven't had one of your tantrums again, have you? You'll push him away, you know, he's a sensitive man, and I know all about it, believe me".' Joan mimicked her mother-in-law, then rolled her eyes. 'But then I heard his dad shout "Phyllis!" down the phone, you know how he does, and she shut up. Tried to get out of it, she did. If only she knew, poor woman. He should try to explain it to her, get her used to the idea. After all, she thinks she knows her own son best, and it's obvious she doesn't! I'm wondering if I should tell her with time, break it to her gently – trouble is, she wouldn't believe me.'

'And you? Are *you* used to the idea?' Rob asked, feeling that Joan was being too cheery for the news she had received. *It's only natural she's in denial.*

'My toe still hurts a bit. It's broken, but it seems to be getting better now. It went black for a while, I think I might lose the toe-nail.'

'No, I mean how are you in view of Terry leaving? Glad to hear it's improving. I shouldn't ask this, but…did Terry hurt you? I mean, I know he wouldn't, but between husband and wife, it might be different. It's just I wondered if it might be that he pushed you when you hurt your toe? That's all, sorry to ask, but as a friend and health worker I'd like to be sure it was an accident and Terry isn't the violent type. I just wondered, that's all…'

'No, it was my fault, Rob, and I'm fine. I stubbed it during a row with him. He was actually quite caring about it. He would never hurt me, but thanks for asking. Well, love, I'll come and see you soon when Pippa comes home,' Joan said, trying to be cheerful. 'She'll be hellish shocked when I tell her about Terry. It's bloody awful, isn't it?'

'Listen, Joan, I think you have to understand how it's been for Terry as well. It's not something that's awful, it's actually quite natural. You must try to understand how he feels as well.' Rob knew he had to talk to her soon; she was being far too cheerful.

'Yeah, I suppose so. Thanks, Rob. This gay thing is all so new to me, I really don't understand it – I mean, after all these years we've been together.'

'Okay, love, I know how it was with your mam and dad. They were always rather stiff about things like that. I can understand how you might feel. Look, er…how about meeting up tomorrow night at the pub and we can have a long chat? I did promise

I would spend some time with you, so let's talk there, eh?'

'Thanks, Rob, I'll do that. See you soon, love, bye.' Joan sighed as she put the phone down. It was always Rob who had been around since Terry had been away. The shower unit, the motorbike and the occasional time with Jordan when she'd had to go out in a hurry. What was the matter with Pippa that she couldn't get on with him anymore?

It was Monday morning. Rob slumped into the settee. On the shelf above the wood-burning stove rested the letter from Grover and Pearson. He knew he could have opened it, but he hadn't considered it a priority. His mind was in so many places. His head was full of Pippa, Joan and Terry.

He sat staring at the envelope. What time was it? *Oh yes, I must go into town and get some food.* That was usually Pippa's job. He needed to vacuum the floor in the lounge where he'd spilt crumbs from a cake he'd eaten the night before, and then there was the washing up. Pippa would normally do those things. In a way, he began to miss her. He knew he shouldn't feel like this because of the housework, but things were beginning to get on top of him. Stephen Carmichael's visit had been very strange. He hadn't stayed long, only long enough to ensure he had the right name and date of birth. 'I'm sorry, I can't tell you any more, except there is this letter for you. It was left with us some years ago. Personally, I have no idea what's in the letter. I was asked to give it to you. I work part-time up here, and my job is with probate. I'm contracted to Grover and Pearson. I happened to be passing through Whitby, so John asked me to call in and see you. I hope it's good news,' he'd said. 'I only had to make sure I was giving it to the right person.'

Rob sat staring at the shelf for a while, then stood up and opened the envelope with care, expecting to see an advert for a solicitor's office in Hull. *Solicitors don't do things like that, though, do they?* Stephen Carmichael had seemed genuine enough; he wasn't selling double-glazing after all.

Inside were two letters. One in a blue manila envelope, slightly tattered, and the other a pristine official-looking letter from Grover and Pearson.

Dear Mr Lambton,
The enclosed letter is for your attention. We have kept it in our files for a number of years for a client of ours.
    When you have read the letter, if you wish to take this further please contact us and we will take the appropriate action.
Yours sincerely
John Grover

Rob held the blue envelope in his hand. *There isn't even a postmark.*

He was careful to slit across the sticky flap on the back of the envelope with a small kitchen knife. *Who has sent me this? It's written on old airmail paper.* Pulling out the flimsy blue paper, he proceeded to read it.

23 April 1979, Berne, Switzerland

My Dear Robert,
By the time you read this I shall be somewhere else, possibly passed away. I am ill. In 1956, I had a child. I believe that child was you.

Rob stopped reading for a moment in shock. *A letter from my real mother, my God, bloody hell. Oh no, this can't be real.* He sat on the sofa, his mouth half open in anticipation of what he was about to read.

...It was a time when they frowned on single mothers a lot more than they do now. I was sent away to an unmarried mothers' home, a disgrace to my family. They took you away from me one night shortly after you were born, I never was to

see you again. I tried to find you and eventually married your father. We had two more children, but the marriage happened quite a few years after you were born, and a few years later we found each other again. At the time he didn't know I was pregnant with you. I wasn't allowed to tell him, and it was impossible to find you. I signed the adoption papers, because at that time it was supposed to be "in the child's best interests". They almost forced me to do it. They put the pen in my hand and said, 'Sign this'. I just signed it and never read it. The last thing I remember is your screaming when they took you away from me. My dear Robert, I have been through hell, believe me. I often wondered if your family kept the name I gave you. I asked the nurse to tell your new parents to keep it. I hope this letter finds you.

Much later, I discovered a family in North Yorkshire had adopted you and that was all I was allowed to know. I told your father the whole story. His name is Dr Peter Haines and he is a consultant surgeon at Hull Infirmary. We live down here. He is…

Rob almost fainted. His mouth was open in awe of the letter, and he couldn't believe what he had read. *That Peter Haines. Oh my God, I've heard of him from work.* He wasn't sure whether to laugh, cry, phone someone or deal with it himself. He read on.

…We live down here in Beverley. He is a specialist in mental health.

Rob's heart beat faster as he read the words "mental health". *You have a younger brother, Bruce, and a sister, Penny, who at the time of writing are living at home with me. It is my wish that one day you will find each other.*

I am sure this letter will shock you and I apologise for the upset it may cause, but you see your father was older by six years, and that was the reason I had to give you away. My

146

mother was strict and old-fashioned in her ways, and she didn't approve. All she could think of was protecting her image. She was well-known in the town. I was only just seventeen and Mum couldn't take the scandal. They sent me away to a life of hardship and much sorrow during the pregnancy. One little mistake and it cost me my happiness. If only I could have found you. Your real father is a good man and we are all proud of him. I have placed this letter with John Grover. He is not only a solicitor, but also an old family friend – he was best man at our wedding too. He has promised to help your father work with the adoption people to find you. It might take years, but I want you to know we have tried. I have given instructions should anything untoward happen to me you should receive this letter. I don't know if they will ever find you, but I gave instructions for John Grover to do his best. My heart aches to think I may never see you. I am writing this because it makes me feel better to know that one day you might read it. If you do read this, please get in touch with the person who gave it to you. I want you to know I always loved you.
Your loving mum,
Fiona Haines

Rob sat with the letter on his knee. He stared at a spot on the wallpaper. The more he stared, the more he thought his life had crashed. He wasn't sure what to do, what to say, whether to stand up or sit down, or call his parents. He sat there, staring into an imaginary void.

Right now, he needed Pippa – well, no, it couldn't be Pippa anymore – but maybe it should be. In his confusion, he dialled Joan. She was the one person who would understand in view of Pippa's absence.

'Hi, Joan, erm…sorry to bother you, it's me…erm, I've had a bit of a shock, a letter from a solicitor in Hull. They've found my real mother.'

'What? Oh my God!' exclaimed Joan, stretching out the words "my God". 'Should I come round and see you?'

'If you want to. I'm not sure what to do about it, to be honest. I need someone to talk to. I'm feeling a bit strange.'

'Okay, I'll be there in about fifteen minutes. I'll ask our Carole to take Jordan, he's playing in the garden. Just need to wash his face and hands.'

On her arrival, Rob handed Joan the letter. 'See this? I'm in total shock…'

Joan read it, her mouth opening and closing. 'Blu-dee-hell, Rob. Oh shit, I don't believe this. You've got a real mam! Wow, this is amazing, how wonderful.'

'Well, it's not quite like that,' said Rob. 'Read on.'

Joan kept on reading. 'You've got a sister called Penny and a brother called Bruce. Oh heck! Are you going to try and find them?'

'For goodness sake, Joan, I've only just read the letter,' Rob reminded her.

'Yes, sorry, I do tend to jump in with both feet, don't I?' she said 'This is really weird, though – and you're sure it's real? This letter, I mean.'

'Oh yes, I feel sure it is now, though before I didn't. I suppose I'll have to tell my real mam and – well, no, not my real ones, I mean *my* mam and dad. Oh hell, this is confusing.'

'I know what you mean, Rob. Yes you ought to phone them and tell them. They brought you up, and they are your real mam and dad in that respect. They're the ones you should tell first.'

Joan read part of the letter again. 'And this guy who is your father is a doctor? That's weird, you being a nurse at the hospital and all that.'

'I know. I ought to tell Pippa before she comes back from Scilly. We have lots to discuss and…shit, there's too much going on. I don't have a phone number for her, she rings me from a call box on the island.'

'I'll support you for now,' Joan said. 'Don't worry, you can tell her at the right moment. It might make a difference to your lives, best not to spoil her holiday under the circumstances. It'll be a huge surprise for her when she comes home.'

Rob didn't hear her last comment. 'But I think my real mother is dead.'

'Oh, Jees. Don't you just wish Pippa was here now?'

'Oh, don't, please, it's all too much.'

Joan began her usual advising. 'It's almost two weeks before she gets back, you must tell her when she phones. I think you ought to phone Benidorm and tell your parents, and then phone the solicitor – that is, if you want to.'

'Yeah, you're right,' Rob said. 'I kind of knew in my heart one day this might happen. In my head I wanted it, but you know I've always been afraid of what I might find, like opening Pandora's Box, that sort of thing.'

'Chat with Ralph and Sally. I mean…they are the parents who brought you up. I'm sure they will help you understand what to do.'

'I'll phone them. It's a pity they're so far away. It's times like these when you need a family member,' said Rob.

'I'm surprised you and Pippa didn't go and live in Spain with them when you had the opportunity.'

'I was studying my nursing career, I didn't want to give it up.' Rob shrugged. He suddenly realised that if he had gone to live in Spain, Daniel would likely still be alive. He tried to stop thinking about it.

'Okay, I know,' said Joan. 'Well…do that, and if you need to talk, then call me – right? Gosh, this is a huge revelation, eh? Bit weird though, isn't it?'

He smiled to himself. *Joan, always there to help.* 'Yes, I know, I'm sad now that I never knew her.' *What the hell am I supposed to do?*

'Maybe you can find your real dad though?' Joan suggested.

'Possibly – I don't know. Anyway, we'll see, eh? I don't want to upset my mam and dad, despite the fact I don't see them much these days. You and I seem to have gone through some bad times recently. It's comforting to know you are there for me at times like this.'

'It should be Pippa you need to thank – not me.'

'No, Joan, you're wrong there – it's more than that. Look at you and your circumstances, and me in mine… We have to try and find a way to get through this, don't we?'

'So what do we do, Rob, this *you and me*? Where will our lives take us next, I wonder?'

'Honestly, Joan, I have no idea. I'll have to make this phone call before I do anything else.'

'I'll have to think about me,' Joan said sadly. 'I don't want to be left behind. I have to make a new start soon for the sake of Jordan, poor kid. One day I'll have to tell him about his dad. I dread it.'

'Joan, it's not so terrible. Terry still cares about you and Jordan, I know he does, he's just not…well, um…not that way anymore.'

'It's a real shit life for me now,' she said. 'I don't think he's coming back.'

Rob had never seen her in this mood; she had always been so positive, old-fashioned and mothering. He liked her for all those things. 'I'm sorry you feel like that, love.' He wanted to help, but his mind was in too many places. 'Let's talk about it another day, shall we? I really do have to sort this matter of Fiona Haines.'

'Okay, Rob, sorry. I'll see you soon.'

Joan left the house. As she was hurrying home to Carole and Jordan, her mind churned over. She always had to pass the place where Daniel took his last breath. She would avoid it today if she could. She knew she was losing both Rob and Pippa; what would she do next? She had to think of how to solve her predicament, but, as she drove along the road in the pouring rain, she couldn't think. Instead, she cried all the way home.

Chapter Fifteen

Time seemed to be closing in fast. Sven had been working again, and Pippa had tagged along and explored the outer islands. She had enjoyed every moment, and not only got to know him better, but felt more comfortable as a birdwatcher and confident enough to know the names of the birds. He had taught her a lot.

'That was a great meal, Pippa, thanks. You can certainly cook. Shall we sit somewhere more comfortable?'

They moved away from the dining table at Gilstone, and Pippa opened a window and closed the kitchen door to keep out the smell of fried food. Sven sat on the settee before sliding down to the floor to stretch out.

'Can of beer for you?' she asked, handing it to him before snuggling up beside him.

'Oh thanks, now this is really cosy.' He fizzed the ring pull and quickly supped the foam from the top of the can.

'So tell me more about your life in Norway,' Pippa said as she settled down and pushed a cushion at her back. She gave Sven a peck on the lips.

'There isn't much to tell really. My life is here now. My father is ill, and my mother takes care of him. He had a small stroke about a year ago and he seems to be improving now. My mother is a retired college teacher – she specialised in teaching English. That's about it, really, except, well, you know… I was going to get married and it's all in the past now.' Sven stroked her cheek. 'Gosh, Pippa, you've had it rough too, haven't you? Far worse than me, for sure.'

'See what I mean? You don't know me. All these things take time for us to learn about each other. Sorry to ask again, but are you really over Astrid now?'

'I think so. I just get lonely here, that's all. I missed the company until you came along. You can have lots of people around you but still be lonely at the same time.'

Sven stared at the cracks in the stone floor as he sat on the multi-coloured rag rug someone had spent hours making many years before. It had left an impression on his legs as he moved to get more comfortable. He put his arm around her and they sat side by side, his brown legs crossed in front of him. He wore a navy-blue Isles of Scilly T-shirt and denim shorts; he'd kicked off his sandals under the coffee table.

Pippa moved closer to him, aware of his regrets as he took another sip of beer with a faraway look in his eyes. It was the warmth of his touch and the cosiness of being in his arms. *Mm, nice.*

'I want to take you to St Agnes. I have a job there in the coming days and I'm expecting Martin back after next week. So we've got plenty to keep us busy.'

Pippa stroked his cheek. 'I can't believe I'm doing this.' She shivered at the thought of going home again.

'Yeah, I feel like that as well, it's all too good to be true.' He kissed her, sensing her soft cheeks with his lips.

Pippa knew she had to stop doubting herself. It might be wrong, but after all she had been through it also felt very right. She hoped she wasn't hiding a subconscious plan to use him; she didn't want him to feel that way.

He kissed her on the lips, but this time it was no ordinary kiss; it was a wanting you, needing you kiss, and she felt the emotion of love welling up inside her. She knew he felt it too and she never wanted it to stop.

He smoothed his hand across her neck and traced a finger to her cleavage. He mustn't make love to her; he would surely lose her. He must show her he cared.

Pippa took hold of his hand and gazed into his eyes, her heart beating faster. She didn't want to think too much about it. 'What are you waiting for?' she whispered.

Sven stopped short for a moment. 'You mean…'

'Yes, I mean…yes.'

'You sure?' Sven's eyes widened.

'Never more sure,' she said, whispering in his ear.

'Pippa, my love, I didn't prepare, er… I mean… I didn't think you would want to. It's too…'

'It doesn't matter, it's okay, my darling. I understand if you don't,' she said softly. It was the way he looked at her, his innocent expression, the way he cupped her face with his hands and looked into her eyes; he really knew what she wanted. Oh, why hadn't she met him before this? *There's no such thing as love at first sight. Why do I feel this way?*

'Oh, I think I do want to, but…' he said with a smile and stroked her cheek. 'I'm not sure, maybe you don't know yourself, my love. You are so fragile at the moment.'

Pippa looked him in the eyes. 'I'm absolutely sure, Sven, honest I am. I want to sleep with you tonight. I need you to love me, issues an' all – honest, there isn't a lot of time left, and what do we have to lose?'

His pause for thought kept her in suspense.

'What's the sudden change of heart?' he asked. 'This is a big jump.'

'Don't you… Oh, all I know is, it feels right.'

'Mm, I think I agree,' he said, kissing her. 'I'm just thinking about you, that's all.'

'Let's stop being sensible and live a bit.' Pippa heard the words she had spoken but it was as if they were coming out of the book she had just read. The words "make love in haste, repent at leisure" went through her mind. One last moment of questioning: did she really know what she was doing? She decided she did.

'It's not very comfortable on this stone floor, and the sofa isn't much better. Should we go upstairs?' she said.

He couldn't find any words to say as he climbed each step to the top. He'd wanted to tell her his feelings were the same. On the landing, he took her hand and pulled her gently towards him. He stroked her neck and licked her lips before kissing her full on, his tongue meeting hers.

Pippa shuddered with excitement; his warm hands stroking her face, his Norwegian words whispering in her ear, had sent her to a new place in her life. The emotion spilling from her heart overwhelmed her.

He led her by the hand to her room, feeling he might not go all the way with her yet, aware of her vulnerable state of mind. What was he doing to himself and to her?

They stood in front of the long mirror, and she watched him holding her in his arms, kissing her hair, caressing her face and telling her how much he wanted her. She wanted to cry and she closed her eyes as he undid the buttons on her blouse.

'You sure, Pippa? I don't want to do something we both might regret,' he whispered. Those scary feelings came flooding back of the first time he'd made love to Astrid. He hadn't had sex with a woman for some time and his body was eager to perform, but with Pippa would he get hurt again? He kissed her and she kept whispering 'yes' to him. He knew he wasn't using her for sex, he was making true love to her, but he kept questioning himself just in case.

By the time he had answered his own uncertainties she was already standing naked in front of the mirror, and he felt the need to kiss her all over, his Norwegian words so full of meaning only for her.

Pippa listened to his words, but didn't understand. But it didn't matter as they sounded so lovely. 'Jeg elsker deg, Pippa, jeg elsker deg.' She felt his breath on her neck as the honeyed Norwegian words kept pouring from his lips. She caught a glimpse of their reflection and saw how his kissing gave her the touching and the adoring she had wanted for so long.

'My God, Sven, you're amazing,' she whispered.

'I want to treasure every moment of today with you, my darling...' he said gazing into her eyes, '...and the next day, and the next.' He led her to the bed, then slipped off his shorts and T-shirt and came to her naked.

Pippa noticed how he was brown all the way down. Seeing him without his clothes provided her with a blissful outpouring of emotion; it made her nervous and she wanted to cry. The only other man she had been to bed with was Rob. What would Sven expect of her? Would she disappoint him? It had been some time for both of them, and every kiss radiated excitement and passion. This Norwegian god of a man who kept telling her how much he cared; she wanted him to love her for the rest of her life. She ran her fingers down his spine and squeezed him closer to her, skin to skin. His hair felt soft and freshly showered, and she brushed it out of his eyes. She had him for herself and wished it would be forever.

Sven stroked her nipples, exciting her. Once again, he asked, 'You sure?'

Pippa's voice faded into a whisper. 'Yes, Sven, I need you, want you, yes, yes and yesss.'

He moved closer, stimulating her libido, responding to her words, feeling for her before he made love to her.

Pippa's cheeks flushed with emotion and she closed her eyes while he rocked her into euphoria.

He wanted his lovemaking to be the experience she would never forget, in case he never saw her again and he could remember the moment all his life. He wanted to be like Sasha, his friendly seal, twisting beneath the sea, surfing the ocean, the freedom of the wild. Every stroke of his hand, every kiss ensuring Pippa felt comfortable in his passion. He must prove to her he was genuine. He knew he had fallen in love with her; he couldn't help himself. It was like the first time all over again – no, better. For some time they lay together, turning back and forth in their passion, until he couldn't hold back any longer. It was now or never. 'Yes, now, oh yes...now.'

Pippa let out an emotional cry. 'Sven' was all she could whisper. 'My lovely Sven.'

She lay there, her eyes watering, overwhelmed in lovemaking. Sven wiped away the tears for her. There was a silence, both looking into each other's eyes; what had she done? She wanted to speak but the words wouldn't come, and it took a moment to recover. She looked down on him, gazing into his face. He was so handsome. Why had he chosen her of all people? She didn't think she was *that* pretty; Rob never told her those things.

'No regrets?' he asked, breathing heavily as she lay on top of him.

Pippa sniffed back her tears. 'Sven, I… I don't know what to say. Is this really happening to us?' She sighed and pulled the sheets over them. His hair was damp; beads of sweat ran down his forehead and she took a corner of the sheet and wiped his brow.

He smiled and kissed her. 'I absolutely adore you, you know that? But you're about to break my heart. Must you go back home – can't we elope?' he said with a cuteness that made her want to melt again.

'Yeah, I know what you mean,' she whispered, 'we're in deep trouble, aren't we? Looking back, I don't think I expected us to go this far so soon. I must be stupid, naïve or something. You are so lovely, Sven, I feel very lucky to have found you. I just wanted you, it felt right.' They kissed and she fell back to lie beside him.

'No, Pippa, you are not stupid or naïve, you must have more confidence in yourself. Who can blame you for wanting to be loved? That was so good – you are good – and stop worrying, everything will be fine,' he said as he hugged her and tickled her ribs. 'Oim sure we'll think of something, my lovely, oi need yew and yew need me,' he said with a laugh as he tried to mimic Don.

Pippa laughed with him; he was glad he'd made her happy. He snuggled himself into her arms. At the end of her holiday, he wondered how he would ever manage to see her again. Leaving her would be a heart-wrenching moment as they said 'Goodbye' on the quay. Perhaps he could go with her, but with work it was impossible.

He couldn't leave his post with Martin being away. Why was his life always so complicated with women? She was right – they had opened up a completely new set of problems they might regret, but no longer did he want Pippa to be his "friend". He wanted her for himself, forever.

That night, as Pippa lay in his arms she knew he would break her heart. How could she go back to Rob and sleep with him after all those wonderful things? Then there was the house in Henrietta Street, the place where she had grown up: she would have to leave it all behind, leave Daniel. What had she done? The situation, so self inflicted, made her wish it could have been different, but Sven…he was everything she could have wanted. But Daniel…how could she be so thoughtless and selfish?

Chapter Sixteen

'Hello, Robert love, how are you? Nice of you to phone,' Sally Lambton said from the Finca Limoneros near Benidorm.

'Mum, I need your help. Something weird has turned up. Is Dad there?'

'Yes he is, what's the matter, love?'

'Well, this concerns all of us, Mum. It's to do with my adoption,' Rob said.

Sally had dreaded those words all of Rob's life. She called for her husband to come and listen in on the extension phone. 'Ralph, it's Robert, he wants to talk to both of us.'

Rob heard the phone go "click".

'Well, Mum and Dad, what I'm about to read you may be upsetting, so I'd better explain. Don't worry, I wish I could be there with you, but I'm not going to do anything drastic, I only need your support and some advice.'

He began his story about the visit from the solicitor's office and then read the letter to them.

Sally's silence worried Rob, and he could hear his father's asthmatic breath wheezing down the phone.

'Mum? Dad? Are you all right?'

At last Sally spoke, her voice low and faltering. 'I knew this might happen some day, didn't you, Ralph?'

Rob knew that tone; it bordered on upset and tears.

'Yes, sure, but the thing is what are you going to do about it, son?' Ralph asked.

'Well, it's difficult, really. I know how hard it was for you and Dad when you first married, and of course, in that way you are my mum and dad and always will be, but I've got a real brother and sister I've never met. Isn't that weird? I don't even know if my real father is still alive. If I ignore it I might regret it, and if I don't, I might regret it. Either way, I can't win.'

'Listen, Rob,' his father said. 'Under the circumstances maybe you ought to go and see the solicitor, find out more and get back to us. I mean, we are your parents, but it was always a worry your biological mother might turn up on our doorstep one day asking to take you back. I knew she couldn't, of course, but it's a fear we had. I suppose it's the same with most parents who adopt. They don't really tell you to expect these things as you get older, but it does happen, kids get curious about their real parents. Life has moved on so fast since we first had you.'

'It seems it wasn't the fault of my mother she gave me away. I know she was forced to do it. Imagine that! I don't even know if she is still alive – I doubt it. She says she was ill when she wrote the letter. Perhaps she had cancer or something.'

Sally sighed. 'It makes me feel rather guilty, but we gave you a good life, good education and lots of love.'

'Yes, you did, and I am forever grateful you were good parents to me.'

His father's voice came down the phone line. 'It was a shocking world just after the war, everything changed. Now you are older and mature we have to leave the decision to you, but we don't have any argument if you want to do it. Be careful you don't get your fingers burned, that's all. I think it would be great for you to find your brother and sister, I just hope they feel the same way. I would love to meet them. It all sounds very intriguing. Good luck, Robert – do what you think is right, and we'll support you.'

'Thanks, Dad. They didn't tell you about my real parents when you adopted me, did they?'

'Certainly not,' Sally replied. 'I had no idea, and nothing as positive as you've got now, love. I've always been very curious to know where you came from.'

Ralph continued, 'So have you thought about what you might do?'

'Well, I'm going to have another think about it and then maybe I'll get in touch. I mean, I could hardly ignore it, could I?'

'Dreadful circumstances about this Fiona woman, eh?' said Ralph.

'Well, good luck, pet. It's very hot here today. Call us when you hear more, we'll be intrigued as well. How's Pippa? What does she say about it?' Sally said.

Rob didn't want to tell them any more; he told them she was fine and he would talk to them later.

An hour passed and Rob spent the time thinking about the conversation with his parents. He held the letter in his hand and read it one more time. *Bruce and Penny, I wonder if they look like me.*

That same afternoon Rob asked to speak with John Grover.

'Oh, good afternoon, Rob, I was expecting you might call – or rather, I hoped you would.'

'I think I'd like to find out more about the Haines family, please,' Rob said.

'Of course. I now have more information on this case. I am sorry to tell you but your real father died a few weeks ago and left a will, and with the will was that letter. I'm sorry I couldn't tell you this before, but I had to exercise discretion and to be sure you were the right person. Stephen updated me on the situation when he got back to the office. He deals with the probates. It had to be for you to read that letter in your own time. It's a very private thing in these circumstances. We were only reconciling for the time being.'

'Yes, I understand. So, it was my real father who died, eh? Oh dear, I thought I might meet him.' Rob felt he should be crying with emotion about his sad loss, but there was no emotion, just a pair of people he knew nothing about.

'I'm sorry. While your father was alive we did our best to try to find you, but it has taken a long time and lots of paperwork. He was, in fact, a good friend of mine, I shall miss him. The point here is that you need to come into our office or meet me somewhere. There is a chance that you have a third share in your real parents' will. They left a clause in the will in case you were found. Your siblings, Penny and Bruce, may want to meet you.'

'Oh hell, this is incredible. Is there any chance I could find them and talk with them?' Rob enquired.

'Yes, I think so, but all in good time, Rob. Give me a few days and we will try to confirm a few things for you. It must be very odd for you, eh? Although I have to explain: your real father was involved in a car accident several months ago, and he hung on, but never recovered.'

Suddenly it all became clearer and Rob remembered something he'd read at work or in the news. 'Maybe I do recall this guy. Wasn't it a hit and run?'

'That's right, how did you know that?' John asked.

'I work at the local hospital, I heard about it. I had no idea he was my father, oh my God!' Rob put his fingers to his lips in shock. 'Look, John, I'm grateful for your help, but you're right – it *is* all very weird. I'm not sure which way to turn.'

'Yes, well…but if I may advise, it's best we take it one step at a time. Allow me to help you sort out a meeting with your siblings. You're sure this is what you want?'

'I think so, but it's a big step. I mean, they might not want to meet *me*.'

'Oh I think they do. Leave it with me – I'll call you next week and let you know. There's a chance you are due some of the inheritance. I have yet to read the will to your family. Your real mother had been looking for you a long time. She got very sick and depressed, I'm afraid, and then later on she was diagnosed with breast cancer. She was in Switzerland at a clinic. Bruce and Penny Haines have had such bad luck, they might welcome this meeting.'

'Oh, I see. It sounds dreadful. And you mentioned an inheritance? Oh my goodness, the other members of the family aren't going to like me nudging in on their patch, are they?'

'I know them well. Fiona Haynes brought them up as good kids. They are not the trouble-making types, they're educated and they wanted to find you as well for the sake of their parents. And now their father has passed away it has brought them closer together. They now know about you and want to meet you.'

'Yes, but this money – surely it will be a bit weird, some stranger coming into their lives.'

'Rob, you are not a stranger, and you are entitled to the money. It's as simple as that. Fiona and Peter instructed it was to happen this way after their death. You are their real son, this is what they wanted. Leave it with me and I'll get back to you, and try not to worry, I understand how much of a shock this will have been for you. I must impress upon you, I don't want you to do anything you can't handle, okay?'

'Yes, I understand.'

'Look, erm… I'll leave you to consider all this a bit longer and I'll get back in touch with you as soon as I know more. It's all very sad.

'Yes, I understand. I lost my young son and it doesn't get any easier. Thanks a lot, John, I'll look forward to it.' Rob replaced the receiver. He'd never felt so alone as right now.

Chapter Seventeen

'Hi, Rob. We need to talk.' Pippa had called him from Scilly.

'Hello, love, how are you? Having a nice time, eh? I miss you.'

Pippa's alarm bells rang loud and clear. His words were a memory from a long time ago. The Rob she used to know, the lovely man she had married. At this moment, she didn't want him to be lovely.

'Pippa? You still there?' he said.

'Gosh, that's a change of heart from our last phone call. What do you mean, you miss me?' she asked.

'Well, I do. Three weeks is a long time to be away. Anyway it won't be long now until you get back.'

He became aware of how quiet she seemed and he thought he should apologise for the way he had behaved in the last few weeks. Perhaps he had better explain; after all, she would be home soon, and their lives would change for the better.

'Look, erm, I've behaved rather badly, I know, and now I can't wait for you to get back.'

'Rob, what's going on? Has something happened to make you have a change of heart?'

'Well, I've had some interesting information. I won't get a chance to tell you everything on the phone, but it looks like we might be due for an inheritance. Someone contacted me, and, to cut a long story short, they have found my real family.'

'What? Oh my God! That's incredible.'

Pippa's insides wrenched sideways. The phone box with its stench of stale cigarettes was hardly the place to take it all in. The last thing she wanted was to go home to Whitby before her holiday was up, but perhaps she should be with him. It was all so confusing.

'Where does that put us, I mean, you and me?' she asked.

'What do you mean, Pippa? You got your inheritance from your dad, and now apparently I'm getting mine. All square, let's enjoy it together.'

Something in his tone of voice sounded like he was getting back at her for not sharing with him.

'Rob, I have shared everything with you. You know Dad gave me the house before we married, it was his wish. He didn't know we would get married. The money was in a trust fund for me until I was twenty-one. I just kept it in my account for us to spend. Remember it was your idea when we married to have separate bank accounts. You weren't working at the time. I just paid for everything, we never thought much about it.'

'Pippa, hush for a moment. I hope you are enjoying yourself down there.'

Pippa went quiet; she had no conversation with him; her mangled feelings stabbed her. Hearing Rob say those words sent severe anger through her. She was tired of his controlling.

'Well, I'm happy for you about the news, but I doubt if this will change things between us. Perhaps you can tell me more when I get back.'

Pippa knew he had been trying to assure her it would be a change for the better and things were going to be fine. He explained about his brother and sister and the phone call with the solicitor. 'I do miss you, honest, I do.'

Pippa wanted to scream. *No, you bloody well don't miss me. Just because you've got some money coming to you, you think that's made a difference?*

'Anyway, Joan is upset now. I think you ought to call her, she has something to tell you about Terry.'

Oh what now? What else can go wrong? Makes me wish I hadn't phoned. 'Can't you tell me?'

'Well, not really, I think it's better coming from Joan, you see…'

The pips sounded, and before she got cut off she garbled the words down the phone. 'Okay, I'll give her a call, bye, call you later when I've got more change.' She didn't feel like putting more money in the slot, and in any case, she didn't have that much change in her purse.

On opening the door of the phone box, she slipped into the fresh air and walked a few steps into the park to sit on a bench. She caressed her own cheeks in contemplation and gazed at the blue agapanthus towering above the shrubs, the sea air drifting into her nostrils. *Oh shit, shit and bloody shit.* She kicked a stone on the path. She needed to tell Sven. What she had with Rob was a husband who was just as mixed up about their relationship as ever, but finding his real parents, would that change everything? There were deep uncertainties about Sven; it could never work, although she wanted to be with him with all of her heart. And yes…how could she love someone after only two weeks? The situation had got out of hand. As she sat in the park it seemed her lovely plans were about to be ruined.

On her arrival back at Gilstone, Sven made coffee.

'Hello, my darling, how did it go?' he said.

'Awful!' she wailed. 'I feel he's scheming to make me feel guilty. He says he misses me, but only last week he was talking about sep-aration and divorce. Hell, this is so hard.'

Sven sucked in a breath. 'Okay, what's happened?'

She told him about the phone conversation and Rob's newfound family. 'I don't think I should go back early. The reason I came here in the first place was his lack of support, why should I support him now? It's always me who keeps the peace in our house. I've had enough of it. I can't live this hot and cold existence.'

'It's quite a story, isn't it?' Sven sensed fear of her return to Rob. He sighed. 'What do you want to do, Pippa?'

'At this moment I don't want to go home. I want to stay here with you.'

Sven smiled down on her and hugged her for the comment. 'Why don't you? – No, I know you can't do that, you have responsibilities.' He remembered the three-week pact they had made and how he couldn't push it. His feelings were being tested to the limit. It had to be up to Pippa. Perhaps Rob might turn the tables on him. He didn't want to think about it. His whole self felt like collapsing in a heap on the floor with the thoughts he might have lost yet another woman in his life. He waited for her to speak.

'I'm going to continue our agreed time here with you, Sven,' Pippa said with a smile. 'Then I'll go home, see what Rob says, and sort it out. Now it's *me* who doesn't want to live with *him*. If he's got money he can find a place of his own now. He doesn't need me.' She lowered her eyes as she said it. She knew Sven had shown her a new path of hope; why would she want to go back on herself? Besides, the chance to stay a bit longer on Scilly with Sven was most tempting.

'Pippa, I want to ask you something.' Sven turned to her, kissing her forehead. She had opened a path for him to say how he felt, and his relief seemed to show.

'Listen, while you were out I was thinking. In view of all this, and I know we have only had a short time together, but could you trust me enough to ask you to be my girlfriend for real, long term, forever – I mean for as long as we both want to be together? I think this pact of ours has gone further than we both intended.'

'What do you mean?' Pippa looked lost for a moment.

'Well, why don't you go home to Whitby as you said, then come back here and live with me at Beachside Cottage? I could help you do it when Martin gets back.'

'Jeeps, Sven! That's one heck of a proposal.' She put her arms around his waist and hugged him. 'You are so sweet, I love you to bits. You can be so impulsive at times, but surely that's not possible.' She chuckled at his puppy-dog expression.

'Well, yes, it is possible. I just want to make you happy, that's all. You've had a hell of a life and you aren't even as old as me yet. We are both kidding ourselves. I know I'm falling in love with you and it's tearing me up.' He gazed upon her sun-freckled face. 'Look, I don't want to steal you from Rob, but if, as you say, things have been unbearable for you, then doesn't it make sense to start afresh? I mean, well… Rob is unlikely to come 500 miles down here to smash my face in, is he?'

Pippa laughed then cried at the same time.

'I love being with you, Pippa, I just can't help it. You're the best thing to happen to me in a long time. I'm going to be devastated if you don't come back to me. Sorry, that's unfair of me, but I had to say it. I didn't want to put you under any pressure, honest I didn't, but things have taken a sudden change, haven't they?'

Pippa sniffed back her tears. 'I don't know what to say. You've blown me away! I'm so overwhelmed I find myself wondering how I got into this mess.'

'Yes, I know, I understand, my darling, but just say "Yes".' He had got her to this point and now he had to try and help her fix it.

'What do I do now?' Pippa asked, feeling both despair and happiness all at the same time. Rob needed her – no, he didn't, he was just saying that – but he was her husband and she should have a sense of loyalty. What was it to be? Loyalty or happiness?

Sven put on a serious face. 'First, I think, before we get too far down this track, you and I will continue as we are. This will give us a few more days to decide if this is real or not.'

'Yes, I agree.' Pippa smiled and kissed him on the cheek. 'What I have here is the chance to get a real life and travel and do all the things I have never been able to do. My only regret is leaving Daniel in Whitby with no one to tend his grave. I couldn't go back very often, and Rob hardly ever goes to the cemetery. My life has been in Whitby, but Scilly has many similarities, and I could feel just as at home here. I would always have to live by the sea. It's a wonderful offer – give me until tomorrow to think again about it. I have to ask myself if I am chasing rainbows. I have a lot to consider back home.'

'That's my girl,' Sven said as he hugged her. 'Very sensible. Perhaps I have a rainbow to chase as well, so let's just enjoy chasing it together while we can. I'm having such a great time with you. I will always support you, my darling, you only have to ask.'

Pippa felt in awe of his proposal to live with him. How could she leave Henrietta Street? It had been her childhood playground. How she had loved going to the beach outside her back door and down the steps. The cobbled street where, as children, she and Joan had played "Jacky Five Stones" on the doorstep with a few other kids – Thomas, Geraldine and little Ingrid whose father was a Danish fisherman. The aroma of the kippers, with their flattened and gutted bellies on racks in the blackened smokehouse, and old Mr Fulton hanging them on tenterhooks ready for smoking. The local kids used to call it the "black treacle house", as the blackened interior glistened in the sun. The number of times they had counted the hundred and ninety-nine steps to the Abbey; they always got it wrong. Pippa smiled to herself; Joan used to argue and say she had counted two hundred.

Now that Rob had changed his attitude, she couldn't quite fathom it. Had he been chatting to Joan? Had she told him to behave himself? She remembered the conversation from a few weeks ago. She and Joan had a heart-to-heart about Terry. Joan was worried she hadn't seen him or had any phone calls. Perhaps this was why Rob wanted Pippa to make a call for support.

Sven glanced at Pippa, who seemed to be miles away in her thoughts.

'Come on, drink up, my sweet,' he said. 'We'll work something out, I know we will.' He held up the mug of coffee. 'Cheers! To our future happiness, no matter where that may be.'

Chapter Eighteen

Rob waited in the pub. He had a date with Joan. It was more an "I'll meet you at the pub for a drink, see if I can help you sort yourself out" kind of date. They had known each other too long for relationships to be anything else but friends. It was how it had always been. Perhaps tonight they could sort out each other's problems, but all Rob wanted was for Joan to talk about Terry; after all, she had been there for him when he discussed about his new family. Right now, he reflected, they probably needed each other.

'What can I get you?' he said as Joan walked into the bar.

'Orange juice, please, Rob.' She sat on the plush red velvet bench and placed her shoulder bag beside her. 'I got a call from Pippa. She told me you'd asked her to phone me. I didn't tell her everything about Terry. I didn't want to upset her holiday. It was difficult. I just said he was depressed and trying to sort himself out. I'll tell her when she comes home.' She tried to change the subject.

'You should have told her, Joan. That was a bit daft of you,' Rob scolded.

'Yeah, well…' She shrugged her shoulders.

The conversation with Pippa had made Joan think she wasn't talking with the same best friend who had left her the previous week; it was the Pippa she had known before losing Daniel. She realised Pippa was having more than a good time. She seemed happy and full of information about birdwatching, visiting islands and going on the boat trips, and the guide who had showed her all the new birds she'd never seen before. She seemed so full of delight, it had made Joan feel she couldn't tell her about Terry.

'How's it going with you?' Joan asked.

Rob thought Joan looked tired and wondered if she had been sleeping.

'I'm fine, I suppose, although it's a bit strange not having Pippa around. There's so much to do at home, I absolutely hate doing housework, and with this family situation, I'm waiting for a phone call from the solicitor. It's all becoming a bit of a nightmare. I'm supposed to be meeting my new family when they can arrange it.' He sighed. 'Then there's all this business of Pippa and me. The other night I was thinking maybe I should just give in. With this money due to me, we could start a new life, try again.'

'Money, money, it's all about money, isn't it?' Joan said with some anger in her voice. 'I would say, first you have to consider Pippa's feelings, Rob.'

'What d'ye mean?' he asked, puzzled.

'Well, there you are counselling your patients, and the one thing you've missed is the feelings of your own wife.'

'Joan, dear.' He lowered his voice in a patronising way. 'I thought we came here to talk about you tonight, to see if I can help you with your future, not for you to help me with mine.'

'Sorry, Rob, but it had to be said. You're a great person, I've always appreciated the way you have been so caring with Jordan and me. Perhaps you need to talk to Pippa when she gets back. I wish things were the same as they used to be, but they're not, are they?'

'Okay, I know what you mean. I'll wait for her to get back, then I'll sit down with her and have a talk, I promise.' He knew Joan was often like a scolding mother, but sometimes he needed it, and she was right. He scoffed at himself.

It was getting dark outside and Rob offered to walk her to the car park. They discussed Joan's future on her own with Jordan, and by the time they reached the car Joan was in tears.

'I can't do this, Rob, face a future on my own. I feel I'm losing you and Pippa – I only have our mam, and I couldn't tell her about Terry just yet. Our Carole is moving to Leeds soon and I won't have a sister or a babysitter.'

Rob put his arm around her and gave her a hug. 'It's going to be all right, honest it is. You and Jordan can have a wonderful life together, and maybe in the future you will find someone else to love you.'

'No I won't. Terry was my life. Who wants a woman with a kid?' She was sobbing her heart out.

'Look, I'll drive you back home and I'll walk back. It will only take a few minutes and it'll do me good.'

He took the keys from her and got into the car. She was sniffing all the way up the hill with a wet handkerchief rolled in a ball in her fist.

On arrival, he got out of the car and escorted her back to the front door.

'Will you be okay?'

'Yeah, Jordan is with our mam tonight. All I need is a good sleep. Thanks, Rob,' she sniffed.

'Well, I think it did us both good to talk, and thanks for the company.' He gave her a hug and kissed her damp cheek. 'G'night, Joanie, see yer, love, and don't worry.'

Joan went to bed even more depressed than the hour before and worked her mind to a frenzy about Terry leaving her in the lurch. She saw the pills on the dresser and wondered if she should take a couple to help her through the night.

Chapter Nineteen

'I've made you a sandwich, Pippa. Thanks for coming round in this awful weather. I just got in about half an hour ago.' Sven was tidying up around him.

'Did you hear the weather forecast? Twelve hour gales, eh? And at this time of year, too!' Pippa replied. 'I'm only here for a few minutes, I have some things to do.'

Outside the wind gusted. With tourists grounded for the day and flights out of the islands cancelled, Pippa realised how easy it was to be isolated here, but it was cosy, and with Sven by her side what more could she want?

'I wondered if you might like to come to St Agnes with me. You haven't been over there yet, have you?' Sven asked.

'Thanks, Sven, I'd love to, but not in this weather,' Pippa replied with an anxious look on her face.

'No, no, silly.' He laughed and gave her a peck on the cheek. 'I thought tomorrow would be nice. It's going to get out fine by the afternoon. I've got a job to do over there and maybe you can help me. We are checking the shoreline for oiled sea birds.'

Pippa's face lit with pride; she could do that. She decided she would tell him about her experiences with the RSPCA in Whitby. 'Oh, that's great,' she said.

'*Elsker deg.*'

'Huh?' Pippa queried.

'It means "love you",' he said with a coy smile.

Now she understood his words from their "love-in" at Gilstone.

When he spoke his native language, it always gave her goose-bumps. She gave him a hug and wanted to stay longer, but couldn't. 'Love you too, but I must go and get some shopping. I've run out of milk and eggs. I'll meet you later, okay?' She picked up her shopping bags, kissed him on the lips, and left Beachside Cottage. She hung on to the bags as the wind pushed her around the next corner. St Agnes would be great and she looked forward to it; she hoped this awful weather would improve as Sven had predicted.

After lunch, Sven left home as his neighbour, Nanette, returned from town. She smiled at Sven over the granite wall. 'Looks like you're havin' a good time, then, young man!'

Sven grimaced. 'And you too, Nan. *Sopskoilt*,' he cursed aloud in Norwegian, thinking how annoying she was. She always wanted to know everything about him; she and Margaret at the office were friends. Nanette had to be the nosiest woman on the islands, peering through her windows each time he left as though she was spying on him. He supposed he didn't really care. He'd lived with it for long enough now.

The following morning Pippa packed a lunch for both of them. As they stepped on board *Lily*, she found a seat at the back; she thought it might help Sven avoid the gossip.

'Hey, man, who's the redhead?' Don asked. He had seen her on the quay chatting to Sven.

Sven pretended to look around the boat. 'Who? What redhead?'

'Your new girlfriend. Wasn't she on the boat last week? I think I've seen her around town – who is she?' Don put the engine into reverse and started out to St Agnes, the sun glistening on the water in St Mary's harbour.

Sven felt cornered. He wanted to protect Pippa, but this time Don seemed insistent on meeting her.

'Pippa!' he shouted above the noise of the boat engine and beckoned her with a smile. 'This is Don. Don, meet my friend Pippa.'

She moved forward in the boat to a seat closer to Sven.

'Pleased to meet you, young lady. Yes, I've seen you two chatting and I wondered if there was a romance in the air,' Don teased. 'Where're ye from, m' dear?'

'I live in Yorkshire,' Pippa replied. 'I've come to Scilly for the birdwatching. Actually, I did meet you a few years ago, but I was a passer-by. You were telling me about the history of your boat—she's quite old, isn't she?'

Don nodded. 'Oh, oi never forget a face.' He grinned at Sven.

Pippa cringed; what if Don really did remember who she was with on her last visit? Her hair always gave her away. She hoped that with all the visitors over the last five years he would have forgotten. If he did remember, he might discuss it with Sven; it was knowing he had met with Rob and Daniel – well, it wasn't that important, just a bit embarrassing.

'Yeah, *Lily* is my pride and joy,' said Don. 'My dear departed wife used to say I love this boat more'n I loved 'er. She was wrong, of course, but the boat is all I gawt 'ere now, 'cept young Sven. He's like a son to me.'

Sven laughed and agreed.

'So, we're awf to Aggie this afe'rnoon. I likes Aggie best, they do a good pint at the pub. On the bowts though, I'm not supposed to drink and droive,' he drolled, 'so I'll 'avta 'av an apple juice or somethin'.'

Pippa beamed at him; no wonder Sven had picked up a Cornish accent, having spent many hours with Don. She realised Sven's look of amusement, and wondered what he was thinking.

As usual, Sven's binoculars were poised against his eyes. St Agnes had no shelter from the lagoon and the sea swell made the crossing choppy. Pippa stood with him and rode the waves, and Sven gave up trying to birdwatch. She was laughing, and the crowd at the back of the boat were making "Woa" sounds as each wave tossed the boat towards the sky. Don adjusted his speed to give the passengers a less bumpy ride.

As the boat pulled into the quay at Kallimay Point, Sven had some jobs to do.

'We have to sort out this tragedy with the oil,' he said. 'There's a shortage of sand eels for the common tern chicks, and the puffins aren't doing well either. It's all a bit of a disaster.'

'So what can I do to help?' Pippa asked eagerly.

'This morning I want to collect the mortalities along the shore, and later on we'll take them to be examined by the vet. The volunteers are also collecting data on the oil spill,' Sven told her.

'Okay, what do you want me to do then?' Pippa asked.

'I'll give you this plastic bag. Don't go picking up any birds without the gloves on. Walk along the beach, and any dead ones you find pop them into the bag. Discard the skeletons, only the recent mortalities,' he called to her as they walked in opposite directions.

She strolled along the beach alone, combing the shingle. She discovered a dead tern, a starfish, and two dead crabs. It was difficult with the oversized gloves on. She took them off, not being able to resist stroking the bird then, and placed it with care in the plastic bag. The softness of the feathers – it was sad to see its lifeless form in her hand. She caressed the bird as she had done with her son before his funeral. It had been a terrible thing to see him lying there. A senseless death: a waste of life. The ghastly vision would always remain and she wished she hadn't seen him like that, but they had made him look so beautiful despite the injuries.

By the time they had been on the beach for an hour, they had found three dead terns and a puffin, and one guillemot, still alive, but unable to fly. She knew a little about guillemots and called Sven to pick it up. He stalked the bird, and then ran a short distance along the beach with the creature helplessly flapping its wings. He stooped down to pick it up. 'Gotcha,' he said.

Pippa ran towards him. 'I took care of a guillemot once. We washed it when Dan was small, and looked after it for six weeks before returning it to the estuary on the river Esk. Dan loved all animals, he was like my Dad.'

'Ah, so you know how to feed them and so on – hm, useful. I'm not surprised about the terns, it's been a hard year for them – all this overfishing. I hope there's not a disaster due soon. We've got too many mortalities in that bag for the short time we've been on this beach.'

They wandered back to the pub, Sven with the 'gilly' nestling under his arm and a hand around its beak. He asked the landlord for a cardboard box in which to place the bird. They would take it back to St Mary's and give it a wash.

They left the box outside at the back of the pub in the shade and continued on their way until Don returned with the boat. As they walked the island, the pungent aroma of chamomile filled the air and Sven pointed out the flora from the field guide.

'Oh my God, what the heck's that?' Pippa jumped back from the path as she said it.

Sven knelt down and picked up a large insect.

'Now here's an interesting thing – it's an oil beetle, a female.'

'Yuk, it's grotesque!' she exclaimed as she gazed upon the black glistening form of a large insect in his hand.

'I think it's rather beautiful,' he said. 'They are known as "oil beetles" because they release oily droplets of *hemolymph* from their joints when disturbed. This contains *cantharidin,* a poisonous chemical which causes your skin to blister, but as long as I don't upset her, she'll be fine,' he explained.

He played with the oil beetle for some time, allowing it to wander over his hand before placing it with care on the grassy verge to avoid someone standing on it.

'Come on, then, we ought to be getting back,' he said. 'You did a great job this afternoon, Pippa. Maybe we can find some work for you here.'

I wish. Pippa rolled her eyes in dismissal.

Before leaving the island, they collected the cardboard box from the pub and showed Don what they'd found. The return journey saw calmer weather as they steered closer to St Mary's. Pippa sat with her hand in the sea, looking down to the clear depths. She noticed Don gazing at her from the wheelhouse – or was it her imagination? Perhaps Sven would explain her circumstances to him. She knew she shouldn't feel guilty, but she did. She had left home to get away from prying eyes, and she was sure Don would wonder about her being with Sven. She dismissed it as paranoia.

Arriving on St Mary's, they took the bird through the office and outside to the old stone sink. Pippa watched as Sven washed the guillemot with a toothbrush and showerhead, using a mild detergent as shampoo – and it occurred to her that maybe she could help him with this kind of work in the future. *The future. Oh gosh! Could I really live on Scilly?* Sven spoke and her train of thought became interrupted.

'Watch your fingers, Pippa. Here, give me that elastic band so he doesn't take a stab at you, and when he's dry again, then we'll feed him some fish. I'll keep him inside, because he has to be given a chance to become waterproof again. He's a "bridled gilly" – you see the white stripe around the eye?'

Pippa stroked the bird, bedraggled and wrapped in a towel. 'Sven, do you think Don remembered me from the last time I was here?' she asked.

Sven laughed. 'I doubt it. He tells everyone that, he's a curious sod, always has been.'

'Yes, but he met Rob and Daniel, you see. I just wondered, that's all. The thing is, Daniel fell over and Don picked him up for me and we put a plaster on his knee.'

'Oh, I see. Well, try not to worry. It won't mean anything to him, and if he does ask me I'll explain. Are you worried about it?'

'Not really, it's just Don seems such a nice guy. I wouldn't want him to think I was bad for you, that's all.'

'Oh Pippa, it's okay, honest. Don's a great person, he wouldn't do that anyway. I promise to tell him soon. He'll understand when he knows about your sad loss. Try not to worry, it's no big deal.'

'I know. Sometimes it's hard for me to put all the little things aside. I was just concerned for some silly reason I can't explain, it gets me like that. When I have more confidence in myself, then I hope all the stupid things will go away.'

Sven stopped towelling the bird to give Pippa a hug and a kiss.

'Come on, let's get this job done and go home. I'll put this gilly under the infrared lamp, help him to dry out.'

In the small storeroom, outside next to the office, Pippa watched as he plugged in the lamp and stroked the head of the guillemot before placing it on a bed of straw. She sensed his caring, and related to the bird's dilemma. It also hadn't wanted to be messed up like this.

Sven let the bird go free on the tabletop and it flapped its wings to shake away the excess water. He turned away with his eyes closed to avoid the spray.

Pippa realised she had also been given a second chance, and perhaps she could learn a lot from the way Sven had provided her with love and care. He had rescued her as well.

Chapter Twenty

Margaret walked into the office and realised Sven was on the phone. She had a piece of paper in her hand with a message, so she left it on the desk.

SVEN. Just to let you know Martin will be back on Saturday lunchtime with the BBC film crew. He says to meet him off the helicopter at noon. Must dash – going into town for my lunch break. Back at the usual time. Marg x

Sven glanced at the slip of paper and cringed. Martin's return was also the afternoon Pippa was going home. He'd wanted to spend those last moments with her.

'Oh, no,' he complained. He was pleased that his best mate was returning, but torn because Pippa was about to leave him and nothing mattered more.

He had taken the afternoon off; his call had been to Charlie James asking if he would step in for him to guide a party of bird-watchers around the headland. He left Margaret a note telling her he would see her in the morning.

Pippa made her way to Porthcressa where she had arranged to meet Sven. They walked up the garden path together towards Beachside Cottage.

'I must get changed,' Sven said, opening the front door. He went upstairs. 'Come on up, see the rest of the house. I have a super bird book up here you can borrow.'

The rooms were smaller than Gilstone where they had spent most of their time. Pippa looked out of the window. *Oh my, what a lovely view of the bay.*

He put on clean shorts. Rob never thought to undress in front of her; instead, he took off his clothes in the bathroom. How he had distanced himself when he could have been helping the romance in a relationship. Yet she always undressed in his presence in the hope he might be more romantic. It didn't seem as if Rob understood true romance. What Pippa had experienced with Sven had blown her mind; how could she go back to Rob knowing the true meaning of affection?

Pippa realised how important Sven had become. It thrilled her to share his life. He pulled on his dark blue sweatshirt with the "Isles of Scilly" logo on the front, and zipped up his khaki shorts, then kissed her cheek. 'We'll drive to the beach. I've got a nice little spot where we can watch the world go by. Here's that book, by the way.'

Pippa took it from him and saw it contained real photos of birds and not drawings. She would take it home later and study it.

After packing a blanket in the rucksack, Sven opened the fridge door and raided the last of the beer before leaving.

'Beer, orange or cola?'

'Cola, please,' Pippa replied.

'Okay, ready? Shall we go, *elskling*?' He saw her puzzled look. 'It means *darling*.'

Pippa picked up her rucksack, smiling at his endearment. *Mm, elskling, what a nice word.* They closed the door behind them.

Driving to Pelistry beach, Sven said, 'It'll be sheltered up here and we can nestle in the dunes. No locals, only a few tourists.'

After a short walk with the picnic in the rucksack, he laid down the plaid blanket in the marram grass and raised his binoculars.

'It's raining over there, probably heading our way. We'll get a chance to eat, and if we're lucky it'll miss us.' The shower headed towards Tresco from the Western Isles. 'Oh look, see the shag,' said Sven, pointing beyond Tolls Island. 'I love it when they pack together in rafts like that. They always look so...how do you say it in English?'

'Snooty?' Pippa offered.

'Snooty? What does that mean? I've never heard of that word, it's a funny one.'

'It means "snobbish" or "toffee-nosed",' she said with a chuckle, and she flicked her finger under her nostrils to show him what she meant.

'Oh, ya, I know what you mean. That's a new one for me. Mm, snoo-tee,' he said with a chortle. 'Am I snoo-tee?'

'Now you're being daft.'

'Daft?' he teased her. 'Your accent always amuses me. Do they all speak that way in Yorkshire?'

Pippa giggled. 'Honestly, you are funny.' She shoved him into the sand where he landed on the blanket with a thud, and then put out her tongue at him. She turned up her nose and laughed. Sven grabbed her and they rolled in the sand together. He was almost of top of her before he kissed her passionately.

Pippa looked into his blue eyes, unable to speak. Her heart spoke passion and adoring every time she looked at him in that way.

Sven sat up, opened a beer, and then dropped the ring pull into his rucksack. Pippa opened the box of sandwiches.

'Always make sure you take these home,' he said, pointing to the ring pull. 'The gannets tend to make nests with all this stuff. Also those bloody plastic things, they get tangled up in birds' feet. You know, the ones that keep the beer cans packed together. The number of birds I've rescued with plastic around their necks too, it's dreadful to see them suffer in that way.'

He watched an older man cross to Tolls Island where, at high tide, the island became cut off from the beach. 'He's left it a bit late to be crossing over there.' Sven checked his watch. 'He should be okay for another hour, though.'

Pippa listened to the sounds of the sea, disturbed only by the lapping of the waves at the turn of the tide. The sun came out and the odour of beached kelp filled the air. Sand flies hopped in front of her as she watched a herring gull snatch a bite of a forlorn sandwich left behind by yesterday's tourist. She heard voices and the sound of footsteps from the path above her that seemed to vibrate a low thud underneath where they sat. Two more people came to the beach and they leaned their bikes on the grass.

'Dad, why do lobsters turn red when you cook them?' a child asked, and his father's answer faded on the breeze.

Peace prevailed. Three small boats rocked gently in the bay, and the Eastern Isles spanned the distant shore. The buzz of a light aircraft broke the peace, but was soon gone. The air soothed, warm over Pippa's skin, and was filled with the perfume of camomile and seaweed, alternating on a summer breeze.

Sven waited. He felt Pippa's calmness, and the time was right to ask questions. 'What was he like, your Daniel? I'd like to know, if you feel you can talk about it.' He put his arm around her.

Pippa smiled as she reminisced. 'Yes, sure, it helps me, I suppose. He was a cheeky little boy, but we had a lot of fun together. He would have been ten next birthday. He was a son that any mother would be proud of. A bit impulsive. You remind me of him, he had blond hair as well.'

'I would like to have children one day.'

Pippa smiled at him. 'That's nice,' she said, trying not to enlarge the subject. He smiled back at her and gave her a kiss.

Visitors to the beach continued to arrive, and the father and son team returned. 'Are you sure this is the right way?' said the young boy. 'And look, there are loads of limpet shells here.'

The man and boy jogged back along the footpath, stopping to do press-ups on the way. There was laughing and joking, the panting of breath as they ran, their voices melding into the dunes.

Nothing could have spoilt their day together. The laughing of the black-backed gulls, the scream of the terns and the wonderful beach to which he had brought her; it all seemed unreal, and Pippa never wanted it to stop.

Sven searched again through his binoculars, across the knoll of

Tolls Island and saw the man returning. Had he left it too late to cross the sand bar?

The man walked down the rocks with his camera swinging. He climbed down towards the shore, not realising that the tide had come in and the water had become deeper.

'Hey, Pippa, see that bloke over there? He's in trouble, I think. I might have to help him.'

'Oh, yeahh…he's not going to try and cross over there, is he?' Pippa peered through her binoculars.

The man seemed surprised to discover how quickly the tide had come in as he stood there looking helpless and marooned. He took his first steps into the strong current. 'Hey!' shouted Sven. 'Don't cross! It's dangerous.' But the man took no notice of the warning. Before Sven could get close to him, he was waist deep in the middle of the sand bar. The current had pushed him sideways and he fell in. He managed to stand up again and continued to wade the short distance to the shore. His pride seemed hurt and his camera ruined, but nothing more.

Sven called to him. 'You okay, sir?'

The man smiled and his voice echoed across the knoll. 'Yeah, I forgot the time and didn't realise how deep it gets.'

'You were lucky,' Sven said. 'You can easily get swept away out there.'

The man thanked him for his concern and walked in the other direction, dripping with every step and looking most uncomfortable.

Sven returned to Pippa. He raised his eyebrows and smiled as the man went on his way. 'I suppose it could have been worse. I can never understand why they ignore the warnings.'

'His camera's probably ruined.' Pippa didn't mean to chuckle. 'Poor bloke. I hope he's got a towel and an understanding wife.'

Sven returned to his cosy spot on the sand and reminded himself of what he had to tell Pippa.

'Oh yes, I forgot, I have to tell you something. Some news. It's a bit difficult really.'

Pippa's heart missed a beat. Was he about to say this was the end of their time together? No, it couldn't be.

'Don't look so worried.' He smiled. 'It's good news. Martin is back from South Africa, and, well… I'm told today that he arrived in Bristol with Andrea. He's bringing the film crew back with him from the BBC. I have to meet him from the helicopter.'

'Wow, how lovely – will I be able to meet him?' Pippa was relieved that for a change it wasn't bad news.

'Yes, sure, but there is a problem – he's coming home the day you leave. I didn't want to be *disturbed*, if you see what I mean. I want to be with you.'

'Oh yes, of course, oh dear. So what will you do?'

'I thought about it and maybe we could all have lunch together. I mean, it's not an ideal goodbye. The timing is all wrong.' He had to find a way to bid farewell to Pippa while welcoming Martin and the film crew; it wasn't going to be easy. 'I think it would be good to meet up for lunch at The Old Town Cafe. You could meet the crew and we could slip away afterwards a couple of hours before the ship sails.'

Pippa agreed and gave a sigh. She was thrilled about meeting The Birdman but was reminded that time was not on their side. 'You know I met that nice couple from Holland? Did I tell you he's very ill and unlikely to live another few more months?'

'No, you didn't. But I've seen them on *Lily* and I thought he looked a bit sickly.'

'Well, I keep meeting them on my travels around the island, such a nice couple. Jan has a tumour – it's a dreadful thing to happen, it made me consider that you never know what's coming at you in life. Then there was a chap I met back home, walking with his wife in the cemetery. He told me I would find my direction around the corner where it's been waiting to meet me. He had lost a family member too. That's so true, you know – he was right. What I mean to say is that my time with you and this second chance could be a lost opportunity. When I look at Jan and Marijke I think how happiness can so easily be snatched away, and with my situation too it's very unfair and I should make the most of it.'

Sven tried to speak and Pippa stopped him. 'Let me go on. You see, I have a plan. You won't be able to contact me directly at home because of Rob so I'll phone you when he's not around. It might take me a while to sort it all out, maybe six weeks. I'll just have to tell him straight about us. I honestly do feel very bad about what I've done to him, but I think it's time I moved on. I really can't imagine myself into old age with Rob the way he is.'

'Yes I agree but…six weeks! I'll never last out all that time.' Sven's face stiffened. 'Once you get home you might change your mind about me.' He took a breath, thinking he might get the wrong response.

Pippa sensed his impulsiveness again. She reached over for his hand, and then hugged him. She kissed him for his words. 'Don't worry, I'll come back.'

Sven lay on his back and looked up at her. 'Six weeks is a long time. I do understand, honest I do, but I don't want us to be apart for *that* long.'

'Yeah, I know,' she said. Could she be brave enough to tell Rob about Sven? Perhaps she should leave Whitby and say nothing; she didn't want him to know she had cheated on him. Just leaving would be easier on them all. She would tell Joan and then leave. Her best friend would find it hard to understand, but this was a chance for a new life and she had to take it.

Sven began to look lost. 'I can't help the way I feel about you. It's a great feeling, but I'm also aware all this could go wrong, and it scares me.'

Pippa, concerned that Sven was upset, tried to smooth things over. Looking in her rucksack, she took out a piece of card and a pen, and wrote down her phone number. 'I'll phone you first – I need to be sure Rob isn't around. Pity you don't have an answer phone at Beachside Cottage.'

'I don't like answer machines. They'd be phoning me all hours, day and night.'

Pippa laughed. 'You shouldn't be such a popular guy.'

The weather closed in over the beach, and they dashed up the dunes and hurried back to where Sven had parked the van.

Within a few minutes, they had returned to Sven's cottage. Sven had gone to the bathroom when the phone rang. Pippa answered it for him.

'Hei, Sven!' said the voice.

'Oh, hello, I am just answering the phone for Sven. He is in the shower at the moment, can I help you?'

'Oh, are you a friend of Sven? This is his mother speaking in Norway.'

'Well, sort of, I'm kind of holding the fort here. Can I leave a message for him?'

'Yes, please ask him to call me back. It's fairly important but not urgent.'

'Oh okay, will do. He'll be down soon I think.'

Pippa felt an anxious mother on the other end of the phone and realised neither of them wanted to get involved in motherly conversation.

'That's fine, and thanks for passing on the message. Bye.'

After his shower, Sven picked up the phone and dialled Norway. Minutes later, he put the phone down with some deliberation and blew out his cheeks. He had done his best to keep his side of the conversation minimal. Hearing his mother mentioning Astrid had given him an acrid taste in his mouth. He could see Mads on the bed apologising to him, and was reminded of the look on Astrid's face when he had walked in on them in the act of having sex and how he'd punched Mads in the face. He had adored her, and the bitch had killed all his faith in human nature. He had worked hard trying to forget her. Why did his mother have to mention her today of all days?

Sven tried to smile to cover up his feelings. It was too late. Pippa had seen it, and he didn't know what to say to her. If this was the time to tell a lie, he had to do it to prevent her from worrying.

186

He would bend the truth. He would tell her how his mother sometimes interfered too much. As he was an only child, there was no one left at home except his father on whom to lavish her attentions.

'Motherly problems?' Pippa asked with a grin. She placed two mugs of tea on the table.

'Yes, she goes over the top sometimes even though I'm not in Norway any more. She wants to come here next summer and for me to go back there before the winter.' He remembered a conversation he'd had with her only three weeks before. He hated himself for lying.

'Will you go?' Pippa asked, wondering how something like that could possibly cause him so much pain.

'I might do, it depends how it goes,' he said. 'I can't go home just like that. She doesn't seem to understand. I have the "Twitchers" month coming up in October, but I might be able to go at Christmas instead – we shall see. Sometimes she just bugs me, always making plans for me instead of letting me do my own stuff. I'm a big boy now.' He grinned. 'They can afford to come here, but I don't earn a lot to go on aeroplanes these days.'

'Aw, Sven, you're lucky to have a mother. She obviously cares about you. I wish I'd had a mother to care for me. Dad was great, but he couldn't teach me to knit or tell me about having babies and all that life stuff – I had to rely on hearsay and friends, and sometimes it was difficult.'

'Well, you and me, we've got a lot to plan in the next three days.' Sven tried to change the subject, but inside he was seething.

'Let's just enjoy the rest of the day together,' Pippa said. 'The weather has changed and it looks nice out there now. Shall we take a walk?'

He hoped there was no need to get upset about it or to worry Pippa. Living on Scilly sometimes made it harder for people to get in touch. Nevertheless, what was his mother trying to tell him? He wished sometimes she would just come right out with it and say what she felt instead of hiding behind her words.

Chapter Twenty-One

Rob arranged to meet John Grover in Harrogate. He had driven there, not knowing what to expect. His father had already spoken with John on the phone a few days before and he seemed fine with his plan, his mother less so.

In the Hotel Royal York, Rob strode into reception and asked for John Grover. The lawyer was already waiting across the room in the hall and introduced himself.

'I've arranged a private room,' he assured his client.

'Oh?' Rob queried nervously.

'First I have to ask you how you feel about getting in touch with your sister and brother, Penelope and Bruce Haines.'

Rob made a face of angst. 'It's rather daunting, all this stuff. I've spent the last week or so thinking about it. I'm not sure really, but I would love to, I suppose, though it's all very odd.'

'Okay, so what if I gave you the opportunity to meet with them this afternoon?'

'What, today?'

'Mm, yes, today.'

'Oh, bloody hell, I hadn't thought about it.' Rob panicked. He placed his hand on his chest. 'Oh, I don't know about today. I think I'll have to sit down, I need a drink.'

'Follow me.' John led the way to a room off the hallway. 'I'll bring you one.'

'Are they in there?' Rob asked with suspicion.

'No, but the reason you are here is that Bruce and Penny Haines

188

are dying to meet you, and I have the will from your parents. I thought we could do this together, but only if you feel you want to.'

Rob's anxiety was all too obvious. He was sweating – it was a warm day, but all these changes were too overwhelming. He hesitated for a moment and pursed his lips, pausing for thought.

'You mean... I'll meet them today?'

'Isn't that what you wanted?'

'Er...yes, of course, but I didn't think...oh heck, this is hard. But okay...let's do it,' he said bravely.

John Grover left Rob by himself for a while. He wanted to check that his other two clients had made it to the hotel and give Rob time to take it all in.

Rob sat alone, terrified he had entered into something he couldn't handle. What was he doing here? A will? Penny and Bruce? How would he get used to it all? For a moment, he wished Pippa were back and he could run out of the hotel, never to be seen again. The door to the street wasn't far away, what if he...? No he would wait.

John discovered Bruce and Penny Haines huddled in a corner of the bar, their glasses almost empty. He held out his hand and in turn they shook it.

'Hello, you two – glad you could make it. Traffic okay? I may as well tell you that your brother wants to see you.' He gave a cheerful but nervous smile.

Penny stood facing her brother. 'Oh my goodness, I'm not ready for this.'

'Don't worry. Rob is as nervous as you are.' John turned toward the door.

'Ready?' he asked.

He led them through the lounge and into the hallway before entering the room where Rob sat.

Startled, Rob turned around. He saw Penny standing there, a young girl with a nose like his, dark hair like his, and the same coloured eyes. Her brother was a little older. Penny wore smart grey trousers and a red blouse with a blue and red striped scarf at the neck. She reminded him of one of the air hostesses he had seen in a *British Airways* advert.

She stepped forward with a look of apprehension as she strode in her high heels across the wooden floor. Immediately her perfume wafted towards him. *Oh God, she's lovely. What do I say?* His heart almost missed a beat. He searched her eyes, and before either of them could speak, he knew she was his sister. *This is weird. Bruce looks so familiar too.*

Penny cried, 'I can't believe it, you look so much like my dad.'

'Oh my God, you two are so…' Rob was lost for words, tears about to flood his eyes. A powerful sense of déjà vu stabbed his feelings.

Bruce wore a blue shirt, grey jacket and jeans. Rob used to imagine how his brother would look if he had one. Bruce looked exactly as he had imagined. He drew in a deep breath and felt a shiver permeate his spine.

Bruce blew out his cheeks, seemingly overwhelmed by Rob. He saw Penny cry and stood back to allow his sister to have her moment.

Rob sensed everything happening at once. He had waited all these years with a fantasy that he would find his real family and here they were, right in front of him. The sensation scared him until Penny put her arms around him.

'They found you. I'm so glad they found you.' She choked back her tears. She kissed Rob on both cheeks and hugged him tight. The resemblance to her father became so familiar it was almost like looking at the photo of him when he was the same age as Rob.

Rob knew this was his real family. As a child, he had wanted a brother or sister before discovering it wasn't possible. Now the emotion was too much to bear and he cried in Penny's arms. His feelings of his bad times with Daniel, his uncertainties about Pippa, and his loneliness about his adoption just spilled out of him. His life had been like the toys that Pippa had stuffed in the wardrobe, waiting for someone to pick them up and love them again. At last, he felt the relief from the unsolved mysteries surrounding his childhood.

When the tears and introductions had died, Rob saw how Penny couldn't keep her eyes off him. Rob couldn't keep his eyes off Bruce; it was like looking at a mirror image of himself. They all kept sighing, chuckling and laughing, then crying again, finding their feelings and calming their emotions.

'Maybe when we get this over you will come and stay with us and we can show you lots of photos of our parents,' Penny said. 'Later on I'll show you a few I brought with me.'

She kept putting her arms around Rob. He seemed to adore all the attention and had to keep reminding himself she was his sister.

'Where's your wife?' Bruce asked.

For the last few hours Rob had put Pippa behind him.

'She's away for three weeks, but unfortunately we've both been through difficult times, like you. We can talk about it later, but I think we'd better chat about us first. I am so thrilled to meet you both, it's been...well, I don't think I need to tell you, do I?'

John Grover tactfully left the room, and a short while later returned, holding a cup of coffee. 'Now, let's talk business. Take a seat, all of you,' he said. 'My colleague, Stephen Carmichael, has already discussed the situation with Rob. It is so sad to think neither your mother nor father will ever know their son. My condolences to you both, and of course to Rob, who I'm sure feels sad about this too. Your father died only six weeks ago. This is also very sad for me because I knew him as a fine doctor and client. He was my friend too. It was only in the last three weeks that I managed to confirm the information about Rob, hence some delays in the reading of this will. It seems that your parents – and by "your" I mean Rob as well – it was their wish for you all to find each other again and share in the family inheritance. It wasn't the fault of Rob that he was adopted, nor was it the fault of your mother. We all know the story now, so I won't go into that.'

John Grover cleared his throat and took out the paperwork from his briefcase. He opened *The Last Will and Testament of Peter Haines.*

'The will states that in the event of your father's death the estate is to be split three ways. We would always have kept Rob's share and placed it into a trust fund. Your father stated that if, by your fiftieth birthday...' he turned to Rob '...if we hadn't found you, the money would be split again between Penny and Bruce.'

Rob looked down at his hands. What right did he have to take away part of their inheritance? He was sure Bruce was thinking the same way.

'It was what your parents wanted,' John assured him.

'I miss my mum,' Penny said. 'I'll tell you about her and Dad. We haven't had an easy time .'

'I can relate to that,' Rob said with a tight smile.

'Okay, shall we continue?' John realised their sadness and bewilderment. He pushed his spectacles further on to his nose. 'I have some documents for you all to sign and then we can arrange for probate to go ahead and money to be placed in your respective bank accounts. There could be some tax to pay, but I'll explain all that soon. Bruce, Penny, your father wanted me to handle the sale of your house, and as you are both at university we can arrange all the necessary details. You are all over twenty-one so there shouldn't be any problems. The house is split three ways and there is the capital in the bank – a substantial sum. Once we get the probate sorted, you should all be comfortable for the rest of your lives. There's something in the region of 300,000 pounds each, plus the sale of the house.'

Rob gulped; his father was a millionaire? He was going to be rich, but it was all too much to take in. He realised he had stepped into a family he hardly knew and they were going to give him part ownership of a house and a share of the proceeds. It was like winning the football pools. For a moment, he thought he was going to be sick. What would he do with all that money? He could hardly believe what he was hearing and naively thought he'd better say something.

'Can't Bruce and Penny still live in their own house? Isn't there a way round this? I mean…'

'Well, they could, but it's a big house and will take a lot of upkeep,' John explained.

'I don't really want to sell the house,' said Bruce. 'It *is* my home after all.'

Rob thought about it. 'Can I help?' he said, thinking it might be possible to leave Henrietta Street and start afresh.

'It's a *very* large house, Rob. Your father had a good job.' John gave a faint smile.

'How large?' Rob asked.

'It's got ten bedrooms,' Penny said. 'Dad used some of it for his private work.'

'Oh heck, that is big.' A spontaneous idea came to Rob. 'Bruce, what are you studying at uni?'

'Medicine.'

Rob chuckled. 'Did they tell you I'm a charge nurse at a local hospital?'

Bruce smiled. 'Really? That's weird – I mean, you kind of following in Dad's footsteps without knowing it.'

'Look, I know this is too soon – I wouldn't want to jump in as a total stranger and take all this away from you – but as I'm here maybe I can help. Perhaps this is something we could discuss in the coming weeks. I fear it might tear us apart, all this money. We have to do something sensible and agreeable to all of us.' Rob realised he had become the older brother already.

Penny hugged Rob. 'Welcome to the Haines family, big brother.'

Rob paused, his real name was Robert Haines, he thought.

He caught the look on Bruce's face; Penny was still quite young and overenthusiastic.

'It's a big relief, Rob,' said Bruce. 'Your absence in our family has caused us a lot of pain over the years. If only Mum could have found you before it was too late – it's so sad.'

John Grover agreed with Rob: it was something they could discuss between themselves. 'Let me know what you decide,' he said. 'I will get back to you within a week or so. In the meantime, I must go now. I have another client to see back at the office. Probate on these matters takes a few months, so don't expect anything to happen immediately. I'll stay in touch so I can explain it all to you. If there's anything you need to ask me in the next few days, call me – otherwise have a wonderful day together, all of you. There's a lot of catching up to do, eh?'

They chorused their thanks to John for his help and he left the hotel lobby.

Rob sat with Penny on the leather sofa in the bar. The hotel was quiet except for a few locals standing with a pint in their hands.

'Isn't this amazing? I'm so sorry to hear about your parents.' Rob suddenly realised he meant his parents, too. 'It's going to take me some time to get used to this, and you guys as well, eh?'

'Do you want to see a photo, Rob?' Penny asked. She took out a large picture of the whole family taken when she was about sixteen years old. 'That's me and Bruce with Mum and Dad.'

Rob held the photo and his heart sank. His mother, Fiona, had been a beautiful woman. Her eyes seemed to reach out to him. His father, dark-haired and handsome, stood proudly with his children. Rob should have been in this photo; it was as if he had died or never existed. He wanted to rage but couldn't do it; instead, he opted to tell them his feelings.

'I'm sad when I see this. Cheated perhaps – lost for words.' He wiped the tears from his eyes, and Penny put her arm around him.

'I know. It must have been awful for you. We've been through so much in the last few years. Mum never gave up looking for you, and it affected the relationship I had with her. We used to argue about it. I could never believe this day would actually happen.' Penny linked her arm with Rob's and couldn't stop gazing at him.

'Oh my God! Where do we go from here?' Rob asked, wiping

away his tears. He was glad to be in a corner of the room where the other customers couldn't see him.

'Tell us about you, Rob,' said Bruce. 'We don't know anything except John said you'd had a dreadful tragedy too.'

'Well, I'm not sure it's appropriate to tell you right now in view of all your own recent problems. For now I'll only say we had a dreadful bereavement too.' Rob knew he didn't have the strength to walk that path again.

'It's okay,' Bruce consoled. 'We're trying to get used to it, but you never do, I suppose.'

Rob told them briefly about Daniel and then tried to change the subject.

'Oh, Rob, I'm so sorry,' said Bruce. 'Maybe we can start afresh, all three of us.'

'So, your wife?' Penny asked.

'We are kind of lost souls. It's a long story. Meeting you couldn't have come at a better time. I rather suspect we might all need each other now. Perhaps you will meet her very soon. She's on a break, getting some respite from our sorrows. I've told her, but she is in Cornwall and hasn't really had a chance to take it all in.'

'I hope she will soon,' Penny said. 'I just wish Mum could have seen you.'

Rob nodded in agreement. 'John told me your dad died three months after having had a car accident that wasn't his fault, eh? It was strange because I heard about it and never thought he was my *dad*. He was so near to me and yet so far away, I can hardly bear to think about it.'

'Yeah, hit and run,' said Penny. 'He lived in a lot of pain for a while and they did everything to save him, but he went downhill and never recovered. We tried to get him a liver transplant, but he passed away before one became available.' She gave a knowing look at Bruce. 'The police are still looking for the person who did this to him.'

Rob sighed. 'This is so dreadful for us all, but we must get together very soon and discuss our future. I'll give you my phone number and I'll come down and see you in the next couple of weeks. I'm so thrilled to have met you. It's going to take some getting used to, isn't it? My adoptive parents are keen to hear how I got on today, so I'll phone them tonight. They are called Ralph and Sally Lambton, which of course means Lambton is my second name. They would love to have met you, but they live in Spain now. Perhaps they'll come back for a reunion party.'

Penny went to visit the powder room before they left, and Bruce waited with Rob to say goodbye.

'I'm sorry about all this, Rob, it's so difficult for me to think I have an older brother, but it seems you're an okay kind of guy,' said Bruce. 'Let's agree to get to know each other better, eh?'

'That's fine with me, honest it is. I fully appreciate you might need time to accept me into the family. I rather suspect we will be meeting up quite a bit in the coming weeks and months. I promise to help you as much as I can.' Rob patted Bruce on the back and gave him a brotherly hug. 'Thanks. You're an okay guy as well. I'm just so overwhelmed today.'

'Yeah, me too – it's all bizarre stuff, isn't it? The things life throws at you. Always when you think you've made it through, something like this turns up,' Bruce said with a smile.

Rob shook hands with his brother and smiled at him as Penny returned.

'Bye, Penny, it was lovely to meet you both. I'll call you soon when my wife gets back from Cornwall.' He gave her a hug, unsure how he should treat her.

As he left the hotel and crossed the road to the car, he took out a cigarette and placed it to his lips, then paused. He removed it and put it back in the packet. He passed a litterbin and popped the packet inside. Today would be the day he gave up smoking.

Chapter Twenty-Two

Joan sat in her kitchen, her chin resting on cupped hands. She'd phoned Rob but he was at work. She wanted to die but remembered she had Jordan. She cried into the tea towel she was holding, never having felt as low as she felt today. The situation with Terry had finally hit her with a stab.

Terry had been home again from the rig. She only knew that because his mother had phoned to ask when she was coming round with Jordan. She thought that she could match make her son back with his wife. Joan thought she had wanted Terry back, but questioned her feelings. Perhaps she should phone him and get him to leave on better terms. She needed him to stay in touch with Jordan, despite what she had told him. She wanted company, someone to talk with, and was now literally left holding the baby.

'Tel, it's me,' Joan cried down the phone. 'Why don't you come round here this afternoon and we can talk?'

'Okay, I will,' he said, relenting. 'See you, love.'

She found it hard to accept it when he still called her "love".

During the afternoon, Terry arrived and embraced her. Touching her was nice, but not in *that* way.

'Hello, you,' he said to Jordan. 'What a big boy you are for Daddy, eh?'

Jordan put out a pet lip. Terry thought he'd better take things slowly.

'I still care for you, Tel,' Joan said, wanting to kiss him. She would try one more time, but somehow what she felt didn't seem right any more.

'Don't, Joan, I'm with Frank now. We are partners.'

'But can't we stay married and be together?' she said, not fully appreciating the partnership thing.

'No, pet, we can't, sorry. I told you I would still care for you and Jordan, and to be honest with you I feel very sorry for you at this moment. Anyway, Rob always seems to be round here these days.' Terry gave Joan a sideways glance.

Joan's anger got the better of her. 'Don't be so bloody stupid, Tel. He's Pippa's husband, and your best friend! He's fixing your bike. I know we get on well, but Pippa hasn't left him, you know. She's coming back home soon. I think now you're being ridiculous.'

'If there was anyone in this world I would rather have to keep an eye on you and Jordan, it would be Rob,' Terry said.

'What d'ye mean? You're his dad, for God's sake. *You* should be looking after us. This is…'

Terry shrugged his shoulders. 'I suppose Rob told you about his windfall. He got 300,000 quid from his real parents and a big house in the country. He has to share it with his brother and sister. He's a rich guy now. He has a new family. He'll take the money and run, and we'll never see him again. By all accounts we might not see Pippa either.'

Joan slumped into the sofa. 'I don't know about that.'

'I'm sorry, Joan – about us, I mean. It isn't fair, is it? Are we going to go ahead with this divorce?'

'No! I don't want a divorce, Tel. I want things as they always were.'

'Joan, pet, you can't do that. I've come out, you know, gay, and that's all there is to it. You have to let me go. We don't have a marriage and never really have had. Start by being honest with yourself, it has to be this way.'

Joan cried, and Jordan, not understanding the situation, thought he had to cry as well. Terry comforted them both and encouraged Jordan to sit on his knee. 'We have to do this, Joanie, really we do. It makes sense.'

'What about our Jordan, *our* son?' she said sniffing.

'I'll stay in touch, I promise.' It was all he could say; he had never been very good in a crisis.

He spent another hour with Jordan and left the house as he had done on his last visit. It was then that Joan realised he may never return.

Carole had taken Jordan to sleep at her house, and Joan tried to busy herself. A bottle of painkillers stood on the coffee table. She had meant to take a couple. She had a headache, a very bad headache. Feeling at her lowest ebb, she wondered if life was worth living without Terry. What if Rob and Pippa left her too? Would Rob really take the money and run as Terry had said? She sat and cried herself ill. Her mind wasn't working properly. With every second she felt sick, and the longer she lay there the more she wanted to die. She knew she loved Jordan, and wished she could rescue herself from the terrible desertion that had happened to her. Pippa's marriage was on the rocks, Terry had left, and now she was going to be alone in her misery. She had always been the brave one, holding the flag for everyone else, and now there was no one to hold her flag when she needed it.

She thought she could hear Jordan crying, but he wasn't at home. His tears and screaming became louder with every second she lay there. She tried in desperation to reach out to him; she was sure she could hear him. On a whim, she did something stupid. She opened the bottle of painkillers, and without a further thought she didn't take one tablet, she swallowed as many pills as she could, forcing them into her mouth and swallowing them with a glass of water. In her frenzy, she wanted to end it all. Nothing happened. Her headache was still there and the sickness got worse. She knew she wasn't dead yet.

Realising what she had done, she tried to retch by sticking her fingers down her throat. 'Oh shit, what did I do? Jordan, I'm sorry. Mummy loves you. Bluurp! I wanna die, let me die!' Her voice was heard by no one. She lay on the settee and awaited her fate, wondering if she should call an ambulance in the realisation she had made a dreadful mistake. She stared up at the ceiling and watched a huge spider crawl along the border on the wallpaper. The creature just got bigger and bigger, and she shut her eyes, hiding her face in the cushion in case it landed on her. The pain in her head became unbearable and she blacked out.

Half an hour later, the phone rang. The ringing noise in her ears made her stir and she reached out a floppy arm and managed to pick up the receiver from the coffee table, but said nothing.

'Hi, Joan – it's me, Rob. Just thought I would call you and see if I can come round to finish the bike. Did Terry come round to see you?' There was a silence on the phone. He could hear sobbing. 'Joan? Joan? It's Rob. Are you there?'

'I'm not going to be here much longer,' Joan sobbed, wishing she hadn't done it because she felt dreadful. The pain was still bad and sleep seemed to dominate her head.

'What the hell have you done?' he said.

'I've taken something, lots of something.' Her voice seemed to crack.

'Where's Jordan?' Rob asked.

'With…ohhh,' Joan said, breathing heavily. '…Feel terrible…' Her voice went quiet.

'God, Joan, stay awake, I'll get some help.'

Rob dialled 999, attempting to stay calm while speaking with the emergency services. Knowing Terry was home, he called him at his parents' house and discovered he had left for Aberdeen. 'Buggeration!' he scolded. He told Terry's father nothing; it was too early to alarm his parents.

He called the ward sister to say he would be late, then raced round to Joan's on his way to work. Much to his distress, he found Joan lying there and the ambulance paramedics trying to revive her.

He escorted the ambulance paramedics to the women's ward and assisted the doctor with her treatment. She looked very white and sick. He held her hand and talked to her to make her stay awake.

'Joan? Joan, love, it's me, Rob.' He was almost in tears seeing her close to death.

He tried for another two hours to keep her conscious. 'Don't leave us, Joanie, it's going to be okay. I'm here, it's Rob. Joanie, come on gal, it's going to be all right.'

She came around for a few moments, sniffed, and tears ran down her face. 'I've got nothing left now, my life is ruined,' she groaned. 'Everything I ever wanted has been taken away. I wanted to die. I hate you for that.' Her voice faded to a croak and then she was sick.

'No, you didn't want to die, surely, and you don't hate me. You were feeling very sorry for yourself, and you can't say it was your fault. You've been through so much in the last few days,' Rob said. 'Come on, Joan, stay with me, love.' He rattled her hand. 'Let's talk about something nice.'

'There isn't anything that's nice any more. I've got nothing left now. I lost Terry to some bloke or another and I feel I'm losing...' She fell asleep again.

'Joan, come on, don't give up. Jordan needs his mum. I care about you. I always will – you're my best friend, remember?' He patted her hand. There was no response.

He waited by her side for another hour and monitored her blood pressure and heart. He did his best to keep her awake. He thought she looked pathetic lying there, pale and tear-stained. It was not the Joan he knew; the woman who was always neat and a bit old-fashioned. He had lost his own son, and now Joan had tried to take her life. *What if she had...* no, he didn't want to think about it. He wasn't going to let his old school friend die as well. In his own way, he had special feelings for her. 'Come on, Joan, stay with me. I can't live with myself knowing I might lose you.'

Chapter Twenty-Three

It was after five o'clock when Pippa returned from seeing Jan and Marijke leave on the boat. She had embraced them, knowing that she might never see Jan again. It was a poignant goodbye moment. Marijke whispered in her ear, 'Follow your heart and your heart will tell you what to do.' Pippa smiled, and Marijke promised to return to Scilly in the future. 'Where can I find you?' she asked.

'Oh, just send a letter to Beachside Cottage, I will be waiting for you,' Pippa replied in a half jest, but the other half of her quip made her wonder if she would manage to return. She hugged Jan and wished with all her heart he wouldn't die. She knew there were people with worse problems than herself. Losing a child was bad enough, but when you knew you were going to die soon, surely that must be the ultimate heartache. Waiting around for it to happen, becoming thinner and thinner with each day, starving to death. Jan had taught her to be strong. She waved them into the distance, thinking that soon she would do the same heartbreaking journey. She turned away and walked briskly into town, trying not to cry.

Sven pulled up in the van at Beachside Cottage. He showered, pulled on a clean T-shirt he'd not ironed, and opened a beer. Sitting in the garden on a green plastic chair, he closed his eyes in the sun and sighed to himself. The Norwegian words in his head were thinking about Pippa. It was her last week on Scilly and he wanted to show her the rest of the islands and do some more birding.

How would he fit all this in with the tour boats? He hoped and prayed Astrid wouldn't phone him. He tried to put it to the back of his mind.

Just then, he thought of an idea to help pull him out of his negativity. An evening trip down the Telegraph Road on bikes would be great; he could include a walk to see the Loaded Camel rock formation on Porthellick Beach. There was so much to see, and so little time. He seemed to have spent it all in bed. He smiled to himself. *She's lovely.*

He wondered how the plan would work when she returned to Whitby. He would wait for her to call him as she had explained; he hoped she would. He could trust her, but maybe Pippa was right – a holiday romance? She might return to her husband after all. The phone rang, disturbing his thoughts.

'It's me, Sven. God, this phone box stinks of fags,' Pippa said as she opened the door to let in the fresh air.

'Oh, hello you. Why didn't you just come round here?'

'Just checking you're back, that's all – save walking up the road for nothing.'

'I'll make you sausage, egg and chips.'

'Now there's an offer a woman can't refuse! Sounds to me like good Norwegian bachelor-pad food. Okay, that's nice, love to.' Pippa chuckled at her own humour.

'I gather you can ride a bike?' Sven asked.

'A bike? Yes, sure, but it's been a very long time,' she said, wondering what he was going to come out with next.

'When you get here I'll tell you why, and I've got some news for you.'

'Oh, okay – half an hour?'

'Half a minute! I miss you.' He laughed, knowing she was only five minutes away.

'Okay, I'll be as quick as I can. See you at your place.'

'Love you.' He replaced the receiver.

*

Pippa dashed home to change her clothes. On her way out again she locked the door behind her. At Beachside Cottage Sven pulled her inside in case Nanette Bell saw her. He promptly closed the door. Once Nanette knew about Pippa, there would be no stopping her. Perhaps it was too late anyway.

'Hello, my love.' Sven kissed her. Then he kissed her again, and yet again. 'Mm…you look gorgeous.'

'Who ironed your T-shirt?' Pippa asked with a grin.

'Oh, I came in and threw it on myself.'

'You need a good woman around here.' She put her arms around his waist and kissed him again. How wonderful she felt in his presence and how much her confidence had grown.

'I suppose I do, really,' he replied with a grin and gave her a hug.

'Now, tell me about this bike thing,' demanded Pippa.

'Our meal is almost ready. We'll talk about it when we sit down, eh?'

Pippa laid the table while Sven brought in the meal: two sausages each, two fried eggs, baked beans, and a mountain of chips. They sat down to eat. Sven patted the bottle of tomato ketchup and the sauce splurged over the chips.

'I got another call today to confirm the time Martin is coming.'

'Isn't he the same guy from that Cornish wildlife programme on the TV?' Pippa was curious, having read a recent local article about him.

'Ya, you guessed it, eh?'

'Wow, he's gorgeous,' she teased. 'How exciting.'

Sven gave a nonchalant reply. 'No, it's me that's gorgeous – or so you keep telling me.'

She giggled at his comment. 'Sounds wonderful.'

'So let's talk about this evening. I thought we'd do a bike ride around the island, go to some places you've never been yet.' He ripped a paper tissue out of the Kleenex box and wiped a blob of tomato sauce from Pippa's lip. 'Looks like you're wounded.'

'Oh! Right. Yes…that would be nice, let's do it! Although I'll have to ask you to ride slowly, because I'm not used to it.' Pippa rolled her eyes at him.

'There is so much to see here, I don't want you to miss it all. We seem to have been so wrapped up in each other, I almost forgot about showing you the rest of the place.'

He put the last chip on his fork and fed it to her. 'For you.'

Pippa closed her cutlery on the plate. 'I'll have to go back to Gilstone and pick up some things, though, let the dinner settle down first,' she explained.

'I'll come round with the bikes and we'll set off at what…say, er…seven?' Sven looked at his watch. 'I gotta go and see someone first about a bike for you.'

'Okay, that's fine.' Pippa stood up from the table. 'I'll get ready now, and let you get on with it. Great sausages, weren't they? Thanks.'

She was glad of the walk; it gave her a chance to think. Whatever Sven had in mind, she had the feeling, judging by his enthusiasm, that it would be fun. Smiling to herself all the way home, she couldn't wait to find out what he'd planned. *Riding a bike, me on a bike! Who would have thought it? It's a pity I don't do more of this at home – too hilly.*

Seven o'clock and Sven waited outside Gilstone with two bikes. 'I borrowed this one, I think it will be the right size. It has six gears. Are you ready?'

Pippa smiled at him. His sea-blown hair probably hadn't been combed since he got up this morning, and it didn't seem to matter. I think it makes him look more desirable, she thought as she straddled the frame of the bike.

She set off and wobbled her first few yards. She felt Sven's steady hand against her back. 'I'm getting the hang of it now. Gosh, it's been ages. You never really forget, do you?'

She rode up the hill towards the church, puffing and panting with Sven behind her.

'I'll have to get you fit. Don't stop pedalling, and put it in a lower gear, Pippa.' He turned left near the top of the hill, and they rode together past the school and along the narrow roads towards the bottom of Telegraph Road.

'We'll come back down that road eventually.' Sven pointed it out to her as they passed the junction. 'First, I want to take you to see the Loaded Camel. You can only see it properly on a side view, and we didn't get chance to take a proper look last week.'

Pippa puffed her way along the lanes until they made it, cycling past the flower farm at Lunnon. Up and down the hills they cycled until she got off the bike feeling breathless. Sven stopped at the top and waited for her.

'Well take a walk.' He pointed and leaned his bike on the grass.

Pippa parked her bike up against a stone wall and followed him down the path towards Porth Hellick Beach.

'There it is, Pippa – look.'

'Oh yes, I see, it does look like a camel with a pack on its back. Oh that's brilliant,' she said, enthralled. She stood awhile, feeling comforted with Sven's arm around her waist, breathless and slightly muscle-torn after cycling. Together they stared out beyond the bay and then Sven kissed her. 'Mm, you are lovely,' he said. 'Come on, let's walk a little further.'

They made their way past a yellow burst of gorse bushes. The soles of Pippa's sandals were muddy, and Sven stepped over a puddle. 'Best we continue on our way now before it gets to dusk,' he said. 'It's not so hilly now, the worst is over.'

They rode on, passing Pelistry, a place Pippa already knew from her ride in the van, and then cycled through the lanes and hedgerows where the honeysuckle and fuchsia bloomed, entwined between the stone walls. They turned the bend towards Holy Vale, a tropical paradise nestling in a small niche in the island's geography. The palm trees and flowers were in full bloom; the blue agapanthus, and the aroma of rosemary and camomile filled the air on a summer evening.

'Wow! Smell that!' said Pippa as she took in the fragrance of the honeysuckle. 'And look at the clematis on the wall of that lovely old house, it's delightful.' She began to feel her muscles had stretched to their limit. 'I'd like to walk a little now.'

'Okay, let's do that – get a chance to talk a bit, too,' Sven replied, hoping to discover more of how she felt about leaving the islands. He got off his bike and walked alongside her.

'What do you want to talk about?' Pippa asked. 'Let's sit on this seat awhile.' She parked her bike against a tree.

They sat together on a bench in a shady spot away from the road and held hands. The bees buzzed in the clover on the grass verge and a helicopter pounded the air as it passed over them. They looked up and watched it disappear over the treetops.

She turned towards him and he cupped her face with his hands and kissed her. 'Pippa, I love you, honest I do, cross my heart I do.'

Pippa's chest pounded with joy; he had told her so many times – how could she turn her back on him now?

'I know. I'll come back to you, I promise. It might take a bit of time to get organised, but I don't want this life any more with Rob.'

'Oh, Pippa, I love you and my life feels more complete now.' Sven lingered in her arms; he laid his head on her lap as he stretched out on the bench, looking up at her.

'You're crying,' he said as she turned her head away from him.

It was a cry she had longed for. At last, someone truly loved her and had told her so. She had to return here; he was the most wonderful person she had ever met. He really did love her, she knew it. Nothing must stop her coming back to Scilly.

'Sorry,' she sniffed, 'you made me very happy when you said those words.'

It dawned on her that the man at the cemetery in Whitby had been her guardian angel. She recalled his words. 'Maybe you'll find direction around the corner where it's been waiting to meet you.' She wiped away her tears of joy. *This is it!* She smiled down on Sven and looked into his eyes, thinking how lucky she was.

Sven checked his watch. 'Let's move on,' he suggested, 'before we lose the light. There are even more surprises at the end of this lane.'

They got on their bikes again, and Sven made her laugh as he cycled "no hands", his arms and fists waving in the air in triumph like someone winning the Tour de France. They were in love; she knew it. They cycled on past the pond on Pungies Lane and took a quick look at the hybrid mallards showing off to their females, flapping their wings and making happy-duck calls.

Sven waited for her at the top of Telegraph Road. 'I'll race you to the bottom,' he said. 'No, better still, change of plan, we'll ride it together. There are a few potholes in the road and I don't want you to fall over.'

Pippa's smile told him more than he could have hoped.

He started the ride from the junction, and they rode hand in hand for a while until the road became steeper. He saw how relaxed she seemed as they freewheeled down the hill with the wind in their faces and the sound of gulls overhead.

He kept looking back at her and mouthing 'Love you'. Her pink shorts and white T-shirt, the curve of her breasts, and her windblown hair: she seemed ecstatically happy. The fact she had bought a pair of open toe sandals reminding him of his own made his heart speak. *You belong to me, Pippa. One day I will make you Pippa Jørgensen, and we can go birding together for the rest of our lives.*

The pace picked up, faster and faster. His hair pressed back against his skull as he willed his feelings to last forever. He wasn't sure if he was dreaming, and wondered if pinching himself might bring him back to reality. He hoped not.

They arrived in town, both feeling renewed. 'That was brilliant,' Pippa said with a grin on her face. 'When I come back we'll do it again.'

Chapter Twenty-Four

Sven had to be up again for work. He looked at Pippa lying in bed, her eyes closed. It was Friday and they had spent the night at Gilstone. In less than a day, she would be gone. His desperation gnawed at the knot in his stomach. She had taken so many risks for him, and now he felt like a man about to lose his sense of normality. He wanted her to stay on Scilly. Should he ask her not to go back to Whitby? It was a pity to wake her, but he had to be at the boat for ten o'clock.

'Come on, my love, time to get up, we have to go to Bryher this morning.'

He prepared the breakfast and put flowers on the table, setting it neatly to impress her.

'Toast?' he asked as he placed the rack of slices on the table.

'Yes please, thanks.'

She seemed miles away, he thought. Well, soon she would be. 'Coming with me today?' he asked, as if it was just a trip down the road in the car.

'Yes, of course,' she said sleepily.

Within the hour, they left and were back on the ocean with Don. She finally got her trip to Bryher.

Sven worked through the morning on the island, discussing work with the islanders while Pippa walked the footpaths and had coffee with the tourists. Later they met to sit on the white sand at Rushy Bay. He had left his wetsuit in a wooden hut along the shore and changed into it, stripping down to his waist. He looked very handsome and Pippa felt an urge for him to make love to her on the deserted beach, but soon realised the beach wasn't that deserted after all.

Sven scanned offshore with his binoculars. 'I want you to see Sasha. I hope I can find her.'

Pippa watched. It was too cold for her to swim without a suit of her own, and she watched as Sven entered the water and sank beneath it.

Moments later, she heard him calling some distance from the shore and looked through her binoculars. A seal had surfaced and then disappeared under the water again. Sven signalled to Pippa that he had found her. Sasha swam around him several times before coming close. As Sven came towards Pippa, the seal followed and made splashing noises with her flippers before disappearing under the water, as if playing hide and seek. As Sven swam closer to shore, he almost persuaded Sasha to leave the sea. Pippa realised the incentive; he was holding a fish in his hand. She laughed. Was there anything he couldn't do? Sasha swam off, and Pippa's sad thought gave her the feeling she might never see her again.

Don arrived and placed a plank between the boat and the beach. Pippa waded into the water and climbed onto the plank to board the boat.

'There you go, young lady, hope you and Sven had a lovely day together. I've taken time out today, bin to the dentist, had a tooth out, it weren't noice,' said Don, assisting her. Sven withdrew the plank and they continued on their way.

As *Lily of Laguna* chugged across the sea, they spotted fulmar resting on the surface and kittiwake dipping their wing tips in the glassy curves. Their calls 'kittiwake, kittiwake' echoed across the lagoon as they fluttered down to catch sandeels in the calmer Atlantic swell. Bishop Rock Lighthouse, the real "first and last outpost", stood on a craggy outcrop, ghostly and proud on the horizon, and

Pippa's senses became heightened as she drew in the tang of salt-ridden air.

Sven pointed to shearwater, puffins and a peregrine falcon nesting close by. Pippa, swept along by the thrill of it all, watched the sun going down on the horizon. Don manoeuvred the boat around the island of Samson and joined the rowers from the Gig Club. Friday night was always Gig Night. In the distance, he heard the visitors cheering on their favourite team. 'Come on, Golden Eagle', 'Come on, Bonnet, pull harder.' He steered towards them to enable Pippa to cheer the gigs as well.

As the last glow of orange was about to leave the sky, they returned to St Mary's. Climbing out of the boat and up the steps, Sven held Pippa's hand. They walked together to the end of the stone pier. Turning to Pippa, he helped her to sit on the wall, then climbed up next to her.

'Look,' he said, pointing over the sea. 'The sun, between the two hills of Samson. Isn't that a sight?'

Pippa laid her head on his shoulder. 'Wow, this is so romantic. You make it very sad for me to leave tomorrow. I feel like running away with you, chasing that sunset.'

'Do you have to go, Pippa? Can't you just phone up and say you aren't coming back?'

'Oh, Sven darling, don't tempt me. You see, it's Rob and the house and all my personal stuff, which is awkward. I have to settle everything first. I might have to sell the house and I can't just throw him out of it. These things take time. I'll have to try and be more delicate and tactful about it. I want to do it that way because of Daniel – it's the right thing to do.'

'Oh, okay,' Sven said. 'I didn't fully appreciate that.' He looked puzzled for a moment.

'You see, the thing is, Rob never questioned that my dad left it to me in his will. It was all a matter of trust, and right now trust is not the most favourable word. I can't chuck him out. I have to make it as fair as possible. We have to talk about it.'

'Yes, I agree,' Sven said, nodding and appreciating her honesty.

She didn't want to discuss how she felt when she had cheated on Rob; she wasn't proud of what she'd done to him. She had never thought her relationship with Sven would go this far and she wondered how she would deal with it all when she returned home. *I can just see it now: Rob storming around the house, throttling me for what I've done to him.* He had often made her feel stupid, and the number of times she had backed down, just to keep the peace. Joan had once said, 'It's a wise woman who keeps her mouth shut.' This time, no matter what, she would be brave, tell him, and let the consequences take care of themselves. Of course, Rob would be angry, but he would get used to it, and he'd get over it, surely? After all, he was the one who wanted the divorce in the first place. He couldn't have it both ways – he'd pushed her in this direction. It was all very sad. Was she doing the right thing by leaving him, and how could she live like that for the rest of her life?

Only the orange glow of the sun remained on the horizon. They lingered on the wall as Don passed by. He'd taken the boat out in the bay to anchor in deeper water for the receding tide and returned in the dinghy.

'Hello, you two love birds. So you're leaving tomorrow?' he said, holding his cheek as he looked at Pippa.

'Oh hi, Don,' Pippa said. 'It was a great boat trip tonight, thanks. I feel honoured you did that for us, especially after you had a tooth out.'

'Oh, I'll be fine.'

'I'll miss her, but she's coming back soon,' Sven told Don as he put his arm around Pippa's waist and gave her a hug as if to be certain she would return.

'I 'ope you enjoyed yer time 'ere, young lady.'

'Oh, I did – it was more than I could possibly explain.'

Sven assisted Pippa in climbing down from the wall, and the three of them walked off together. As Pippa strode along the quay, hand in hand with Sven, she wondered if her life would ever be the same again.

'Birdman's coming back tomorrow, Sven,' said Don.

'Yeah, thank God, it's been too long. I'm picking him up in the morning, before lunch.'

'Gawd, that man's got a good job, eh? Flying 'ere and thur.' Don looked at Pippa again and laughed. 'No doubt you and Sven will be gallivantin' awf hither and thither soon – 'n me? I'm a Scillonian. I don't think I'll ever leave this place. I've got everythin' I want 'ere. I 'aven't bin awf this island in the last six years since Millie died.'

As they walked towards The Mermaid, Don invited them for a drink.

'Sorry, Don, we can't, not tonight, but thanks anyway. It's our last night and Pippa is packing.' Sven knew his best mate would understand.

Pippa agreed; she didn't want to be with anyone other than Sven, but it was kind of Don to ask.

As they walked up Hugh Street together, Sven didn't feel he needed to hide the woman in his life and blatantly walked arm in arm with Pippa along the road. No one noticed. They were only a couple in love, walking along a street. Pippa smiled at him as he pulled her closer to him; she felt like waltzing up the road so everyone could see them, but in her head she was very aware of how she had cheated on Rob, and the dread of what might happen next filled her thoughts. How would Rob take it, his wife leaving him for another man? It sounded dreadful when she thought about it in that way, and she wondered if she really had been stupid.

As he walked along the road, Sven smiled at Pippa. He was glad he had made her happy, and his life would be complete when she returned to Scilly. Yes, he would miss her so much. Inside his heart was breaking; he wanted to plead with her not to go home, but with the house and everything, she had to sort it out to win her freedom. He understood. He would keep in touch with her every day.

That night they stayed at Gilstone. Pippa folded her clothes into the rucksack. She needed to talk. 'I really don't know what I'm going to tell Rob. Maybe I'll start by saying...'

Sven interrupted her and put his finger to her lips. '*Elskling*, I don't wish to interfere but I suggest you let *him* open the conversation. Stay quiet and see what his other news brings. It might open a new dialogue for you to do something positive.' He slowed his words, speaking more softly and looking into her eyes. 'See how it goes. Don't sit there worrying or practising your opening lines, just go with the flow – that's what I would do. Let him lead the way. It's not easy for me either. I don't want to steal someone away from their marriage, but I love you and that's the way it is. It's also a huge risk to my morale that you might not make it back here.' He kissed her on the cheek.

'I suppose you're right, but what if he makes a huge fuss? Oh God, there's so much to sort out, I need to find a way to tell him about us – how can I do that without a row? I can't give him the house. Dad wanted to give me a good start in life. That house might take ages to sell, and do I really want to sell it? My roots are there. But...'

'Try not to worry, my love. Surely Rob can stay there until he needs to move? Maybe give him a deadline or something. I mean, if he has all this money now he can survive on his own, surely? How do you really feel about him, anyway?' Sven asked, looking for some reassurance.

'Well, he hasn't always been this bad. We've had a few ups and downs – he tends to be very unpredictable, always has been. I don't know the full story on his adoption thing, but I do feel very sorry for him in that respect. His parents didn't tell him until just before we married. His insecurities seem to have rubbed off on me in recent years. The only regret I have is leaving Daniel at the cemetery.'

Sven hugged her. 'I understand, but at some point we can go there together and you can show me around Whitby. You can visit your son – we can be discreet about it, surely?'

'I don't know, darling, maybe it's time I moved on too. All this has come at the right time. I wish I could let go of Daniel and allow him to become a fond memory for the rest of my life. I can't begin to tell you how it's been.'

Sven could see she was regretful. 'Give it time. Time is a good healer.

Pippa held his hand as he led her to bed. It was a warm, sticky night and Sven opened the windows as the temperature had risen and the house was slow to cool down. He wrapped the white sheet over them and, like the proverbial peas in a pod, they became one as they slept.

Chapter Twenty-Five

The following morning Sven rose early and made Pippa a cup of Yorkshire Tea, her favourite brand. She had brought tea bags with her on the train. With The Birdman arriving later that morning, Sven had to leave to meet him from the helicopter.

Pippa watched as he put his arms into a T-shirt and pulled it down over his head. With his hair tousled and not brushed, he looked quite unkempt; it made her want to drag him back to bed and cosset him to death. He pulled on a pair of frayed denim shorts and zipped up the fly. He borrowed Pippa's hairbrush and smoothed the waves of his natural style to make it straighter.

'I'm going now. Sorry this is such a rush, but I have to be at the office and discuss things with Margaret before I go to the airport. Don't forget, twelve o'clock.'

'Okay, I won't.' Pippa yawned and then blew him a kiss.

'Come up the hill on the bike, and down the other side and you're in Old Town. The café is on your left before the bend, you can't miss it.'

'Thanks, I know where it is,' she assured him.

'You look gorgeous this morning.' He paused for a moment to slip into his sandals. 'I wish this wasn't happening, but must go. Bye, Pips.' He kissed her and then dashed down the stairs without taking breakfast, rushing out the front door to the van. Pippa heard the engine start and then silence as the van disappeared up the street.

Lying in bed, she thought about everything that had happened to her. It seemed as if Sven had swept her off her feet, often quite literally.

Her trip to Whitby would be the worst journey of her life, but could she stay here forever and not return? Perhaps she could miss the boat and go back a few days later than planned. No, that would be putting it off, and cowardly too. In the old days Rob had been good to her most of the time, but this "old friends thing" seemed to have got in the way of the meaning of true love. It occurred to her she might have been too young when they married.

Aware of what Joan would say to her when she got back, Pippa wanted her friend to understand that she hadn't deliberately set out to do this. It wasn't like that. She would make sure her best friend appreciated the reasons for her departure. Maybe Rob had already told her about their conversation on the phone. Joan liked to spend time with him; they'd always had a good rapport, and Pippa knew that Rob would remain friends with Joan. She had been a good ally. Perhaps he had married the wrong person! Joan would probably never move on in her life; she wasn't made that way. She was a local lass and always seemed happy in her own world of Terry and looking after Jordan. Pippa had often wished that Rob paid less attention to the Marshall family and more to her. He had said he owed it to Joan for all the kindness she had provided during the months after Daniel had died.

Pippa fiddled with her wedding ring; perhaps now she could remove it. After all, its significance no longer held any meaning. She looked down at her hand and imagined herself free again to do what she liked. This had to be the end of her marriage; Rob had driven her away. So why should she keep his ring? She tugged at her finger with sadness in her throat and the ring seemed to slide away easily. She held it between her fingers and blew out her cheeks before placing it into her make-up bag and sealing the zipper.

It was 11.30. Pippa got on the bike Sven had left outside the front door. She was early. They had promised to have lunch with Martin and his entourage. As she reached the top of the hill, she stopped to look at the view. If she had been able to write a poem, this would have been her chosen moment. *Wow! This is stunning.* As she looked back, masses of pink, purple, orange, and cream Livingstone daisies covered the walls, their colours flowing to the ground. She cycled further down the hill and there it was, in front of her: Old Town Bay in full blue tide with the church on the foreshore. With the sun glistening on the water in the bay, it was paradise ten times over. Her sense of completeness. Perhaps she had fallen in love not once, but twice, during her stay. Life here seemed so unspoiled, and she hoped it would remain so forever. Sven had shown her how vulnerable these islands were with the oil spill and how important it was to protect them from the ravages of the outside world. 'These islands are the height of vulnerability itself,' he'd told her. 'Take what you have and cherish it all your life.' She had to support his quest. He'd told her how he wished everyone could make a difference to the world by doing one thing in their lives to save the environment. It was as if he alone was attempting to take on the battle of the elements and the human race.

Pippa freewheeled further down the hill and arrived at the café. She parked her bike, ordered a coffee and watched the people passing by her table. She caught a whiff of coffee and cake from the next table and it reminded her of the first time she had met Sven. She closed her eyes in the sun and waited for the arrival of The Birdman.

Martin, looking well-tanned from the African sun, arrived with his wife, Andrea. He was taller than Sven, and, not unlike his colleague, he wore shorts and open-toe sandals and a *Greenpeace* T-shirt. The film crew followed behind him, carrying bags, tripods, and camera equipment.

'Hi, mate!' Martin embraced Sven. He introduced him to the crew. 'Pete, Larry, meet my colleague, Sven Jørgensen, the only Viking on Scilly!'

Sven shook hands with the camera crew.

'Hi, Sven, great to see you.' Andrea waved at Sven, then welcomed him with a kiss on the cheek. 'Come on over for a meal tonight, I'll make us something special.' She turned to Martin before she left. 'Darling, I'll get home now.' She had ordered a taxi. She kissed her husband. 'Bye, love, don't be long, will you?'

Martin explained, 'She's gone back home to sort things out, and anyway you know she doesn't like travelling in the van.' He chuckled. 'Where did you say you were going, Sven – Old Town Caff? I'm starving. We can all take a break there. Good idea.'

'Ya, Martin, erm…there's someone I would like you to meet.'

'Who's that?'

'Oh, you'll see, bit of a surprise.' Sven gave a big smile as he walked beside his friend.

'Oh yeah?' said Martin.

'Come on, let's go.' Sven felt a touch of anxiety.

As she left the airport, Andrea waved goodbye and Sven responded with a thumbs-up. Her blue denim mini-skirt and sea-green blouse showed off her suntan. Sven watched her go. It was good to have her back after her trip to Bristol to meet Martin, and he wondered if she would befriend Pippa. He hoped so. He'd worried about Andrea last winter, being on her own while Martin was in the Antarctic. Nevertheless, she always seemed to manage. She was the kind of person who could make something delicious with very little effort. He admired her enthusiasm and humour.

'How are things?' Martin asked. 'You look great, Sven. Glad we're back, it's been a long tour.' He patted Sven on the shoulder as they left the small airport terminal.

Sven took the wheel of the van and drove into Old Town with the entire luggage and film crew in the back. He filled in a few gaps from Martin's absence from Scilly, feeling relieved he had more support now.

Pippa sat at her table, admiring the view and drinking her coffee. She could hear the familiar sound of the van coming around the bend. She peered through the windscreen. *Yes, it's Sven!*

The group almost rolled out of the doors, and Sven smiled

to see her sitting at the table. He decided to be brave about the introductions.

Pippa saw all the new faces invading her space. She waited, wondering how it would be now The Birdman was back.

'Erm, Martin…this is my girlfriend, Pippa Lambton.'

Martin looked astounded. 'Girlfriend?' He smiled warmly at Pippa, then grinned at Sven.

'Yes, I've seen you on the telly.' She began to think how different he looked: taller and even better looking than she had seen him on TV. She shook hands with him. He seemed so friendly and outgoing. He waved at the café proprietor and then at someone in a car who passed by with a toot of the horn.

His sense of humour mingled with his manners; he seemed the perfect gentleman. Holding onto Pippa's hand, he grinned at her. '*Enchantez*, Madam.'

Sven laughed. 'Hey, man! She's *mine*.' Then he reminded himself she wasn't his yet.

Pippa decided to match Martin's charm. 'My God, are all your friends this handsome, Sven?' They laughed at her comment, and Sven jokingly whispered in her ear, 'Only the ones who do any work on Scilly!'

'I've been trying to get Sven fixed up with a girl for the last five years. I go away, and I can't trust him five minutes – sneaky bugger goes behind my back!' Martin pushed Sven's arm in play.

'This has to be a moment for a photo, eh?' said Pete.

Photos could mean trouble, they might end up in the press, Pippa thought.

With quick thinking, Sven replied, 'Oh, no photos, *please*, let's have some lunch. Pippa is returning north this afternoon and we don't have much time together.'

'Thanks,' she whispered to Sven from the corner of her mouth. 'Anyway, I hope to come back in the next few weeks,' she assured them. She thought Martin seemed very talkative and confident.

'Pippa won't have met Andrea yet, of course?' asked Martin.

'No, but I'm sure she will soon, anyway. I've told her what a good cook she is. We've been trying to beat the "Scilly Grapevine", so we didn't tell anyone about us,' Sven explained.

'Ha! Sure. Well, Pippa, when you come back, go and see her. She needs a new friend – well, I think she does.' Martin grinned.

'I will. Sven has told me a lot about her and what a great team you are.'

Pippa saw Martin give a knowing look to Sven and wondered if she had met with his approval. After all, Sven and Martin were part of a long friendship – would she fit in?

Having completed his winter filming, Martin seemed happy to return to his beloved islands. The five of them sat together and ordered fish, salad, a bowl of chips, and wine. After lunch, Sven bought a huge Dame Blanche ice cream for Pippa and a holiday atmosphere prevailed.

Pippa listened, fascinated and in awe of Martin's stories about his trip to Africa. It helped to take her mind off the afternoon, the ferry back to Penzance and the train ride north. She held Sven's hand and put her foot on his under the café table. Sven smiled as she played "footsie" with him and he gave her a knowing look. Martin tried to cheer them up; he had also felt the tension of her departure.

'Hey up, lass, 'ave a glass of wine, stop yer from bein' sea sick on't ferry.' He over-mimicked Pippa's Yorkshire accent. Pippa giggled. She already liked him.

Sven stood up from the table. It was time to leave. He saw Pippa's bike propped against the side of the café and decided to leave it there; he would collect it later.

They all squeezed into the van. There were no seats in the back, and they sat on a blanket and some cushions. Martin picked up the van keys where Sven had left them on the table. 'I'll drive,' he said. Sven looked at Pippa and made a grimacing face when he thought Martin wasn't looking. He whispered to her, 'I hope you're ready for this.'

'I see they still haven't fixed that big hole in the road,' Martin said as he drove towards Hugh Town.

'Oh, yes, it's been fixed twice, but the bad weather we had this winter didn't help,' Sven informed him.

Pippa was laughing with Pete and Larry as they sat in the back. Martin's driving habits were unpredictable and she soon began to understand Sven's comments.

Larry shouted from the rear. 'If I wanted a ride on a roller coaster, I'd have bloody well paid for it. Ouch, my arse,' he called above the sound of the engine.

'Sorree,' shouted Martin. 'I forgot we're not on the African plains!'

Pippa couldn't stop laughing, and Sven turned round to see what was going on. Pippa was hanging onto Pete in the back as they kept sliding forward on the downhill route. She laughed so much that her tears began to show. Pete offered her a sheet from the roll of kitchen paper that Sven had hung on a wire behind the seat. She took it, still laughing and crying, as they went over another bump in the road.

The group arrived in town, passing Porthmellon beach and the view across the bay with the boats in the harbour. Pippa could see the *Scillonian* at dock, and each moment reminded her it would soon be time to leave. Martin and the crew got out of the van. They offered to meet later for a drink.

'Bye, Pippa, come back soon, and have a good journey up north,' said Martin.

Pippa was still grinning at Sven as he drove home. Her cheeks ached from laughing so much.

'I didn't realise his driving would be that bad,' she said, stroking her face and trying to bring her cheeks back to normal.

'Oh, that's Martin. He arses around and shows off sometimes. What you see on the TV isn't the same as when he's at home. He can be a bit of an idiot at times, but he's a fun guy.'

'I liked him. You really are a team, aren't you? And...there's Don, of course.' All Pippa could see in her head was Sven and Don riding the waves on *Lily*. She smiled to herself, thinking how wonderful it would be to belong to the team and come home on bikes each day down the well-remembered lanes.

There was one last thing Pippa had wanted to do. 'Sven, darling, will you walk up the hill to The Garrison with me?' she asked.

'Of course,' he said, holding her hand.

Arriving at Gilstone, they picked up Pippa's rucksack from the porch. She looked around to ensure she hadn't left anything behind. The last thing she recalled was Sven sitting at the table on his first visit to the house.

'So long, house. It's been amazing – I'll be back soon.' She left the door key in an envelope as Janice had requested, and with sadness closed the front door behind her.

Sven drove towards the quay; the ferry would leave in an hour. The ship's whistle would soon call the passengers to return.

'Will you walk with me to the seat at the top? It's the place I had the happiest memories of Dan during our last visit, and then maybe I can leave here knowing I'll have done what I set out to do.' She turned her eyes away from his face.

'Ya, sure, Pippa, I understand.'

Together they walked up the hill, Sven with binoculars swinging on his chest as usual and Pippa feeling proud by his side.

On Pippa's favourite bench, they admired the view of the islands in the lagoon. A gull mewed loudly below the cliff as Sven began to talk. He waited until the bird passed over him.

'Promise me you'll call the minute you get back.'

'Yes,' replied Pippa, reassuring him. 'Of course I will. We're a couple now, and nothing'll stop me from coming back to you.' She prayed that her words would be true.

'I love you so much,' Sven whispered. 'You know, Pippa, you're amazing, and especially the way you have changed since we first met – I'm so proud of you.'

'Well, if it weren't for you I wouldn't have got this far – I mean, I feel very different now.' There was a mutual silence and a sense of belonging.

Sven held her hand and kissed her. 'Pippa, I'm scared,' he admitted. 'Scared you won't be able to come back. You know we have to be together, nothing else matters.'

'Of course I will, I *absolutely promise* I will. I love you so very much, but I have to do the right thing.'

In the distance, Pippa imagined she could see the figure of the small boy, the one she had seen before, standing looking out to sea and pointing. It was as though he was trying to tell her something. It would always be a special place, somewhere to sit when things were not quite right in your life and you could contemplate how to repair your sorrows. Pippa knew Jan and Marijke had discovered that too. She kissed Sven. 'This one is for the view,' she said. 'Darling, you are so kind to me. There have been days when I wondered how I'd survive, but I suppose I do, and now this, you and me, sitting here looking out to sea. I wonder if one day, when we're old and grey, we will be sitting here again on this very spot, remembering our time and us – together. It's been great. When I get back, I'll have to try to be brave. This has to be the hardest decision for me: leaving you, having to sort out such sorrow at home.'

'I know you are a good person, Pippa.' He kissed her again. 'If things haven't been right for a while, then you have to do what's best, I suppose. I'm just a bit scared, that's all, because you'll be so far away from me.' He sighed. 'Can't you…*accidentally* miss the boat this afternoon?'

Pippa chuckled. 'Yeah, I thought about that one too. You know…' She paused. 'I think I will always feel I belong here. I loved Telegraph Road, the bike ride, the islands, everything! There are no words to describe it. I'm going all that way back to Whitby. I never want to stop thinking about you and all of this. I'll come back, I promise. I want to watch the birds, to help conserve nature and do all those things we both enjoy so much.' She hesitated for a moment. 'Do you know what *tot ziens* means in Dutch? Marijke said that to me when she left. She told me one night when we walked home together. It doesn't mean goodbye forever. It means "until I see you again".'

'Yes, I know, it's like *auf wiedersehen* in German,' Sven said. He squeezed her tight and kissed her. 'Come on, darling, let's go and do the goodbyes, shall we? Time is getting on.'

As they strolled down the hill, he thought she looked lovely walking along the track, her wispy auburn hair blowing in the warm breeze. He wouldn't let her down, he was sure. Would she have the strength to end it all with Rob? He must trust her; it would be awful if anything went wrong. He didn't want to think about it.

Martin was on the quay. He flicked his hand in a casual wave as he chatted to Don.

'Nice girl he's got,' said Don.

'Yeah, amazing, isn't it? I had no idea he had a girlfriend. I hope she comes back. Great legs!' Martin said with a grin.

Don laughed. 'You've been leaving that good wife of yours for too long.'

Sven took Pippa to a secluded corner of the quay and kissed her before walking to the ferry. He fussed over her. 'Now, do you have everything with you? Your train ticket, my phone number? You're at the youth hostel tonight, aren't you?'

When Pippa whispered in his ear, 'I love you, Sven' he wiped away his own tears, wishing he could blame them on the wind and the salt spray. Helping her with the rucksack up the gangway, he stopped at the top, holding her in his arms and gazing into her eyes.

'You know, Pippa, when you fall in love, it's a kind of madness. I'm sure we can sort it all out – I know we can. I know we were meant for each other.'

Pippa's heart thumped; he had given her hope to return to Scilly, the place she had dreamed about since school. She felt sure there was a wonderful life ahead for both of them and the plan to live with Sven would be possible. Despite being scared at having to tell Rob, her confidence had grown and she now knew what she wanted. Once she had told Rob about her plans, it would be just a case of how and when she would leave. She dreaded the "telling him" bit most.

'Come back to me, Pippa,' Sven almost pleaded. 'I love you so very much.'

Pippa jumped as the ship's whistle sounded. Time to leave. They laughed together, and she flung her arms around him. 'I love you too. I will come back, I promise. Thanks for everything. I think you know how much this has meant to me – sharing your life, the birds, the islands, just everything. You've been fantastic. I'll call you.' She sniffed into her handkerchief. Sven stepped onto the quay and as the crew raised the gangway she waved to him.

Sven blew a kiss, caught her eyes, and mouthed the words 'I'll never stop loving you.'

Tourists stood on the quay with Sven as he watched the ship reverse to sail around the bay towards St Agnes and out to sea. He waved as long as he could, and with a heavy heart made his way home.

As the ship left the lea of St Mary's, Pippa stayed outside on deck. She had waved until she couldn't see him any more, standing there with tears in her eyes. Her heart screamed, 'Go back, go back.' Why had she done this to herself? Too late: she had left St Mary's with dreadful sorrow.

She hid in a corner of the upper deck and watched the islands disappear over the horizon. The sea crossing was lumpy and she began to feel queasy, cursing herself for not taking her travel-sickness pills. She had been fine on the little boats, but the movement of the ferry felt different and she wished she hadn't had the glass of wine with her meal.

After a few minutes she threw up and felt ill most of the way. An hour later, the Cornish coast came into view and she threw up the contents of her stomach into the sea for the third time, and concluded that she wanted to die rather than suffer seasickness. How she wished she hadn't had the ice cream.

Pippa arrived in Penzance, took a taxi to the youth hostel, and met with Mike on reception. She had made conversation with him on her outward journey.

'It's good to see a familiar face,' she said, feeling she might vomit again.

'Hello, Pippa! Are you all right? You look all in – was it the ferry?' Mike guessed. 'I was expecting you around now, I have your booking down here.' He pointed to the diary.

'Yeah, I feel terrible, I was seasick.'

'Oh dear, it often happens, but how was Scilly?'

'Awesome – no, it was more than awesome, it was incredible.'

'Glad you enjoyed it. Can I make you a cup of tea?'

'Oh, Mike, I would love to say yes, but… I feel awful.' She wanted to talk about her time with Sven, the birds, the boats, Don, Martin, the islands, everything. 'I'm so shattered, I want to sleep, and I think a cup of tea might not be a good idea right now. But thanks for the offer.'

'Despite the seasickness it sounds as if you did have a good time,' he remarked with a smile. 'You'll be fine in a few hours. Call me if you need help, okay?'

'Maybe we'll chat later.' Pippa let out a deep sigh.

Mike carried her rucksack to the top of the stairs and found her a room where no one was sharing. She thanked him and closed the door behind her, almost falling on the bed. She felt as if she was about to keel over. What had she done? Was it all real? Would she make it back? *Oh, the pain of it all.*

As she lay on the bed, the room seemed to be going up and down from her boat trip. It was getting late; she felt hungry, but couldn't eat any food in case she was sick again. She slept, then woke again an hour later, still feeling the motion of the ship. She would drag herself downstairs to the phone; it was 9.30 in the evening.

There was a tall mirror in the room, and as she raised herself from the bed to wash her face, she looked at her reflection: tanned, wearing shorts, open-toe sandals, her eyes red with tears. *God, this is unreal. Dad, I need you.*

She dialled Sven's number. It rang for a long time. She tried twice more; she assumed he was at The Mermaid drowning his sorrows with Martin.

Again, she felt desperately sick and decided she would try again in the morning. She set her travel alarm for six o'clock to catch the train at 7.30. Perhaps a shower would be the answer to her nausea. An hour later, she had cried herself to sleep.

Now that Martin was home, Sven deliberately busied himself. Andrea had invited him for an evening meal and had prepared a cheese fondue with baked potatoes and salad. She produced a bottle of her homemade mulled wine and proceeded to pour a glass for each of them.

Sven tried to drown his sorrows, explaining to Martin and Andrea how it had all happened.

'Oh, you haf no idea how she has shanged my life,' he said after drinking his third glass of wine, plus three cans of beer. 'I've felt quite different while you guys have been away.'

Andrea realised his intoxication and smiled to herself. 'I said you needed a woman in your life,' she chuckled.

Martin joined in the conversation. 'Well, when Andrea and I got together, we were the same. I met her on holiday too, but we had a *normal* relationship. Nothing as whirlwind as you and Pippa, so...' He paused. 'Do you think it'll work, being so far away and all that?'

Sven looked right at him and sighed. 'You know, I've never been so sure in all my life. I'd be devastated if I was wrong. I'm missing her already. You know she is married, but things are not going well.'

'God, Sven, is she?' Andrea said.

'Well, it's a bit complicated, but she's had a dreadful time. When she came over here I could feel something was wrong, and you know me, I asked her about it.'

Martin slumped further in his chair. 'Don't be so hard on yourself, Sven mate. You go for it, but watch you aren't cited in a divorce case. Pippa could lose a lot and you'll end up in trouble.'

'What do *you* know about divorces, Martin?' Andrea shook her head and 'Tut-tutted' at him.

'I know…well…nothing, really, I only want Sven to take care.'

'I'll be careful. You know, she lost her son in a dreadful accident. He was only six. That's why she was here, and her husband is not… well, it's a long story.'

'Oh my God, is that right?' Martin said.

'Ya, I know. She might tell you herself about it when she comes back.'

Sven recognised Andrea's expression. He knew that "sisterly" look too well. She seemed shocked that he'd become involved in someone else's tragedy and was meddling in their marriage. Even so, she had to keep reminding herself he wasn't the young twenty-something that first came to Scilly some years before. Sven was a good friend, and she didn't want him to be the laughing stock of the island gossip.

'I don't think you need worry about me,' said Sven. 'Even if it was a holiday romance, it was the best time for some years. I know how I feel, but I'm trying to be realistic, despite what you might think.'

'Another beer, Sven?' Martin asked.

'Yeah, go on, we may as well drown my sorrows.' Sven laughed. 'Well, I mean, she is a beautiful woman, don't you think?' He seemed in his own world of love, and leaned on the sadness Pippa had left behind.

'I've left the washing up to drain in the sink. I'm not going to dry it tonight, I'm too tired,' Andrea sighed. 'One of these days you might buy me a dishwasher, 'cos you never do it.'

'Oh yes, bugger the washing up, love, come and join us. Have another glass of wine.' Martin clumsily grabbed hold of his wife and hugged her. She kissed him a peck on the lips.

'I'm thinking of going on a trip myself soon,' Andrea announced as she sat on Martin's knee, fiddling with the bleached hairs on his legs and stroking him. 'The girls from the darts club are considering a long weekend trip to Amsterdam. Would you mind if I went too, darling? We can fly from Exeter or Bristol. It just gets me off the island now and again. I love it here, but *you* know how it is, Sven. When did you last leave St Mary's?'

'Oh, ages ago, but maybe that will change soon,' Sven replied.

'Nice idea,' Martin said. 'No going down the Red Light District, though, do you hear me?' He chuckled.

'Don't be dull, of course we will!' she exclaimed. She took a second glance at Martin. 'I don't think I can stand kissing you any more with that on your face.' She tugged at his facial hair and shook her head.

Turning towards Sven, she asked. 'Do you think Pippa really will come here?'

'Don't put doubts in his head, love,' said Martin. 'She's a nice girl, you'll have to meet her.'

Sven's speech began to slur. 'I hope so 'cos I love her to bits.' He slunk down into his chair and stretched his long suntanned legs in front of him.

Andrea loved Sven's quirky personality; it was endearing, and she would flirt with him and tease him about his "Nor-ways" if only to cheer him up. The age gap between them was not too wide, but she had always felt from day one that Sven needed guidance. She hoped Pippa would do the right thing by him; he certainly did not need any more hurt in his life. He was a good man and knew his job well, a valuable asset to Martin and to the islands. Now her husband was a TV personality, her own life had changed too.

Martin fell asleep on the settee; he still felt the effects of jet lag. Andrea seemed to have enjoyed her time in Bristol with him. They had no children yet, but she hoped they would start a family soon.

She hadn't been ready, but now she was thirty-five she began to think perhaps it was time, before it was too late. Maybe she should talk it over with him again soon.

Slightly the worse for his beer, Sven chatted with Andrea. 'I should get a call from Pippa tomurro. I can't wait t'zee how she is doing.' His mouth wasn't working with his brain and his Norwegian accent was more pronounced than usual.

'Well, I hope you do,' said Andrea. 'It would be a shame if she got back and had second thoughts. Maybe you should be at home now waiting for her to call.'

Sven didn't seem to be listening. 'We had such a great time.' His words had become glued together. 'You know we did that thing I told you about, you know, you know, the bikes. It was awesome, you gotta try it.'

'Actually,' she said, 'I did try it, in April this year. Margaret and I freewheeled down Telegraph to see who could get to the junction first. It was fun. Martin thought I was bonkers when I told him. He thought we were like two kids.'

She pointed to Martin, who had his eyes shut and let out a loud snore in the back of his throat. She rolled her eyes and Sven smiled at her.

Andrea poured another glass of wine, and while Martin was breathing even louder, Sven began to close his eyes.

'Don't you fall asleep as well, Sven.'

'No, no, must go now, Pippa might call me.'

As he stood up, Andrea realised he was in no fit state to walk alone up the road. She suggested he go upstairs and sleep over on the spare bed. She helped him climb the stairs and managed to guide him to the bedroom.

'Sshhh, you'll wake Martin.' Sven laughed and giggled in his alcoholic state. In low voices they sang *Show Me the Way to Go Home*. In the spare room, Andrea helped Sven into the single bed, still wearing his shorts and T-shirt. She took off his sandals, and Sven told her, 'Don't bother taking anything else off – I'm really shy when I'm drunk.' Andrea giggled as she tucked him up in bed. She put out the light and closed the door.

'Whew, men!' she exclaimed aloud as she went down the stairs.

A voice from the bedroom said, 'I heard that, Mrs Birdman, go fook yerself!'

Andrea heard him and couldn't help laughing. Sven always swore when he was drunk, but it sounded quite comical. She knew it was another side of him she'd seen many times on those days when they'd all had too much to drink. She hoped the evening had helped him to overcome his parting from Pippa. He really was in love, she could tell. Andrea thought that she knew more about Sven than he knew about himself. The Birdman and The Viking were a team, and she was proud of them both. She hoped the new love of his life wouldn't let him down, and it worried her.

Pippa was about to leave the youth hostel that morning and passed the time with Mike until the taxi arrived to take her to the station.

'I can't begin to tell you what a wonderful time I had on Scilly,' she said.

'I hope you are feeling better this morning – you didn't look at all well last night. I hope to see you again, Pippa, you're one of those people I found it hard to forget when you left here. We had such a lovely chat on your last visit. I suppose… I remembered the colour of your hair… I bet everyone says that, though.'

'Oh yes, Mike, I'm used to it now, but thanks. Look, I might be coming back this way soon. I hope you are still going to be working here, it would be nice to chat with you. I could be *living* on Scilly soon.'

'You've got a job over there?'

Pippa beamed. 'Nope, I've got a new man in my life.'

'Oh, that's a shame. I was hoping to ask you out. I missed my chances, didn't I?' He laughed.

'Oh, Mike, that's so sweet of you. Yes, we did have a nice evening chatting and eating our fish and chips last time. I appreciated the company.'

'Never mind, you know where I am if you need a friend.'

'Sure do. Don't forget to come and see me on Scilly. I will call in and see you soon, and thanks for being so nice to me. It's hard when you're on your own, but I hope all that will change soon. See ya. Bye.'

Pippa picked up her rucksack as the taxi was waiting. She knew there was no point in trying to contact Sven just yet; he would be fast asleep in bed; it was too early to call. She imagined him, his hair tangled in the pillow, breathing quietly to himself. She would try calling him later before the train arrived.

The next morning, after Andrea had insisted he ate a good breakfast, Sven made his way home. On arrival, Nanette informed him that his phone had been ringing. He tried to appear calm.

'It's ringed twice fer ages. I 'eard it when I was in the garden,' Nanette said with the usual curiosity in her voice.

I knew I shouldn't have left the house last night. He was annoyed at himself for getting drunk when he had wanted to come home. *It could only have been Pippa who called, surely? Oh fuck, I've let her down.* He couldn't phone her back, and still lived with the fear that Astrid might call him. What if that had been her on the phone, and not Pippa? He told himself not to be so stupid. What did he have to be afraid of? He'd done nothing wrong, but his head was full of self-scolding.

He knew he couldn't contact Pippa just yet. The waiting was agony; he missed her a lot and wished in a way it could have been different. He had the phone number but was unable to contact her. She'd asked him to hold back until she had spoken with Rob. Sven sighed and began to get impatient. Wild thoughts went around his head; he might have lost her forever. All he knew was that she lived on Henrietta Street in Whitby. Panic. What if she didn't phone to give him permission to use the number? What if he really had been just a bit of fun on holiday? He tried not to think about it.

Chapter Twenty-Six

Rob stood waiting at Darlington for Pippa. It was his day off and he felt good but not confident about his plans for the future. He was anxious to tell her about Joan and Terry, and all about his new-found family. He wondered how Pippa had managed with her holiday. Would she be more relaxed around him?

Poor Joan, he thought. He was glad she was in recovery now. He would visit her and try to arrange some care for her and Jordan. Perhaps seeing Pippa again would make her feel better.

Pippa felt tired and hungry after her long journey. In the late afternoon sun, she arrived in Darlington and made her way to the front of the train to look for Rob. Her heart was aching, her eyes swollen with tears – what would she tell him?

She searched the platform but couldn't see him. Then, as the train pulled out of the echoing station, she caught a glimpse of him waiting. At first, she couldn't believe her eyes: he'd been to the hairdresser and he looked smart and good-looking again. It was a feeling of surprise more than anything, but it was still Rob. The moment she saw him she wanted to turn around and go back the way she had come.

She dropped her luggage on the platform as he came towards her and flung his arms around her. Her body went limp.

'Hey, how was it? I missed you,' he said, giving her a peck on the cheek.

Pippa said nothing. Why was he being so affectionate? She gave a weak smile. 'I'm very, *very* tired,' she said, closing her eyes. 'The journey from Penzance was long. I've been travelling since yesterday when I left Scilly.'

'Yes, you look tired, and your eyes are very swollen. Are you okay?'

'Yes, I suppose so. I was very seasick.'

He tried to kiss her again, but she bent down and pretended to fasten the shoelace on her trainers. He never kissed her when she left three weeks ago from this very station. What was he doing?

On the way home, she tried to think of anything and everything that could possibly stop her from crying. She kept nodding and agreeing with everything he said.

Later, they reached Whitby. Rob put Pippa's silence down to the long journey she'd endured. They travelled along the moor road and Pippa had fallen asleep. The next thing she knew Rob was patting her knee.

'Come on, Pip, home time. We're almost there, love.' He sounded like her father, and for a moment she was a child in the back seat of the car, wrapped in a blanket and woken by a parent after a long journey.

'Huh? Oh yes, Whitby,' she said, remembering where she was. It made her realise how much she wished she was back in Cornwall and the islands. The journey through the industrial part of Middlesbrough had sent her heart to her feet. The old railway tracks, the grimy Victorian buildings and deserted docklands, close to the station, made her want to turn around and take the next train back to Penzance.

They passed over the swing bridge in town and Rob parked his car in the side street, then carried Pippa's rucksack. He tried to hold her hand, but frowned as she darted into a shop for some chewing gum.

Pippa thought that if she was chewing, he might not want to kiss her. He waited for her and they walked on together down the cobbled street. She kept her arms close to her as she walked.

As she entered the house on Henrietta Street, the odour of fried bacon hit her nostrils. On the table rested a photo of Daniel, and one of her father staring back at her. A wedding photo of her and Rob back in 1976 stood on the dresser, along with another photo of Terry, Joan, herself, Rob, and Daniel taken by a local photographer on the day of the Whitby Regatta. She wanted to scream. What was the point?

'I'll put the kettle on, love, and then you can tell me all about Scilly,' Rob said, trying to lighten the mood.

Pippa sat quiet. She had nothing to tell him; all her news was about Sven. Her heart was five hundred miles away, and with Sven's face in her head, how could she tell Rob anything?

'I was very ill yesterday. It might take me some time to recover,' she said as she put the chewed gum in the bin. 'I had a wonderful time. It was fantastic.' She started to open up to Rob, but wished he would leave the house so she could phone Sven.

After an hour, Rob sat down with her. 'Look, er... I've some good news and some bad news. Joan is in hospital. We didn't want to tell you because I knew you were coming back. Anyway, it only happened a few days ago.' He proceeded to explain all about Joan and Terry.

Pippa looked away, sighing, and allowed herself to cry. 'Oh my God, I didn't expect this. How is she? Something told me Terry was depressed. I've talked to him a few times about it, but he kept clamping up. He's a bit of an oddball, but now it all makes sense. Why didn't she tell me on the phone? I just don't...'

'Well, it's a bit more than that, but let's take one thing at a time.'

Rob explained Joan's failed suicide attempt and brought Pippa up to date with her progress. He said they could visit this evening if Pippa felt well enough. She dabbed her eyes, her eyelids drooping; she couldn't take any more.

Rob tried to comfort her, but each time he came near, she

made an excuse not to be close to him. Avoiding his affections, she wondered how long she could go on in this way. It must have showed.

'Make me a coffee please, Rob, I need it right now.'

'Oh…okay, in a minute.'

Pippa gave a heavy sigh.

'I also have a wonderful bit of news.' Rob thought he would save it until last. 'We came into some money, but a whole lot more than…'

Pippa seemed to go into a trance. She stopped listening. 'Rob, sorry, I have to go to bed, I feel quite ill.'

'Oh, I thought you might be happy for me. And I've given up smoking. I thought you'd be pleased.'

'Oh, good for you. Of course I'm pleased, but I only just got back and you have to give me some time. I'll talk later about it if you don't mind. Why don't you let me sleep, and perhaps you go and have a beer or something? Then I'll be able to take it all in afterwards.' She paused a moment. 'We need to talk as well. I feel in view of all this, things might change for us.'

'What d'ye mean?' Rob frowned.

'Oh, just with your situation and how it was before I left for Scilly.'

'Oh, I see,' said Rob sharply. 'Look, I think you're right, I will go to the pub. You have your sleep. I'll see you in a couple of hours, okay?' Right now he needed a cigarette.

Pippa looked into his eyes; it had all been too much. She liked his new hair-style, but it didn't seem like the Rob she had left behind three weeks before. The husband who talked divorce, who made excuses not to tell her he loved her. What was he trying to do to her feelings? He wasn't going to make her feel guilty right now; it was too late. He'd come into some money, and if he thought that would change things, then he was wrong. She had decided she didn't love him; she had learned what love meant, and it wasn't with Rob. The situation had taken a sudden change of tack.

*

Rob left the house, and Pippa sat brushing her hair and wondering what she should do. She put the brush on the dressing table. She noticed the blond hairs tangled in the brush and smiled to herself, then almost cried again. This could be the only evidence she had of Sven. She had to phone him now. *Yes, now.* Why couldn't she contact him last night and today? She supposed that communication on the islands was going to be very difficult.

She dialled the number and the phone rang several times, but no one answered. She felt like a tormented cat. An hour later, she tried again, but no reply. Where was he? Her heart cried out for Sven to pick up the phone. Perhaps the goodbye had been forever.

Chapter Twenty-Seven

'Afternoon, guys and gals,' Sven walked through the door into the yard to greet the volunteers.

'Hi, Sven, how's it going?' said Jacqui.

'Fine. I think we're winning now, but it's been a huge job, eh? I want to thank you all for your help.' Inside him, he wanted to say all was *not* fine. He was in love and couldn't do a darned thing about it. Why hadn't Pippa phoned?

'What is it with Charlie these days? Sometimes he can be dead nice and other times he's dead grumpy.' Beth gave a sigh. 'I can't get on with him.'

'He always tells me he canna understand a werrd I'm sayin',' Linda explained with a grin.

'I do.' Sven grinned. 'We used to be neighbours once upon a time, up there in Shetland. Isn't that where you used to live, Linda?'

Linda nodded. She knew what Sven meant.

Martin was listening. 'Still, we mustn't complain. He does a good job, which brings me to consider our tasks today. I think we might be lucky this time with these birds, but if you people could collect the ones we found this morning, maybe give them a wash, and then we'll collect the rest for the helicopter. They can go to the RSPCA on the mainland. We don't have the room here. I got three gannets yesterday, vicious little buggers. Watch your eyes, Beth.'

The volunteers stood around the sink and each filled a washing-up bowl with water. Bottles of mild detergent stood on the work surface, and Linda took one of the razorbills out of the cardboard pet carrier and held it over the sink. 'God, yuk! This one is so emaciated. Alan, look, I can feel its breastbone sticking out.'

'Yeah, give it a scrub. It'll be all right, we'll feed it later,' Alan replied.

Sven joined in. 'The good news is that the oil spill seems to be dispersing. Some foreign tanker has apparently leaked into the Irish Sea. Bloody idiots! We've been lucky. Scilly might have lost all its tourism and God knows what else.' He picked up a gannet from the box. 'Aren't they good-looking birds? Look at this one – despite the oil, I think it's going to be fine. I love their eyes.' He took the bird outside the shed.

Beth whispered to Jacqui, knowing Sven wouldn't hear, '*He's* a good looking bloke too, isn't he?' She nudged Jacqui.

Jacqui smiled. 'Do they really call him The Viking?'

'Oh yes, he's always been called that from the first day he arrived here,' said Beth. 'The Birdman and The Viking. It sounds like a film title.'

'What're you two whispering about?' said Alan.

'Men!' Beth grinned.

'Oh, don't even go there,' Alan replied. He took the shower out of the basin and pointed it at Beth.

'Alan! I'm soaked, you Aussie git. Ahh, don't,' Beth squealed.

'I'm not an Aussie, I keep telling you that. I'm a Kiwi. You only say it to annoy me.'

'You remember Mrs Arginson had some kittens to give away?' Linda announced in one of her dreamy moments. 'Well, I found a home for two of them, and I took one back to the mainland for my niece.' As she spoke, she tied an elastic band around the beak of a guillemot to stop it ingesting the oil. She looked as if she was miles away.

Beth was laughing at Alan; neither of them listened to Linda. When Sven returned, he smiled when he saw how they flirted with each other. Scilly stirred all kinds of feelings for romance. He dangled a sand eel in front of the guillemot he had finished drying. It tried to open its beak, and at the right moment he pushed the food down its throat. Success! Once it had the idea, he continued the feeding process. Clever little devils, he thought. *The gannets will be more of a challenge.*

'The sooner we get these big buggers back to sea, the better!' he exclaimed. 'They don't feed easily as they're plunge divers, and it can be rather dangerous trying to get food down *their* throats. They love to take a stab at you.'

An hour later, the *Scillonian* arrived with yet another boatful of tourists. Sven finished his bird-cleaning job and went down the quay to see Don. As he leaned against the rails all he could see was himself kissing Pippa as she left on the ferry. The whole place seemed empty now without her.

'Bet yer missin 'er then, eh, Sven?' Don called from the boat below.

'Ya, it's like someone stole a part of me,' he said with a sigh.

'Heard anuthin' then – phone call?' Don was wiping the seats on *Lily.*

'No, not yet, but I've hardly been home and I was round at Martin's last night. I'm just so busy with this bloody oil spill. I'm knackered. I know she'll phone me, no problem.'

The crew tied up the ship and they stacked the luggage on the back of the lorry ready for delivery.

Don had to take *Lily of Laguna* out to anchor in the bay. Sven made a decision to go with him. He needed the company. He would go home after this and wait for Pippa to phone. Now realising the importance of having an answer phone, he promised himself he would order one soon.

As they started the outboard motor for the return journey, something made him turn around and look towards the quay. Two girls were standing on the pier. He thought he was mistaken and checked through his binoculars. As he got closer, he swung the outboard motor around the other side of the quay and Don almost fell in the water.

'What the...*fuck* is she doing here?' Sven exclaimed.

'Sven, mate, what the hellya doin'?' Don asked, looking shocked.

'Bloody Astrid!'

'Huh?' Don had no idea what Sven was talking about.

'She's the reason I came to Scilly. I suppose that's the only thing I have to thank her for. It's my mother's fault, she shouldn't have told her I live here. She's touring the UK, apparently, with her friend.'

'Who is she, mate?'

'Only the woman I almost married!'

Don turned down the corners of his mouth in sheer surprise at Sven's announcement. He'd no idea, and Sven had never mentioned her before.

'Why the hell can't she leave me alone?' muttered Sven.

He wasn't able to see the girls any more as they had turned the corner of the pier. He would approach from the other side; thank God she hadn't seen him. Was it really Astrid? No, it couldn't be. He recalled the conversation with his mother.

'She wants to see you again.'

He hoped that if it was her, she had come on the day trip and she would be gone by five o'clock. At least, he *hoped* she would. He could avoid her and she might get the message.

If he did it right, he could moor the dingy some distance away from where she was standing and walk along the pier from behind her. Perhaps, if he was lucky, she might be gone soon. He couldn't believe she had actually come to Scilly; this was the second time she had tried to contact him over the last few years. If all she wanted was to apologise and free herself from her own guilt, then he didn't wish to be part of it.

Don found it amusing, but kept his amusement to himself.

'I'll drop you here, mate. I'll go round and approach from the other side, Sven, if that's okay?'

Sven climbed the steps and looked around. *Phew! She's gone.* It couldn't be her – wasn't her – but it was too much of a coincidence. He reached The Mermaid and then he saw her in front of him, a short distance up Hugh Street. *Oh shit, it is Astrid – and Kjerstin.* He would hang back and go home another way. He walked over The Garrison to avoid her.

On arrival home, he plonked himself on the sofa. He shut his eyes, puffing out his cheeks. *What have I done to deserve this? What if she comes knocking at Beachside Cottage?* He hoped no one would tell her where he lived, but it seemed likely they would.

Seeing Astrid standing on the quay was as if she had never been away from him. They'd had good times together, but he could never forgive her. Why did she have to come here all the way from Norway? Was she stalking him? He would scold his mother for doing this to him. He ought to have told her about Pippa.

The phone rang. He didn't know if he should answer it.

'Sven's phone,' he said.

'Darling, it's me. I got back safely, but I won't have much time to talk. Rob has gone out and I'm waiting to speak with him.'

'Oh, Pippa, thank goodness you phoned. I've been so worried about you. Are you okay, *elskling*?' He wanted to jump for joy on hearing her voice, but something in her tone made him realise all was not quite right.

'I'm very tired, and there's been some difficult things happening here. I don't have time to tell you everything except Joan is ill, Terry has left her, she's in hospital, and Rob's got himself a few hundred thousand pounds more than he had when I went on holiday.'

'God, that's amazing – will it change anything? I miss you,' Sven said quickly. 'Come back soon.' He realised he might not have time to say everything.

'I miss you too, but it's going to be hard to talk at the moment. Just wanted you to know I'm doing my best, nothing's changed. I still love you.'

Sven let out an enormous sigh of relief.

'I'll phone you later, okay?' she said in a hurry and trying to be caring at the same time. She heard Rob coming through the front door. 'Must go, sorry, back soon, bye,' she whispered.

She put the phone down, and feelings of abandonment crept into Sven's skin. He knew she would phone him back, but it was all so frustrating not being able to be with her, knowing she was back home with Rob. *I wonder if she's told him.*

It was five o'clock and Sven wanted his self-imposed internment to end. It might be safe now to go out on the street. He was glad he had missed Astrid's visit; he was sure it had been her, and she would be gone by now on the ferry back to the mainland. Was his mind playing tricks with him? He was thrilled Pippa had phoned and, after he'd thought about it, he understood why the call was short and sharp. Maybe she would change her mind about them being together if Rob had all this money. Somehow, he didn't think money mattered to Pippa; she only wanted happiness, but what if he was wrong? *Maybe it's always going to be like this.* How long would he need to wait for her to return to Scilly? He was missing her so much he thought his heart might break. They were meant for each other and he kept repeating those words to himself.

His thoughts turned to Astrid. What did she want to have come all this way? Three years before, he had gone home to Norway and discovered she frequented the same bar as he used to visit. Now it seemed more than coincidence. He could never forgive her. Did she still care about him? Well, too bad, Pippa was part of his life now – or was she? The stress overwhelmed his thoughts.

He needed a drink. Being on his own again was not what he wanted. Those empty feelings made it seem as if Pippa had never been on Scilly; a figment of his imagination in the last three weeks. He walked down Hugh Street and called in at The Mermaid.

The guys from the Gig Club were drinking together. The barman said a 'Hi Sven' and Sven ordered a beer. He sat on the stool at the bar with one foot on the floor and another resting on the stretcher, a pint in his hand, lonely again, his mind mostly on Pippa and the things that might have been.

Someone put money into the pool table and the balls came clattering down the ramp; the noise was too much. He thought he would take a walk along the beach. It wasn't going to get dark until late. He gulped down the last dregs of beer and left the pub.

He walked a long way up and over the headland, the prints on the soles of his sandals making patterns as he walked along the sandy footpaths with the occasional look through his binoculars at a passing bird. With the call of the wild around him, and the voice of the sea, a lump came to his throat. Why did he have to do this to himself each time he found someone he loved? Every time – snatched away. The sound of the waves comforted him, but his legs dragged and his heart felt as if it would stop. He needed to go home to wrap himself in a blanket and hide for a day.

On Sven's return to Beachside Cottage, exhaustion overtook him. From his room he looked across Porthcressa Beach at the incoming tide. He was about to go to sleep when the phone rang. Should he answer it? What if it was *her?* It wouldn't be Pippa or Martin at this time of night, surely. He let the phone ring and put his head under the pillows. He was too tired to be bothered to go all the way downstairs. What if it really was Astrid calling him? She'd often phoned late at night when he was in Norway. The duration of the ringing phone got the better of him. What if it was his mother calling about his dad? He decided to answer it. Before he could pick it up, it stopped. He knew he was being stupid, but he couldn't go through all that again. The person would call back if it was urgent. He returned to his bed. Pippa was his soulmate and he needed her right now. If only he could phone her.

*

The following morning Sven met with Martin at the office. He needed to catch up on the events of the last three months. Margaret had left him a message on his desk.

Hi, Sven,
A young lady came in here yesterday, she said she was from Norway and was asking about you. She left the attached envelope for you. Apparently, she was a friend of yours from some time back. Marg.

Sven banged his fist on his desk. *What does she want from me?* It occurred to him that perhaps he was making a big thing out of it and he should just relax. He had loved Astrid, but how could he go back in time and forgive her? Pippa was his love now, and all he wanted was to take care of her. They needed each other; he realised that now.

Each time the phone rang, he thought twice about answering it. He'd better talk to Margaret.

'Hey, Marg, erm…can you vet all my calls before you put them through? I'm a bit busier than usual. I'd rather not talk to anyone right now – and don't let anyone in my office, please. I want everyone to make appointments to see me. I'm too busy.'

'Oh, okay,' Margaret said, looking surprised. 'I didn't think you were *that* busy now that Martin's back, but okay, I'll do it.'

Sven wondered if he should open the letter immediately. Perhaps it could wait, but, as an afterthought, he reckoned it might provide some insight into why Astrid was here. If he opened it now he could clear up the matter and get on with his life. He decided to be brave about it.

He slit open the envelope and immediately recognised the writing in his own language. It really was from Astrid! What was she doing here?

246

Dear Sven,

*Hope you don't mind me getting in touch like this. I had coffee
with your mother a couple of weeks ago; she looks well. Anyway,
she told me you are working here on the Scilly Islands. Kjerstin,
my best friend, you might remember her, we are doing a tour
of the south of England. We love Cornwall. We were in Devon
a couple of days ago and caught the train to Penzance. We
found a nice little bed and breakfast on St Mary's and took
a risk that maybe after all this time we could put our past
behind us and perhaps meet up for a coffee. There are things
I would like to tell you. I will understand if you don't want to
see me. I mean, last time wasn't exactly under the best of terms.
I just wanted to put it all to rest. I will be on the Garrison
tomorrow lunchtime and I will ask Kjerstin if she wouldn't
mind doing her own thing so we can talk. If you can make it,
I will see you at 12.30pm.*

Love Astrid x

Sven held his breath. The kiss at the end of her name didn't seem
right. He didn't really want to see her. What could she possibly
have to tell him that he did not already know? And yes, to dig up
his feelings like this, after all this time – *typical Astrid.* She had
chosen a place to meet, a place so dear to Pippa's heart – she knew
how to annoy him all right! He realised she couldn't have known,
it just made him angry. She must have realised how it had affected
him all those years ago when he found her with Mads, and now
this waiting, waiting for Pippa, his heart all tangled and torn, no
wonder his head was in turmoil.

Chapter Twenty-Eight

'Pippa, come to bed, love,' Rob shouted. 'It's getting late. We can talk.'

Pippa sat in the lounge wondering what she should do. He might want to "do it" and she knew she couldn't, and he would ask why, and she would have to tell him. For sure, it would be a long night, and she knew a dreadful row was brewing. She couldn't take it after her long journey. Perhaps she should spend time talking and boring him to sleep. How was she going to get out of this one? Tonight was not the right time to discuss their future.

She undressed in the bathroom and pulled on her least sexy pyjamas. She smoothed cream on her face in the hope she could turn him off. She would sleep in the other room; all she wanted was some breathing space from her journey and a chance to think about the best time to explain everything.

Instead, he opened his arms to her and made to kiss her on the lips. Pippa

withdrew from him. 'I can't do this, Rob, I don't feel like it, sorry.'

'What do you mean – *sorry*? You've been asleep most of the day, you've been away from me for the last three weeks – how am I supposed to behave?'

'I know I have, but…' She turned away from him. She was about to tell him she was leaving him when he pulled her down on the bed in play and put his hand up her pyjama top.

'Come on, Pippa, it's been a long time. Let me hold you.'

Pippa stiffened in terror. Her thoughts were screaming 'No, no, I don't…want…to…do…it. Don't make me do it.'

'What's the matter with you? Why don't you want to?' He noted the white ring around her suntanned finger. She wasn't wearing her wedding ring. Yet she had been wearing it; perhaps she'd left it in the bathroom.

'I can't,' she said, thinking she was being unfaithful to Sven and not the other way around. She pulled him away. 'Rob, for God's sake, you have to give me time.'

'How much *more* bloody time do you need? Come on, give us a bit,' he said in a last desperate attempt. 'I need you. You're my wife and we're supposed to love each other.'

Pippa lay there in sheer torment. She didn't know what to do; she felt pinned to the bed. 'Rob, let me go, *please*.'

He released his grip. 'For god's sake, Pippa, what're you trying to do to me? We haven't done this in months, you go away, and now you won't let me near you – what the hell is going on?'

'Let go of me, Rob, don't do this. I don't want sex with you,' she screamed.

'Look, Pippa, we can't carry on like this.'

'You bet we can't. I'm not sleeping in here tonight. I don't want to be with you any more.' She stormed into Daniel's room and Rob followed her.

'But…Pippa, love, things have changed since you went away. We've got money now, and you have to let me explain. Things will be different, I've changed. I have a brother and sister now and well… you have to let me…Oh shit! Why do I bother?'

'Go away, we'll talk in the morning. Bloody money – is that all you care about?' she growled, turning away from him.

'Pippa, I think I still love you. We have to sort this out, I'm sorry.'

'You didn't love me two weeks ago when you said you wanted a divorce, and last month, and the month before that. I don't want to talk about it, go away. You're such a mixed-up person, I don't want to be with you any more. All this counselling and stuff hasn't changed you one bit.'

'*I'm* not mixed up, it's *you* who is mixed up. Things have changed. I keep trying to tell you.' Rob cajoled as best he could.

She pulled the duvet over her head and closed her eyes, denying herself the thoughts of what life might be like if she stayed in Whitby.

'Come on, Pippa, just let me show you, I want you back.' He put his arm around her.

'You're lying, Rob. Don't think I haven't noticed *things* over the last few years.' Her voice was muffled from under the bed covers.

'What things?'

'Hm! Look, just leave it, will you? Give me time to think about all this stuff with you, that's all. I'm not in the mood.'

'You're never in the mood, this has to stop,' he said firmly. He grabbed her again.

'Get lost, Rob, when I say no, I mean no! This is typical of you. You don't know how to love someone, it's all grab-grab and wham-bam. I hate it. You'll never change, I know that now. I want to talk to you in the morning, and maybe we can sort this whole sordid business and get on with our lives.'

The following morning, after Rob had left the house, Pippa tried to phone Sven again, but couldn't reach him.

Feeling as if she had lost Daniel all over again, she wrote to Rob and told him she didn't want to stay with him. She couldn't face him. Then she threw the letter in the bin. When she couldn't find Sven at home, she rang his office; it was all too much.

'Sven is out at sea at the moment,' said Margaret. 'Just gone over to St Agnes. He'll be back soon, though.'

Pippa left a message to say she would phone later at home.

Oh shit, what's happening to me? Was Sven a man of his word? Was he avoiding her now she had left the islands? How could she tell Rob her intentions with Sven so far away, and no news? She began to write it in her head: *Holiday Romance Scandal – grieving mother had sex with birdwatcher.*

Chapter Twenty-Nine

Sven decided the best course of action was to go and see Astrid, and then he could put it all behind him and get on with his life. He felt increasingly concerned about her reason for visiting him. There had been a five year gap since he last saw her; she would have changed, and he had no feelings for her any more, so perhaps it couldn't do any harm.

He raced up The Garrison in his lunch hour, forgetting to take his sandwiches with him. His mind was in too many places, trying to put everything back into perspective. When would Pippa phone, and how had she got on with telling Rob about leaving him?

As he walked up the hill, Astrid hadn't arrived; he was a few minutes early. He sat with his arm across the back of the bench and waited with anger in his thoughts.

Then he saw her, and his heart raced. Old memories began to stir: his time in bed with her; the way she used to tickle his toes; the time they made love in the snow on the forest floor on Christmas Day, and how he'd almost had frost bite on his buttocks. Astrid had taken all his fun away.

As she came towards him, her dark blonde hair blew on The Garrison breeze. She wore black leather clogs and a long flimsy blue-green wraparound skirt, which flapped in the wind like a loose sail on a yacht. Sven stood up to kiss her on both cheeks, to show politeness. She put out her arms to give him a hug.

'Hoi, Svennie, it's good to see you again. How are you? Glad you came. I wasn't sure you would. You look different somehow

– you never used to have long hair, and you were always…' She hesitated.

'Smarter?' he offered with some sarcasm in his voice.

Astrid didn't reply; instead, she sighed.

Sven tried to restrain his thoughts. 'How do you like my islands?' he said, looking out to sea and attempting to be somewhere else.

'Shall we sit down?' Astrid suggested. 'I wanted to see you because I was very sorry about what I did to you. I've never forgotten you, and the reason Mads and I got divorced is purely that I made some dreadful mistakes. I think I still love you, Sven.'

'Oh, Astrid, here we go. Emotional blackmail.'

'No, Svennie, you've got to listen, please. You see, the thing with Mads and I, it was a spur of the moment thing, and we didn't want to hurt you. It was a one off and a stupid thing to do. A final fling, you might say, before our wedding day – a kind of juvenile silly joke that went wrong. I'll regret it for the rest of my life, honest I will. I would never have told you about it, because it was stupidity. I didn't meant to hurt you so bad. You left Norway before I could explain. It all seems such a long time ago now.'

Sven turned to her. 'I can't imagine what brought you this far thinking I might come back to you at the drop of a hat. There has to be another reason.'

'Kjerstin and I decided to take a holiday in the south of England. I felt I should take the opportunity to come and tell you this, as your mother told me you grieved about me a long time. She thought you were still upset, as you hadn't found anyone else in the last five years. We had a long chat and we both thought you might like to talk about it. I'm on my own now, and I still think about you, Svennie.'

Sven waited a few seconds before replying. 'I think you came here on a mission which has failed, Astrid,' he said coldly, annoyed she had got his mother involved in this.

Not being sure about his relationship with Pippa, he took a risk. Seeing Astrid made him realise he still had *some* feelings for her, but not the same feelings as he'd once had; she had broken his heart. He had to be blunt with her.

'I already have a girlfriend and we are very close.' *Close* was not the word; distance was the biggest bugbear, and he might be throwing away something he would regret for the rest of his life. Astrid or Pippa? He mustn't even think about it. He had no choice, and anyway, Pippa was his love now. He must have faith that she would make it back to the islands.

It was then that the inevitable question seemed to flow from Astrid's lips. Her eyes gazed upon his sandal-clad feet.

'Oh, I see, how long have you been going out together?'

'Not long,' he said, avoiding the truth. It was none of her business anyway.

Astrid came closer. He could almost feel her breath upon his face. 'Sven, I miss you so much,' she said as she linked her arm with his.

'You should have thought about that when you got into bed with Mads. You hurt me, Astrid, hurt me real bad, and I can never forgive you.' Sven turned away from her. 'Did you really think by coming to Scilly you could persuade me to come back to you after all this time? You must be crazy.'

'Sven, listen, I travelled all the way from Norway to tell you I'm sorry.'

'What! After five years, you come to tell me you married the wrong guy? You had *me* – me who loved you – and you blew it.'

'Please, Svennie. I do miss you.' Astrid's tears fell down her face.

Sven stood up. 'Don't do this to me, not now,' Sven said, knowing he had to get back to work soon.

She sobbed, the queen of sobs. He thought she sounded genuine and he put his arm around her to comfort her. She looked up at him and she kissed him full on the lips.

For a few seconds he felt confused. It was the kiss he remembered when he proposed to her. He pulled away from her. 'Astrid, stop, don't do that. You and I, we…'

'Don't tell me you don't love me any more.'

'The truth is, after I left I lost all faith in love, women, and sex – everything after I lost you. I came to Scilly to start a new life. The last thing I expected was you to follow me here five years later to apologise to me. You're sick, you know that?' He stood up and moved away from her. 'I'm sorry, Astrid, but I can't do this, and how do I know you wouldn't do it again, huh?

She looked distraught, and Sven's natural kindness returned. He sighed as he began to feel sorry for her. He felt some remorse about what he'd just said.

In a quiet moment, Astrid spoke. 'I lost our baby, Sven. I mean *our* baby.' She looked into his eyes.

'What? Now I know you are really crazy.' Sven almost felt sick with anger. He stood up from the bench and looked again at the view of the other islands.

'I was pregnant when Mads and I were...well, you know. I never told you because I didn't know. I got to seven months and she died within me. I know she was yours. I had morning sickness for a few weeks before Mads and I got together for that one time. I had no idea it was a pregnancy, I assumed I was a bit ill.'

'Astrid, are you stupid or something?' Sven turned to her.

'I didn't know about how it would be to have a baby then, or how I was supposed to feel. I was only twenty-two at the time. We were young and knew nothing. The baby had to be yours. They told me at the hospital she was longer term than I thought. I worked out the dates. I saw her, Sven, she lay in my arms so small and sweet, then they took her away and we had a small funeral. Mads never knew the baby wasn't his until I had to tell him. I made some terrible mistakes and I'm sorry. You have no idea what it did to me – and Mads, too. I'm just a stupid person, Sven, I only came to tell you I'm sorry. You had to know about it, that's all. I had to tell you the truth.'

'Astrid, if this is true, why didn't you tell me until after all this time? I mean, are you saying it was my child? How could you do that?' His insides thumped with anger. His child was stillborn and his ex had married his best friend instead. How was he supposed to feel? He wanted to hide from her, wishing he had ignored her. With this new revelation, his day, his whole life had turned upside down.

Astrid sobbed. 'I'm sorry, Sven, I'm so, so sorry.'

He held her in his arms to comfort her again. What was he supposed to do about it? He wanted to believe it wasn't true. He had to meet Don in twenty minutes, and fifty passengers were going to St Martins. How could he go on the trip with his mind on this? He felt sick at her revelation, and time wasn't on his side. How could he let his birdwatching group go on a walk without him? Martin was busy catching up on his work; he couldn't possibly ask him to help. He took a deep breath.

'Astrid, look, I'm sorry, and at this moment I know it seems a bit thoughtless, but I have to go back to work. I only get an hour for lunch and then I have a tour on the boats. How long are you staying on the islands?'

'Two more nights.' Astrid sniffed into her handkerchief.

'Oh, I see. Maybe I'll find time for a drink before you go back. Please don't ask me to commit to you. I have Pippa now and we have a wonderful relationship. I can't be part of your life any more, sorry. A child makes no difference. I don't feel anything. It's like you're talking about someone else.' He wasn't sure if he had told the truth.

He looked into her swollen eyes, with the tears still rolling down her face. The thought that he might have been a father confused him. He would always have remembered how unfaithful she was. Her revelations didn't mean a lot to him; he felt numb and unconvinced, not sure what to say to her. He would never have come to Scilly, led a wonderful life and met all these lovely people if she hadn't gone with Mads. Perhaps in her own way Astrid had given him a chance he would never have had if they hadn't parted. How was he supposed to feel? He didn't know anything any more.

'I'll meet up with you before you leave. I'll buy you and Kjerstin a drink and we'll have a chat together. I don't want to leave you on bad terms, but I have Pippa and I could never let her down or upset her in any way. She lost someone close to her in a road accident and there is no way I could hurt her. Besides, I love her very much.'

'Oh…I see…Where is she today?' Astrid sniffed into her paper handkerchief.

'Er…she's away in the north of England for a week, gone to sort out some family business.' Sven realised he shouldn't have told her. He knew he was just an honest bloke and not very good at telling lies.

'Well, maybe she would understand how it's been for me, too.'

'Look, Astrid, I'm sorry. Life goes on. It makes no difference. Sorry, but I have to get back to work, I'm afraid. Come on back into town with me and we'll meet with Kjerstin. I remember her from college – is that the same person?'

Astrid sniffed back her tears. 'Yes, she knows you, she told me.'

'I am shocked, of course. I mean…but I can't say it'll change anything. I have a wonderful life here and I really don't want to come back to Norway. It's a lot warmer down here, less depressing in the winter, and, well, it's – idyllic! Would you blame me?' he said with a smile and a raised brow.

His hate for her began to subside. If only Pippa would come back; if only he had an assurance that she would leave Rob. I love Pippa, he kept telling himself, I do, I do, I do. Going back to Astrid would never be an option; he knew she couldn't be trusted. She should have told him about the child. Why had she married Mads? Was it because Sven had left and she needed a father for the baby? Surely not.

Chapter Thirty

Rob tried to smile, but couldn't. 'I have to go and see Joan at the hospital, I promised her I would. When I get back, we have to talk. We can't go on like this any more: something has to give. I really did expect you to come back from Scilly feeling happy, but instead you have turned into the saddest person ever! I've never seen you this way since Daniel. What's going on, Pippa?'

She looked into his eyes, feeling battered. 'Rob, I'm leaving you.'

'Come on, don't be silly. Try to pull yourself together, Pippa. What's the matter?' He tried to treat her like his wife and not one of his patients. He leaned to get closer to her, thinking he'd make it up to her.

'Get away from me,' Pippa cried. 'You almost raped me last night.'

'No, I did not! I was so frustrated and I was trying to cheer you up. Look, I'm truly sorry for what I did. It's not like me to behave in that way, but I needed you and you weren't there for me.'

The tears leaked down her cheeks. All she could see was Sven holding out his arms to her.

Rob held her hand and she let him. 'Come on, Pippa, we can have a wonderful life together now. We can go on those holidays we could never afford, and have a new family life with Bruce and Penny, my brother and sister. It will be amazing. Come here, let me hold you.'

Pippa's tears burst forth into wailing. Sven had said the same words in the bird hide. Rob held her in his arms, but it was not Rob, it was Sven who kissed her.

'Come on, love, it's going to be all right,' said Rob.

'No, it isn't.' She pulled away from him with a determined air in her voice. 'I'm leaving you. I've found someone else in my life and I can't go on like this any more. You have money now, a new life. I have the house and no ties.'

'What? You've got another bloke?' shouted Rob. 'Pippa, how could you do this to me? Who is he?'

'Someone I met on the Isles of Scilly,' she sobbed loudly.

'Ha! A holiday romance. I knew it! I thought I could trust you. That's what all that palaver was about last night – now I understand. How stupid can you be? How stupid am I? Did you have sex with him? I bet you did! You are so naïve, aren't you? He only wanted you because you're on your own – men do that, Pippa, easy pickings. It's the same old story women fall for every time, a bit of cheap fun on holiday. No wonder you didn't want to open up to me last night. I get it now, I see.'

'No, it wasn't like that,' Pippa pleaded.

'Now, come on…for God's sake.' He stood glaring into her face. 'You need some help to understand your inner self. I've had enough of this.'

Pippa thought about his final words. Was she losing her mind? No, she bloody well wasn't.

'Rob!' she shouted. 'I do *not* need counselling, all I want is to live with nature and have some freedom away from this dreadful life we have together. This is the only way. I don't want to be with you any more. If this is all about money – forget it. You and I can live independently. We don't need each other any more.'

'You can't leave me, Pippa, where will I live?' All Rob could think about was the timing of the situation. He needed a cigarette and realised he'd given it up.

'I've thought about it. You can stay here until the house is sold. You'll have plenty of time and your own money will be through by then.' Pippa saw the forlorn look on his face and decided she needed to say more. 'Rob, listen to me.' She softened her tone. 'This is our chance to start afresh, don't you see? We had a great time together, but with Daniel gone, it's all gone, every single bit we ever had – vanished. I lost my mother, then my dad, and then our son, and now I'm choosing to leave. I've had enough. This is our chance to move on in our lives. We've spent too long with Joan and Terry, and as much as I adore Joan, I think she realises it too. Anyway, you spend too much time with Joan and not me. Don't think I haven't noticed.' She wondered how she would tell Joan about Sven. Was it necessary? Joan seemed too sick, and Pippa was putting off visiting her for another day or so.

Rob stood in anger and walked out of the room. Pippa heard the front door slam behind him. For a moment, she felt a silence she'd only heard once before, the day he'd told her Daniel had died. She sat down and fixed her eyes on the empty grate in the stove. She had done the same thing when she returned from hospital, staring at the glowing embers and wishing she had died with her son.

'Sven's phone.'

'Hi, Sven, it's me.'

'Oh, thank goodness. Hello, my love – are you all right? My stomach is in such a knot, I'm so worried about you.'

His Norwegian accent sang down the phone line. For one moment, she was back on the islands with him, sitting on the white sand with her back against the rocks on Porthcressa Beach.

'Sven, I'm so confused. I told Rob – well, I didn't tell him who you were. He's gone out to see Joan. She's out of hospital, I have to go and see her later. You've gotta help me here, what do I do? Should I just pack up and travel back to Scilly?'

With those words, Sven's heart gave a jump. Astrid was still lurking on the islands. He had to make sure she got back on that ferry.

Pippa started to cry again, and Sven longed to be with her – to hold her in his arms and love her to bits.

'Do you still want me?' she cried. 'I don't know what to do.'

'*Elskling*, of course I want you. He's bound to make it difficult, but the decision has to be yours.' Sven wanted to assure her he would take care of her for the rest of his life. 'I love you, Pippa, with all my heart – come back to me.'

Pippa cried down the phone. 'I don't know how to do this, and then there's Daniel in the graveyard. How can I leave him?'

'Pippa, my love, sometimes you have to find that direction – remember what you told me? Perhaps this is your one and only chance, but you have to make this choice yourself. Believe me, no one understands right now more than me about making choices. I came to Scilly after a broken love affair, remember? I thought we were made for each other, but it's you I love, Pips, honest I do. I just wish you were back here, loving me. We're both feeling very lonely right now and very insecure.'

Pippa thought she knew what he meant. She was feeling more than insecure right now, but time wasn't on her side to think too long about it.

'Yes, me too. Can I phone you back? Rob will be home soon. I love you too, Sven. There has to be a way. I'll call you this afternoon when he's gone to work.'

Sven made kissing noises down the phone. 'I'll be at home around three. Call me then, okay? I'm coming home early today. Bye, *elskling*, and good luck – hope to see you soon, as I have an idea that might please you. I'll explain when you phone back. Love you lots, bye.'

Pippa slowly replaced the receiver, his lovely voice echoing in her ear. 'You know we have to be together, nothing else matters.'

Sven knew he had to talk with Martin. He'd never been to Yorkshire; perhaps a holiday would do him good. Get away from the insular lifestyle of Scilly for a week.

He wanted to tell Pippa about Astrid, but if he told her now, she might change her mind. The revelations about her having his baby all those years ago, losing it after long term, and never having told him had made him both angry and sad. Pippa would surely understand. Perhaps he wouldn't bother to tell her at all; it might spoil her feelings towards him. Well, maybe he should, but not now. He would choose the right moment when she returned.

'Yoo hoo, Sven, it's me-ee,' Andrea shouted through the porch.

Sven stepped into the lounge from the kitchen. 'Hi, Andrea, how lovely. This is a surprise.'

'I brought you your favourite – chocolate brownies,' she said. 'I thought it might cheer you up.'

'You're too good to me, you know that.' Sven chuckled as he took the Tupperware box from her hand.

'Everything going well, then? Martin's gone over to Tresco today so I thought I'd call in. We missed you while we were away. It was lovely to see you again the other night.'

'I have to thank you for letting me sleep over. I was rather pissed, wasn't I?'

'Nooo, of course you weren't! Just happy, that's all,' she said, laughing. 'Have you heard from Pippa? She sounds lovely, I am dying to meet her. Is she coming back to St Mary's soon?'

'Well, yes, I've had some good news and some bad.' Sven sighed. He proceeded to tell Andrea the whole story about Astrid. Relieved that Andrea had paid him a visit; he needed to offload.

'Is there anything I can do?' she asked. 'You never told us about her, but I suppose it was none of our business.'

'Just be there for me, Andrea, please. As a woman, I'm sure you understand how other women think. I don't have anyone else I can talk to except Don, and he belongs in the last generation. He's a bloke – so I need to talk to *you* right now.' Sven was only half-joking.

'Of course, I'm always here for you, Sven, you know that. So... Pippa is coming back soon, eh? May I ask you if you really love her?

I mean, enough to spend the rest of your life with her? You hardly know each other, I suppose,' Andrea said, playing the role of parent.

'I know what you mean, and it's been hard not to see Astrid as we used to be. We had such great times together. I absolutely idolised her. She was my soulmate, and that's why I asked her to marry me. The trouble is she kissed me yesterday – you know, in *that* way. Of course, I spurned her, but it stirred all kinds of things in me. I hated doing that and it did give me an odd feeling, but when I got home I realised she could destroy me again and again.' He shook his head and turned down the corner of his mouth. 'With Pippa…yes, she has some grief and stressful baggage to overcome, I know, but when she does come back here, it'll be just a matter of her getting a divorce from her husband. I love Pippa very much. Besides, despite the fact we have only been together a short time, she loves the things I love. She and I have something far more special now. Astrid never understood my love of nature, and I don't think I could ever love her again.' He decided not to mention the baby thing: best not complicate it further. He must tell Pippa first.

'When is Pippa coming back? I mean, a three week relationship has to be something extraordinarily special.' Andrea gave a sympathetic smile.

'It *is* special. I don't know yet when she's coming, I want to speak with Martin. I have an idea. Astrid is going home soon. I hope she's not here when Pippa comes back – that'd be the end for me, my worst nightmare. I think it would destroy her.'

'The way I see it, Pippa seems right for you, and the way you described her the other night, you seem completely bowled over by her.'

'I know – you're right.' Sven smiled at her comment. 'But all this is confusing me.'

'I like Pippa already,' Andrea told him, trying to sound positive. 'She sounds like one of us, but you are really going to have to be very careful, Sven – you're treading on dangerous ground. I'm worried that you will end up being hurt again.'

'Mm, I know,' Sven said pensively. 'It's just there's something about her which tells me she is genuine and understands me. It's not the same as when Astrid and I were together, it's more, well... more grown up, if you see what I mean.'

'Don't worry, everything will turn out fine. You only need to see Pippa again, and, well, Astrid...she's another problem you have to try and sort out pretty soon. Look, sweetie, I must be on my way now – sorry to cut this short. You will come round and see us soon, won't you? Let me know how it's going. The only advice I can give you right now is to follow your heart.'

Andrea wished Sven good luck and left him with the chocolate brownies.

'Call me if there's anything I can do, you know I'm a good listener. And why don't you have a chat with Don anyway? You know he thinks a lot about you.'

'Thanks, Andrea, I just needed to talk, that's all. You know what it's like here.'

Sven watched her as he waved goodbye. 'Thanks for the brownies,' he called with a smile as she walked down the garden path. *Good old Andrea, Martin is lucky to have her.* He knew that was how he wanted his relationship to be. Travelling the world with the woman he loved: genuine support for each other, and a perfect partnership. There was no doubt Pippa had the same interests. He didn't wish to leave Scilly and go back to Norway, and it was all such a long time ago. Anyway, if Astrid could lie to him once, she could do it again. Besides, she had also lied to Mads. No, it was best to do it this way. Fate had certainly taken a hand, he thought.

Chapter Thirty-One

'Your blood pressure is a little higher today, Joan,' Rob said as he tugged the band away from her arm. He pulled down her lower eyelids. 'Mm, nice and pink. I would think in the next few days you'll be fine. You look a lot better than the other day when I saw you in hospital. I'll tell Dr Kumar I called in to see you.'

'Our Carole had Jordan today for me and she did my hair. Yes, I know I made a stupid mistake the other day. I was so down about Terry and the thought of being left on my own… I'm still feeling lonely. How are things with you?' Joan asked, wondering why Pippa hadn't been to see her.

Rob realised she wasn't ready to talk about her suicidal frenzy, and he didn't want to talk about Pippa either.

'Okay, I suppose. Perhaps now isn't a good time to discuss it.'

'What's the matter, Rob? Is it Pippa?' Joan asked, looking into his eyes.

Rob nodded. He hadn't come to see Joan to discuss Pippa, but he supposed it was inevitable. The two women were friends, but for how much longer he didn't like to guess.

Joan patted Rob's arm. 'You know the way I see it both of you need your heads banging together, and the same goes for me. I suppose none of us likes change. It's unsettling, especially when you are left alone to cope with it.'

'Joan, I have something to tell you. I'm sorry, but it's not very good news at this difficult time. Pippa told me this morning she has found someone else.'

'What? Another bloke, you mean?'

Rob nodded grimly.

'My God, when did this happen? Rob, I'm so sorry.' Joan wondered what Pippa had been doing since she'd been to Scilly. Everyone was leaving her, and what was she supposed to do? She began to feel abandoned again.

Rob gazed at the floor; he had failed. His son was dead, his wife had betrayed him, and now he knew how Joan must have felt when she took the pills.

Joan put her arm on his shoulder. 'Rob, how do you feel?' She had meant to say 'How do you *really* feel?'

'A bit of a failure at the moment,' he said, turning down a corner of his mouth. 'But my training keeps me positive, I suppose. I have to believe this is not happening, but somehow it's like… I don't have any feelings at all. I was hoping with all this extra cash from my real parents we could do something different. At the moment my world's turned upside down.'

'Money doesn't buy happiness, Rob. We all know that. I'll talk to Pippa later and see how she is. I don't want to be left on my own. I'll miss you both, and then what am I supposed to do with my life?'

'You and me, Joan, it seems we have been through such troubled times in recent months,' Rob said. Joan was sweet and kind to him, and he needed it right now. She had always known how to talk to him; she had been stronger than Pippa in many ways, but she hadn't had a tragedy in her life until Terry had left. She had Jordan, and he was her pride and joy. *She'd obviously blocked the kid out of her mind when she took those pills.* He adored little Jordan, and he'd often looked after him when Joan had gone shopping. He thought about how much they needed each other right now.

He kissed her on the cheek. 'Must go, Joan, I'm off to work this afternoon, pet. I'm feeling a bit lost for words.'

'It's understandable,' Joan empathised. 'I mean, you have both been through such a lot of pain over the last few years.'

'Let me try and fix this, Joanie. I'll come and see you later, and please don't worry. These things have a habit of sorting themselves out. I have the feeling Pippa might not be around much longer, and I can't stand living like this any more. I need love and understanding, not a daily boxing match where I get knocked out with every bloody round.'

Joan smiled at him, feeling a bit "piggy in the middle". 'You're right. It's awkward, isn't it? Let me know if Pippa is really going. I'm upset about it. Who's this bloke she's got?'

'Some bastard from the Isles of Scilly – no idea. I'm worried in case it's all a stupid phase, a holiday romance. She won't go back there, surely? It's too far. I daren't ask her about it, she just clams up. I'm on nights again tomorrow, in bed all day. God!'

He wanted to kiss Joan again for her caring, but at the last moment he got cold feet and gave her a hug instead.

Joan smiled a quick, flirtatious smile. 'Promise to come back soon.'

'I will. Now you go and get some rest, I'll be late for work.'

She looked at him and he caught her glance. 'I wish…' Before he stood up to leave, she held onto him in a lingering way.

'Rob?'

He smiled at her, conscious of the way she looked at him. Their eyes met.

'Rob, I've been thinking…'

'I know,' he said with a smile. 'Give me a bit more time…'

Chapter Thirty-Two

'I suppose I can do without you for a few days,' said Martin. 'I think you deserve some time out. Anyway, Sven, let's talk about it this afternoon at the office.'

Sven had waited for Martin to say the right words. He didn't wish to inconvenience his colleague by asking for time off when Martin had just got back from his tour, but knew his friend might understand.

After a brisk walk into town, he took his sandwiches and sat on a step at the top of the quay, his mind a million miles away. He dangled his feet over the edge. There were tiny fish in mini shoals, and he watched a small crab claw its way along the bottom of the sea. He took a bite of his chicken and lettuce sandwich, and some of the crumbs fell in the water. The small fry came to the surface to nibble.

He pondered if he should hire a car or catch the train. Then he realised the worst of his problems would be when he got there. It might be awkward. What if he met Rob and there was a slanging match? He didn't want to think about it. He knew the train journey would be arduous; he would ask Andrea if he could borrow a map of Great Britain for when he hired the car.

How he missed Pippa. Each time he thought about her, he wanted to make her happy again. Take her away from the misery of her life with Rob. He had visions of her living in a quaint cottage like his, and her husband ignoring her all day. How could she possibly have an amicable divorce? Perhaps Rob needed a fresh start as well. Anyway, going north would get him away from Astrid – she might decide to stay, and it would get him off the hook if he left the islands. He was about to take a risk, but would he regret it?

Behind him, someone tapped his shoulder. 'I'm leaving today. I'm so glad we talked.'

'Oh, er, hi, Astrid, erm…yes, I see.' Sven shook himself out of his world.

'I shall never stop loving you, Sven, but I realise I can't have you.'

'Let's just say you could have had me, Astrid, but it was not to be, and let's leave it at that, shall we? I'm only here because of you, and I suppose I have to thank you for that. I'm very happy living on Scilly, I don't want to come back to Norway. You do understand that, don't you?' He stared hard into her in the eyes, he definitely wasn't going to change his mind.

'You are lucky, you know, your life here looks great. It really is very beautiful around these islands. I've enjoyed myself despite everything. I'm sorry, Sven, I hope you'll forgive me.'

Sven became aware of the look on her face. It was a look of "you've got to feel sorry for me". He'd seen it all before.

'I named our baby Petja. I hope you will at least have a name for her now. I think maybe she looked like you, but she was so small, it was hard to tell. I lost her in the January in the year we were supposed to…you know…get married. Perhaps your girlfriend understands how I feel. Will you tell her about me?'

'She knows,' he replied coldly. 'I'm glad you see things in a different light now, Astrid, thank you. I'm so sorry about the baby.' He realised what he'd just said; it was as if the baby was in his imagination and not his child – and perhaps it wasn't. Maybe Astrid wanted sympathy for her wrongdoings; it was hard to tell. He ought to give her the benefit of the doubt. He made his apologies, telling her he had to get back to the office. He hugged her, and she kissed him one last time and then burst into tears.

'I can't do this, Sven, please let me stay with you. Please, darling, let me…'

Kjerstin called to her in English. 'Come on, Astreed, de boat is leaving.'

'I'm not going, Kjerstin, I can't do this, I want to stay here with Sven,' she replied.

'Astrid, you *can't* stay here – you have to go home,' Kjerstin pleaded. 'Please don't mess up our holiday.'

Sven realised he had to be strong. 'Kjerstin's right – you have to go. These islands are not the place for you, Astrid. I'm sorry, but I don't love you any more. Please just go home – it's too late for all this, far too late.' He ushered her, almost pushed her, towards the *Scillonian*.

Kjerstin held onto her arm and drew her towards the ship. The crew were taking up the gangway. She urged Astrid to get a move on.

Astrid sobbed as she made her mind up whether or not to leave. Sven couldn't take it any more. He and Kjerstin walked along holding one each of Astrid's arms, escorting her to the gangway. 'Go home to Norway, Astrid. I really don't want you here, okay? Sorry, Kjerstin, can you calm her down when you get on the ship and make her see sense?'

Astrid broke down in floods of tears as Sven looked away from her.

Kjerstin nodded. 'Come on, Astrid. We have to go. Say goodbye to Sven and let's get on this boat.'

'I'm sorry, Astrid, but I love Pippa now and, well… I'm not changing my mind. Goodbye, and maybe one day I'll see you in Norway. Who knows where our lives will go in the future? Good luck.' He didn't kiss her goodbye and knew he'd pushed her on the boat. He smiled at Kjerstin apologetically. He hated the way he'd treated Astrid, but he really didn't want her any more; he knew that now. *I have to go and find Pippa.*

The local boatmen stood and watched, unable to understand what was going on. Astrid had no right to make a fool out of him in front of the islanders.

He made certain the gangway was up and walked away as they set sail. He gave an apologetic wave and caught a glimpse of her sobbing. *A baby? I never thought…* He shook his head in disbelief. She was obviously very insecure, but it could be true, and secretly he wanted to believe he could father a child.

'Hi, Sven, let's go into my office and then we can talk in some peace and quiet. God, I've had a busy morning, and everyone wanted to ask me about my trip.'

Sven sat down, his mind perplexed after his farewell to Astrid. No one he knew had ever carried on in that way.

'Tea?' Martin asked, starting to fill the kettle.

'*Please,*' he said, feeling grateful.

'So Pippa is coming back after all, eh?' Martin sat down on the swivel chair at his desk and stretched with his hands clasped behind his head.

'I hope so.' Sven was quiet. He hoped Martin could spare him time off.

'Well, I've been thinking about this since I got back. I hear you've done a great job, I'm very grateful for all the work you put in. Anyway, I have some good news for you. Head Office has given me the chance to renew your contract with the Wildlife Trust on a more permanent basis.'

Sven's chest pounded. He thought he had come to discuss Pippa and his time off. He stirred his tea and preferred not to have the milk that Martin was pouring into his cup; it looked a bit suspect anyway.

'Oh hell, I haven't really had time to think about it, but yes, it is something I would like to do very much. I mean, stay on here. I couldn't imagine leaving Scilly now,' he confessed. 'That's wonderful news.'

'From all accounts you've made a name for yourself while I've been away. I see "The Viking" has become an icon,' grinned Martin. 'I think if they were to end the contract I would be in deep trouble with the folks on these islands. As long as there is funding for you, we can keep going.'

270

Sven smiled. 'Hm... I'm only doing my job, but that's great news.' His mind was still feeling the negativity about Astrid and the look on her face as she left on the boat. He wasn't proud of his actions.

Martin continued, 'Now, because of this, and with the situation between you and Pippa, I've had an idea. In view of what you told me about her teaching skills and her enthusiasm about wildlife, I feel she would be a valuable asset to these islands. I was told this morning they are going to fund an education officer for us.'

'Oh, hang on, Martin, I don't know if she will... I'll have to ask her, but... My God, that's fantastic! You think...' Sven stopped before he jumped too far ahead.

'Margaret retires next year and we could consider Pippa as her replacement – but in the meantime we need someone to go into the schools and help with our wildlife projects and so on. Having a qualified teacher as part of the team would be great. What do you think? I could interview her when she gets back.'

Sven smiled, feeling grateful, but his mind jarred for a moment – what about following local protocol? 'Well, I think that's great, but it's rather premature – and shouldn't we be giving this job to an islander?'

'I know what you mean, but I have been asking around. There's Sue Carruthers on Tresco who seemed interested, but then she gave up on the idea. One of the local teachers said she would like to do it and promptly changed her mind because of the extra commitment, and then I thought about Margaret helping us part time, but she wants her retirement. I shall put up an advert in the library and on the door of our office, and I might put one in the local magazine too, to be fair.'

'Okay, I'll see what Pippa says when we get together. Thanks, Martin, that's a very interesting offer.'

'You say you want to go north and bring her back? Won't she be able to come here on her own again?'

'It's awkward, she needs me right now. You see it's not that easy for her at the moment. We've made this, erm...arrangement?'

'Sven, you idiot, you don't have to ask, of course you can go.' Martin laughed at Sven's expression. 'When do you want to do it?'

'In an hour?' Sven joked.

'When I saw you both on the quay, I don't think I've ever seen anyone more in love than you two. She seems a lovely girl. Congratulations. I hope it works out. I would like to meet with her again when she gets back, get to know her better, and generally find out what she can do for us.'

Sven's life began to blossom. His time with Pippa had been wonderful, but this offer had exceeded his expectations.

'How about if I pack my gear later this afternoon and fly out tomorrow? I can drive up to the airport and see if they can take me in the morning. I might have to stop over at the youth hostel and then go up north the next day. The YHA is handy – it's cheap and pleasant enough. Pippa told me she stayed there too.'

'Fine, Sven. Do it.'

'I think I'll go by train and then hire a car. It's a long way to drive on my own. I'll have to borrow a map. Does Andrea have one I could use? She does a lot of driving on the mainland, doesn't she?'

Martin smiled, and almost chuckled. 'I can tell you already had this planned in your head, mate, eh? Are you usually into rescuing damsels in distress, Sven?'

Sven laughed. 'Is it that obvious? I don't suppose I am really, but I don't think I could live with myself if I didn't at least try.'

He finished his tea and couldn't wait to burst out of the office. The phone rang. Martin answered it. He was chatting to someone Sven couldn't hear.

'You've got an injured gannet? Where is it…? Oh, I see – on the airfield…? Yes, sure, have you caught it…? Right, okay. Well, Linda is still with us, I'll ask her to drive up there and fetch it. If necessary, she'll take it round to the vet… And while you're on the phone, Colin, Sven might want to ask you something. Hold on.' He handed the phone to Sven who raised his eyebrows, now realising who it was.

'Oh, hi, Colin. Have you any flights for tomorrow morning? It's only for me.'

Colin checked the list. 'No, sorry, none in the morning, but in the afternoon…' He checked down his list again. 'Yeah, plenty, we've got four seats free. D'ye wanna book it?'

Sven left the office not believing his luck. He would phone the youth hostel next, and then make enquiries for the train and car hire in Darlington. His nerves were holding up. Where did he really stand in this love knot? Pippa might be annoyed at him for coming up north, and besides Rob was still lurking around. He could end up with more than a broken nose.

He waited at home, and as promised at three o'clock the phone rang.

'Hi, Sven, it's me.'

'Hi, Pippa. How are things?' He thought she sounded tired.

'Awful. I'm worried in case this isn't going to work. I mean, how can I get to you? I've never walked out on anyone before.'

'Well, listen, my darling,' Sven continued. 'First I have some good news. How about if I come to Whitby? Martin has given me a week off work, and my contract has been renewed. Do you love me enough to be with me for the rest of your life, Pippa?'

'Oh, Sven, you're so lovely. Congratulations on the contract. Yes, yes, yes. Please come to me. I need you right now, except we'll have to be careful Rob doesn't see us together. I don't want you to be meeting him in a pub. It's a bit like Scilly here, everyone knows everyone else. Word might get around. I'm feeling so lonely. Joan is telling me not to do it, and then she said did I really mean it? They say I am stupid and it's a holiday romance. It's as if they have all turned against me. Rob thinks I need grief counselling. I know I love you. I want to live my life with you, the birds, the wildlife, the freedom. Who could blame me for wanting all that?'

'Then let's do it.' Sven smiled down the phone. 'I'll call you as soon as I'm on my way. Stay with it, Pippa, rescue is at hand.

273

I know we're both mad, but that's what our relationship is all about – this crazy madness. I didn't want to break up someone's marriage, but I have and I feel…bad enough. Listen, my love, you and I were meant to be together, it's that simple. The hard part is leaving, but don't worry, we'll sort it.'

Pippa giggled with tears in her eyes. He still loved her. *What a relief.* Could she hold out until he made it to Whitby?

Chapter Thirty-Three

Sven almost ran around Beachside Cottage with joy. He was going to the mainland at last! It had been fifteen months since his last visit.

His time with Astrid had sealed his finality over his relationship with her. He now had no regrets; he knew he could father a child, and understood some of how it must have been for Pippa when she lost Daniel. Astrid had shown her own grief, and perhaps he should have spent more time with her. But no, there was nothing more he could have done. He was destined to be with Pippa. Perhaps one day they would have children of their own. He would tell her soon about Astrid and the baby. All he wanted was to go north and find her. Perhaps he was making the biggest mistake of his life if it all went wrong – and would she change her mind? He tried not to think too much about it – now or never – and then there was Rob...

The following afternoon he landed with the helicopter at Penzance, then called in at the youth hostel and met with Mike.

'Can you spell your name for me, please?' Mike asked as he leaned over the reception desk.

Sven commenced the spelling. 'Jor...gen...sen.'

'I gather you've come from Scandinavia.'

'Yes and no. Actually I live on the Isles of Scilly, but yes, I'm Norwegian.'

'Oh, right. I met a girl going to Scilly the other week. Her name was Pippa. Smashing girl, she was. We spent a short time together on her first trip, and then a quick chat when she went back up north. She's got herself a boyfriend over there now.'

'Ha! That's funny, she's my girlfriend.'

Mike smiled to himself. 'Lucky you, it seems I missed the boat there.' He chuckled. 'She's a really nice girl, seemed a bit lonely when I first met her. Anyway, you're in room twelve on the next floor. If you need help, just ask.' He hoped he would see them both again. Pippa had mentioned the local artists on the islands, and he was an art student after all. 'Good luck, anyway. Please send my regards. Here's your key. Okay, see you later.' His eyes followed Sven as he climbed the stairs with his rucksack slung over his shoulder.

It was early morning as Sven boarded the train to Bristol, where he'd change trains for Darlington. He expected to arrive in Whitby that evening, and would collect the hire car and go to the Abbey Hotel to check in for his reservation.

On the phone, Pippa had told him where she lived, but he couldn't possibly go there. What if he bumped into Rob? Not that he knew what Rob looked like. Chasing after a woman he'd only known for three weeks had never been his way of doing things, and Sven knew his Scandinavian looks and the way he spoke stood out in the crowd.

The following morning he awoke to the familiar sound of herring gulls calling on the rooftops. His attention turned towards the white cottages and buildings on the narrow streets and alleyways of Whitby. The scenery looked all too familiar, but the ring and bustle of a mainland seaside town felt different from the unique sounds of island life. He could hear traffic – lots of it, the squeal of brakes and doors slamming below his window. After breakfast, he took a walk into town and pretended he was window-shopping. He daren't walk past the house, yet it was so tempting to turn up and say, 'Hi, I'm here.'

As he stood at the end of the street, he scanned the view of the harbour, which gave him a feeling of being home again. He wandered down to the sea, and stood on the beach in case Pippa looked out of the bedroom window above him. He smiled to himself, deciding he loved the place and hoped he might return in the future.

He longed for Pippa to walk out of the door, and lingered for a while at the end of Henrietta Street. It gave him a tight feeling in his chest being so near to her and yet so far away. He must phone her, it was the only way.

'Rob Lambton.'

Sven froze, and the gap between the pips and the voice was enough for him to put the receiver down. Rob was at home. What had gone wrong? Didn't he work nights? Perhaps he'd got the shift wrong. No, he'd just phoned a bit too early. He had to tell Pippa he had arrived. Or had she changed her mind?

An hour later, he tried again and gave a sigh of relief.

'Hello,' Pippa said in a whisper.

'Hi, Pippa, I've arrived in Whitby.'

Rob was still marauding around the house.

'Oh hello, er… Joyce,' said Pippa as Rob passed by in the hall. 'Haven't seen you in ages, where are you? Nice to hear from you.'

'Abbey Hotel,' Sven whispered down the phone.

'Oh! Er…yeah…erm… Okay, I'll come. Be round there soon. We can have coffee together and catch up, eh? I've just got back from holiday, so can't be long. I need some fresh air.'

Hearing Sven's voice and knowing he was around the corner up the hill made her heart jump with joy. She would have to act as if Joyce had turned up wanting a coffee until Rob had gone to work. She waited for him to leave, and the wait seemed tortuous.

She busied herself in the kitchen, making plans inside her head about what she was going to do. How could she possibly leave Whitby and go to Scilly with Sven? What did he have in mind? He really was crazy, but oh so full of love and caring.

Rob was about to leave the house, and he muttered 'Bye' to her as he wandered through the open front door onto the street. Pippa hoped she wouldn't bump into him on her way to see Sven. She would give it five more minutes.

Rob didn't go to work immediately. Instead, he went to see Joan.

'Just thought I'd call in and check on you,' he said.

'You didn't tell his mam about me, did you, Rob?'

'No, did you?'

'Oh, thanks, love. I didn't want her to worry, I haven't told her about Terry yet. It scares me, and she'll find a way to blame me, you know. She's going to ask me why I haven't been round with Jordan. I'll have to go and see her. His dad is very sympathetic about it all. He rang me when Phyllis had gone out shopping. And, oh yes – I spoke with Pippa on the phone, but she told me very little about this guy she's met. I'm afraid nothing is going to change her mind, Rob. You're going to have to consider your future too.'

'Life's not fair, is it?' Rob shook his head.

'I don't know. I mean, you seem to have done okay with your inheritance. I'm not sure what to say about it – I mean, Pippa's completely changed. She was so full of her time on Scilly I hardly got a word in edgeways. I tried to get her to see sense.'

Rob was sitting on the edge of the sofa, and Joan had the blanket strewn over her knees.

'Here, let me wrap you up a bit more,' he said. He pushed the blanket towards her, and in doing so touched her leg. Her smile caught his feelings.

'It's summer, Rob! No need. Look, pet, I've been thinking,' she said. 'I mean, I feel very alone at this moment, and I know you do too. Perhaps... I mean, while Pippa is still with you, it doesn't feel right, does it? Especially with Tel being your best mate and all that. Maybe we should just continue being friends.'

Rob stiffened for a moment, not sure what to say. He tried to move the conversation on. 'I think we've both lost Terry, you know. I suspect we might only see him when he visits Jordan.'

'It wouldn't surprise me if we never saw him again,' Joan admitted. 'It's awkward.' She paused for a moment. 'So what are your plans for the future?'

'I'm waiting on Bruce and Penny contacting me. I have to go and see them at the house. It's very sad the way they lost their parents, and my real mother going through all that stress and illness. They might lose the big mansion house they live in – it's too big for them, and we thought we might have a meeting to see if we can do something about it. Not sure what we can do, but it's worth talking to them. I want to be certain I fit in. I feel strange because it's their house and it doesn't feel as if I belong, but with time and lots of meeting up I am sure I can come to some arrangement with them. They're such nice people, and Bruce looks like me – it's dead weird! Maybe...' He looked at Joan and then stopped.

She gave him a kiss on the cheek. 'You are so good to me. Thanks, Rob.'

He turned towards her and stroked her face. 'You're a bonny lass, our Joan.'

He didn't know what he wanted any more, but he wanted to hug her. She was right, it was awkward. Perhaps when this was all over...he thought about the holiday he'd always wanted in Italy. What if he'd married the wrong person?

Chapter Thirty-Four

Pippa closed the front door behind her. With her car keys in her hand, she walked to the car park to find her red Vauxhall Nova. She started the engine and drove up to the Abbey Hotel on the cliff top.

Confident that no one would know her up there, she went to reception and asked to speak to Mr Jørgensen. It felt strange asking for him by that name. The receptionist called him. Pippa waited, fidgeting with her hair and earrings.

'Just go up to Room five. It's on the landing through that door.'

Was it really Sven staying at this hotel? She couldn't believe it.

She knocked, and he opened the door slowly at first, then his head appeared. He was wearing his usual summer gear, looking brown and welcoming. Pippa almost fell through the door as he spoke. He opened his arms, and she sank into them as if nothing else mattered.

'Is it really you?' he said, pulling her inside and closing the door.

Pippa cupped his face in her hands. 'We did it. How on earth did you manage to come all this way just for me?' Her voice gave a cracked whisper as she gazed into his eyes.

Sven ran his fingers through her hair and kissed her tenderly. 'Cos I love you, Pippa. How I missed you.'

'I feel I've been to hell and back. It's been torture. What a wonderful surprise. I never thought you would actually come up here.'

Sven kissed her again, his hands smoothing down her back and caressing her neck. 'Mm, love you.'

'I can't believe you're here, you know. It's kind of weird – no one has ever gone to such lengths for me before.'

'You deserve it, my lovely, my *elskling*. We are going to be together at last.'

Pippa prayed he was right and that nothing else would go wrong. All she wanted to do was to find out what Sven had planned.

'How quickly can you pack up your stuff?' Sven asked. 'I want to take you back to Scilly before the end of the week.'

'What? Oh, bloody hell, it's all so sudden. I need some help, I can't just leave in two days. I have the house to sort out.'

'I thought the house…surely you can just leave it for a few weeks and come back when you need to discuss with Rob about what he wants to do?'

'I don't know.' Pippa looked lost in thought, unsure of what was to happen next. The thought of leaving Henrietta Street made her sad, and yet she knew Sven was right. Scilly was by far the best offer of her life and a chance to make wonderful changes. She didn't have to worry about the house any more; she could sell it in a few months' time and give Rob time to sort himself out.

'Yes, you're right, good plan,' she said. 'Rob's on nights for the rest of the week. You and me, we can spend more time together in the evenings.'

For the next two days, Pippa tactfully moved her clothes out of the house when Rob wasn't around. She packed the essentials in a suitcase and prepared to leave Whitby.

She took a risk and stayed overnight at the Abbey Hotel, an old mansion above the town. She slept long in Sven's arms, hardly daring to move. By now she knew he loved her and would always do the right thing by her.

While she was still sleeping at five in the morning, Sven got out of bed and left her a note. He laid it on the table next to the electric kettle.

When she awoke and Sven was no longer by her side, Pippa panicked. Scared to look, she read the words.

Hi, Pips, love you. Back soon, gone birding, hope you don't mind. Can't be here in Whitby without a quick twitch! Thought you might like to sleep a bit longer before we leave. Back in time for breakfast. Sven x x x x x PS Did you know that on the day I came back to you it was my birthday? Too much going on, we can celebrate it together now, eh?

Pippa laughed; she needn't have worried, and now she knew everything would work out. She smiled to herself then blew out her cheeks – *don't give me any more shocks like that.* She must learn to trust him more. Rob would wonder where she was at this time of the morning, but she often took an early morning walk, so she didn't have to be concerned. All she needed to do was act as normal as possible, but the nerves were beginning to set in and she wished Sven would hurry back.

Armed with binoculars, which he rarely left behind, Sven walked along the harbour. He stood on the sea wall looking down the river, staring at the rolling grey waves of the cold North Sea at the river mouth. There were cormorants, or herring gulls as he knew them back home, which made him feel more desperate to leave. It was warmer on Scilly and he felt a shiver on his bare legs. He had become used to living without cars, traffic lights and traffic jams; he wanted to get on with his journey to Cornwall and go home to Scilly where it was more peaceful. He hated the confusion of the mainland. He gazed across the river at Pippa's house and his mixed feelings about taking her away from this lovely old harbour gave him a sense of guilt. Whitby was unique, a seaside town with ancient monuments and dramatic scenery. He trained the binoculars on the house in Henrietta Street but couldn't see anyone inside.

He must tell Pippa about Astrid at some point. It was going to prove difficult; he couldn't tell her now, she might change her mind – and anyway, it wasn't his fault Astrid had left him. Yes, he would wait a little longer. The weather had clouded over, and with a brisk pace he returned to the hotel.

As he walked over the old iron swing bridge and up the hill, he reminded himself it was time to leave Whitby. Pippa would be waiting for him. On arrival at the hotel, he paid the bill and went up to the room.

Pippa kissed him. 'Glad you enjoyed yourself. Look, erm… I've got a couple more things to do. Give me half an hour and then we'll go south.'

She walked down the main street towards her house. She had the key, but decided not to go back inside. She stood at the bottom of the 199 steps, then turned around and looked down the cobbled street.

'Goodbye, Henrietta Street. Bye, everyone,' she whispered, and left a note for Rob, posting it quietly through the letterbox. He would be in bed, and a letter was best.

Bye, Rob, sorry it turned out this way. I think we made a mistake, and I know you and Joan are loyal to each other. I haven't had my eyes closed all this time, you know. Please tell her I won't be angry. I know too well that look on Joan's face every time you walk in the room! You two have always supported each other. Tell her she has been loyal to all of us and I bear no malice. I still love you all in a very special way. I was drowning in my own sorrows, and I couldn't see any of us changing. One of us had to see sense – one of us had to go. Poor Terry has suffered too, I suppose. Maybe I understand how difficult it has been for him. I always loved you as Daniel's dad, but we have changed, grown up, seen the worst kind of grief, and it's time to leave it all behind. You can live a new life, and so can I. Today I am slipping away from you so you can just get on with it – I hate goodbyes.

Good luck to all of us in the future, I'll will call you about your plans. I will always remember our time together as

a family. Now it's all broken up, what is the point in staying together? Enjoy your new life. We came into this relationship, all four of us, as friends, and now I want to walk away as friends. I hope that's possible. Again, sorry. Please visit Daniel. Bye.
Love, Pippa x x x

An hour later they had set off for Cornwall. Sven took his left hand off the steering wheel and patted her knee while watching the road. She remembered he had done that some weeks ago on Scilly. It was comforting.

'I'm sorry you lost Daniel in that way. I can't begin to understand how much you've suffered...'

'Wait! Stop! Turn left here, up the hill,' Pippa ordered.

Sven looked at her. 'But the Moor Road is that way, isn't it?'

'The cemetery is that way. I have to say goodbye to Dan.'

Sven smiled. He didn't say a word, but simply carried out her instructions.

'I have to do it, sorry,' she said.

'That's okay. Do you want me to come too or would you rather be alone?'

'I think I'd rather be alone for a while. Stay in the car, I won't be long. Do you mind?

'No, not at all. Okay, I'll take one last look through the town and then I'll come and pick you up. Give you time to reflect, eh? No rush, but remember we have a long journey ahead.

'Thanks, Sven, I appreciate it.'

Pippa stood by Daniel's grave and reflected on her life with him. There was a seat near the boundary hedge, and she sat there thinking about her son and if she was doing the right thing leaving him. What if he was watching her? She heard footsteps; perhaps it was the man she had met on that day who had told her she would find her direction.

Instead, a familiar voice whispered, 'I thought I might find you here. Call it gut instinct. I read your letter, it seemed obvious you would come up here to say goodbye to Daniel.'

Pippa jumped in shock. 'What the hell are *you* doing here?'

'He was my son too, Pippa, or have you forgotten?'

Pippa's heart raced; what if Sven came back?

'I gather you are going away?'

'Well, yes, but I didn't expect…'

'Expect me to be up so early? Oh my, you haven't been all that discreet, you know.'

'Look, Rob, I didn't want it to be this way.'

'Yes, I know, Joan told me.'

Pippa looked horrified, wondering if Joan had betrayed her.

'I wasn't going to stop you, but I hope you aren't making a fool of yourself.'

'Rob, sorry, I don't want to talk about it. I have to leave. I can't live like this any more.

'Okay. All I wanted to tell you was I accept your decision. Things have changed for me, I've found happiness too.'

Pippa's face looked terrified in case Sven sounded the horn in the car park or he came to see her and met Rob.

'I have to go, Rob. Sorry.

'Let's say goodbye to Daniel together, Pippa, eh?'

They stood side by side until Pippa couldn't take it any more. Her eyes filled with tears , she walked briskly away.

'Bye, Rob. Have a good life, and thanks.'

'Where are you going?' he asked.

'I'm catching a train, and don't try to stop me.' She had to lie in case Sven turned up.

'I won't, but…'

Pippa walked briskly away and didn't turn around until she got to the gate. Rob had gone. She waited a full ten minutes and Sven didn't come. Her heart pounded; what if he had seen her with Rob?

A few minutes later, his car appeared and he pulled over to open the window. 'Sorry I was so long, the swing bridge was shut and I had to wait. I was worried in case you wondered where I had gone.'

Pippa opened the car door as if her life depended on it, and she supposed it did.

'Stratford upon Avon here we come,' said Sven. 'Now we really are eloping.'

There was silence for the first hour of the journey; Pippa needed time to calm her feelings, and Sven understood.

'Any regrets?' Sven asked as they reached the A1 dual carriageway.

'Of course I do, it's only natural, but it's you I love, and I feel like a different person since we met.'

He signalled right to join the A1 on the slip lane, then switched on the radio; the DJ played Carly Simon's "You're So Vain". Pippa mouthed the words and they sang it together as Sven drove on.

'I could live in Yorkshire – it was so wild on the coast, and I saw the whalebone this morning. I'm not exactly a supporter of killing whales; I have to keep my lips sealed when I go back home. You seem to have the best of both worlds, the moors and the sea, but from tomorrow you're an island girl.' He chuckled.

In Stratford, they stayed in a bed and breakfast. Over dinner that evening, Sven discussed with Pippa about living in Beachside Cottage and having Nanette as her neighbour. They both laughed before a brief silence fell. Should he tell her now?

'I'll have to phone my parents in Norway this weekend. They'll wonder what happened to me in recent weeks. They don't know about you yet.'

Pippa smiled. 'You know, I hadn't thought of your parents. You only mentioned them briefly. I see you've got a picture of them at home, and then there was the phone call you had from your mother. Does she still want you to come for Christmas?'

Sven hesitated and opened his mouth. For a moment he couldn't speak, and he decided the time wasn't right. 'I don't know. I, er…haven't spoken with her yet.'

The candle on the dinner table glinted through Pippa's hair. The way she smiled at him, her joy at being together at last – he could hardly spoil the moment, but he must tell her soon.

'Well, they're great folks, and I hope you will meet them one day. We could go there. They live in Vormstad, a small town, and our house is outside the city. I miss my own culture, but Scilly holds so much more for me since I left.'

'I bet it does, though I bet Norway is lovely too?'

Sven paused for a moment. He remembered he also had something else to tell her. Perhaps this news would make it easier and prove he meant everything he said. 'Now I've got a surprise for you. Martin wants to see you when you get back home. I think he has a job for you.'

'What sort of job?'

'Teaching at the school.'

'Bloody hell, you two didn't waste time, did you?' She laughed.

'Well, my wages aren't going to be fantastic, and it's best you have something to do during the day.'

Pippa continued reassuringly, 'And you say Martin is keen to help me? I'd better see him about it. I don't mind living on Scilly with less money. There aren't many shops to spend it in, and I do have some savings. We only need food and lots of love. Anyway, I'm with you and that's what counts the most.'

'Still, I think we have some serious planning to do.'

'Wow! I never thought I would have the confidence to go back to work. Martin is such a nice person, I shall have to thank him. Oh, Sven, I forgot something – it's your birthday today, isn't it? I wanted to buy you a present, but we didn't have time.'

'It's okay, *you* are my birthday present.' He blew her a kiss.

*

287

The couple left Stratford the following morning and drove the long journey to Penzance. Sven had phoned ahead to see if they could stay at the youth hostel.

Mike answered the phone. 'Of course. I'll try and find you a family room so you and Pippa can be together, is that all right?'

They arrived at the youth hostel and Sven shook hands with Mike. Pippa smiled at the way he always walked around the youth hostel barefooted. There was carpet on the floors and she assumed he was more comfortable without trainers.

'I've finished for tonight,' Mike said. 'Great to see you two again, now I can match you up. You make a great couple.' He chuckled. 'Fish and chips again tonight, Pippa?' He winked and grinned at her. He remembered how he'd given her a lift up the hill back to the youth hostel and they'd eaten their fish and chips together in the communal kitchen.

Sven looked at him, puzzled.

'Come on, Sven – you like fish and chips, surely?' Pippa said.

'Ya, sure.'

'You must come over to Scilly soon, Mike. Please come and see us and visit the galleries there, you being an art student. The scenery will be fantastic for your paintings,' she suggested.

'I will. Expect me next year.'

'Come on, let's go and get some food,' Pippa said. 'Best fish and chips in town.'

They crossed the road and stood in the queue at the fish and chip shop.

'We'll walk down and sit on the harbour a while. The ferry should be back now,' Sven said, opening up his meal. The battered fish and golden chips with the aroma of salt and vinegar steaming through the paper made him hungry.

The following morning the *Scillonian* was tied up in the harbour, but Pippa told Sven she couldn't stand another journey on the ferry.

'Perhaps we can go on the chopper?' she suggested. 'It will be fun, I've never been on a helicopter before.'

'It's quite expensive compared to the ferry, Pips, I don't think I can afford to pay for the two of us. The end of next week I get paid.' Sven hoped to do some birdwatching at sea.

'Don't worry, I'll treat us. I have some money. I'll have to go to the bank before we leave, though. Please say yes – we'll get there a lot quicker. Consider it a birthday present from me.'

Sven kissed her as a thank you. 'If you're sure?'

'What about the luggage?' asked Pippa. 'It's a bit heavy.'

'Don't worry. Let's go over to the ferry, I've got an idea. We can unload the car there before we return it to the hire company.'

Sven went to see his mate, George Taylor, a member of the crew. George greeted them. 'Hi, Sven, how are you? I 'eard you was on the mainland. Yeah, I'll take yer stuff on the ship, and you can meet us later on when we dock on the other side, okay?'

Sven laughed to himself. He hadn't been away long – now everyone would know about Pippa, he was sure.

He made the final arrangements and booked their tickets at the heliport. Within three hours, they managed to book a flight. The sun shone on a perfect morning. He phoned the office, and Charlie answered the phone.

'Martin isn't here. Can I take a message for you, Sven?'

'Just tell him Pippa and I are coming back on the next chopper flight,' Sven replied.

Charlie seemed to be in one of his light-hearted moods and wished Sven a pleasant trip.

'Thanks, Charlie, for the support – much appreciated.'

'Okay, mate, see you then,' Charlie said as he closed the call.

'This is like coming home,' Pippa remarked.

'I'm so glad you see it like that.' Sven kissed her again.

Chapter Thirty-Five

Later that afternoon they boarded the helicopter in Penzance, and within a few minutes took off from the heliport, surging forward over Land's End and the Atlantic. Pippa smiled at Sven, and they held hands most of the way. After a twenty-five minute flight, she could see the islands below. The blue sea and white beaches, the shapes of St Martin's, Tresco, Bryher and St Mary's below her.

'That's an awesome sight, eh?' she said. 'I can see to the bottom of the sea. It's wonderful.'

The helicopter circled around St Mary's before coming to land on a windswept grassy airport. Pippa looked out of the window. There seemed to be a lot of people milling around the terminal as she stepped down with her bag on her shoulder. Everyone was waving. She looked behind her to see whom they were waving at, and as she got closer she recognised Charlie, Martin, Linda, Alan, and a dark-haired woman standing with Martin who she presumed was Andrea. They held out a long banner: *Welcome back, Pippa. Who's the blond guy?*

Pippa stopped for a moment with tears in her eyes.

'You're crying?' Martin said as he gave Pippa a friendly embrace. 'I'm glad you came back.'

'I'm happy, very happy.' She sniffed back her tears. 'Those guys out there sure know how to welcome you back.' She took in a breath of sea air as the wind blew a gust over the runway and her hair tangled around her face.

Martin smiled. 'Come on, then, you want to learn more about

birds? Well, you've got the right blokes to teach you. Welcome back, Pippa. Hi, Sven. Hope we can all work together soon, eh? I'll tell you what, we were all willing you to make it back here. Everyone, I mean *everyone* around town, is waiting to meet you. It's been quite an adventure for us too, you've been keeping us all guessing.' He turned to the dark-haired woman behind him. 'Pippa, this is my wife, Andrea.'

Andrea gave her a hug. 'Welcome back. I hope you'll come round to see us soon.'

'Welcome back, Pippa. He found you, eh?' Linda said with a welcoming kiss on the cheek. 'We had to do this today, we are all so happy for Sven. Martin suggested it, but we didn't need to be asked twice. We all love The Viking, you know.'

Pippa laughed. 'My goodness, I didn't expect all this for me. Hi, Charlie, great to see you. I feel like a celebrity.'

'Hi, Pippa,' Charlie said. 'Glad you got back, now you can come and help me with some work on the reserve.'

'I have to get her fit first – more bike-riding, I think,' Sven said, looking at Pippa and laughing at his own comment.

Andrea chipped in. 'Don't let him boss you around, Pippa.'

They squeezed into the green van and Martin drove them to Beachside Cottage. His driving seemed to have calmed down since Pippa's last visit. Linda followed in her battered pale-blue Ford Escort with Charlie and Andrea and the others.

'I don't need you for the next two days,' Martin told Sven. 'Take the weekend off to relax and get yourselves sorted. I realise you've both had a traumatic time – I think it would be nice if we can start with a clean sheet on Monday morning.'

'Thanks, mate, I appreciate it. I agree, we have a lot to talk about.'

Sven put the kettle on to make coffee. Pippa knew the routine off by heart. She looked around the room at Sven's few possessions and decided she would make it more homely for them both. She would ask him what he thought about it.

'I suppose I'll have to get a new double bed now,' Sven joked. 'We can't go back to Gilstone, Janice is fully booked for the summer. I'll have to order one from the mainland. It might take a couple of weeks, so it'll be cosy!'

Pippa turned to him and kissed him. She could taste the salt from the sea air on the lips of the man who had made her feel wonderful.

'I still can't believe I'm here, darling,' she said.

'Didn't we do well?' said Sven. 'Mm, I hope I don't wake up tomorrow morning to find it wasn't real.'

Later that afternoon, Sven drove down to the quay and collected Pippa's luggage from the ship. When he returned they sat down to an early dinner.

'Happy birthday, my darling.' She raised her glass. 'To us!'

'I don't think I have ever been this pampered,' Sven told her.

'Well, you'd better get used to it,' Pippa chuckled.

It seemed the right time; he must tell her about Astrid. He held her hand and kissed it. In a quiet moment, he began to speak.

'Pippa, I have something to explain. I didn't want to spoil things when we drove down here, but I have to do the decent thing and tell you something that wasn't my fault. It's not serious – only Andrea knows a bit about it, and my love for you hasn't changed. Okay?' He looked her in the eyes and tried to smile.

Pippa looked at him with suspicion. 'What?'

'It's okay. I tried to explain it while we were in Whitby, but we got so wrapped up in each other. I know I ought to have told you, but it's like this, see. While you were away, my mother made a silly error. My fault, I should have told her about you. Remember that phone call I had from Norway? Well…she gave Astrid my phone number, and one day last week she actually came to the islands to visit me. She was on holiday. I couldn't possibly tell you because I didn't think she would do it, but there was a reason.'

Pippa's jaw dropped. 'Here on St Mary's? What, all the way from Norway?' She sat there stiffening, wondering what terrible bombshell he was going to drop on her.

Sven nodded. 'She was on holiday and decided to visit the islands. My mother told her where I was. God, I was so angry.'

'So what did you say to her?'

'I was very straight with her. She wanted me to come back to her, and it got a bit complicated. Look, my darling, to put your mind at rest before I go on with the story I want you to understand nothing happened and everything is fine with you and me. It was quite odd, really, she made a bit of a fool out of me. Her friend Kjerstin and I, we almost had to carry her back on the ferry. It was unbelievable – and to prying eyes somewhat comical, I suppose.'

'She's gone back to Norway then?' Pippa's relief was obvious.

'Yes, but she told me something, and I hope you can be understanding about it. To be honest, I'm not sure whether to believe her or not. I promise you I knew nothing about it until a few days ago. I'm afraid Astrid lives in a world of her own and this is why I didn't want to get involved with her ever again. I don't feel there will ever be a right time to explain all this.'

Pippa puffed out her cheeks in more horror, looking as if she'd made a terrible mistake.

'Before we were supposed to…you know…get married, she told me she had been pregnant, but at seven months the baby was stillborn and I never knew. She claims it was mine. She came here to relieve her guilt. She actually married Mads, and I think she made out it was his child, can you believe that?'

'A baby? Oh my God, Sven! Do you believe her?' She had to keep reminding herself he had come all the way to Whitby to bring her back to Scilly.

'Honestly, Pippa, I didn't know anything about it. I don't know if it was true. Please believe me. She's so immature. I told her about you and that nothing would change my mind. After all this time, I don't know how she could possibly think I would go back to her. I needed to tell you the truth. I never wanted you to find all this out from someone else.'

Pippa sat with her hands cupped around her face, looking around the room. There was that silence again, the one she knew too well. She realised he had never tried to tell her any lies, and the look on his face showed how upset he was. She calmed herself.

'I suppose I understand her motives, losing a child no matter what stage of pregnancy or age of the child. Perhaps she felt closeness to you because of the baby. How do you feel? I mean, you might have been a father.'

Sven sniffed. 'Mm, well…it's hard to believe.' He shook his head.

'What do you want me to say?' Pippa sighed, seeing how upset he seemed.

'I really don't know. I'm so sorry, Pippa, I only wanted you to come back to me. You should have seen me trying to avoid her. I think you would have laughed. I mean, everywhere I went, she was there, and I got phone calls late at night and daren't answer them. She used to do that to me in Norway before I left for Scilly. I hoped it wasn't you – well, I wanted it to be you, if you see what I mean. That's why you might not have been able to contact me. Will you forgive me, darling?' Sven kissed her hand again.

'I'm glad I wasn't here. I don't think there is anything to forgive. You've told me the truth and I trust you. I remember the look on your face when your mother phoned and I wondered what might be wrong. You should have said.'

'How could I? You were so happy, I didn't want to spoil our precious moments together – and if I'd told you, we wouldn't be here now, surely? So nothing's changed.' He looked at her for reassurance. 'Sorry I had to tell you after your arrival here, but I couldn't find the right time to explain it all.'

'We ought to move on and be happy,' she said. 'Some things are best left behind.'

How could this Astrid woman think she could just waltz back into his life? He was right, she must be crazy. Still, it was something Pippa understood, especially the guilt and sorrow.

'Can you really forget her, Sven?'

'Yes, of course I can! It just shocked me, that's all.' Sven widened his eyes and sighed.

'You shocked me too. I thought for a minute I'd come all this way for nothing.'

'Sorry, darling.'

Pippa hugged him. 'You're amazing, you know that?'

Sven raised his glass. 'To our future, *elskling*. Thanks for being so understanding.'

'Well, let's say I hope you've seen the last of her. I love your honesty.' She smiled and kissed him on the cheek. At least he could father a child. Perhaps one day they might have children of their own. She hoped Astrid would go away never to return.

A few days later, Pippa arrived at Martin's office.

'Sven tell you about the job, Pippa?'

'Yeah, brilliant. I would like to help if I can.'

'How about the end of September after the school holidays? We're anxious to get the project off the ground now we have the funds. You can liaise with Margaret, she'll explain about the general run of things around here. In the coming weeks, if you work with Sven each day you can get to know the routine a little better.'

Pippa thanked him. There was nothing she would like more than to be with Sven discussing the job. At the end of the interview, which was more like a friendly chat, she made her way back to Beachside Cottage. It seemed her life was complete. As she walked along the shore, she stopped and looked beyond the bay out to sea, thinking about what had happened to her, the journey to Scilly – and back! The job would be perfect; it would get her out of the house, stop her moping, and she could start afresh.

At the cottage, she saw Sven in the garden. She thought he looked so much at home in his own environment. Everyone knew him and he knew everyone. He was hoeing around some lettuce. She had startled him.

'Oh…hello, darling.' He kissed her.

Nanette came out of her front door with a broom in her hand. 'Mornin', Sven.'

'This is Pippa, Nan.' Sven had dreaded this moment.

'Oh, I 'eard abowt you,' she said. 'Welcome to St Mary's.'

'Thanks, Nanette, good to meet you.' Pippa smiled at Sven.

Nanette seemed to linger on her doorstep as the postman drew up in his red van. At the garden gate, Pippa took the mail.

'Morning, Pippa,' he said. 'Enjoying your time here then?'

'It's great.' She thanked him for the letters and gave them to Sven.

She realised that the grapevine had finally grown regarding her living with Sven. She didn't mind; this was her home now. Soon she would have to see a solicitor and speak with Rob, but she didn't want to think about it yet.

'Oh look,' said Sven, 'there's one here for you from Holland. It must be from your friend Marijke. How on earth did she know you were going to be living here?'

'Let's go inside.' Pippa opened the front door and carried on talking. 'Yes, I told her to send it here.'

Sven gave her a questioning look. 'But you…'

'Well, I hoped I would come back. I prayed it would happen. I knew you were right for me all along. I just hoped I could keep my promise to you.'

Sven chuckled. 'Love you.'

Pippa slit the flap on the white envelope. She feared bad news.

Hallo, Pippa,

I wanted to tell you that we arrived home safely. I hope you get this letter. Jan has asked me to write, we want to thank you again for being our friend. He has gone back into hospital and I am sat by his bed as I write this letter. It is a matter of days now before he leaves us. I hope to come back to Scilly, but I will be afraid I will be alone. We are not positive about the future. Please stay in touch, am thinking of you and Sven. I hope your lives are wonderful together. Much love, Marijke and Jan x x x

Pippa sat on the settee. She wanted to cry alone, but Sven was with her.

'*Elskling*, you look a little sad, what is it?'

'Well, yes, Jan is in his final days.' She held the letter close to her. 'I'm so glad we did this, you know.'

Sven sat by her and put his arm around her waist. 'I love you so much. This is all yours to share with me, this wonderful scenery on our own doorstep. Isn't it great?'

'I know. You see, Marijke and Jan provided me with the confidence to make the right decision.' She sighed, hoping Jan's final days would be peaceful. She would write to Marijke soon and she would never forget them. Perhaps she and Marijke would become pen friends.

She turned to Sven and kissed him. 'Love you.'

'Let's try and cheer ourselves up, shall we? I have an idea. Let's go swimming again. You know, I'll never forget our first kiss.'

Pippa smiled. 'Great, good idea, I'll go and get changed.'

She wore her green bikini and picked up her bag, pushing her hairbrush inside. As she walked to the cottage gate, she looked behind to see if Sven was following.

On Porthcressa Beach, across the path, Sven put his arm around her as they leaned against a sun-warmed rock.

'Mm, this is lovely,' Pippa said, closing her eyes to the sun.

He pressed his lips to the back of her ring finger where the white mark from her wedding ring had begun to fade. 'When all this is over I would like to make you Mrs Pippa Jørgensen.'

Pippa lowered her eyes. 'I wouldn't change this for the world.'

With a smile on her face, she wrote *Pippa & Sven* in the sand.

The End

Acknowledgements

My sincere thanks are due to Will and Maggie Wagstaff, Julie and Dave Love, Liz Askins, Linda Thomas at Radio Scilly and Beth Hilton, Co-editor, *Scilly Now and Then* Magazine. To Lydia Birch, and to my dear friend Huberta Hollauf in Austria, in memory of Franz.

Thanks also to my editors at Cornerstones Literary Consultancy and SilverWood Books who rescued me from the void. Also to all my friends of the Romantic Novelists' Association.

Lastly, a note on *The Gardeners Curse* by Lady Laura Maconochie (1887–1972). Lady Maconochie wrote this poem in response to complaints about visitors stealing cuttings from the Scottish National Trust Garden at Inverew, Scotland, and I wish to remind visitors to Tresco through the poem how fragile the gardens can be from both visitors and the elements.

For more information about the author and her work visit
www.itslinhere.wordpress.com

Lightning Source UK Ltd.
Milton Keynes UK
UKHW04f0730110718
325503UK00009B/12/P

9 781781 323465